ALEXANDER CAMERON WAS PASSION, RAW AND PRIMITIVE, AND SHE KNEW SHE WOULD BE LOST THE INSTANT HIS FLESH TOUCHED HERS AGAIN

But he did not touch her again. He lowered his hands by his sides and took a precisely measured step back.

"You will oblige me by dressing for dinner. You will accompany me to the party later this evening and you will be on your very best behavior or so help me God . . . I shall assume you have no further desire to see your England or your precious Lieutenant Garner ever again."

With the tears still bright along her lashes, Catherine tilted her head defiantly upward. "At the cost of your own soul, Mr. Cameron?"

"I have no soul, madam. It died in my arms fifteen years ago."

She took a deep, shaky breath. "You are indeed a loathsome creature. You have no scruples, no morals, no faith, no conscience . . . not one single redeeming quality that should permit you to walk upright on two legs."

Alex stared a moment, then offered a sweeping bow. "A man always appreciates knowing where he stands in a woman's estimation."

"You stand, sir, with one foot on the road to hell, and I do not envy anyone who chooses to stand alongside you."

Marsha Canham

The Pride of Lions

A DELL BOOK

Published by
Dell Publishing
a division of
Bantam Doubleday Dell Publishing Group, Inc.
1540 Broadway
New York, New York 10036

The trademark Dell® is registered in the U.S. Patent and Trademark Office.

ISBN: 0-440-22457-8

Reprinted by arrangement with the author

Printed in the United States of America

Published simultaneously in Canada

November 1997

10 9 8 7 6 5 4 3 2 1

OPM

To Peter, my mainstay, who puts up with the insomnia, the forgotten meals, the constant doubts, and biweekly threats to heave the typewriter through the window . . . any window. . . .

To Lesley, who says she has yet to see her name in any of my books, and to Suzie and Lindsay, whose mother insists they be twenty-one before they *find out* if they are in any of my books.

To the various friends and acquaintances who step lively through these pages, I hope they realize they do so out of affection.

And to my son, Jeffrey, who was just a little boy the last time I looked up from my desk and now . . . well, *he* calls *me* Shorty.

DERBY
July 1745

I

Catherine reined in her horse at the top of the forested knoll and waited, her eyes sparkling, her heart pounding within her breast. She could detect no signs of pursuit through the deeply wooded grove, but to be doubly sure she urged her roan down into a hollow and cantered behind a dense copse of fir trees. Sitting there, panting to catch her breath—her cheeks flushed pink from the excitement—she took time to appreciate the irony of the brisk morning hunt, where the fox only *appeared* to be the quarry.

Laughing, she dismissed the feeble efforts of the two-legged bloodhounds who had tried to follow her into woods she knew as well as the back of her hand, and with a smug twinkle in her violet-blue eyes, she leaned forward to praise her roan.

"Well done, my beauty; we seem to have outrun them. I should think this calls for a reward."

She glanced around to get her bearings and recalled an isolated glade a few hundred yards ahead, cut by a stream that ran cold and clear and tasted faintly of soft green moss and rich black earth.

"We could both use a cool drink, could we not? Let the hounds and hunters wander in circles as they may."

Catherine earned a soft nicker in response and guided her roan toward the deeper woods. In the distance she could hear the faint braying of the dogs and the eerie, hollow echo of the trumpet calling the riders back into formation. She ignored the sound, even preferring after a while to slip out of the saddle and walk alongside her horse, her attention divided equally between the tangle of new saplings that caught at her skirts and the secretive whispers of the breeze chasing through the silver-backed leaves overhead. She was happy to be home in Derby. The tranquillity of the country was a shocking change from the endless rounds of balls, masquerades, and cotillions, but after three months of dancing until dawn and sleeping through to the afternoon, she had actually begun to look forward to the end of the London season.

Here in the lush, blue-green countryside that surrounded Rosewood Hall, the days were long and lazy, the nights painted with starlight, fragrant with the perfume of roses and honeysuckle. She could unfasten the cameo brooch that held the collar of her white silk blouse tight to her throat—as she did now—without fear of creating a scandal. She could strip off her gloves, loosen the buttons of her blue velvet riding habit, even free the pearl closures of the fitted satin waistcoat and scratch deliciously at the tight bindings of her whalebone stays.

Since she was alone and had every intention of remaining so for the time being, she removed her tall, veiled hat and tugged at the wide ivory combs that kept her hair in a restrictive knot at the nape of her neck. She shook the thick golden cascade free and ran her fingers through the curls as she walked, the temporary distraction causing her to veer into a low snarl of brambles. The hem of her skirt snagged on a thorn, dragging her back, and it was while she was leaning over to release it that she felt an unaccountable prickle of alarm scratch down her spine.

Her first thought was that she had been found out, and she whirled around, fully expecting to see the grinning face of a scarlet-coated hunter. Only the trees, however, green and sparkling in the filtered sunlight, met her startled gaze, and as she waited for her heart to settle back into her chest, she acknowledged the birds bickering in the branches above and the squirrels rustling through the dense undergrowth that surrounded her. She smiled inwardly, even imagining she could hear the crackling voice of her old governess scolding her. *You should never go out walking alone, young missy. It is a sure invitation to trouble. The woods are full of gap-toothed boar hunters who'd as soon ruin an innocent babe as stop to ask the time of day.*

Catherine's smile was a little sad as she continued walking, for Miss Phoebe had died of the fever two summers ago. As stern and as uncompromising as she had been, at least the governess had genuinely cared for her charge. The same could hardly be said of Catherine's mother, Lady Caroline Ashbrooke, or of her father, Sir Alfred, a recently elected Member of Parliament who rarely spared more than a quick, passing thought for anyone in his family, let alone a daughter who seemed determined to challenge him into early gray hairs. In truth, Catherine had only her brother, Damien, to turn to for advice or comfort, and even he was distancing himself more and more these days. He had established a law practice in London and seldom found time to commute to Derby. He was here now, for a few too-brief days, but only because it was her birthday and she had all but threatened him at gunpoint to be here.

It wasn't every day a girl turned eighteen, nor was it every girl who could boast of receiving six proposals of marriage in the past twenty-four months—so many, in fact, that the faces of the petitioners had begun to run together. She hadn't had the heart to tell them their efforts had all been in vain. She had already made her choice, and that choice was garrisoned right here in Derby.

Lieutenant Hamilton Garner was tall and heartbreakingly handsome. He had the lean, sinewy body of a fencer and, indeed, was Master of the Sword for his regiment of the King's Royal Dragoons. He was twenty-eight, the son of a London banker, and from the moment Catherine had first set eyes upon him, she had known he was the man worthy of her affections. The fact that he never lacked for beautiful and willing companions did not discourage her, nor did the reputation he had brought back with him from the Continent. The rumors of his quick temper, of his dueling escapades, and his many scandalous affairs only made the challenge of bringing him to heel all the more intriguing as far as Catherine was concerned. His very nature dictated that he seek the most popular, most sought-after heiress in Derby for his own, just as her nature demanded a conquest of equally momentous proportions. And because he had spent the past three months practicing drills and formations on cow pastures while she had been at the heart of the whirlwind in London . . . well, he would undoubtedly be champing at the bit to stake his claim.

To that end Catherine had made grand plans for the stroke of midnight. Thoughts of them made her skin tingle and her pulse race, and her footsteps turned swift and light as she rounded a thatch of tall junipers. There she stopped so suddenly that her skirt and petticoats creamed against her ankles like the backwash of a ship.

The glade she sought was directly ahead of her, wide and slightly misted from the small pool at its center. The sunbeams, bolder and broader here, exaggerated the brilliant greens of the leaves and ferns, silvered the surface of the water, and immodestly flared around the naked torso of a man kneeling in the lush, thick moss that grew along the embankment.

Jolted by the unexpected sight, Catherine stood absolutely still. His back was to her and she could see the muscles rippling with the motion of his hands as they splashed water on his face. She had no idea who he was— a poacher? He did not have the ragged, hungry look of a thief about him; his breeches were clean and well-tailored to his long, powerful legs. His boots were fashioned from expensive leather and polished to a mirror gloss. A shirt and coat lay nearby on the moss, the shirt of fine white linen, the jacket of rich, claret-colored wool.

Black hair curled wetly down his neck, dripping on shoulders that were broad and gleamed like newly sculpted bronze. As Catherine watched, he raked his hands through his hair to remove a bright shower of excess droplets and leaned back on his heels with a long, refreshed sigh.

The question of why he had stopped was apparent; the question of how he had come to be there was quickly answered by a shrill whinny from the opposite side of the pool. An immense black stallion stood there, his ears pricked warily upright, his nostrils flaring taut as he caught the scent of the mare. Catherine had not seen the beast at first because of the hazed streamers of sunlight, but the animal had obviously seen her. And the man, hearing the snorted alarm from his horse, pivoted swiftly, his hand a blur of motion as it stretched out toward the pistol that lay hidden beneath the folds of his jacket. The sight of the gun and the speed with which he whirled, cocked, and aimed it startled a cry from Catherine's lips. She dropped the hat and gloves she was carrying and sent her hands flying up to cover her mouth.

For a moment the two stared at each other without further sound or movement. His eyes commanded most of her attention; they were as black as the ebony mane of his hair, as dangerous as the barrel of the pistol he pointed unwaveringly at her breast. He blinked once, as if to confirm what he was seeing, then quickly lowered the gun.

"Has no one ever warned you against sneaking up on a man when his back is turned?" His voice was harsh with anger, startling enough to cause a similar sharpness in her own.

"Has no one told you, sir, that it is singularly unhealthy to trespass on private property?"

He blinked again and some of the wild, savage look went out of his eyes. "I beg your pardon?"

"This is private property," she repeated tersely. "And you are trespassing. If I were a gamekeeper, or if I were armed, I would have been well within my right to shoot you out of hand."

"Then I should count myself lucky that you are neither." The dark eyes narrowed. "May I ask what *you* are doing out here in the middle of nowhere?"

"You may not. What you *may* do is gather your belongings and leave here at once. This land belongs to Sir Alfred Ashbrooke, a man who does not take kindly to trespassers . . . or *poachers*."

The stranger studied her a moment longer, then slowly stood up, straightening to an impressive height of well over six feet.

"It has been a long time since anyone has accused me of poaching"—he smiled faintly—"and lived."

Catherine's temper flared. Her skin was still reacting to the boldness of his stare, but she had no hesitation in responding to his insolent humor. "There are forty men riding within the sound of my voice. A single scream and—"

"At least you have sense enough to be frightened," he interrupted, his grin broadening. "I think you should have listened to your nanny years ago when she warned you against walking alone in the forest."

Catherine's eyes widened. "How did you know—"

"Doesn't every abigail worth her vinegar warn her charge against the perils of venturing off on her own?" He leaned over to pluck his shirt off the ground. "In your case, you should consider yourself lucky you didn't run across someone who possessed fewer scruples and had more time on his hands. Someone who might not be deterred by a sharp tongue and an equally sharp disposition."

"Someone with fewer scruples? You flatter yourself, sir. And what do you mean by a sharp disposition? My disposition is perfectly fine."

The calm, unnerving stare pinioned her again, holding

her without evasion, long enough for a flush to spread down her throat. His gaze followed, lingering on the parted edges of her collar before descending to where the fabric molded attractively over her breasts. As if that was not audacious enough, he showed his teeth again in another wolfish grin.

"My first guess tells me you might be related in some way to this Sir Alfred Ashbrooke?"

"I am his daughter," she admitted with a small lift to her chin. "What of it?"

"His daughter." The rogue's voice purred around the word, and Catherine was aware of him taking several slow, measured steps closer. Neither her feet nor her pride would respond to an inner command to turn and run, but her horse sensed her sudden nervousness and snorted a warning. This, in turn, instantly challenged the enormous black stallion into thundering several paces across the clearing.

"Shadow! Stand!"

The stranger did not take his eyes away from Catherine's face, but she was shocked enough to look past his shoulder and see the huge stallion skid to an immediate halt. It stood, sable head held erect, eyes smoldering like coals, and flanks trembling with the desire to attack. Her astonishment was complete when she realized the diversion had allowed the man to close to within arm's reach; further, he was going so far as to extend a hand toward the velvet-soft muzzle of her roan.

"She'll tear your fingers off," Catherine cautioned.

The hand hesitated, but only fractionally before continuing toward the long, tapered nose. The mare's nostrils quivered and her eyes widened with hostility, yet she made no overt move to avoid the stroking fingers. The stranger had donned his shirt, but it hung carelessly open, and Catherine, caught between him and her horse, had nowhere to look but at the immense wall of his chest, at the cloud of dark curling hairs that did little to soften the hard planes and contours of the muscles beneath. She lifted her eyes slowly, settling first on the lean, square jaw and wide, sensual mouth. His voice was deep and cultured, betraying more education than his manners supported. Up close, his eyes still appeared to be obsidian, but a stray shaft of light revealed midnight blue depths that hinted at dark secrets and dangerous passions. Arched above were eyebrows the same ebony black as his hair, one of them slashed through with a thin white scar—a dueling scar?—to give his arrogant features an added saturnine twist.

His arm accidentally brushed against her shoulder as he stroked the roan, and Catherine flinched as if touched by fire.

"Excuse me," she said tartly, "but this is my horse. It is, in effect, my clearing as well, so if you don't mind I would prefer that you leave here at once."

Amused, he raised an eyebrow. "And if I said I preferred to stay?"

She drew a slow breath. "I would say you were a nuisance and a trespasser, as impudent and lacking in scruples as any man I have ever had the misfortune to meet. And one who no doubt has had thoughts of poaching, even if he has not done so already."

He edged closer, and Catherine felt the heat of the midnight eyes rake her again.

"Indeed, I am beginning to have thoughts, Mistress Ashbrooke," he murmured. "But not of poaching."

She stumbled back a step and came up hard against the roan's warm flesh. The stranger moved with her, placing his hands on the horse's neck, effectively trapping her between. He was near enough that she could smell the sunshine and sweat on his skin; she could see the beads of water glittering in his hair, dropping onto the white linen of his shirt and dampening it so that it clung to the broad shoulders in darker patches. The top of her head barely reached his chin, and she felt small and insignificant and terribly vulnerable in the lee of his imposing frame.

"S-since you refuse to leave, sir, then I shall," she stammered, shocked by her total lack of control over the situation. There was hardly a man in Derby who would dare accost her in such a way, nor was she accustomed to dealing with anyone not instantly overwhelmed by her position, wealth, and beauty. She was the daughter of a Member of Parliament, not some coltish serving wench to be waylaid and frightened into submission. No gentleman who laid any claim to the title whatsoever would dare speak to her the way this creature was speaking. Or presume to stand so close. Or stare so boldly.

And yet, a glance up into the dark eyes warned her that despite his fine clothes and implied gentility, he was not a man who would follow any rules other than those of his own making. There was something raw and primitive about him. Something reckless and sinful that made her heart pound within her chest and sent the blood singing through her veins.

She swallowed with difficulty. "If it is m-money you want, I'm afraid I have nothing of value on me."

She saw the flash of strong white teeth above her and felt the heat of his breath on her temple.

"So, now I am a highwayman rather than a poacher? I don't know if I should be flattered or insulted."

"P-please, I—"

"As for you possessing nothing of value"—he shifted even closer, and Catherine's heart throbbed up into her throat—"you underestimate the temptation of a silent forest, a bed of soft pine needles, and a fresh young minx sorely in need of a hard lesson in reality."

"A lesson that you, of course, feel capable of delivering?"

The sarcasm in her rebuttal only brought forth another laugh and deepened the roguish cleft that divided his chin. "My services are yours to command, Mistress Ashbrooke."

A golden tendril of her hair stirred against her throat, and she realized with a start that his long fingers were toying with several shiny strands. She tried to pull away again, but his hand was suddenly cupping her chin, tilting her face abruptly up to his. His eyes held a shuttered watchfulness as he studied the play of sunlight on her skin and hair, and their midnight intensity, combined with the contact of his hand on her flesh, sent a shiver of cold fear trickling down into her limbs, numbing them.

The intense scrutiny drifted down to the opened collar of her blouse, and she felt as if the layers of silk, linen, and lace were being stripped away until there was nothing left to shield her from his burning gaze. She would not move, could not even close her eyes to escape the mortification, and with a growing sense of horror she realized she was entirely at his mercy. She could scream, but he could easily silence her. He could as easily rip off her clothes, throw her onto the forest floor, and use her until she had no more breath or strength left to fight him.

His hands descended to the narrow indent of her waist, and Catherine suffered a sickly wave of light-headedness. Her mouth went slack as he drew her slowly against him, crushing her close to his chest. The pressure from his hands increased and be began to lift her, making her shockingly aware of the friction of silk and lace against his heated skin. Her own hands were braced on the bunched muscles of his upper arms, and as he lifted her higher, her fists closed around the loose fabric of his shirt, nearly tearing it at the seams.

She drew a breath, tensed to scream, but instead of ravaging her, as she so fully expected him to do, he continued to lift her until she was suspended high above his shoulders. With a mocking twist to his lips, he plumped her unceremoniously onto the roan's saddle and bent to gather up the reins.

"I am truly sorry to have to disappoint you, but I am a little pressed for time today . . . and not really in the mood for disciplining children. Should we meet again, however, and should the circumstances be more . . . advantageous . . . I daresay I could rouse the inclination to oblige."

Catherine's jaw dropped. "Why, you arrogant, insolent—"

He laughed and slapped his hand across the roan's flanks. Catherine jerked back in the saddle, her hair flying, her skirts whipping up in a froth of lace petticoats, blinding her until the mare had spirited her away from the clearing. Her cheeks were on fire, her hands trembling as she sought to grasp hold of the reins and slow the startled charge through the woods. She could hear the deep resonance of his laughter following her, and for the first time in many long years, her eyes flooded with tears of humiliation. Too late she remembered she had left her hat and gloves behind, but she was not about to turn around and go back. If she'd had a gun she might have been tempted. In fact, if she'd had any weapon more threatening than a short leather riding crop, she would surely have gone back and used it with the greatest of pleasure!

Catherine rode into the courtyard of Rosewood Hall, the roan's hooves beating an angry tattoo on the cobblestones. A groom, alerted by the sound, came rushing out of the stables and arrived by her side in time to catch the tossed reins.

"See that she is given an extra rasher of oats," Catherine ordered. "And walk her well: She has had a hard run."

Still bristling over the encounter in the woods, she barely heard the groom's muttered response as she strode toward the main house.

Catherine's furious pace slowed as she followed one of the many garden paths around to the front of the house. Rosewood Hall was built in the Elizabethan style, a two-storey manor with white plastered cornices and pilasters accentuating the rows of tall, multipaned windows. Columns of ivy and lichen clung to the red brick walls and climbed as high as the steeply sloped gray slate roof. There was no porch or terrace fronting the main entrance, but the double doors were housed between two massive turrets consisting of floor-to-ceiling bow windows. The pediment over the doorway was engraved with the family crest, a testament to the noble lineage of the Ashbrooke name.

Catherine was feeling anything but noble as she neared the porticoed entrance. One of the carved oak doors swung open just as she was about to reach for the latch, and her brother stepped out into the dazzling sunlight, his lean form looking especially handsome in a chocolate-brown broadcloth coat and fawn breeches.

"Whoa up there. Has the hunt run the course and left you behind?"

"No, it has not. I simply decided it was not worth all the sweat and bother. The sound of braying dogs leaves me with a migraine, as does the sight of grown men cheering while a pack of blood-crazed hounds tears apart a cornered fox."

"My sister the humanitarian," he chided wryly. "The same one who goes quail hunting and shoots helpless little feathered creatures full of lead shot."

"Those helpless little feathered creatures provide us with dinner, brother mine, while hapless little foxes only provide bloodthirsty men with a morning's diversion. And why are *you* not in *your* scarlets? Has Harriet Chalmers had the good sense to snub you again?"

Damien Ashbrooke offered up an easy smile. He was of medium height, not much taller than Catherine, with pale blue eyes and a shock of long, wavy chestnut hair worn neatly clubbed at the nape of his neck.

"No, the lovely Mistress Chalmers has not snubbed me. If anything, I was hoping to use these few brief hours of solitude to catch up on my reading."

Catherine's eyes narrowed. "She will have you wed, regardless of how you try to avoid her company."

"Is that so? Well, unless I have missed something along the way, the man is still the one who does the proposing."

She stuck out the tip of her tongue and pertly misquoted, "Thou dost protest too much, methinks. I have seen the way you ogle Harriet: like a wide-eyed lapdog, oblivious to everything but the wealth of charms that pour over the top of her bodice."

He arched an eyebrow as he took in the tumbled state of her hair and clothing. "Can that be the voice of jealousy I hear? Or just envy over her sense of proper fashion?"

Catherine followed her brother's gaze and swatted at a fold of velvet that had become stuck in the cuff of her boot. "And just what should I be envious of? The way her bosoms threaten to spill out of her gowns at every breath? Or the fact that they probably already have, and your hands have been most willing to catch them?"

Damien's cheeks darkened beneath a flush, and she huffed. "There, you see? And you still insist you have some control over your fate? A month, brother dear, and five gold sovereigns say she will have you so frustrated you will be dragging her to the altar."

"You're on," he murmured. "But only if we can set the same time limit and stakes on your conquest of Lieutenant Garner."

"Have your money ready," she said tartly, "because he has already proposed. He intends to speak to Father tonight at the party so we can make the announcement official."

"Well, I'll be damned." He was genuinely impressed. "I thought for sure he was only playing at courtship."

"Only because you sadly underestimate the extent of my own charms—spilling forth or not."

"Does Mother know?"

Catherine's smile turned bitter. "A better question might be: Does Mother care?"

"She cares enough to have been conspiring with Father to marry you off to Pelham-Whyatt for the past three years."

"Him!" Catherine wrinkled her delicate nose in distaste. "He is an absolute *boor*. He wears clothes ten sizes too big and ten years out of date. He speaks with a lisp and smells suspiciously as if he hasn't bathed since I pushed him in the duck pond when we were children."

"He is also in line to inherit the land that borders ours. He is rich, and not too dreadfully ugly—"

"Not ugly! He's missing most of his teeth, and his skin is so badly pocked it is a wonder he can shave it. The last time *he* rode to hounds, he fell headlong into the pack of dogs and they started to chew on him, mistaking him for the fox! Marry him? I would sooner marry myself to a convent, thank you very much."

"You should not speak in haste, darling Kitty. Father has promised that and much more besides if you dare involve the good family name in any further scandal."

"Scandal? It is usually considered an honor when one man duels another for the sake of his lady's reputation, is it not?"

"Not when her champion gives the distinct impression he enjoys running a man through with his saber."

"Good heavens, you talk as if Hamilton *killed* Charles Waid. The fool isn't dead, he merely suffered a scraped cheek."

"Only because Lieutenant Garner knew a novice when he saw one and had no desire to be brought up on charges of murder."

"Charles challenged Hamilton. What choice did he have?"

"He could have waited until the fool sobered up and realized the gravity of his error."

"His error was to offer me an insult within Hamilton's hearing," she countered primly.

"Brought on by your trying to make the good lieutenant jealous. Well, it worked. And even though I know you were suitably repentant, I shall still warn you to be careful around Father until you are safely wed and away from his parliamentary eye."

Catherine's anger prickled warmly in her cheeks, as it usually did when she was caught at fault and boxed into a corner. "Since you seem to show such concern for my well-being, perhaps it would interest you to know I was accosted in the woods today. *That* is why I am home from the hunt so early, and why my appearance invites such sarcasm."

"Accosted?" Damien's features hardened instantly. "Where? By who?"

"By *whom*, my Oxford-graduate brother. By a poacher, that's who. A vagrant. A trespasser. A cutpurse hiding in the woods. An arrogant brigand who had the nerve to accuse *me* of being where I should not have been."

Damien relaxed slightly. He knew his sister well enough to recognize the bright flecks of indignation in her eyes and to know it was only her temper that had been accosted. It explained the cutting edge to her wit and the sharp remarks directed at Harriet—her best and closest friend since childhood.

"He sounds interesting. Was it anyone I know?"

"I would not doubt it for a moment. He looked the exact type who would keep your company in gaming houses and . . . and other places a lady would be no lady if she mentioned. On further consideration"—her eyes slitted vindictively—"I believe five gold sovereigns would be a small price to pay to save Harriet from committing a horrendous error in judgment. I shall speak to her the instant she returns from the hunt. By tonight, Damien Ashbrooke, you will be able to count yourself among the fortunate if she so much as glances your way."

With a toss of her long blonde hair, Catherine walked past him into the foyer and began mounting the wide, massive wooden stairway to the upper floor. Damien followed her to the bottom step and rested his hand on the carved mahogany newel post, his thoughtful blue eyes admiring the agitated swing of her skirts. He had no fear of Catherine's threat coming to pass—she had schemed too long and too hard to awaken him to the fact that Harriet Chalmers had outgrown her pinafores and developed into a beautiful young woman. What she could not know was that his and Harriet's commitment to each other had already gone well beyond the stage of casual flirtation, and it was only because there were so many other houseguests staying under the same roof that Harriet was forced to share Catherine's bed, not his. A moment here and there had been all they had managed to steal so far, and with everything happening so fast . . .

"Kitty?" He half-expected her to ignore him and keep climbing, but she didn't. She stopped on the first landing and glared down at him over the dog-gate, a delicate eyebrow raised askance.

"I was just thinking—" He hesitated and offered her the smile she knew was reserved for her and her alone. "We could make it a double announcement tonight. I think I could scrape up five gold sovereigns from somewhere."

Catherine stared at her brother's handsome face. He did not approve of Hamilton Garner—what brother would? He considered the lieutenant pompous and overbearing, cruel to his junior officers, and indifferent to anyone not directly beneficial to his career. Be that as it may, Damien loved her dearly. He had been more than just a brother to her; he'd been father, confessor, adviser, and friend when it seemed as though she was growing up all alone in the vast emptiness of Rosewood Hall. He wanted her to be happy, and if winning Hamilton Garner—if becoming

Mrs. Hamilton Garner—would make her so, then he would support her choice all the way.

She took a deep breath and released it on a wistful sigh. "That would be wonderful, a double announcement. I could not wish for a happier way to welcome in my eighteenth birthday."

"Then it shall be so," he whispered. "Happy birthday."

2

The festivities at Rosewood Hall progressed through an afternoon of croquet and archery contests. The younger ladies squealed with delight and vied for attention as their chosen champions displayed their skills. Heavily corseted matrons and chaperons hovered nearby like a swarm of blackbirds, for although scarcely able to breathe without the ominous creaking of whalebone ribs, they would sooner be dead from suffocation than miss a single word of gossip.

By four o'clock the bustle moved indoors, where preparations began in earnest for the banquet and evening ball ahead. Corsets and stomachers were loosened to permit a few hours of normal respiration. Huge vats of water were supplied for the dozens of slender hands that needed to dip and splash away the effects of the day's heat. Hair was crimped and curled and tortured into elaborate pilings. Some added enormous wire contraptions to existing coiffures and then had false curls of horsehair pinned and woven in place before faces were shielded by funnels while clouds of flying white rice powder were applied to the whole. Artful additions of flowers, ribbons, jewels, even small artificial birds and animals were set to roost in the heights, making the ability to balance such a headdress an essential skill for a young woman of substance and fashion.

Catherine took her sweet time in the upper chambers, adjusting curls that required no adjustment, fussing over a smudge of rouge or a faded line of kohl. She was moderately pleased to see that no one had dared attend her birthday party in a gown anywhere near as sumptuous as her own. The rose-colored watered silk, cut in the latest Paris style, molded snugly to her narrow waist and pushed her breasts high enough to mound impressively over the bodice. The sleeves were tapered to the elbow and from there flared to allow the falling cuffs of her chemise to spill forth in a delicate profusion of creamy lace. The skirt was full and bell-shaped, spreading its width sideways over panniers, while the front and back panels fell in straight, shimmering folds to the floor. The hem of the skirt was pinned up in scallops to display the richly embroidered petticoats beneath, which consisted of more tiers of exquisitely delicate French lace.

She had chosen to wear few adornments that might detract from the effect of the rose silk. A single strand of blazing white brilliants circled her neck, drawing attention to the long, slender arch of her throat and the two soft half-moons of her breasts. Free of horsehair curls or dull dustings, her hair shone with gold and silver threads in the glow of the candlelight. Studying it critically in every mirror she passed, Catherine was almost thankful for her intolerance to rice powder; even the lightest coating caused her eyes to start weeping and her nose to leak and—horror of horrors—her skin to break out in a spiny rash of itchy red bumps.

"Lieutenant Hamilton Garner should be honored I am even considering his proposal," she murmured, giving her ostrich-feather fan one last flick to gauge the effect. Satisfied, she tucked her hand through Harriet's arm and walked out of the bedchamber and along the corridor.

"Considering?" Harriet frowned as she glanced over. "Whatever do you mean, considering? I thought you had already accepted."

"A girl can have second thoughts. Or thirds. Or fourths."

Harriet's soft brown eyes grew rounder. She did not possess Catherine's classic beauty. Her eyes were overly large in a rather plump face; her mouth was a shade too generous and there was a persistent spattering of freckles across the bridge of her nose despite the mercury wash she used day and night to bleach them away. All of her features combined to produce a cherubic countenance, one that contrasted dramatically with the luscious hourglass shape of her body. Men stared with the aplomb of guttersnipes, and it was just as well she had been enamored of Damien Ashbrooke from the tender age of three. She and Catherine could never have been friends otherwise; she would have been too much of a rival.

"On the other hand," Catherine said, pausing at the top of the staircase and tipping her head as if to appreciate the strains of music drifting out of the ballroom, "he hasn't exactly put his proposal into so many words."

Harriet, in the middle of descending a step, reached out and clutched at the balustrade in an effort to maintain her balance. "What? *What did you just say?*"

"You heard me." Catherine glanced over her shoulder to see if anyone had noted the startled outburst. "And for heaven's sake, keep your voice down. Of course he has asked me. I mean, he has hinted broadly enough, it's just that—"

"He hasn't . . . actually . . . proposed?"

"I'm sure he is only waiting for the perfect moment. Tonight, for instance. What better way to wish me happy birthday than to offer me a pledge of undying devotion?"

"But you told Damien—"

"Hush!" Catherine pinched her arm as a couple strolled past. Harriet smiled and nodded, and waited until they were well out of earshot before nearly exploding with impatience.

"You told Damien that Hamilton was going to ask your father's permission tonight. You told him you were going to announce your engagement!"

"Well . . . he was baiting me. He was being a brute and teasing me and . . . and I simply said the first thing that came to mind. I wasn't *lying*. Not completely. Hamilton *does* want to marry me; everyone in Derby knows that.

And he would be a proper fool indeed if he let someone else steal away my affections, now, wouldn't he?"

"Yes, but—"

"Nor could he make a better marriage for himself if he courted one of King George's fat old daughters."

"Catherine!"

"Well, it's true. I have the dowry my grandmother Augustine left me. I have *some* social graces, and now that Father has been elected to Parliament there's no telling what influential friends he might acquire. A young, healthy, handsome lieutenant in the King's army could do a good deal worse than marrying me, and if he does not act soon, I may just leave him to it and accept Pelham-Whyatt."

"You don't mean that," Harriet gasped.

"I certainly do. Tell me I could not walk into the great hall this very instant and receive a dozen proposals within an equal number of minutes if it became known that Hamilton Garner was out of favor."

"I am not saying you couldn't. I'm just saying . . . well, perhaps Hamilton would resent being the subject of such a wager as you and Damien made this afternoon. He is rather . . . strong-minded."

"Content in his bachelorhood, you mean? Well, it's time he opened his eyes. This is 1745, and there are simply not enough bachelors left in England to go around. Nor will there be in the near future with everyone breeding daughters like rabbits."

"Catherine!" Harriet gasped again and blanched beneath the mercury wash. "Where do you hear such things?"

"In the finest London drawing rooms, of course." Catherine's violet eyes searched the foyer below, and Harriet had to lay a gloved hand on her arm to draw her attention back to the present crisis.

"What if Hamilton hears about the wager? I mean, what if Damien offers a toast or tries to congratulate him on the upcoming nuptials?"

"He won't," Catherine insisted. "Not until midnight anyway. When he plays, he plays fair."

"This isn't a game," the voice of doom persisted. "What if Hamilton simply smiles and says happy birthday to you at midnight with a bouquet of periwinkles?"

"Then he shall wear them emblazoned on his forehead the rest of his sorry life. But he wouldn't dare. And he wouldn't have continued courting me after the duel with Charles Waid if he had no intention of doing the honorable thing. Why else does one gentleman fight another if not to claim the lady's hand himself?"

"If that were true he should have a score of wives by now," Harriet murmured, instantly regretting the words when she saw her friend's mouth compress into a thin white line. "Well, you cannot deny he has earned himself quite the reputation as a lady's champion. They even say—"

"I don't want to hear what *they* say," Catherine interrupted coldly. "*They* are most likely jealous old cows who have nothing better to do than wag their tongues and spread malicious bile. All I want to know is . . . are you with me in this or not?"

"Of course I am with you, but what can I do?"

"You can keep Damien occupied elsewhere until I give you some sort of a signal."

"A signal?"

"Just before midnight I shall invite Hamilton out onto the terrace for a breath of fresh air. If all goes well, when I return I shall be carrying . . . a rose." She paused and smiled conspiratorially. "I wagered five sovereigns with Damien this morning. I am prepared to give you half as much again if Hamilton does not pluck the rose himself and hand it to me."

Marveling at Catherine's confidence and determination, Harriet could not help but return the smile. "By midnight?"

"Midnight," Catherine agreed.

"You are not giving yourself much time."

"I don't need much time. After all, he is only a man."

Only a man. Harriet mouthed the words silently, then

had to lift her butter-yellow skirts and run to catch up as they approached the opened doors to the ballroom.

Catherine's violet eyes sparkled with the brilliance of a dozen fountainous chandeliers as she stood under the arched doorway. She had no doubts whatsoever that she would have a rose in her hand by midnight. Hamilton might well be fiercely protective of his bachelorhood, but the time was ripe for him to mend his ways. It was a perfect match for both of them. Just the thought of the commotion it would cause when their engagement was announced sent a delicious thrill down her spine, for her peers would be seething with envy. Each and every one of them had watched and waited, hoping she would fail as they so miserably had. Jealous, the lot of them. Jealous because they could not hold his interest. Jealous because they knew there wasn't a man alive who could escape a net as fine as the one she had cast for Lieutenant Garner.

She spied him instantly, even though the room was awash in crimson tunics, bewigged heads, and gowns in every shade of every color known to man. He was standing with her father, smiling at something that had caused Sir Alfred's many chins to quiver with laughter.

"Good," she mused. "He is already ingratiating himself with his future father-in-law. Sweet merciful heavens, but doesn't he look magnificent?"

If ever there was a man suited to wear a uniform, Catherine decided, it was Hamilton Garner. His shoulders filled the scarlet tunic with a power and grace that rippled clearly from every taut inch of muscle; his legs, long and lean, stretched the snow-white nankeen of his breeches in such a way as to turn a lady's heart faint. It could only be a bonus that he was exceedingly hand-some—*indecently* handsome, with a squared, angular jaw and large, seductive eyes the color of warm jade. He had seen service with King George's brother, the Duke of Cumberland, and had returned from Fontenoy a hero.

He had recently been given his own company of dragoons and was expecting a full captaincy any day now.

Standing with Hamilton and her father were several other wigged and powdered gentlemen, among them her uncle, Colonel Lawrence Halfyard, a short-tempered, gruff man who spoke in staccato sentences that sounded like gunfire. He was Hamilton's commanding officer, and as such was sure to be encouraging his protégé into a union with his niece.

"It could not be more perfect," Catherine murmured. "Now remember—you must keep Damien away from Hamilton until I give you the signal."

Harriet offered up a small groan. "That might be rather difficult. He is talking to Hamilton now."

"What? Where?" It was proof of her single-mindedness: she had not even noticed her brother standing slightly to Hamilton's left.

"You don't suppose—"

"No. I don't," Catherine said flatly. "Not with Uncle Lawrence and William Merriweather standing in their tawdry little group. If they aren't discussing Charles Edward Stuart again, I will eat every feather in my fan!"

Harriet groaned again, this time with genuine dismay. "Politics, *again*? I swear if I have to listen to one more argument about Stuarts and Hanovers and who rightfully belongs on what throne—" She looked down at her own fan, which was made of painted lace and seed pearls, and grimaced. "I may seek out Pelham-Whyatt myself."

"The Stuart line is finished," Sir Alfred said loudly, trumpeting his nose into a linen handkerchief. "Why the deuce these papists cannot seem to grasp the idea, I do not know. Y'd think they would be tired of fighting a losing battle, tired of defending a cause that has nowhere to go but the bottom of the sea. England is not going to stand for another Catholic king on the throne, and certainly not one who speaks with a Highland brogue."

"Ek-tually . . ." William Merriweather was a neighbor

and friend of the family, as short as Sir Alfred and equally stout, making the pair of them resemble two round balls of dough when they stood together. He liked to play devil's advocate and to argue just for the sake of arguing, regardless of the topic. "James Francis Stuart speaks as clearly as you or I. If anything, he leans more toward an Italian influence, having spent nearly forty years in exile there."

"Papists," Colonel Halfyard snorted. "The Old Pretender is an old fool. Maintains a royal court in Rome! Who does he think he is?"

"The rightful heir and King of England, Scotland, and Ireland," Merriweather drawled. "Ousted from his throne by a German usurper."

"King George is a direct descendant of James the First."

"Through the daughter's succession, not the son's."

"James Stuart is a fool, like his father before him," Sir Alfred insisted. "He should be thankful he was only exiled and not beheaded for his papist spoutings. Smartest thing Cromwell ever did, you ask me, lopping off any fool notion Charles might have had to try to reclaim his crown. A pity we don't have generals like him today . . . er, present company excepted, naturally. At any rate, why these Jacobites persist in making threats and screaming treasonous accusations is beyond me. Only last month they arrested one of them right in the Commons!"

"Cheek of them," the colonel agreed. "Cropping up everywhere. Can't be trusted. Don't know who your friends are anymore."

"One thing we do know is that Louis of France will never mount another invasion fleet to support the Stuart claim. Not after that sorry fiasco last year."

"Lunacy." Halfyard nodded. "Launching a fleet in February. Crossing the Channel in the dead of winter. Eleven good ships lost. Hundreds . . . thousands of stout lives lost for no good reason."

"A pity Charles Edward Stuart did not go down with the rest of the fleet."

"Yaas." Merriweather pursed his lips. "The insolent pup. Imagine him declaring to all and sundry that he will not rest until he has returned victorious to England and won the throne back in his father's name. Such impudence deserves a watery grave, what?"

Sir Alfred harrumphed emphatically to show accord. His complexion was ruddier than normal, an indication that he had been enjoying a liberal quantity of Spanish Madeira wine. The lace that was bunched around his throat and cuffs was sprinkled generously with the crumbs he had taken away from the dinner table, some of which parted company with the cloth as he gestured angrily with one hand.

"I say we should hang all the blasted Jacobites we can lay a hand to. The higher the better."

"That would likely involve laying waste to a vast portion of Scotland," Hamilton suggested blithely, "since most of the Pretender's support comes from that quarter."

"Nothing but savages," Sir Alfred sputtered. "We should have driven them all into the sea when we thrashed them raw back in '15. But what did we do? We gave 'em amnesty, that's what we did. We gave 'em back their land and built them military roads better than our own. All of Scotland was to be disarmed and subdued thirty years ago, but tell me, can you walk anywhere in that godforsaken land and not find one of their skirted warlords brandishing a bloody great broadsword across your face? Especially now that they've found themselves an idiot who actually believes he can rouse them into conquering the world."

"Not all of Scotland is eager to fight for a Stuart king," Damien pointed out cautiously. "Most of the population is as wary of stirring up old feelings as we are. As for their being savages, I daresay there were as many Scots at Cambridge and Oxford as there were Englishmen."

"Bah! Is that why I sent you to law school, boy? So you could sound like a lawyer? Where is your anger? You lost a grandfather and an uncle in the last Jacobite uprising, and I'm not ashamed to admit you damned near lost your father from sheer terror. Not savages, eh? They live in mountain caves and dress like wild men. They walk about in woolen petticoats, which they are not in the least modest about casting aside when they need their sword arms free. Dash me, can you even begin to imagine the sight of a horde of naked, hairy-legged creatures charging at you across a battlefield like bloody fiends out of hell—screaming and flailing those great bloody swords and axes of theirs like scythes? Not savages? They hardly know an intelligible word of the King's English, for pity's sake, and spend all their waking moments plotting thievery and murder on their neighbors."

"We should recall the army from Austria, I say," a gentleman strolling past the group interjected. "If law and loyalty cannot be brought to them by persuasion and logic, then by God we should carry it there by musket, bayonet, and gibbet."

"Hear, hear," came the general consensus.

"In truth"—a thin, nervous-looking guest adjusted his pince-nez and thrust a finger forward to insert a comment—"the clans are quite ferocious in their loyalty and strictly law-abiding within their own sects. They regard their chief as father, magistrate, juror, even somewhat of a king with inherited rights and powers that the lowest of the tacksmen would not dream of disobeying."

"What the devil are you on about, Faversham? You consider yourself an authority because you have spent some months up there plotting maps?"

"Good gracious, no, not an authority. It would require a born-and-bred Scotsman to fully understand the way a fellow Scotsman thinks. But I must confess my opinions of them in general were forced to change somewhat after having traveled the length and breadth of the country."

"And now you mean to convince us they are amiable, honorable hosts?"

The sarcasm caused the little man to adjust his spectacles again. "Actually, they were most hospitable, indeed, once they determined I was there for peaceful, scientific reasons only. As to their honor, I made the unknowing error of intimating to one particular chief that some of his people had not behaved toward me with the civility I had come to expect. Damn if he didn't clap a hand to his sword and say that, if I required it, he would send me two or three of their heads for the insult. I laughed, thinking it a jest, but the chief insisted he was a man of his word, and . . . faith . . . I believe he would have done it."

"You use this as an example to demonstrate their degree of civility?" Lieutenant Garner's mouth curved sardonically. "I should think it better illustrates their baser instincts to be so ready to sever a man's head from his shoulders."

"Perhaps I have explained it poorly, then," Faversham said in defense. "I meant only to show that to a Scotsman— and to a Highlander in particular—honor is everything."

"Show me a Highlander," Lieutenant Garner countered dryly, "and I'll show you a thief."

"I do not recall that I ever lost anything among them but a pair of gloves—and that I owed to my own carelessness."

"You sound as if you harbor some respect for them, sir."

"Respect, Lieutenant? If anything, I find it prudent to respect that which is so simple and basic it cannot be ignored. Or destroyed."

"Hah!" Colonel Halfyard slapped Faversham so soundly on the shoulder, his pince-nez jumped off his nose. "There you have it. By our own admission— simpletons!"

While the others laughed and applauded the colonel's wit, the cartographer fumbled to reseat his pince-nez. "No, no. I meant simple in its purest and strictest sense. Honor, to a Highlander, is honor. There are no where-withals, no provisions for exception. They swear their oaths before God and man, sealing them with their lips placed upon a dirk. Should they ever break that oath, they accept the fact that they forfeit their lives to the steel of that same knife. How can one not respect such stalwart faith?"

"Are you now saying, sir, that because they kiss knives and show a willingness to have their hearts impaled for telling little white lies"—Garner's voice dripped with sarcasm—"that we should tremble in fear and do nothing if they decide to swarm across our borders and dethrone our King?"

Faversham reddened painfully under the silent glares of the men. "I only meant to imply that if they have made a vow to return the Stuart monarchy, it should not be taken lightly."

"And I state plainly and clearly, here and now, that the whole of the Scottish rabble assembled together could not pose enough of a threat to dampen my collar. They have no regular army, no guns, no artillery, no navy. Only bagpipes and swords to send against the most powerful, well-disciplined, well-equipped military nation the world has known."

Saying this, the lieutenant turned his back on Faversham, rudely dismissing him as a nuisance. The gentleman darkened to a throbbing shade of crimson as he started to slink away, and was as surprised as the rest of the company to hear a voice come to his defense.

"I myself have always been of the opinion that it is healthier to take precautions against an enemy than to underestimate him completely."

In the sudden silence that followed, Hamilton turned slowly to address this new, quietly spoken challenge. The man was a stranger to the group, a business associate of Damien's up from London.

Garner's jade-green eyes narrowed. "Montgomery, isn't it?"

"Raefer Montgomery," the man acknowledged with a slight bow.

"And you share Faversham's opinion that the Scots pose a real threat to the safety of the English monarchy?"

"The opinion I share is that I would not want to be too hasty in dismissing them as inept savages. They have, after all, managed to keep their own borders relatively sacrosanct for the past thousand years or so. Not even the Norman conquerors dared to invade in any force."

"Possibly because there was nothing across their borders to merit conquest," Garner said evenly. "The land is barren, the weather unpredictable. You would have to be as thick-skinned as the savages themselves to survive there any length of time."

Montgomery smiled. "Yet we pay prime prices for their beef, mutton, and wool, not to mention the thriving black market that deals with their finer . . . uh . . . liquid spirits. Unless my palate has grown rusty on French wine, I detected a distinct Caledonian musk to the whisky we are enjoying this evening."

Sir Alfred cleared his throat noisily and started to splutter some hasty excuse, but no one was paying heed. All eyes were intent upon Montgomery and Hamilton Garner.

"Might I ask your business, sir? And if I may be bolder still, your accent eludes me."

Montgomery swirled the contents of his glass in his hand. "I grew up on the Continent, Lieutenant: France, Italy, Spain. As to my business, it is import and export, and to that end I travel extensively in search of interesting and profitable acquisitions. My interest in politics—assuming that to be your next question—extends only insofar as it affects my profits and losses. However, like Mr. Merriweather, I enjoy examining both sides of an argument . . . and like Mr. Faversham, I am able to keep a relatively open mind during such examinations."

Lieutenant Garner studied Montgomery as closely as if he were studying an imminent opponent. The exquisite cut of the merchant's indigo-blue frock coat, together with the silvered blue waistcoat and breeches, reeked of money and easy living, yet there was nothing soft or negligent in the strong, tapered hands or the broad, heavy shoulders.

"Accepting your declaration of neutrality for the moment," he mused, "and acknowledging that your interests are purely financial, you must agree a stable government would be more to a *shopkeeper's* liking than outright war."

Montgomery absorbed the thinly veiled insult with a slight deepening of his smile. "On the contrary. If I were strictly a profiteer—hypothetically speaking, of course— I would be extremely anxious to see the two countries go to war. There are always incredible sums of money to be made in chaotic situations, just as wars undoubtedly provide grand opportunities for ordinary, mundane soldiers to hack a bloody path to prominence and promotion."

Garner stiffened visibly. His hand slid up to rest on the filigreed hilt of his dress sword, and the skin across his cheeks and over the finely chiseled flare of his nostrils paled with tension. "I would hardly equate the two professions, since the one exists to defend life and liberty, while the other . . . the other was created by parasites to feed on the spoils of defeat."

Damien Ashbrooke was the only one to gasp out loud, but his surprise was obviously shared by the others as they waited, expectantly, for an explosion of violence to erupt between the two men. It was, however, an explosion of a very different kind that burst into their midst. An explosion of color and laughter and soft swirls of silk.

"All this serious talk and all these serious scowls," Catherine scolded prettily, "on my birthday? Shame on you, Hamilton. And you too, Damien. Poor Harriet and I were beginning to feel as neglected as one of the potted palms."

"Mistress Ashbrooke!" William Merriweather bowed flamboyantly over her hand. "And Mistress Chalmers. Have you truly been feeling neglected, or do you say it simply to tease these poor ravished heartstrings?"

"Positively perishing of boredom," Catherine insisted.

"But for that charming bit of gallantry, you may claim the honor of my birthday dance."

Her violet eyes flashed toward Hamilton to mark his reaction at being passed over for the privilege—but her gaze did not make it past the gentleman standing beside her brother. His face had been partially turned away in profile, but at the sound of her voice he had turned, and at the first glimpse of those dark, penetrating midnight eyes, her breath became trapped somewhere between her throat and her lungs.

There was no mistaking those eyes, no misreading the slight curl on his mouth that took another subtle stretch upward when he saw the shock register on her face. For despite the formal attire and neatly bound periwig, it was the same rogue who had accosted her in the forest that morning.

3

Catherine stared at the stranger for what seemed like half an eternity. Her reaction did not go unnoticed; Damien, for one, saw the flush flow into her cheeks and the violet of her eyes darken with outrage, and if he had not known better, if he had not known that Raefer had arrived from London only that afternoon and had never met any of the Ashbrooke family before, he would have sworn his sister was regarding him as she would a life-long enemy.

Acutely aware of the strained relations between Montgomery and Hamilton Garner, Damien attempted to cover the awkward silence with introductions.

"Raefer Montgomery, I don't believe you've had the pleasure of meeting my sister, Catherine."

The tall merchant stepped forward and bowed politely over her hand. "A very great pleasure indeed, Mistress Ashbrooke. And my warmest felicitations on your birthday. I arrived rather unexpectedly, and Damien was kind enough to invite me to stay for the party—although he neglected to mention he had such a lovely sister."

"I'm so glad you could join us," she said frostily, her eyes flicking to her brother with a promise of retribution.

"Er . . . and Mistress Harriet Chalmers," Damien added lamely. "Mr. Raefer Montgomery."

Montgomery's smile widened and changed from one of amusement to one of genuine pleasure. "Mistress Chalmers. I have indeed looked forward to meeting you. Damien has spoken of you many times, but if I might be allowed to say so, his descriptions have not done you justice."

"Why, thank you, sir." Harriet blushed furiously, conscious of Catherine's black glare.

As to the latter, she was fighting hard to control the indignation coursing heatedly through her veins. She had come perilously close to slapping the sly grin off Montgomery's face, and certainly would have if not for the presence of her father and Colonel Halfyard. That and the fact she could not afford a scene tonight, of all nights.

"I do not recall my brother ever mentioning your name, Mr. Montgomery. But then I suppose some lawyers prefer to keep their . . . um . . . less palatable clients anonymous. You aren't, by chance, a murderer or a highwayman?"

Damien was horrified, but Montgomery only laughed—the same deep, resonating sound she had heard following her out of the forest. "Rest assured, Mistress Ashbrooke, I call upon your brother's expertise for purely financial matters."

"Raefer owns a shipping venture based in London," Damien explained quickly.

"Slaves or black market?" she inquired sweetly.

"At the moment . . . ladies' petticoats," Montgomery replied, not the least perturbed. "The market is extremely lucrative in the present climate for anyone able to carry cargoes of silk, lace, and brocade. With trade to France cut off, goods from the Orient are commanding top prices."

"How interesting," Catherine declared, opening her fan with a bored snap. She turned to William Merriweather and favored him with a devastating smile. "I believe I hear the orchestra tuning for the next set."

With an artful sweep of her wide skirts, she accompanied Merriweather to the dance floor, where other partners were forming two long lines. The music was a minuet, elegant and stately, the steps executed with precision and grace. Catherine determinedly avoided looking in Montgomery's direction, though she was aware of his dark gaze following her through the intricate pattern of steps.

"Such an odious man," she said conversationally when she and Merriweather closed together to turn a pirouette. "Ladies' petticoats indeed. I'll wager he does not waste the sail to bring goods all the way from the Orient. I'll wager he smuggles them from France despite the embargoes."

"Rather too brusque a character for my liking," Merriweather agreed. "Yet he does have a certain boldness. Not afraid to speak his mind at all; he and the lieutenant were warming to each other just before you arrived."

"Really? About what?"

The lines parted and the dancers traced through several stations of the dance before coming together again.

"What does anyone argue about these days?" Merriweather sighed. "Politics, of course. I admit to a certain penchant for poking the odd hornet's nest meself, but our bold Mr. Montgomery came right out and whacked it with a stick."

"He advocates war?"

Merriweather pursed his lips thoughtfully. "Dash me if I know what he advocates. Or for whom."

Catherine frowned and stole a peek over her shoulder. Montgomery had detached himself from the group somewhat, though whether it was by his choice or a subtle move by the others to close ranks against him, she could not tell. Either way, he did not seem overly concerned. He had enough to hold his interest, what with every female eye in the room vying to catch his attention.

Despite her intense dislike for the man, she had to admit he presented a strikingly handsome contrast to the shorter, less muscular guests who were either bewhiskered members of the local gentry or scarlet-coated officers who all tended to blend together in form and features after a while. He stood half a head taller than most of the men in the room—Hamilton being the immediate exception—and she knew for a fact that very little of the shaping beneath the indigo frock coat was due to the skill of a tailor with cutting and padding. Further, there was an indefinable air of self-assurance about him, as if he knew he was the subject of most of the whispered conversations in the ballroom but couldn't care less. In addition, Hamilton's back was as stiff as an iron rod, and he was glaring at the merchant as if he would like nothing better than to bare his fists and finish their interrupted conversation.

Catherine moved instinctively through the final routines of the dance, her mind racing well ahead of the music. Hamilton's vanity had already been pricked once by the stranger; could she use it to her advantage? A casual flirtation might just be the motivation her lieutenant needed to spur him into an impassioned proposal. She would have to be careful, of course. Montgomery had been boorish and unforgivably rude this morning, and she did not want to fuel his arrogance with any false impressions, but midnight was fast approaching and she could not afford failure where her own vanity was concerned.

The minuet ended on a trickle of applause, and Catherine was escorted back to her father's group.

"I thank you, Mr. Merriweather," she said with a smile and released his arm. "You have managed to quite steal my breath away. Hamilton—" She glanced up at him from beneath the thick fringe of her lashes. "Might I impose upon you for a glass of cool water?"

He bowed curtly. "Of course you may. I won't be but a moment."

"Thank you. Oh, and Father . . . I believe Mr. Petrie is looking for you."

"Petrie?" Sir Alfred perked up like a hound scenting blood. Hugh Petrie could always be counted upon, on any occasion, to dispense with the nonsense and frippery and get down to the more serious business of whist and backgammon. "Well . . . er . . . *harrumph!* Lawrence— what say we look him up and see what he is wanting? Something that warrants our immediate attention, no doubt."

"No doubt, no doubt." The colonel nodded and was

rapidly ushered away. Merriweather lingered a moment longer, but the temptation of a rousing good game of cards was too much to endure and he made his excuses as well, leaving Damien and Harriet and Raefer Montgomery.

Catherine caught Harriet's eye. "A gavotte," she said, tipping her head toward the music. "One of your favorites, is it not?"

Harriet's eyes widened, but she slipped her hand through the crook of Damien's arm and won an invitation to join the dancers. Catherine watched them until they were out of earshot, then turned to Montgomery.

"Tell me, sir, do they teach music appreciation in poaching school?"

"Dance appreciation too," he said, offering his arm. "May I?"

She studied the rakish grin a moment before accepting. She was aware of the heads swiveling to follow them as they walked past a row of whispering matrons, even more conscious of a pair of jade-green eyes spearing them from across the room as they merged with the dancing couples.

Montgomery's movements were fluid and assured, amazingly light and graceful for a man of his size. She did not anticipate so strong a reaction to the feel of the steely muscles against her fingertips or the memory that came flooding back of him stripped to the waist, his black hair dripping water onto his naked flesh. She did not expect the liquefying reaction in her own body each time he took advantage of the music to draw her boldly into his arms.

"I must apologize for being so abrupt this morning," he said, leading her in a delicate circle. "I had been riding all night and was suffering a general lack of patience, having lost myself several times on the forest paths."

"Apologies hardly suit your character, Mr. Montgomery. But why did you not say you were a friend of my brother? It would not have excused your abominable behavior, but it might have helped explain it."

"He counts poachers and highwaymen among his friends?"

"I have been to his offices in London. I have seen some of the company he is forced to keep."

They parted, exchanging steps with other partners in their quadrangle before dancing together again.

"An apology from you would not be remiss either," he said thoughtfully.

"An apology from me?" She tilted her head up with a frown. "Whatever for, may I ask?"

"Creeping up on me unawares. Standing in the shadows watching me bathe."

Her mouth dropped open. "I certainly was not *watching* you, sir. Had I known there was anyone bathing in the clearing, I would not have gone within a hundred yards of it. I was merely attempting to water my horse and—" She stopped and clamped her mouth shut. The maddening, all-knowing smile was back on his lips, encouraged by the distinct gleam of amusement in the blue-black eyes. "Please take me back now. I see Lieutenant Garner has returned with my refreshment."

"My dear Mistress Ashbrooke—" He raised her hand to his lips and pressed the heat of his breath against her gloved fingers. "It has been many long months since I have held such an incredibly lovely woman in my arms, and I am loath to forfeit the pleasure just yet. I'm afraid the lieutenant will have to wait."

"I hardly think—"

"Do I still frighten you? Even in a crowded room?"

She caught her breath and stared up at him. Hamilton was moving toward the edge of the dance floor carrying the tiny crystal glass of water. The orchestra was playing and couples were moving all around them. Montgomery was smiling, challenging her, calling her bluff.

She raised her hand and settled it around his wrist. She felt his hand tighten on her waist again and imagined she could hear the swelling of whispers that rippled around the room as she accorded a *second* dance to the stranger from London. It was scandalous behavior, as scandalous as the way his midnight eyes held her, demanding her full attention, relegating all else—the music, the laughter, the buzzing of conversations—to the distant background. She was only dimly aware of the flashes of colored silk that passed them, of the brilliant splashes of candlelight that reflected off the panes of the windows and doors. She was not sensible at all to the fact that he whirled her away from the close confines of the ballroom and danced with her out onto the terrace, around and around, swirling her away from the lights and the noise until they had only shadows and the dusting of starlight overhead.

Drawing her closer, Montgomery embraced her in a way that made her feel molded to the hard contours of his body. The circles they inscribed became smaller, their footsteps slower, until they were barely moving at all, hardly swaying to the strains of the music. Catherine felt a mindless drumming in her blood and knew he was holding her too close. The night was too dark, the air too fragrant with the scent of roses. She lowered her gaze a fraction and it was no longer his eyes that held her transfixed, but the sensual curve of his mouth—a mouth that was descending toward hers even as his hand slid up from her waist to cradle the nape of her neck.

His lips touched hers, and the shock trembled through her body. A feeble protest shivered free on a sigh, but she could not even summon the strength or wit to make it sound convincing. All of her senses became centered around the feather-light pressure of his mouth, on the teasing, taunting dalliance of his tongue as it sampled, tasted, prepared her for the bold intrusion that followed.

His arms tightened and his lips slanted more forcefully over hers. A second gasp gave him the opening he sought, and his tongue slid possessively into the shocked heat of her mouth. Catherine felt her knees give way and her stomach turn to jelly, hot jelly, heavy as molten lead that slithered downward into her limbs on each silky, probing caress. Her fists clenched and unclenched. Her fingers spread open across the velvet thickness of his frock coat and inched higher . . . higher, until her hands were circling his neck, clinging to the powerful breadth of his shoulders. She pressed eagerly into his embrace, thrilling to the strength in his arms as they enfolded her.

She thought she had known every kind of kiss a man could offer—what mystery could still remain in the simple touching of lips? Hamilton's kisses, to be sure, warmed her deliciously and sent tiny shivers of satisfaction through her body, more so than those of any other man before him. Yet he had never inspired this surge of liquid heat that was now setting her veins on fire. His body had never commanded hers to melt against him, to move with him, to question the cause and cure for this incredible, burning tension. Even her skin had grown tauter, tighter, and her belly was fluttering with urges that made her want to move closer, to feel the heat of him with her bare flesh.

She was kissing him back, she knew she was, but Montgomery ended the kiss suddenly, breaking away with an abruptness that brought a cry of disappointment from her lips. His face was in shadow—she could barely discern more than the black slash of his brows—but she sensed a shared feeling of surprise. As if he had not expected the rush of pleasure she could feel thundering through his chest.

He held her away from his body, as if he did not trust any further contact, and when he spoke he tried to make his words sound light and casual.

"I did warn you about unscrupulous rogues who would not hesitate to take advantage."

"So you did," she murmured. "You also threatened to teach me a lesson in reality. Was that it?"

"Reality?" he whispered. "I'm not even sure I know what that is anymore. I thought I did. . . ."

Catherine shivered as he brushed his fingertips along the curve of her throat. She turned her head slightly, the better to feel the warmth of his flesh on hers . . . and her eyes opened wide in horror.

The figure of a man was standing less than five paces away, his silhouette framed in the glare of lights that spilled from the open french doors. His hands were rigid by his sides, the fingers of one fist crushed around a tiny crystal glass.

Catherine gasped and jerked out of Montgomery's arms. "Hamilton!"

"I hope I am not intruding," the lieutenant said, his voice cracking with anger.

She took several halting steps toward him. "Hamilton . . . it isn't what you think. . . ."

"Is it not? Pray then, by all means, tell me what it is. You send me for a glass of water, then dance away with a fellow to whom you have only just been introduced. Ten minutes later I find you wrapped in his arms and"—he finished the sentence with a sneer—"you tell me it isn't what I think."

"Hamilton, please . . ."

"I think, madam, you were kissing this gentleman, and with no great show of reluctance. The act hardly requires more explanation than that . . . unless, of course, you have recently formed the habit of kissing perfect strangers and see nothing untoward in the deed."

Montgomery gave up an audible sigh. He reached to an inside pocket and extracted a thin black cigar. "You are not giving the lady much of a chance to explain. If you did, she might be able to tell you the kiss was entirely my idea, and that she simply . . . endured it."

"*Endured* it?" Garner's face remained impassive, carved out of stone, as he watched Montgomery strike a sulfur stick and touch it to the end of his cigar.

"It is her birthday, is it not?"

"And you thought to take advantage of the situation by forcing yourself on her good nature?"

"I did not force anything on anyone," Montgomery said quietly. "I was merely expressing my felicitations."

Hamilton's fist tightened around the crystal glass. "Catherine . . . I think you should go back inside now and rejoin the party; the air has developed a distinct chill."

"Will you come with me?" she pleaded in a whisper.

"Not just yet. Montgomery and I have not finished our conversation."

She reached out and touched the sleeve of his tunic. "Hamilton, please—"

"I said, *go inside.*" The iced green eyes turned to her as he pulled his arm away. "This is between Montgomery and myself now."

"On the contrary," Raefer said, studying the glow of ash at the tip of his cigar. "If there was anything further to discuss, it would be between me and Mistress Ashbrooke. However . . . if an apology will put an end to this simple misunderstanding, then I offer one freely. I had no idea the lady's time was spoken for."

Hamilton ground his teeth together. "Catherine's time is her own. If she chooses to throw it away in the company of unprincipled bastards, then so be it."

Montgomery stared at the dragoon officer for a long, taut moment. When he spoke, his voice was low and deceptively silky. "I have offered my apologies. If you will excuse me—"

He bowed politely to Catherine and started toward the french doors. There was a shrill whisper of steel on leather, and an instant later Hamilton's saber slashed down in front of Montgomery, the flashing silver point touching the ruff of lace at his throat.

"An apology is not enough," Garner hissed. "Not unless you beg your further pardon for being a *coward* as well as an ill-mannered boor."

"What the deuce is going on here?"

Catherine flinched at the sound of her father's voice booming out across the terrace. What little color she had remaining in her face drained down to her toes when she saw him striding out of the doors with Damien, Harriet, and Colonel Halfyard close on his heels.

"Well? Speak up! What is the meaning of this? Lieutenant Garner, put that damned thing away and explain yourself."

"Indeed," the colonel barked. "You are a guest in Sir Alfred's house. This is no place for swordplay."

"Nor for insults, which this . . . *gentleman* . . . has seen fit to tender to both myself and Mistress Ashbrooke."

"What? What manner of insult?"

Catherine wished she could shrink away into the shadows. Damien and Harriet were both gaping at her as if they knew, somehow, she was the cause of it all. Colonel Halfyard had his hand on the hilt of his own sword and looked prepared to cut down the first person who dared to move.

Sir Alfred's face darkened through several shades of crimson. "I said, put the sword away, Lieutenant. If there has indeed been an insult tendered, we shall get to the bottom of it."

The sword wavered, then descended slowly from beneath Montgomery's chin. With a sudden, well-practiced flourish, the blade was whipped about and flashed into its sheath again.

"Now, then." Sir Alfred's voice was grave. "What manner of insult would have you drawing swords under my roof?"

Montgomery had not so much as blinked since Garner's saber had appeared. He did so now, as he turned to address Catherine's father. "It was a simple misunderstanding, for which I have already apologized."

"The apology was a mockery," Garner declared. "Delivered out of the side of his mouth, and for that I have demanded satisfaction."

Raefer continued to hold Sir Alfred's gaze. "I have no desire to kill this man."

"Kill me?" Hamilton surged forward. "It would be my pleasure to let you try."

"Hamilton, for God's sake—" Damien stepped forward quickly, placing himself in the lieutenant's path.

"Raefer?" He turned and searched the placid features for an explanation.

The dark eyes flicked to Hamilton's face, and he allowed a slight smile to tug at one corner of his mouth. "The lieutenant seems to have taken offense at my bringing your sister out to the terrace for a breath of fresh air. He seems to feel I was out of line, yet he says he has no claim on the lady himself. To my way of thinking, that leaves the decision up to Mistress Ashbrooke as to whether there was an insult delivered here tonight or not."

"No claim?" Damien cursed under his breath. "They're engaged to be married, for God's sake."

Hamilton's gaze broke away from Montgomery's long enough to cast a startled—and even angrier—glance in Catherine's direction. She felt her cheeks blush a hotter, more humiliating red, and she had to blink hard to keep the sting of tears from blinding her.

"Well, daughter?" Sir Alfred's voice came down on her like a gavel. "We're all waiting. Did this gentleman insult you or not?"

She looked helplessly around the ring of hostile faces, wishing she had never ridden into the forest that morning, never learned to dance a gavotte, never been born eighteen years ago this night.

"At least tell us the nature of the supposed insult," her father insisted, his patience nearing its limits.

"He . . . he . . ." Her words were barely above a whisper, and she needed to swallow to make any sound at all. "He kissed me."

"Kissed you?" Sir Alfred leaned closer and peered into his daughter's face. "He *kissed* you? Against your will?"

"I . . ." She curled her lower lip between her teeth and bit down savagely on the fleshy pad. What could she say? If she said no, she would lose Hamilton as surely as if she slapped his face in public. If she said yes, his damned code of honor would require him to defend her reputation. "I . . . One minute we were dancing, and the next . . ." She faltered again and lowered her eyes. "I did nothing to encourage the liberty."

Colonel Halfyard sucked in a deep breath and glared at Montgomery. "Explain yourself, sir!"

Montgomery's attention remained fixed on Catherine's face a moment longer, then switched indolently to the colonel. "There is nothing to explain. It is a beautiful night, I had a beautiful woman in my arms; I saw something I wanted and I took it."

The colonel's nostrils flared through a hot gust of indignation. "Insolence, sir! It appears Lieutenant Garner was justified in taking offense. By God, in his place, I'd likely do the same."

Hamilton's mouth flattened into a sneer as he glared at Montgomery. "Will you or will you not give me satisfaction?"

Raefer exchanged a dark look with Damien before he answered the lieutenant's challenge. "Where and when?"

"Tomorrow. Dawn. Kesslar's Green."

Montgomery smiled faintly. "I have pressing business in London. By dawn tomorrow I plan to be well on my way down the road. I would as soon have this over with by then, if you don't mind."

Garner's expression became whiter, more pinched at this additional mockery. Even Sir Alfred stared at the tall merchant, surprised by his audacity.

"Then you shall meet here and now," he declared. "The courtyard in front of the stables, in one half hour. Damien—since Mr. Montgomery is here by your invitation, you shall act as his second. Weapons, gentlemen?"

"The lieutenant seems to be comfortable with sabers," Montgomery said wanly. "I have no objections."

"Hamilton—" Catherine raised imploring eyes to him one last time. "No, please. He has already apologized. . . ."

"Daughter! You are a little late with your concerns." Sir Alfred took her roughly by the arm. "I have no doubt you were more than slightly at fault here—if, indeed, not entirely to blame." He started to propel her toward the door, leaning close to hiss in her ear as he did so. "I warned Lady Ashbrooke we should have married you off years ago. I warned you as well, young lady, that I would tolerate no further scandals. You will take yourself to your room at once, and there you will remain until I decide what is to be done with you!"

Catherine could no longer hold back her tears. They brimmed over her lashes and streaked down her cheeks, dripping dark stains onto the rose silk of her bodice.

"Father—"

"Now! At once! Do not even dare ply me with any of your missish tricks. Your days of having your own way are over. Over, do you hear me!"

Catherine heard nothing over the frantic beating of her heart. She fled the terrace, fled past the startled, staring guests in the ballroom, and did not stop until she was safely locked away in her room, with her head buried in the muffling blindness of her bed quilts.

4

A ring of brass lanterns had been set up in the courtyard. Light fog had drifted in from the river, no more than a haze, but enough to blur the yellow posts of light and distort the ghostly shadows on the damp cobbles. Word of the impending duel had spread through the party like a bushfire, and every man worth his salt was present, forming a second murmuring ring around the lanterns. Some of the more daring women, cloaked and hooded to preserve a semblance of modesty, huddled in small, excited groups by the stables. Servants, liveried coachmen, and grooms perched on the carriages, hung from window ledges and doors, eager anticipation on their faces.

Two stories above, her hand clutching the sheer lace curtains, Catherine stood at the window of her bedroom, grimly watching the scene unfold below. Her face was damp with tears, her eyes polished and red. Harriet stood behind her, twisting a lace handkerchief to shreds.

"Someone has to stop this madness," Catherine whispered. "I never meant it to go this far. I didn't want anyone to be hurt. Oh, Harriet, you do believe me, don't you?"

"I believe you," Harriet murmured, giving the lace another savage twist.

The truth was, Catherine often hurt people—herself included—simply because she acted without thinking and worried about the consequences when it was too late. There was goodness in Catherine, and kindness, but she was too stubborn to admit she was vulnerable, too proud to reveal to anyone that she wasn't nearly as strong or self-sufficient as she professed to be.

"Did Lady Caroline say anything when she came to see you?" Harriet ventured to ask.

"Mother?" There was a derisive sigh. "She was more irritated at having her tryst with Lord Winston interrupted. I don't think she listened to a word I said. Perhaps I should have told her Montgomery raped me; that might at least have roused some curiosity."

"Oh, Catherine . . ." Harriet bit her lip, not knowing what to say to comfort her friend. One of the reasons they *were* friends was that they understood the loneliness of growing up in an empty household. Harriet's mother had died giving birth, leaving her to be raised by indifferent nurses and nannies. Catherine might as well have been an only child—and an orphan—for all the attention her parents had given her. "You shouldn't speak so harshly of your mother. She cares for you, she just . . . doesn't know how to show it."

"She knows how to show it to her lovers. Oh . . ." She dropped the curtain and whirled around. "Why is this happening? Why? It was such a stupid little thing. A kiss, for pity's sake. I've kissed dozens of men before tonight. Why make such a fuss now? And why could Hamilton be satisfied with nothing less than a duel?"

"Because he is Lieutenant Hamilton Garner of His Majesty's Ninth Dragoons," Harriet said on a gust of exasperation. "What did you think he would do, Catherine? What were you playing at when you let Mr. Montgomery take you out onto the terrace?"

"I didn't *let* him take me anywhere. We were dancing and . . . and I didn't even realize where we were until it was too late."

"You didn't realize where you were? It must have been some dance . . . and some kiss."

Catherine felt her cheeks warming in response to

Harriet's accusing tone, but how could she possibly explain what had happened? She couldn't even explain it to herself. It was as if Montgomery had cast a spell over her, had swallowed her into his eyes so that she could not think or move or even breathe without his command. And the kiss. . . . Her lips still burned with the memory, but that was all it had been: a kiss. A simple kiss that was threatening to turn her whole life upside down. Undoubtedly it would cost her any hope of winning a proposal of marriage from Hamilton. And likely it would cost the London merchant his life. The lieutenant was a master swordsman, an instructor for his regiment. Catherine had heard stories about his instinct and agility, and despite Montgomery's bravado—or perhaps because of it—Hamilton would take delight in cutting him to bloody ribbons.

"Oh, God." She leaned her brow against the cool pane of the window and saw a new commotion below. Hamilton had emerged from the shadows around the courtyard and was walking with his seconds—two junior lieutenants—into the center of the lighted ring. He had removed his scarlet tunic and decorative white leather belts and wore only his nankeen breeches and collarless white linen shirt. He halted by the stone fountain while one of his seconds unsheathed his sword and handed it to him. He held it lovingly, running a finger down the gleaming surface of the steel before he held it in both hands and flexed the supple blade in a slight arc. He whipped it free almost at once, slicing the air with spirals and deadly swift slashes to warm his wrists.

A smaller stir rippled through the crowd at the opposite side of the courtyard as Raefer Montgomery and Damien approached the ring of lanterns. Montgomery had also removed his frock coat and satin vest, his fancy lace jabot and starched neckcloth. His shirt was silk, opened at the throat. The formal wig had been discarded, and his jet-black hair lay like splashes of ink against his neck and temples.

Catherine's hand twisted into the curtain again. Hamilton moved like a dancer, preparing for the macabre performance ahead; Montgomery stood motionless, the smoke from his cigar rising in thin tracers above his head.

"Why didn't he leave?" Catherine asked in a horrified whisper. "Why did he not just get on his horse and leave? He didn't seem to care what anyone thought of him earlier; why should he care if they think him a coward now?"

Harriet moved up beside her. "Men call *us* proud and vain, but I daresay everything we learned, we learned from them."

Catherine was only half-listening. Colonel Halfyard had apparently been chosen to act as adjudicator, for he was walking solemnly into the center of the lighted ring and holding a hand up for silence. The window was open enough to hear the hush fall over the crowd and the colonel's voice when he called the principals forward.

Hamilton strode confidently toward his commanding officer. Montgomery drew deeply on his cigar one last time and dropped it onto the cobblestones, grinding it beneath his heel before he took his sword from Damien. He wore a curious smile on his face, but there was nothing amusing in the way he carved an invisible *Z* through the air with the slim steel-blue blade.

"Gentlemen." The colonel's voice boomed out through the dampness. "I am bound by convention to appeal to both of you to settle this *affaire d'honneur* without bloodshed. Lieutenant Garner . . . will you accept an apology if tendered?"

Hamilton shook his head. "A mere apology is insufficient."

"Mr. Montgomery." The colonel glared at him from under beetling white brows. "Do you believe there is any other way of settling this dispute?"

"The lieutenant seems to have his mind made up, sir. I can but oblige."

"Very well." The colonel nodded brusquely to the

seconds. "If everything is in order, we shall proceed. Is there a doctor in attendance?"

A barrel-shaped, bewigged gentleman stepped forward importantly and raised his hand. "Dr. Moore, at your service."

The colonel looked gravely at each combatant. "At the command *en garde*, you will take up your positions. I understand first blood has been waived by both parties? Very well. God have mercy on your souls. Gentlemen, take your marks."

Hearing this, Catherine backed away from the window, her face as pale as wax. "They have waived first blood?" she whispered in horror. "That means . . . the duel is to the death?"

Her heart pounding painfully against her rib cage, she turned and ran for the door.

"Catherine! Where are you going?"

She did not stop to answer. Flinging the door wide and gathering the voluminous folds of her skirts in her hands, she flew along the hallway to the stairs, then down and through the double oak doors as if a demon were snapping at her heels. She ran along the fine gravel of the drive and onto the manicured lawns, slipping on the dew-laden grass and giving her ankle a painful wrench in the process. She did not stop. She kept running toward the rear courtyard, and long before she rounded the corner of the house, she could hear the angry bite of steel on steel, the shrill metallic screech of offense and defense.

The duelists faced each other, left arms bent and raised for balance, right arms in straight thrust, parrying, engaging, counterthrusting without a break in the stride or rhythm of their movements. It was like a ballet—a lethal, deadly ballet that had the crowd holding its collective breath, knowing from the first few strokes that these were no fainthearted academy duelists who would be worried more about the art of their footwork than the presentation

of their blades. Each step was precise, calculated for the
most efficient use of speed and strength. Each thrust and
riposte was effected with a terrifying grace and beauty; a
less experienced swordsman meeting one or the other
would have been dead after the first pass.

Hamilton had been pleasantly surprised by Montgomery's level of skill. It meant he could display his own
without fear of censure for having taken advantage of a
lesser opponent. With that in mind, when they came
together, their blades sliding to the hilts, Hamilton spun
away, feinting to the left while he cut an agile backhand
low across Montgomery's exposed thigh. The crowd
gasped as first blood was drawn, and, as was the custom,
the men parted and paused a moment to acknowledge the
point of honor.

Montgomery waved away the physician with an impatient gesture, then raised his blade in a mocking salute.
His face was hard, his jaw squared, his eyes catching the
glow of the lanterns and smoldering like embers in a fire.

At the call to *encore*, Hamilton went on the full attack,
his teeth bared in savage delight. A slash. A stinging whip
of steel on steel, and Montgomery was pressed briefly
back into the shadows. Instinct found another opening, and
the tip of the lieutenant's blade sliced the flesh from Montgomery's temple, just above his right ear. A dark red
ribbon of blood spilled from the wound, running down the
smooth-shaven jaw to splash the front of the white silk
shirt. He barely registered the injury or the further cries of
approval from the crowd of onlookers. He bared his own
teeth in a snarl and launched himself at his adversary, the
power of his counterattack driving Garner from one side of
the ring to the other, their swords scattering the guests like
leaves in a strong gust of wind. Montgomery forced him
all the way into the lee of the stable, where a thundering
riposte reversed the impetus again, carrying it back into
the circle of yellow lantern light.

The crowd was cheering now, wagering among
themselves as both men, drenched in sweat, began to

show signs of strain. Hamilton bore cuts to his arm and neck; the front of his shirt was slashed open from shoulder to waist. Montgomery's thigh was bleeding profusely, and the entire left side of his face and throat was wet with blood. Garner suspected the merchant's last attack had cost him in stamina—such a sustained onslaught could not help but weaken the wrist, deplete the reflexes. He could even detect the subtle shifting in the fluid stride as Montgomery began to compensate for the wound in his thigh. He willed aside his own fatigue, for he knew his victory would come at any moment. He could feel it, taste it, smell it in the damp, dark air as they fought and slashed a wide, furious circle around the stone fountain.

The opening came with the next double touch, when both blades struck exposed flesh and came away red. Montgomery flinched and retreated, but Garner followed through, putting every last ounce of strength he possessed into the thrust. Montgomery appeared to fall, to stumble off balance, but at the last unlikely moment he shifted his weight forward in a maneuver that should have been impossible to execute. For a certainty Hamilton had not expected it, not this late in the contest. The two blades careened sharply together, the sparks exploding from the steel as Montgomery forced two, three inconceivably swift turns along Hamilton's saber, causing the lieutenant's wrist to roll and break tension. A further twist tore the hilt of Garner's sword out of his numbed fingers and sent it cartwheeling across the cobblestones.

In shock and disbelief Garner watched as Montgomery recovered his stance and brought his saber lunging forward for the coup de grâce.

The tip of the blade, aimed unerringly for a point at midchest, veered, in one blink of the eye to the next, to plunge instead into the soft flesh between two ribs. The impact of the cold steel punching through muscle and tissue took his breath away, and Hamilton staggered back, his gaze fixed with a kind of fascinated horror on the blade as it sank hilt-deep into his flesh, piercing clean through to the other side. There was no pain, not immediately, only a curiously shrinking, sucking sensation that was more pronounced as Montgomery leaned back and pulled the saber free. It was smeared with blood, glinting red in the lantern light, and the lieutenant stared at it, waiting, knowing it would be piercing him again as Montgomery drove for the heart. Hamilton stood his ground, steadfastly refusing to give way to the urge to sag to his knees, although on the next gasped breath he had no choice. His limbs folded beneath him, bringing him down heavily on the damp cobblestones, the crunching of his tall leather boots the only sound in the otherwise hushed courtyard.

Hamilton folded his hands over the rapidly spreading bloodstain and raised his eyes to Montgomery.

"What are you waiting for?" he demanded hoarsely. "Finish it, you bastard."

Montgomery straightened, the unnatural glow fading slowly from his eyes. He stared at his sword for a moment, then, as if it had suddenly become something repulsive to him, threw it aside and took several steps back toward the flickering row of lanterns.

Hamilton's seconds rushed forward and grabbed him beneath both arms to offer support. Montgomery was dimly aware of Damien pressing a wad of folded cloth into his hand, then guiding the hand up to staunch the flow of blood from his temple while someone else poked at the cut on his thigh.

"Come on," Damien urged quietly, aware of the goodly number of Hamilton's fellow dragoons in the crowd. "I don't think you have made any lasting friends here."

"Montgomery!"

The London merchant stopped and turned. Garner was on his feet again, swaying against the efforts of his men to lead him to the side of the ring.

"Don't you walk away from me, you bastard!"

Montgomery's eyes narrowed. "I have no further quarrel with you, Lieutenant. Take your life and leave it at that."

"Leave it? I'll leave nothing." He shrugged off the hands holding him and lurched forward, the spittle tinged pink as it foamed on his lips. "You think this makes you the better man? You think this makes you any less of a *coward*? You were lucky, that's all. Lucky."

"As you believe, Lieutenant. I'll say good-bye to you now, however, with sincere wishes that we never meet again."

"Bastard." Hamilton's jaw clenched through a shudder of pain. "*Bastard!* You're damned right we'll meet again, and when we do you'll regret you turned your back on me. *Do you hear me, Montgomery? Don't you walk away from me!*"

His seconds caught him as he collapsed under a wave of pain. His eyes rolled back so that just the whites showed, and he slumped unconscious into their arms. Two men hurried over with a long plank; he was placed on it and carried into the house, the doctor issuing anxious orders by his side.

Damien, meanwhile, led Montgomery to the tack room at the rear of the stables, where he was induced to remove his shirt and breeches. The cut on his temple required some patience to staunch the bleeding; the thigh wound was deep enough to warrant stitches, but Damien thought it prudent not to wait on the doctor and sent instead for the groomsman who usually tended the Ashbrooke horses. The stitches were put in place slowly and painstakingly, and when the actual sewing was done, Damien sent him away and helped wrap the wound himself in tight cotton strips.

"The sooner you are away from here the better," Damien muttered. "God*damn*, I should have known something like this would happen."

Raefer bit the end off a fresh cigar and lit it. "Because

of me or because the lieutenant is an arrogant sonofabitch who likes to play cock of the block?"

Damien glared. "You may think all of this is amusing, but Garner meant what he said. He doesn't forgive and he won't forget."

"You're saying I should have killed him?"

"It might have saved us both a lot of trouble."

Montgomery's response was delayed as he leaned over the water barrel and rinsed his face and throat. When he straightened, his gaze was drawn to the door of the tack room, where Sir Alfred Ashbrooke stood, his multiple chins quivering in the lamplight.

Damien turned. "Father!"

Sir Alfred ignored his son. "Mr. Montgomery. I felt obliged to come and compliment you on your skill. I do not believe I have seen such fine swordsmanship in all my days."

Montgomery finished drying himself and pulled on a pair of clean breeches. "It is not the kind of compliment I seek on a day-to-day basis, but I thank you nonetheless."

"I thought you might also be relieved to know the wound in the lieutenant's side, while certainly serious, is not likely to be fatal. The doctor feels it was quite a precise cut, missing most of the vital organs, and he anticipates a full recovery in time." He paused a moment and clasped his hands behind his back, swaying slightly against a wave of alcoholic vapors. It was obvious he had been drinking heavily, his usual belligerence heightened by the effects of strong brandy. "I am encouraged to see your own wounds are minimal. Your . . . wife and family will be grateful to get you home in one piece."

Montgomery's eyes flickered again as Colonel Half-yard loomed up in the doorway behind Sir Alfred, his nose just as red, his eyes just as bleary. "I appreciate the sentiment, but I am not married."

"Ah." Sir Alfred smiled crookedly and nodded to the colonel, who in turn gave a signal to someone standing out of sight. That "someone" proved to be six armed dragoon officers, their uniforms tinting the shadows scarlet.

Montgomery scanned the hostile faces before arching an eyebrow warily. "Have you come to arrest me, then?"

"The duel was fairly fought," Colonel Halfyard declared. "Fairly won. No need for an arrest."

Montgomery shrugged his big shoulders into a clean shirt. "In that case, I assure you the escort is unnecessary. I have no intentions of overstaying my welcome."

"The escort, sir, is to ensure your cooperation in fulfilling the rest of your obligation."

"The . . . rest of my obligation?" Montgomery frowned. "I'm not sure I understand."

"Neither do I," Damien said. "Raefer was challenged, he met the challenge, and won—honorably, as Colonel Halfyard has already noted. What else is expected of him?"

Sir Alfred pursed his lips and rocked back on his heels like a lecturing prelate. "You were challenged for taking liberties with my daughter. You accepted the challenge. You won. These men are here to see that you assume your full responsibility."

Montgomery retrieved his cigar, but it did not quite reach his lips. "My . . . responsibility?"

"Indeed. Your exact words were, I believe, *I saw something I wanted and I took it.* You fought for my daughter, sir, and you have won her fairly. Both she and the Reverend Mister Duvall have been taken to the library to await your cooperation in this matter."

Montgomery said nothing. Damien gaped at his father as if he could not possibly have interpreted his meaning correctly. "You can't be serious."

"I assure you, I am very serious. Deadly serious, in fact, as are each of these six young men who are more than willing to see that Mr. Montgomery does the honorable thing to salvage your sister's reputation . . . unto the death, if necessary."

Montgomery stared. Hard. Only the squared ridge of

his jaw betrayed the control it was taking to keep his anger in check.

"Let me get this straight," he said through the grating of his teeth. "You expect me to marry your daughter? Here? Tonight?"

"By your own admission, sir, having neither wife nor family, you are free to do so."

"You know nothing about me."

"I pride myself in being an excellent judge of character," Sir Alfred countered smoothly. "And I judge you to be more than adequate to the task of managing my daughter's somewhat headstrong tendencies. Further, as a businessman, I am sure you can appreciate the fact that a union with Catherine does not come without financial rewards. She was bequeathed quite a handsome dowry by her maternal grandmother—a dowry I am prepared to match, a pound to the penny."

Damien stepped forward, his face a tight white mask. "You're talking about Catherine as if she were a commodity, a piece of dry goods available to the highest bidder. She is your daughter, for Christ's sake. Your own flesh and blood."

Sir Alfred's face reddened. "As such she should know I am a man of my word. I warned her—especially after the last escapade—that I would not tolerate such behavior, yet she seems determined to defy me time and time again. And unless you can produce irrefutable proof that Mr. Montgomery is a liar or a cheat, a thief, a murderer, or a carnivore, I can see no reason to deny him his just rewards! If he is any or all of those things, then these selfsame fine officers will be more than happy to escort him to prison where he belongs."

The muscles in Damien's jaw worked furiously. "Does Catherine have nothing to say about this?"

"Not one single thing," Sir Alfred said bluntly. He looked at Montgomery and swelled out his chest. "Well, sir? What shall it be? Six more stout young duelists . . . or a quiet ceremony in my library?"

"He could refuse to marry her, and he could refuse to fight," Damien persisted. "What would then be your recourse, sir? To shoot him out of hand?"

Sir Alfred pursed his lips. "Nothing quite so drastic, I assure you, but his refusal would pose some difficulties, to be sure. Difficulties that could take weeks, perhaps months to resolve to everyone's satisfaction. Mr. Montgomery would, of course, be detained in the colonel's gaol until such time as the King's court could be petitioned for a ruling—he seems to have a great deal of knowledge about black-market goods, for instance, and his references would have to be investigated thoroughly, including his business interests and associates."

"That's blackmail!" Damien gasped and looked at Montgomery. "They can't force you to do this."

Raefer's jaw clamped down hard enough on his cigar to break off the end. "They aren't leaving me much of a choice. Unfortunately, I have neither the time to waste rotting in their gaol, nor the inclination to fight any more of your sister's misguided champions." He sent the cigar hissing into the barrel of water and tucked the loose ends of his shirt into the waist of his breeches. "Let's get it over with, gentlemen."

"Your waistcoat, sir. Your jacket?" Sir Alfred snatched up both as Montgomery brushed past him out the door.

The tall Londoner stopped and cast a fulminating glance downward. "If you want me that badly, you'll take me as I am."

He strode past Colonel Halfyard and walked angrily out into the courtyard. There were still some guests lingering in the mist-shrouded lantern light, talking excitedly among themselves, replaying every detail of the duel. They fell instantly silent when they saw Montgomery with his escort of dragoons, and most of them, picking up the scent of a new scandal, moved hurriedly to follow them into the manor house.

Once inside, Sir Alfred's much shorter legs had to

scramble considerably faster to overtake the merchant and lead the way up the stairs and along the corridor to his library. He flung the doors wide and waited for Montgomery, Colonel Halfyard, and a dazed and disbelieving Damien Ashbrooke to enter before closing them again, leaving crisp orders with the dragoons that no one was to enter or leave without his express permission.

The library was a dark and somber place with its wood paneling and ceiling-to-floor bookshelves. A single three-pronged candelabra had been lit and set on the enormous gumwood desk, supplementing the less than enthusiastic flames that licked fitfully at the charred logs in the fireplace. Harriet Chalmers sat on a red damask settee and sobbed quietly into the shreds of her handkerchief. The Reverend Mister Duvall, invited as a guest to the party, looked both bewildered and uncomfortable as he waited by the hearth, his hands worrying the pages of a Bible.

Lady Caroline Ashbrooke sat on a leather chair near the reverend, and fussed with nonexistent wrinkles in her skirt. She was a beautiful woman, straight-backed and slender, whose fine, delicate features had been luminously duplicated in her daughter. Her hair was still a soft honey gold beneath the layers of rice powder, her complexion smooth and pure enough to disdain the use of paints and washes. Her eyes were a deeper shade of violet than Catherine's, but where her daughter's were bright and vibrant, sparkling with life, Lady Caroline's were dull, as indifferent to her surroundings as twenty years of a lackluster existence could render them. Her affairs were no secret to anyone in the immediate family, not even her husband, who had taken his own mistress three weeks after their marriage.

She looked up now as Raefer Montgomery's arrival caused the air in the library to fairly crackle alive with tension. Harriet stopped sniffling long enough to cast a shocked glance in Damien's direction—a glance that was interrupted by Sir Alfred summoning the reverend forward.

"We have arrived at an amenable arrangement, Mr. Duvall. Mr. Montgomery is more than willing to accept the hand of my daughter in marriage."

The reverend cast a helpless glance toward the deeper shadows beside the window embrasure. "And, er, Mistress Catherine?"

She had been standing there so still, so utterly motionless, neither Damien nor Montgomery had noted her presence when they entered the room.

"Catherine!" Sir Alfred held out his hand, indicating she was to join them by the hearth. "You will oblige your mother and me by coming out of that damned corner at once. We have the means at hand to repair at least some of the damage you have brought about tonight. Catherine—*do you hear me?*"

The minister trembled visibly at the violence in Sir Alfred's command. "R-really, Lord Ashbrooke, I don't think—"

"Precisely. Do not think. Simply read the blasted ceremony and say the right words."

"B-but the legality—"

"I am quite prepared to pay generously for any special dispensation you may require. In fact, I am willing to pay for a complete new roof for the chapel, if that is what it will take to dispense with any further delays."

"It . . . it isn't that, Your Lordship. It's just . . ."

"It's just what? God's blood, speak up!"

"You cannot force your daughter into a marriage by threats and coercions. It would not be morally legal."

"Poppycock! It's been legal, morally and otherwise, for centuries gone by. That's the root of most of society's troubles these days, allowing flighty, empty-headed children to decide what is best for their future. My daughter will be married this night, sir. If not to Mr. Montgomery, then to the first thick-fisted lout I drag in from the stables."

Catherine moved slowly out of the shadows. Her face was pale, the skin almost translucent where it was stretched over her cheekbones. For the briefest of moments she met and held her mother's eyes, for Lady Caroline's marriage had been arranged: a prudent union between two families of substance, with no thought whatsoever to affection, or even to whether the two parties concerned could tolerate each other. Catherine had hoped for so much more. . . .

Damien hastened to her side and grasped both of her ice-cold hands in his. "Kitty . . . you don't have to go through with this. He cannot force you. You can come back to London with me and—"

She raised a hand and pressed her fingers over his mouth. "My dear brother, my dearest friend . . . he is not forcing me. He has simply explained the advantages and disadvantages of refusing to do as he asks. It will be all right, I promise. *I* will be all right. Just . . . help me get through this unpleasantness, and you'll see. Everything will be all right."

She was calm. Too calm, Damien decided, and far too docile when she should have been screaming and breaking things. She was up to something. There was a definite glimmer in her eyes and a shallow, calculated quality to her breathing that was making her mouth dry and her pulse race.

The Reverend Mister Duvall cleared his throat and Catherine took her place before him. There was one final moment of tension as the thunderously dark-featured Raefer Montgomery let his frosted gaze settle briefly on each face in the room, imposing his contempt and disgust upon them in equal measures. With the barest breath of a curse he moved to Catherine's side and stared straight ahead, his fists clenched as tightly as his jaw.

The reverend began droning the oft-repeated rites and vows of the marriage ceremony. He dared not look either participant in the eye, but directed the promises of love, honor, and obedience to the lofty bookcases. Only once did he make the mistake of focusing on anything more animated, and then only because the cut over the groom's eye had begun to leak again and a bright red spot of blood dripped onto the front of his shirt, staining the stark whiteness of the silk like an omen of tragedy to come.

5

Catherine Ashbrooke Montgomery stood in numbed silence watching a small battalion of maids swarm through her armoires, dressers, tables, and sideboard to select the possessions she approved before packing them quickly into two enormous wooden trunks. A nod or a shake of her head decided the fate of dozens of gowns. Those she rejected were set aside, not to be burned, as she had initially commanded, but to be distributed among the servants. Her new husband had informed her in curt, cold tones of his intentions of departing Rosewood Hall with all due haste. He had stalked out of the library immediately after the perfunctory ceremony, and she had not seen him since.

Numb was exactly how she felt. Her mind, her body, her senses—it was as if she hung suspended somewhere in the air above the room and could watch but not participate as someone else said yea or nay to the selection of gowns. Someone else was watching Harriet burst into tears at every turn, and that same someone else was unable to cry herself. What good would it do? She was married to a man she did not love, did not even know beyond Damien's halfhearted attempts to assure her he was educated, civilized, and reputed to be a gentleman in every sense of the word.

Twice she had thought to go and see Hamilton, and twice she had stopped herself at the door. The doctor, she had been told, had labored over his wound for more than two hours before declaring it might be safe to move him from the table in the kitchen to one of the guest rooms.

What must he think of her? What *would* he think of her when he found out she was Mrs. Raefer Montgomery? Would he consider himself lucky to have escaped her clutches with only a few scars to show for his misguided interest?

Catherine stepped around the clutter of discarded garments and headed for the door again.

"Catherine?" Harriet sniffed and looked up. "Where are you going?"

"I must see him," she said softly.

"See him? See who?"

"Hamilton. I must try to explain . . ."

"Oh, Catherine, no. Why torment yourself? Why torment Hamilton? There is nothing either one of you can do about it now."

Catherine squared her shoulders and went out into the corridor. It seemed strange that there should still be music and laughter drifting through the hallways, but her father had not seen the need to halt the celebrations, only to add a new toast to the bride and groom. The laughter, she was sure, was all in her honor; she would be fodder for the gossips for many months, probably years, to come.

She was still dressed in the watered-silk gown, and the skirt made a soft whispering sound as she made her way toward the guest wing. There were candles alight in the wall sconces. It was nearly four o'clock in the morning, and thankfully, she met no one coming from or going to any of the rooms she passed.

The door to Hamilton's room was slightly ajar and Catherine approached it warily, not knowing who or what to expect to see inside. She could smell, even out in the hallway, the lingering odor of the herbs and unguents Dr. Moore had used to treat the wound. A single candle sat on the bedside table, its flame weak, the wick trimmed to assure the minimum discomfort for the patient. The glow it cast illuminated the sheer canopy that hung like a massive cobweb over the four-poster bed. It also lit the features of the servant who had been assigned to watch over Hamilton Garner while he slept.

Catherine put a finger to her lips and signaled the woman to leave them alone for a few minutes. She edged closer to the bed, her hands pressed over her breasts, hoping the rapid pounding of her heart would not wake him. Hamilton's eyes were closed, the lids flickering sporadically beneath a film of sweat. Droplets slid from his brow and temples, turning his tawny gold hair into a damp, clinging cap. His flesh seemed to have turned gray, and his hands, resting along either thigh, were clutched around the blankets, trembling with each wave of pain. His clothes had been removed and he lay bare to the waist. The thick, wide bandage that was wrapped around his midsection was oily yellow from the doctor's poultice and tinged pink with blood.

Catherine moistened her lips, uncertain now whether to stay or go. He was asleep, drugged most likely with the tincture of laudanum that sat in a blue vial on the night-stand. Hot, fat tears welled over her lashes and slid down her cheeks as she leaned over and gently rearranged the covers he had tugged aside.

"No," he snarled, and a hand shot up, grabbing at her arm. The jade eyes bulged open, but it took several seconds for him to focus and recognize her through the pain. "Catherine? Catherine, is that you?"

"Oh, Hamilton, what have I done to you?"

She sank down onto her knees beside the bed, her head bowed over his hand, her tears wetting his skin.

"You were not to blame for this, Catherine. It was entirely my fault. I underestimated him and . . . and he proved to be the better man."

"No. No, Hamilton! Not a better man. He's vile and devious and coldhearted—"

"Catherine—" He swallowed with difficulty and his hand tightened on her arm. "Dear God, Catherine, did you do it? Did you really marry him?"

"I had no choice," she sobbed. "Father forced me. He was in a rage, he threatened to throw me out into the night, to disown me, to marry me to the first stable hand he could pull out of the haystack."

"You *married* him?"

"I had no choice," she cried weakly, raising her tear-stained face. "He would have done it. He would have thrown me out of the house, and where could I have gone? What could I have done? Who could I have turned to knowing that you hated me, and Damien hated me, and—"

"Hate you?" His eyes burned feverishly, and fresh beads of moisture broke out across his forehead. "I don't hate you, Catherine. You're mine, dammit. *Mine!* And no strutting, arrogant bastard is going to touch you, not while there's breath left in my body."

He started to struggle upright, to push himself off the bed, his hand flailing angrily at Catherine's attempts to stop him.

"What are you doing? Your wound—"

"He's not going to have you, by God! I'll kill him before I'll let him take you away from me!"

"Hamilton, no! You're too weak. Your wound will open again and—"

"You're mine, Catherine. Mine!" A searing jolt of pain lanced through his side, twisting his handsome features into a mask of agony. He slumped back onto the pillows, the sweat pouring from his face in rivers. His mouth moved and he tried to speak again, but there was no sound.

Catherine bathed his face with a damp cloth and tried to soothe him. "Hamilton, you know I love you. You *must* know that I love you."

His eyes shivered open. "No one makes a fool of me," he hissed. "No one. If he tries to take you away, I'll follow. I'll track him to the ends of the earth if need be. He can't get away with this. He *won't* get away with it, I swear."

Hearing footsteps out in the hall, she leaned over and whispered in his ear. "You mustn't do anything until you get well. Please, Hamilton, please promise me you will not do anything until you have your strength back."

"It was a trick, you know. It had to be. I don't know how he did it. No one has ever bested me before; no one ever will again. Yes . . . yes, somehow a trick—"

"Hamilton . . . I want to stay with you, but we need time. Time for your wounds to heal, and time for Father to realize what a dreadful thing he has forced me to do. No, listen to me—" She placed her fingers gently over his mouth to prevent an interruption. "I will leave with Montgomery in the morning, as planned. I must. But at the first inn we come to, I shall tell him I intend to go no farther. I will wait for you there, Hamilton, and . . . and we can run away together. I will go anywhere you want me to go, my love. Anywhere."

"Montgomery is your husband. He can force you—"

"He cannot force me to do anything," she declared vehemently. "And I did not hear him rushing eagerly to repeat his vows. He wants this marriage less than I do, and I am sure he will have no objections to finding someone to annul this entire mockery at the first opportunity. What's more," she said, leaning even closer to whisper against his lips, "I am eighteen now. When the marriage is annulled, the dowry my grandmother left me will be mine. I shall insist Montgomery sign it back as the terms of our parting."

The glazed eyes stared up at her, fighting to absorb everything she was saying.

"He will not touch me, Hamilton, that much I swear to you. As long as you love me and want me, I am yours. No other man shall have what belongs to you alone."

His hand snaked up and curled around the nape of her neck, pulling her roughly forward, crushing her mouth over his. The kiss was anything but gentle and loving; his teeth bruised her lips, his tongue was hot and sour where it thrust into her mouth. But she shuddered away her revulsion, knowing it was a kiss of desperation, of anger, of helplessness.

"Tell me you love me," he commanded harshly.

"I love you, Hamilton. With all my heart."

"Tell me you want me. Only me."

"I want only you," she whispered ardently, aware that they were no longer alone in the room. The servant had come back, and on her heels, Dr. Moore. "Rest now, my love. We will be together soon, I swear we will."

The coach pulled up to the front of Rosewood Hall just as the dawn light was painting the horizon pale blue. The last of the brightest stars still winked overhead and the ground shimmered under a carpet of mist and dew. Catherine stood in the foyer, her gray velvet traveling suit covered beneath the wings of a light woolen cape. Her hair was protected against the morning dampness by a muslin cap trimmed in lace, surmounted by a small gray felt hat. Her hands were gloved, her slippered feet tucked safely inside leather pattens to guard against mud and water.

She was determined not to cry. Her expression was taut, her eyes heavy and strained from sleeplessness, and it gave her some measure of satisfaction to see that Sir Alfred was not bearing up well under her accusing stare. His bloodshot gaze avoided meeting hers. His lips were held in a tight pucker that made him look a bit like a stuffed chicken; his neckcloth was loosened, his jabot askew, the front of his shirt spattered with stains.

"Kitty?"

She turned from her father's discomfort and allowed a small sigh as she leaned into Damien's supportive embrace.

"Kitty, I don't know what to say. . . ."

She had been tempted, seeing the terrible, haggard look on his face, to tell him her plan—hers and Hamilton's—but she had to be certain nothing else would go wrong. He had told her she could go to London and live with him there, and she was counting on him to uphold his promise once she was away from Montgomery.

"It isn't as if I am the first daughter in the world to be

tossed away like so much excess baggage," she said bitterly. "Mind, if I were you, I would be quick about having the banns read for you and Harriet ... before someone takes it upon themselves to destroy *your* life and happiness."

The sarcasm was not lost on Sir Alfred, who reddened further and cleared his throat with a vengeance. But if she hoped for an apology or some sign that he truly regretted his decision, she was sadly disappointed again.

"Stay well, daughter. Behave yourself. Show this fellow Montgomery what stock we Ashbrookes are made of. Say good-bye to your mother now and promise to send her your address in London so that she may deliver her felicitations."

Catherine's eyes stung with tears, despite her resolve. She felt Damien's arm tighten around her shoulder, but it still took every last ounce of strength she had remaining to appear calm as she turned to Lady Caroline. There were signs of a long, sleepless night etched on her mother's face, but somehow Catherine doubted they were the result of any overt concern for her daughter's welfare. Her mouth was puffed and tender-looking, her cheeks and throat were chafed pink. It was more likely that she and Lord Winston had made up for the brief interruption in the library.

"Good-bye, Mother," she said coldly. "Try not to worry about me."

Lady Caroline offered a weary smile. "There is far too much of my blood in your veins for me to doubt you will eventually come to make the best of this situation. Your husband is rich, he is handsome, he is incredibly"—she took a slow, deep breath while she searched for the precise word—"*male*. Do bring him home for a visit now and then. You know you will always be welcome."

Catherine turned away.

"Catherine! Catherine!" Harriet came through the front door like a small hurricane, her hair straggling down her back, her gown rumpled from her having fallen into a fitful sleep in a chair. "You weren't going to leave without saying good-bye, were you?"

"You were up with me most of the night," she murmured, the words muffled within a frantic hug. "I did not have the heart to disturb you."

"I want you to write me every single day, do you hear? *Every day*, no matter what!" She lowered her voice to a fervent whisper. "And if that brute mistreats you in any way, Damien and I will fly to your rescue. We will absolutely *fly*."

"I will write," Catherine promised softly, her heart lodged in her throat again. "I promise. Every single day."

The desperate exchange of embraces ended abruptly at the sound of approaching hoofbeats. Raefer Montgomery, his broad frame cloaked in a flowing greatcoat, rode into view. He was astride the gigantic black stallion Catherine had seen in the clearing, and his face, glowering out from beneath a tricornered beaver hat, was as bleak and grim as the cloud-ridden sky. Dressed all in black, with his black eyes and his black stare, he seemed a larger-than-life specter out of some terrifying nightmare.

"Well, Mrs. Montgomery? Have you dispensed with your farewells?"

Catherine flushed at the coarseness in his manner, at the deliberately mocking inflection he gave her new name.

"I'm ready." She gave her brother a final, quick hug before stepping up to the coach.

Montgomery waited until Damien had handed her inside before he touched a gloved finger to the brim of his hat. "My thanks for an interesting and eventful evening. We must get together and do it again sometime."

Damien opened his mouth to respond, but Montgomery had already wheeled the stallion around. The attending coachman closed and latched the door, and before Catherine could lean fully out and wave a hand, the driver was cracking the whip over the heads of the matched bays, reacting smartly to a barked command from her new husband.

Sir Alfred had spared one of the smaller carriages, a vehicle that could seat Catherine and her personal maid, Deirdre, in relative comfort, as well as transport her two massive trunks in the boot. Constructed of glossy black oak, the side panels were chased in brass and emblazoned with the Ashbrooke family crest as well as the stamp identifying Sir Alfred as a member of the British Parliament. The team of bays was handled by a driver and coachman, both on loan until Montgomery reached London.

Judging by the speed at which they raced along the road, Catherine assumed he wanted to set a new record from Derby to London. The trunks rattled and shook so much she feared the bindings would not hold. The thunder of the horses' hooves was so loud and incessant that a constant vibration hummed in her ears and she could not relax, could not even contemplate trying to recoup the hours of sleep she had lost during the long night. Deirdre O'Shea, normally a bright and cheerful companion, was pale from fear and doubtless could not have bolstered her own spirits, much less those of her mistress.

Montgomery made no attempt to see her or speak to her during the long morning, and it was not until well past noon that he deigned to spare a thought for her mental or physical comforts. By then she was in fine fettle, ready to slap his face or gouge out his eyes at the least provocation.

"How thoughtful of you to inquire after my necessities," she said seethingly. "How considerate of you to stop every few miles that we might stretch our legs or ease our thirst with a sip of water. And how *very* kind of you to instruct the driver to slow down for bends in the road and to do his utmost to avoid every pit and rut across the county."

Montgomery was standing by his horse, stroking the

beast's neck, but showed no reaction to her outburst aside from a faint tug at the corner of his mouth.

"Have you nothing to say?" she demanded, stamping her foot with frustration.

"If the accommodations were not to your liking, you should not have come."

Her eyes blazed violet fire as she planted her hands on her waist. "You know very well I was given no choice in the matter."

"People always have choices."

"Really? And what were yours, pray tell? You looked even less pleased than I did—*if that is at all possible*—and yet you went through with the wretched ceremony anyway."

His eyes lifted from their indolent study of her mouth. "It seemed the most expedient way of getting through an awkward situation."

"Expedient? You call entering into a marriage that neither of us wanted . . . *expedient*?"

"That . . . and a damned nuisance. I told you, I was pressed for time. I still am, so if we could dispense with the rest of your righteous indignation, I'd like to see if we can't reach Wakefield by nightfall. With luck we should be able to find a sympathetic—or greedy—magistrate thereabouts who will legally annul your father's error in judgment." His smile broadened and he arched a saturnine brow. "Unless, of course, I have misread the lovely flush in your cheeks each time you are addressed as Mrs. Montgomery and you would prefer to keep the designation a while longer?"

Catherine's anger drained away in a dizzying rush. She stared up at his bronzed features, totally at a loss for words. She was not even sure she had heard him correctly.

He laughed softly. "My dear Mistress Ashbrooke, while I will admit to a certain misguided attraction to your more earthly charms, I would not now, or ever, consider them worth relinquishing my freedom. I would not relinquish that for you or, indeed, for any other woman."

The candor heightened the flush in her cheeks. "You have an aversion to marriage, sir?"

"Distinct and everlasting, madam. But aside from that, do I honestly strike you as the type of man who would take an unwilling wife to hearth and home?"

"I suppose . . . if I thought about it . . ."

He laughed again. "If women thought about a tenth of the things they *should* think about, I warrant the world would be a far less complicated place to live in."

"Are you suggesting this was *all* my fault?" she asked, her eyes narrowing with renewed vindictiveness.

"Are you trying to tell me you considered the consequences—*all* of the consequences—of using me to rouse your lover's jealousy?"

The heat in Catherine's cheeks reached a searing level. "Lieutenant Garner is not my lover."

"A moot point. Obviously no one has ever cautioned you against pricking the vanity of proud men or wild animals; neither is completely predictable."

"And which of those categories do you fit into?"

"I'll leave the choice solely to your discretion," he mused and bowed solicitously. "And I am still in a hurry, so if you don't mind—" He tilted his dark head in the direction of the lunch Deirdre was laying out on a blanket, and with a haughty swirl of her skirts Catherine walked away. He followed the play of her hips beneath the gray velvet skirt, then all but ignored her for the next hour while he shared his cigars and chatted with the coachmen.

6

The afternoon passed in as much discomfort as the morning. Catherine's only consolation for the bumps and bruises was the promise of speedy salvation at the end of the trek. An annulment at Montgomery's suggestion was the best possible solution she could have hoped for. No arguments. No questions asked. No claims against her dowry. He was actually being quite civil about the whole thing, rather good-natured . . . almost indifferent. In fact, if she thought about it she could conceivably become just as angry at him for the exact opposite reasons. Did he think he was too good for her? *An aversion to marriage . . .* the scoundrel should have counted himself the luckiest man alive to have won the hand of Catherine Augustine Ashbrooke at the small sacrifice of a cut temple and a skewered thigh!

"We are outside of Wakefield," Montgomery announced, his cloaked form suddenly filling the coach door.

Catherine was startled upright, amazed to discover that she had actually managed to doze off, even more amazed to see the dusty purple hues of twilight framing Montgomery's shoulders.

"I would appreciate it if you ladies would remain inside the coach until I have completed arrangements with the innkeeper."

"And the Magistrate?" Catherine asked hopefully, rubbing her eyes.

"Unfortunately, that will have to wait until morning."

"Well . . . as long as there are clean sheets on the bed

and a hot bath waiting in my room," she grumbled. "And food. I am famished."

He stared at her a moment. "I'll see what I can do."

Catherine leaned back on the seat. She felt grimy and dusty, but somehow elated to have the worst behind her. Three or four days, a week at most, and Hamilton would be in Wakefield to rescue her. With her annulment in hand they would not delay in making new vows, proper vows this time between two people who loved each other and belonged together for all time.

She heard the returning crunch of boots on the hard ground outside and gathered the folds of her skirt and petticoats in anticipation of disembarking. The door swung wide again, and Montgomery reached a black-gloved hand inside to offer assistance. Primly she accepted it, and daintily she ventured one petite foot out onto the coach step, but that was as far as she got before stopping dead and gaping in horror at the "inn."

The building was no more than a run-down country cottage. The walls were mud and mortar, the roof was thatch, rippled like the surface of a pond. Wooden shutters leaned drunkenly from the oilcloth windows, and there was more smoke escaping through cracks in the roof and walls than from the half-rotted chimney.

"Is this some kind of joke?" Her voice cracked with fury.

"On the contrary. The landlady takes her hospitality very seriously. It may not be much to look at from the outside, but I am assured of the tastiest meat pasties in two counties and the best black ale in all of England."

"A tavern. You have brought me to a *tavern*?"

"You shall have a clean room for the night. It will not be as fancy as you may be accustomed to, but—"

"The walls could be painted with silver and the floor with gold," she hissed. "The King himself could be lodged in the next room, for all I care. I will not spend so much as a single *hour* in this hovel, much less challenge providence by sleeping under that roof."

"My dear Mistress Ashbrooke—" He slipped his hand

under the crook of her arm, but she jerked back angrily. "All right, then, my dear Mrs. Montgomery—" His arm curled around her waist and he lifted her clear off her feet, crushing her to a shocked silence against his chest. "You can either walk through that door and up to your room under your own power, or you can be carried up the stairs like a sack of grain."

She gasped. "You're hurting me."

"Madam, you do not know the meaning of the word," he said silkily, "but if you would care to learn . . ."

His voice was as ominous as the dark gleam deep in his eyes, and Catherine pushed her fists against his chest to break his hold. "You are even more despicable than I had imagined. Morning cannot come too soon to please me."

"I share your sentiments completely, madam, but until then you will behave yourself. You will walk inside the inn and you will smile pleasantly at Mistress Grundy, for she is quite beside herself at the thought of providing for a lady of *quality*."

Catherine bristled at the sarcasm and wrenched out of his grasp. Deirdre, stepping out of the coach behind her, clutched the portmanteau she was carrying tighter in her arms and joined her mistress in staring at the posting house.

"Faith, Mistress Catherine . . . is it here we're expected to sleep?"

"So I have been informed," Catherine replied tartly, her gaze clashing with Montgomery's. "But only for the one night. Tomorrow we shall endeavor to find *respectable* lodgings where we need not tolerate *any* manner of vermin."

She took Deirdre's arm for support as they walked toward the lighted doorway. An effort had been made in some century past to plant a garden along the pathway, but the weeds had long since taken over. Inside the rickety door, the prospects were no less discouraging. The lower floor was an ale room, dark and airless, smelling of rancid food and unwashed bodies. A fireplace occupied one wall, hung all around with pots and cooking utensils and vile-looking strips of dried meat. A dismal fire was producing more smoke than light or heat. The ceiling sagged threateningly between thick-hewn beams, and a narrow flight of steps—more like a ladder than a stair-well—rose from the center of the room, dividing the public tavern area from what she supposed to be the living quarters. She could only suppose, because there was a sagging rope bed visible behind a sheet of canvas hung to provide privacy.

Of course, there could be some other purpose for the bed and curtain being there, something to do with pro-viding *hospitality* to the patrons, but she did not care to contemplate it.

She took a reflexive step backward, only to come up hard against Montgomery's body. She flinched from the contact and spun around to glare up at him, convinced he was doing this deliberately. Out of spite, perhaps? Or revenge for the humiliation of being forced to marry her?

"I wish Hamilton had run you through. I wish it with all my heart."

"Perhaps next time."

"You doubt there will be a next time, sir? Lieutenant Garner is not so easily pushed aside. If he says he intends to finish what he started, you had best believe he will."

"In that case, perhaps I should give him a good reason," he murmured. "Perhaps we should finish what we started out in the garden last night."

Catherine gasped and stumbled back out of his reach. A very short, very stout, very red-nosed woman scurried out of the taproom and executed a clumsy curtsy.

"Milady. I'm ever so sorry for the mess 'ereabout. We wasn't expectin' 'Is Lordship ter bring a lady back with 'im. I'll 'ave the linens in yer room changed in a lick."

"Her Ladyship would also appreciate a bath, Mrs. Grundy." Montgomery's smile oozed charm like snake oil. "Is that possible?"

"Wa-a-ll, I trow I could send up a washtub."

"That would be fine." Prodded by a gentle nudge from a black-gloved hand, Catherine moved toward the stairs. The banister, as such, was a frayed length of ship's rigging, which she held gingerly as she placed her feet carefully on each cracked and sagging riser. Deirdre, who had observed the exchange between her mistress and presumed new master, followed at a discreet distance, her knuckles white where she gripped the portmanteau that contained all of Catherine's personal articles and jewelry.

The upper floor, Catherine discovered, was partitioned into four small rooms, none of them as large as her dressing room at Rosewood Hall. Having braced herself to expect the worst, she was somewhat relieved to find the tiny bedchamber surprisingly clean. The walls were wood, not canvas, and whitewashed; the bed was old, but solid and draped in a canopy that was not more than a decade old. The only other furniture was a small spindle-legged nightstand and stool. There was no rug to cover the bare planks of the floor and no curtain on the high square window.

"I'll 'ave the washtub sent up right away," Mrs. Grundy said, offering another lopsided curtsy.

"Please . . . do not trouble yourself," Catherine murmured. She caught a warning glance from Montgomery and added, "I'm much too tired to bother with a bath tonight. A simple wash will do fine."

"Aye, I know what ye mean, milady. Never ye mind. I'll send yer up some nice 'ot broth and mutton pies ter fill yer belly."

Catherine forced a smile. "That would be lovely."

She peeled off her gloves and tossed them on the faded coverlet, dimly aware of the landlady excusing herself and bustling off down the stairs again. She leaned her brow on the bedpost and sighed, suddenly weary beyond all recollection.

"That wasn't so difficult, was it?" Montgomery asked. "And you must admit, the room is reasonably clean."

Catherine straightened and faced him. "I will admit,"

she said quietly, "that I would prefer not to have to look at your face again until the morning."

After a brief hesitation his husky laugh pricked the fine hairs across the nape of her neck. "It would be my pleasure to oblige, madam."

He bowed with a flamboyant swirl of the black cape and departed, leaving Catherine to stare at the closed door. She heard his boots echo on the floorboards and mentally cursed every step he took, hoping against hope a plank would give way and plunge him to his death below. The footsteps went only as far as the room next door, however, where they were met by the scrape of a chair and a muffled greeting.

Deirdre, seeing the weariness on her mistress's face, set the pormanteau aside and hurried over to check if there was water in the cracked pitcher that sat on the nightstand.

"Oh, Mistress Catherine, I do wish there was something—"

"What the bloody hell did you bring her here for?"

Both Catherine and Deirdre were startled by the outburst and turned to stare at the partition wall. They waited, holding their breaths, but whatever was said next was ordered into more reasonable tones by Montgomery's sharp reprimand. It was Catherine who noticed a bright sliver of light halfway up the partition—a knot in the wood or a crack from aging—and, curious despite herself, she tiptoed over to the wall and pressed a rounded violet eye to the gap.

Deirdre was plainly shocked. "Mistress Catherine!"

"Hush. I just want to see who he is talking to."

There were *two* other men in the room with Montgomery. One was of medium height, rangy-looking and thin, as if he had not had a good meal in some time. His cheeks had only the sparsest of dirty brown hairs covering them, making him appear to be not much older than Catherine. The second man, who'd had his back to the wall, paced forward in thought, turning at the far wall to provide a glimpse of his face. He was almost as tall as Montgomery, but lean and graceful in his movements, with the somber, contemplative features of a man who might have been a poet or a philosopher. Both of the strangers were dressed casually in loose-fitting homespun shirts, leather jerkins, and plain breeches.

"She won't be a problem after tomorrow," Montgomery was saying as he moved away from the door and stood directly in Catherine's line of sight.

The philosopher leaned into the light and inspected the fresh cut on Montgomery's temple. "Her husband give you that?"

"It was . . . a slight miscalculation on my part. Nothing to worry about. We should be more concerned about the rumors we heard in London. They were true. The colonel tells me several regiments are making preparations to move north; they expect to have their orders by the end of the month."

"So they suspect something?"

Montgomery nodded grimly. "They know our friend is not in Normandy anymore, and they don't believe for a minute he has gone back to Rome. Some are even convinced he has already crossed the Channel with an army."

"The colonel told you this?"

Montgomery removed his tricorn and tossed it on the bed along with his greatcoat. "It was a risk, meeting up with him in Derby, but the reports he passed on were too important to trust to regular couriers. He's concerned—with good reason—that the English army knows too damned much about our business. Too damned much for the information to be coming from their people alone."

"Information goes both ways," the philosopher said quietly.

"Aye, an' the colonel's no' one tae talk, bein' *Sassenach* himsel'," the younger man noted.

Catherine lifted her eye from the peephole, momentarily taken aback at the sound of the broad Scots accent and the vilification placed on the word *Sassenach*—a vulgarism used by the Celts to denote anyone of English birth.

"Is something wrong, Mistress?" Deirdre asked in a whisper.

"Shhh. I ... don't know." She leaned forward again, pressing her ear instead of her eye to the crack in the wall.

"... much longer can you expect to use the name Montgomery?"

"As long as it remains useful, although I was beginning to grow rather fond of it. For that matter, I must confess I was beginning to grow fond of everything to do with Raefer Montgomery's lifestyle."

"Then it's long past time ye came home, cousin. Yer brithers need ye, yer clan needs ye, an' if that's no' reason enough, happens we should be smugglin' yer father, Old Lochiel, back tae Scotland, no' you."

"Perhaps you should be, Iain," Montgomery agreed. "And for your troubles he would have been the first man the English arrested and hanged without the benefit of a trial."

"What makes ye think ye'll fare any better? There's still a price fixed on yer heid—ten thousan' crowns, the last I heard. When the Duke o' Argyle kens ye're back at Achnacarry, like as not he'll double it."

"I would like to be there when he does," Montgomery said flatly. "The look on his face alone would be well worth the trip."

"I, for one, would prefer to look inside his head," came the more reasonable voice of the philosopher. "You can be sure he'll do more than simply raise the reward."

"Aluinn's right," the younger man agreed. "He'll do somethin'. The duke has a long memory, an' so do his clansmen. They've no' forgotten how ye cut down the sons o' a powerful laird an' lived tae tell about it. Furthermair, it's no' so much the Duke ye've tae worry about, but the third whoreson ye let live. *He'll* be the one who'll stir the whole bluidy lot up again. He'll have every Campbell wi'in a hundred mile screamin' that ye got away wi' murderin' his brithers. He'll have them sharpenin' their *clai'mors* an' searchin' every road an' rut that leads tae Achnacarry."

"The Duke of Argyle will control his clansmen and his nephew," Montgomery said flatly. "A raid on Cameron land now, after all these years, would unite the Highlands faster than if Prince Charlie landed with the hundred thousand Frenchmen he has promised. The English government would not be too pleased with the Campbells either, since they know my brother Donald is the last nail holding the lid on the powder keg."

"Aye, an' mayhap that's why yer brither has sent f'ae ye, knowin' yer presence at Achnacarry could blow the lid off faster than any pitch-soaked fuse."

"Donald is a man of peace—a diplomat, not a fighter. The last thing he wants is a war with England."

"Aye, but mayhap he kens one is comin' in spite o' all the talk an' blather. Mayhap he kens the time f'ae talk is over, an' he needs someone beside him who can lead the clan tae war. Men listen tae Young Lochiel, aye, but they'll fight f'ae you."

"I can't believe that is Donald's intention."

"Do ye doubt his loyalty tae the Stuart cause?"

"Loyalty and stupidity are two different things."

The reply was shot back, stiff with indignation. "Ye believe our fight tae see King Jamie back on the throne o' Scotland . . . a stupid thing?"

"At this particular point in time I believe the world is full of righteous fools who think it their divine right to chase each other around in circles. A prudent man might want to consider which fool has the larger, stronger army before he decides to join the chase."

"King Louis has promised tae send troops," Iain objected.

"*If* and *when* the Highlands raise an army of their own."

"He wouldna betray his own cousin!"

"King Louis," Montgomery said grimly, "would betray his own mother if he thought there was a profit in doing so."

"If ye believe so strongly, then, that we're after wastin' our time, why did ye agree tae come back?"

"Damned if I know" was the dry response.

"An' you, Aluinn MacKail?"

There was barely a pause. "I go where Alex goes."

"By all tha's holy," came the slow, disbelieving rejoinder, "I never would ha' guessed it if I hadna heard it wi' ma own ears. The *Camshroinaich Dubh*, tremblin' at the thought o' a few Campbells takin' wind o' him; fearin' the thought o' a wee war wi' the *Sassenach*. By Christ, ye've forgotten who ye are! Ye've forgotten whose bluid flows in yer veins!"

"I haven't forgotten," Montgomery replied, his voice cold as steel.

"Then ye've misplaced yersel' somewhere along the way," Iain spat derisively. "For ye're no' a Cameron. Ye're no' the same Alexander Cameron what slew the dragons from Inverary Castle!"

"Those dragons were made of flesh and blood. They died as easily as you or I could die tomorrow. For God's sake, don't make the mistake of canonizing me over an act that was cold and brutal and ugly."

"Ugly? Aye, it were tha'. But no' as ugly as what I see afore me now. They've made a coward out o' ye, cousin. A *Sassenach* coward."

The sound of angry footsteps and a slamming door brought Catherine's ear away from the peephole long enough to verify that the furious young man had exited the room, leaving the other two occupants staring at the door, then at each other.

"A little rough on him, weren't you?"

"He's exactly the kind of hothead who's going to push Scotland into a war she's not ready for," Montgomery said on a curse.

"Yes, but he's all of what . . . nineteen? Twenty? Not

much older than you were when you thought you could take on the world single-handedly."

"My fight was personal: a life for a life. And if we're speaking of windmills, I recall you jousting at a few of your own, my temperate friend."

"Only because I had to watch your back."

"No one asked you to."

"No," MacKail agreed. "No one asked me to. I ascribe it to a kind heart and an addled brain myself. Also to the fact that there isn't a day I don't wake up wondering what the devil you're going to throw us into next. It has made for a fairly interesting life, so far."

"I'm glad I have amused you," Montgomery said dryly and walked over to the small window.

"Alex . . . why *did* you agree to come back?"

"We've been in exile fifteen years. Isn't that long enough?"

"Iain was right about the Duke of Argyle; the Campbells still want to see you hung for murder."

"They still have to catch me first."

MacKail sighed and raked a hand through his light-brown hair. "Don't you ever worry that your luck is going to run out?"

"Why should I? You worry enough for the both of us."

"That is probably why I have the distinct feeling I should have stayed tucked comfortably in the bed of the luscious Countess de Mornay."

Montgomery laughed. "It was only a matter of time before her husband noticed the horns growing out of his head . . . and besides, you were just as anxious to go home again as I was."

"Just a couple of sentimental bastards at heart? Well, you're right about one thing: This should prove to be an interesting challenge. The borders are being patrolled day and night; the Black Watch is out in strength searching for rebels, inventing them when none can be found to fill their quota. A few thousand Argyle Campbells will be sniffing behind every bush for blood and reward money."

He paused to let a wry smile twist his lips. "Have I missed anything?"

"If Donald did not think we could make it through, he would not have sent Iain to meet us, and he certainly would not have suggested we travel through England."

"True enough, though I doubt he would have gone so far as to suggest we do it in a carriage emblazoned with the crest of a Member of Parliament."

Montgomery swore again. "It's a long story. I don't suppose we could discuss it over a few pints of ale and some of those meat pies I'm smelling? I haven't eaten anything to speak of since I left here Thursday."

They moved toward the door, and Catherine, on the other side of the partition, backed slowly away from the wall, her mouth dry, her heart pounding in her ears—and no wonder! The man she was married to, however temporarily, was not at all what he had presented himself to be. He was *not* a London merchant. *He was not even an Englishman!* He was one of those bare-legged, skirted savages who belonged to a race of warmongers as barbaric and primitive as the barren land they inhabited! He was a Scot. And a Jacobite. Her father would have taken a pistol and shot the rogue out of hand had he known a papist traitor was masquerading as a gentleman . . . and under his own roof!

A Scot! She had known, had *sensed*, there was something unnatural, something sneaky and underhanded about him from the very beginning. How could Damien—a lawyer and a keen judge of character himself—have been duped so easily into a friendship? God in heaven, his career would be ruined if word leaked out that he had been doing business with a Jacobite spy. Everyone knew the Jacobites were in the business of smuggling, kidnapping, extortion, theft, treason, murder . . .

Murder! Raefer Montgomery was wanted for murder! There was a price on his head of ten thousand crowns! And he wasn't even Raefer Montgomery—he was Alexander Cameron, a Jacobite spy, a cold-blooded murderer, and God only knew what else! No doubt he had brought her to this filthy inn under false pretenses, with no intentions of letting her go or of taking her into Wakefield to have the marriage annulled. He would annul it himself with a pistol or knife, then dispose of the body where no one would ever find it.

Catherine raised a trembling hand to her temple . . . then nearly jumped out of her skin when she felt a hand settle on her shoulder.

It was Deirdre, who jumped nearly as high and gasped nearly as loud as her mistress whirled around.

"Deirdre! I'd forgotten you were here."

"Well, I am," the maid said, her hand clasped to her throat. "And no happier for it at the moment."

"Oh, Deirdre—" Catherine reached out to grasp her arm. "Did you hear any of that?"

"Some of it was muffled, mistress, but I heard most."

"Then you agree, we are in terrible danger. We must find a way to get out of here . . . to get away from those men . . . to alert the authorities and have them arrested!"

"But . . . how?" The maid cast worried eyes around the small room. "There are only the two of us, set in the middle of nowhere for all I can see."

Catherine stiffened again. Montgomery—*Cameron*—had said they were in Wakefield, but for all she knew they could be fifty miles north or west or east of any familiar towns. Even so, they were still well within England's borders, and there had to be a garrison of militia nearby.

She walked on softly placed feet to the door and tried the latch. It moved freely enough, but in her mind's eye she could see the stairs and the taproom below and knew there was no possibility of slipping unseen out of the tavern.

She turned and pressed her back flat against the door. There was nothing in the room they could use as weapons, either to attack or to defend themselves. There was a musket in the boot of the coach and a pistol under one of the seats. She had shot her fair share of grouse and pheasant and had no doubt she could shoot a man if he stood between her and her freedom, but first they had to find a way to reach the coach.

"The window, mistress?" Deirdre whispered, her thoughts obviously following along the same lines.

Catherine hastened over to the small, paneless aperture and pushed the shutters fully back on their hinges. The window was not much wider than her shoulders, and the drop to the ground seemed a long way down, but right outside stood an old, gnarled oak, the branches thick as a man's arm, one of them stretched temptingly close to the window. It had been at least ten years since Catherine had even dared to think about climbing a tree, and then never more than a few token feet off the ground to impress her brother.

She started to shake her head. "I don't know . . ."

Deirdre, one of thirteen children sired by an estate game-keeper, had spent half of her life clambering through the forests behind her eight older brothers, and she saw the clear and obvious solution. "See, mistress, how the branches stick out like steps all the way down? Indeed, they look a good deal sturdier than the ones we used to climb up here. I can make a quick try of it first, if you like, but it looks as simple as climbing down a ladder."

Catherine chewed savagely on her lower lip and glanced at the door. "Yes. Yes, you go first. But not just to prove it can be done. You must keep going and try to find help."

Deirdre's soft brown eyes rounded. "I couldn't think of leaving you, mistress, not to the likes of *them*."

Catherine gripped the girl's arm. Deirdre had been her abigail for seven years and was fiercely loyal . . . but this was not the time to prove it. "It might be our only chance. These men are murderers, traitors! You don't actually think they will let either of us live beyond tonight, do you? For all we know, they have already slain the coachmen. This is life and death. And it's no time to argue who will go and who will stay."

Deirdre studied her mistress's desperate features a moment, then bent over and hoisted her plain black skirt and single layer of petticoat up over her knees. Strapped to her upper thigh, just above her stocking garter, was a thin, deadly-looking dagger no bigger than her hand. She slid it out of its sheath and held it out so that a flare of light glittered off the wickedly sharp blade.

"It has come in useful many a time, with many a frisky houseman," she explained, "You take it, mistress. Tuck it here, like so—" She carefully fitted the knife beneath the bodice of the gray velvet traveling suit and adjusted the lace, tucking a piece to shield the heel of the hilt. "Should we become separated for any reason or should one of them try to do you harm, take no chances and aim right between the legs. You needn't be too accurate or strike too hard to have them rolling helpless on the floor."

It was Catherine's turn to study Deirdre's solemn features, this time with new respect. It was a shameful admission to have to make, and one that came at an awkward time, but she had never really paid much attention to the Irish girl before. Servants had been taken for granted all her life, and Deirdre had behaved no differently from any of the other shadowy figures who worked with silent efficiency tending to the comforts of the residents of Rosewood Hall. Yet Catherine and Deirdre were the same age, nearly the same height and build. Had the glossy brown hair been curled and styled instead of scraped back in a severe knot at the nape of her neck, it would have softened a face that was as smooth and fine-boned as any well-born lady's.

"Bless you, Deirdre," she murmured, taking the girl's hands in hers. "I am ever so grateful for your company, and your loyalty. I don't know if I would have half so much courage if I were alone."

Deirdre flushed under the unaccustomed praise and gave her mistress's hands a returned squeeze for encouragement. "Shall I go now, then, or shall I wait? They spoke of sending us food—"

"No. No, I don't want to spend a single moment longer

in this wretched place than I have to. Moreover, if we wait," she added on a more honest note, "I may think too long on the obstacles against us. Hurry now, before they—"

A sound out in the corridor froze them both. Deirdre still had her skirts raised and a hand on the window ledge as the door opened and an equally startled face loomed up pale in the wash of lamplight.

"What the devil are you two up to?"

7

"**D**amien!" Catherine was so surprised to see her brother standing in the doorway that she could do little more than gasp and stare. "What are you doing here?"

"Well . . . I've come to take you home, for one thing. For another—" He was prevented from saying any more by the armload of sobbing female he suddenly found himself holding. "Hello? What's all this? What is going on here?"

She could manage nothing coherent through the sobs, and he soothed her as best he could while he rummaged beneath his greatcoat for a handkerchief.

"There now," he said, guiding her to a seat on the edge of the bed. "Blow like a good girl and tell me what this is all about. You act as if you've been frightened half to death."

"Oh, Damien—" She looked up at him, her eyes swimming in a pool of tears. "Damien, thank God you're here."

"Didn't Raefer tell you I was coming?"

"He . . . h-he *knew*?"

"Of course he knew. We made arrangements last night—well, this morning, actually. I was to follow, meet you here at the inn, witness the annulment, then take you back to Rosewood in the morning."

Catherine gaped up at him in astonishment. "He . . . *told* you to meet us here?"

Damien took the handkerchief out of her hand and wiped the wetness off her cheeks. "He may be a rogue and a bit unpredictable, but he isn't without common sense. He suspected Father would regret his actions when he sobered up, but he couldn't very well send you home alone, without an escort, and he certainly couldn't take you back himself."

"He really was going to go through with the annulment?"

"Of course he was. He isn't in the habit of collecting wives, not that I know about." He stopped and frowned. "Did you think—Good God, is that why you were about to scuttle out the window, to avoid your wifely obligations? Now, really, Kitty—"

"Damien! Exactly how well do you know Raefer Montgomery?"

"How well do I know him? Why do you ask?"

"*How well do you know him? What* do you know about him?"

His frown deepened. "I know about as much as I need to know, I suppose. I met him three or four years ago in Brussels, and since then he has sent a great deal of business my way."

"What *kind* of business?"

He looked bewildered. "Import, export. He's a merchant. . . . Catherine, what is the matter? Why are you asking me all these questions?"

She swallowed hard and clutched his forearms as much to brace herself as to prepare him. "Damien . . . he isn't who he says he is. His name is *not* Raefer Montgomery. He is *not* a London merchant. He isn't even an *Englishman*!"

"Isn't . . . ? Catherine, what are you talking about?"

"I'm talking about *him*," she whispered fiercely. "He isn't who he says he is. He's a *spy*. A *murderer*. I heard him admit it from his own lips that if anyone knew they were here, it could start a war."

"A war? Come now, Kitty, I know you're tired and your imagination is active at the best of times, but—"

"Did you see the men he was with when you came in?"

"There were two other men in the tavern," he admitted slowly.

"Well, they're his cohorts, or his partners, or something—I don't know what. I only know they were here at the inn waiting for him when we arrived. And when they leave, they are heading north." She leaned forward through a dramatic pause and added, "They are *returning home* . . . to *Scotland*. They are spies, I tell you. Jacobite *spies*."

"Catherine"—Damien's handsome face took on the dubious look of a man who believes that a loved one has gone completely mad—"I can understand why you wouldn't like the man, but really, Raefer is neither a—"

"His name isn't Raefer. It's Cameron. Alexander Cameron, and he's wanted for the murder of two men near some place called . . . Archberry. If we had time I'm sure you could check it out for yourself."

"And if I did I'm equally certain we would find some logical explanation. Men change their names for all sorts of reasons, but it doesn't make them spies and murderers."

"Mistress Catherine is telling the truth," Deirdre said quietly. "I heard him say he was going home to Scotland and how they would have to be careful to avoid the border patrols and the Black Watch."

Catherine's eyes gleamed triumphantly. "There is a bounty on his head. Ten thousand crowns. And he was definitely at Rosewood Hall last night to meet up with some colonel—good sweet merciful heaven, you don't suppose it could have been Uncle Lawrence!—to receive reports on army movements that could not be trusted to regular couriers. Damien, can you not see that he's only been using you, using your friendship and your connections to disguise his real activities?"

Damien's face had paled, and although there was still the shadow of doubt in his eyes, there was also the glimmerings of belief.

"When did you say you heard all of this?"

Catherine pointed to the crack in the wall. "I could see and hear everything perfectly. They obviously didn't realize the walls were so thin."

Damien continued to stare at the peephole—so long that she grew impatient.

"What are we going to do?"

He turned to look at her. "Do?"

"They're spies. They're traitors to our King and country. We cannot simply let them mount their horses and ride away."

Her words startled some color into his cheeks. "What other choice do we have?"

She thought about it a moment and grasped his hands again. "If what you say is true, if he really does plan to go into Wakefield tomorrow to arrange an annulment, all we would have to do is tell the judge the truth and he could have Cameron arrested on the spot and thrown into gaol where he belongs."

She leaned back, proud of her plan, pleased at her own ingenuity. Her earlier panic had given way to confidence and, admittedly, some excitement at the prospect of capturing a dangerous criminal. Her conduct the night of the party would be exonerated, and she would be given a heroine's welcome home. Hamilton would be bursting with pride, eager to claim her as his wife. Her plan was perfect, flawless, and far less risky than scrambling down a tree in the dead of night.

"Well? Is there or is there not a detachment of militia in Wakefield?"

"An entire regiment, if I'm not mistaken," Damien murmured. "But the risk—"

Catherine allowed a small, vindictive smile. "He kept us cramped in that horrid coach all day and hardly stopped long enough for food and water. He did not deign to tell me his intentions of annulling the marriage until well past noon—and you can imagine the state I was in by then! Worst of all, he did not even have the common decency to ease my suffering by telling me you were following behind. I'm so angry right now, I could scream for help and hang the risk."

"You don't want to do that," Damien cautioned hastily. "In fact, for this to have any chance of success, you are going to have to act as if nothing has changed. As if you haven't noticed or heard anything out of the ordinary."

"I would rather scream."

Damien rubbed a hand across his brow. "I should go back downstairs myself. They might become suspicious if I stay up here too long."

Catherine clutched his arm. "You aren't going to leave us here alone?"

He stroked gently at a strand of golden hair that had fallen across her cheek. "I am going to go downstairs—exactly as I would have done if you hadn't accosted me at the door. I am going to sit with them and drink with them and, now that I know who and what they are, I am going to listen very carefully to everything they say and perhaps learn something that will be of use to *our* side. You, meanwhile, are going to try to relax and get some sleep. You will need all of your strength and courage tomorrow. And remember: You are perfectly safe as long as you do everything they expect you to do."

Catherine's lips were bloodless, her eyes wide and shiny with fear again.

"Deirdre is here with you," he reminded her. "Good God, they wouldn't dare kill all three of us—plus two coachmen, who, I might add, are engrossed in a game of dice in the stables. Just as a precaution, however, I will be sure to mention that I told at least a dozen people where I was bound and why."

"You will be careful?" she pleaded in a whisper.

"I shall be the soul of discretion. It will be difficult, since I rather liked the fellow up to now. But I admit I like my own skin more." He planted a tender, brotherly kiss on her forehead and moved toward the door. "Remember now: eat and sleep. No more thoughts of vaulting through the window, and no more hysterics. I need you to be strong for me tomorrow."

Catherine managed a weak smile. "I will be. As long as you promise that when this is over, you will exaggerate shamelessly to Father and all our friends about how brave and fearless I was."

Damien grinned. "I shall shout it from the rooftops."

His grin stayed in place until he pulled the door closed behind him. But by the time he had arrived at the bottom of the rickety stairs, his brows were drawn together in an unbroken slash and his hands were balled into fists by his side.

The three men were seated in front of the fire. Raefer Montgomery had his back to the wall, his long legs stretched out and crossed at the ankles. He cradled a pewter tankard, half filled with black ale, in his hands.

"Well?" he asked without looking up. "What did I tell you? Alive and well, although if this fiasco had been for real, your sister might have found herself nursing a well-tanned backside. Pull up a chair and help yourself to some ale or wine. You must be cold from the long ride."

"I am cold, but not from the ride." Damien's gaze shifted to the two men seated opposite Montgomery. The younger one, his expression gloweringly distrustful, was staring back. The third man actually started to offer up a friendly smile, but the gesture was halted with Damien's next words. "My sister has just finished telling me a very interesting story. It seems the walls between the upper rooms are very thin. So thin, in fact, that both she and her abigail heard every word the three of you said. They know who you are and what you are."

Alexander Cameron's midnight eyes turned from the fire, though he was the only one who did not flinch when Damien's fist came smashing down on the tabletop.

"Goddammit! Why weren't you more careful? I pleaded with you . . . I *begged* you to watch what you said and did in front of her. Good Christ, it was insane enough that you went through with the marriage, let alone that you brought her here."

Aluinn MacKail raised an eyebrow. "Marriage? What marriage?"

"You mean he didn't tell you?" Damien snorted with contempt. "Why doesn't that surprise me? What's to tell, after all? Only that he showed up bold as brass at my home and single-handedly managed to piss off half a regiment of dragoons. Only that he fought a duel over my sister's honor and was forced to marry her while her wounded fiancé screamed for vengeance overhead. Not an entirely wasted evening by any standards, though possibly not as extraordinary as I supposed it to be if neither of you seemed concerned enough to ask how he came by the wounds on his temple and thigh."

Cameron patted his breast pocket and produced a cigar. "You're becoming a little overexcited, aren't you?"

"Overexcited? You appear unannounced on my doorstep, jeopardizing both our positions. You antagonize half the guests at the party by defending the politics of a rebelling country, then compound the situation by whisking my sister—who just happens to be the fiancée of an officer in the Royal Dragoons—into the garden, where you make damned sure Hamilton Garner sees what you are about. You goad him into challenging you to a duel, after which my father forces you at gunpoint to marry Catherine! You bring her here and frighten her half to death with stories about spies and murderers! And you accuse me of being *overexcited*?"

Aluinn and Iain both gaped at Alexander Cameron, who calmly struck a match and held it to the end of his cigar.

"In the first place," he said slowly, savoring a long drag of smoke, "there was no way to forewarn you that I was coming to Derby—we missed you in London by half a day. Second, I did not deliberately set out to antagonize any of your guests—pompous, bigoted, anarchist fools that they are. And third, your sister was asking for trouble. I may have taken advantage of that particular situation, but if it hadn't been me it would have been someone else. Furthermore, you know damned well I tried my utmost to avoid accepting the lieutenant's challenge; he just wouldn't let it lie. As for the absolute legality of the wedding ceremony—"

"Ye mean it's true?" Iain blurted with a grin. "Ye really are married tae the wench?"

Damien glared at the younger man. "I'll thank you to remember that the 'wench' is my sister. My *only* sister, whom I love very much. And in case you have forgotten, she also knows who you are."

Alexander clamped his teeth down on the butt of the cigar. "Now, that truly *is* an unfortunate turn of events."

Damien sighed as the fight went out of him and reached for a tankard. "Having the pox would be an unfortunate turn of events right now. Having Catherine ready and eager to drag you in front of the local militia, however . . ." He shook his head and splashed ale into the mug.

"We can't afford any trouble just now," Aluinn said quietly. "She'll have to be kept away from the authorities—at least long enough for us to get across the border into Scotland. The last thing we need right now is more patrols searching for us."

"I fully agree," Damien said. "I just don't know how you're going to do it. When she has her temper up—and believe me, it's at full cock now—you'd have an easier time taming a cobra."

"Ye could always tell her ye're one o' us, *Colonel*," Iain said with a smirk. "Mayhap she'd wear a white cockade under her bonnet as well."

Damien's pale blue eyes iced further at the sarcasm. "I doubt that very much. She would probably scream twice as loud, twice as long."

"Are you saying you don't think you can control what she says or does over the next few days?" Cameron asked.

"I'm saying . . . she has confused priorities at the moment, compounded by a stubborn streak a mile wide. I think as soon as she is set free all hell will break loose. She'll have every hound in England set loose to hunt you down, and if she even suspected I was involved in helping you, she would send them after me as well."

Cameron took a deep breath, uncrossed his ankles, and stood up. "What if the consequences of such actions were spelled out to her?"

Damien studied the hard, uncompromising set to Cameron's jaw. "I don't want her frightened any more than she is already."

"Threats don't usually come sugarcoated."

"Maybe I can talk to her. . . ."

Cameron tossed his cigar into the fire. "We can't take the chance she won't listen."

He strode across the room and went up the stairs. Damien started to follow, but Aluinn was there to block the way.

"He can be diplomatic when he wants to be. And extremely persuasive."

Cameron used his boot to kick open the door, not bothering to slow down or knock before he entered Catherine's room. The force tore the iron latch out of the wall and sent it cracking against the wood with the report of a gunshot. Deirdre, in the middle of undressing Catherine's hair, scattered a handful of steel pins across the floor. Catherine jumped to her feet, her cheeks instantly flushing with two hot spots of indignation.

"What is the meaning of this? How dare you burst into my room uninvited!"

The dark eyes held hers for the span of several throbbing heartbeats, then flicked to the maid. "Leave us alone for a few minutes."

"Stay where you are," Catherine cried and reached out to grasp Deirdre's hand. "Whatever you have come to say, sir, you can say to both of us."

He nodded, his eyes now narrowing. "I suppose that is only fair, since you will both undoubtedly be sharing the same fate."

"And just what is that supposed to mean?"

"In plainer language? I understand you have been eavesdropping on my business. Eavesdroppers often hear things they shouldn't—things that prevent them from remaining healthy for too long."

Catherine glanced at the shattered door. "Damien," she whispered. "What have you done to him?"

"Nothing. Yet."

"I want to see him. I want to see my brother."

Cameron crossed his powerful arms over his chest, posing a formidable threat. "You are hardly in a position to make demands, madam."

"What do you plan to do . . . *Mister Cameron*? Kill us? Damien told Father he was coming after me. If anything happens to us they will send every soldier in England after you. They will catch you and drag you before a tribunal, and they will see that you die a slow, terrible death as a traitor and murderer before they hack you to pieces and feed you to the dogs!"

"My, what a picturesque imagination you have. But just how do you propose your father—or anyone else, for that matter—will find me, let alone catch me?"

"Your arrogance is misplaced, sir. You sadly underestimate my father's influence with the army."

"On the contrary; I warrant he and his hordes of avenging devils would not hesitate to turn London upside down in their search for the elusive Raefer Montgomery. But how long would it take them, do you suppose, to realize Mr. Montgomery no longer exists?"

The truth of what he said struck Catherine like a cold, cruel slap. No one outside the walls of this inn knew that Raefer Montgomery was a disguise. Even Hamilton, who had sworn to come after her, would instinctively follow the road to London, searching for clues to her disappearance. By the time the deception was discovered—if it ever was—their slain bodies would be long overgrown with weeds.

"What do you plan to do with us?"

"That, madam, depends entirely upon whether or not we can come to an agreement."

She crossed her own arms over her chest and studied him belligerently. "What kind of an agreement?"

"I will tell you what I need from you"—the dark eyes narrowed—"and then we can decide what method of persuasion to use to win your cooperation."

"Never," she said promptly. "I will never cooperate."

"I need a week," he continued, as if he had not heard the interruption. "I need time to reach the border, cross into Scotland, and ride up into the Highlands without anticipating a shot in my back every step of the way."

"A musket would be too merciful. They hang spies, you know. They draw and quarter them and stick their severed heads on pikes until they shrivel and blacken like figs."

Cameron grimaced wryly. "You have been reading too many novels."

"And you, sir, are without a conscience, without a soul. The punishment fits the crime, to my way of thinking."

"You can petition for any manner of punishment you see fit . . . providing you give us the week we need."

"Nothing you say or do could induce me to make such a rash promise."

"Nothing?"

"Nothing," she declared flatly.

His eyes descended from the blaze of defiant violet down the slender curve of her throat to come to rest where the soft white flesh of her breasts plumped temptingly over the edge of her bodice.

"Have you forgotten, madam, our participation in a certain poignant ceremony last evening? I believe it gave me . . . shall we say . . . some rather specific rights and privileges."

Catherine refused to acknowledge the cool shiver that rippled down her spine. "If you are referring to conjugal rights, sir, you could indeed claim them, but in doing so you would be adding the charge of *rape* to your already illustrious array of crimes, and I fail to see how doing so would win my silence. If anything, it would only increase my desire to see you crushed beneath the heels of justice."

Cameron felt his temper rising, felt a desire of his own to crush something with his bare hands. "What if I said that to refuse your cooperation would mean you would never see your brother alive again?"

Some small part of her had been expecting the threat, yet it still took all of her strength to keep her expression clear of any emotion. "I do not believe you would kill him so easily," she said quietly. "Damien befriended you."

"I am required to befriend a good many people in my line of work."

Her hands inched up toward her bodice, toward the concealed hilt of Deirdre's knife. "He ... invited you into our home. He defended you against Hamilton and the others."

"He is a lawyer. He defends people for a living."

"And you could kill him? Without suffering a single qualm?"

"If, as you say, I am without a conscience or a soul, what is one more murder? Or three, for that matter?"

Catherine clasped her hands over her breasts and stared into the bottomless black eyes. She saw the surprise register in their depths a moment before she drew the knife and sent it slashing toward his face. He sidestepped the attack and was able to catch her wrist with insolent ease, using more force than was necessary to twist her hand cruelly around and up into the small of her back. An expert pinch on the appropriate nerves produced such an excruciating flash of agony that her fingers sprang apart and her knees buckled beneath her. The knife fell to the floor and was instantly lost under the swirling confusion of her skirt.

Deirdre lunged after it, pushing aside the crush of velvet and lace, scrambling to find the hilt and rise to her mistress's rescue. She saw the gleam of metal on the floorboards and was reaching for it when a second strong pair of arms went around her waist and lifted her bodily away from where Catherine still thrashed frantically to free herself from Cameron's grip. Aluinn Mackail cursed aloud as Deirdre's hard-soled shoes gouged his shins with several well-placed kicks. He flung the Irish virago aside and was reaching for the knife when the maid launched herself at him again. This time he swung his arm up to protect his face from the threat of clawing nails, but instead of deflecting the attack, his fist slammed solidly into Deirdre's temple. The blow snapped her head to one side with enough force to send her sprawling to the floor.

She did not move again.

Catherine ceased her struggles instantly. "You've killed her! Oh, my God . . . *you've killed her!*"

Aluinn knelt quickly beside the maid's prone form and pressed his fingers against her throat. He looked almost as relieved as Catherine when he found a pulse.

"She's all right. She's just out cold. I'm sorry, I didn't mean to—"

"Murderers!" Catherine screamed. "Traitors! Spies! I'll see you both hung for this! If it is the last thing I do, I will see you hung! Hung and drawn and—"

"Oh, for the love of Christ." Cameron leaned forward, scooping Catherine up and over his broad shoulder. He carried the shrieking, flailing bundle out into the hall and down the stairs, dumping her unceremoniously by the hearth.

Damien rushed to her side, a wild eye on Cameron as he helped his sister right herself. Instead of cringing into his arms, Catherine flung herself at the Highlander again, vilifying him with every curse and expletive she could recall hearing. Damien had to grab her around the waist and physically haul her back.

"Let me go!"

"Catherine, please—"

"Let me go! What difference does it make what we say or do, they're going to kill us anyway. They've already tried to kill Deirdre!"

Damien glared at Cameron over the top of her head.

"What is she talking about? What have you done to Deirdre?"

"Nothing. *She* was the one who pulled a knife and tried to settle accounts. The maid got in the way and was knocked out."

"Murderer," Catherine spat. "Traitor! Spy!"

"Damned nuisance," Cameron muttered and searched his pockets for another cigar.

MacKail came back downstairs then, his face tight. "She'll likely be out for a couple of hours, but she's all right. Nothing is cracked or broken."

"What happened?" Damien demanded.

"More to the point," Cameron said, "what happens now? With or without a sugarcoating, your charming little sister is refusing to listen to reason." He arched an eyebrow warningly as she opened her mouth to offer up a retort. "And if I hear one more word from you, madam, I won't be responsible for what condition your hide will be in when and *if* you live to see daylight." His gaze shifted back to Damien. "I'm open to any suggestions you might have. We need time. A couple of days at the very least."

"Let Catherine and Deirdre leave. Keep me with you as a hostage to guarantee their silence."

Catherine whirled around, horrified he could even propose such a thing. "Damien—no!"

"It is the only way, Kitty. They need assurances."

"Or a stout shovel tae dig graves," Iain remarked dryly.

Catherine twisted her hands around fistfuls of her brother's jacket. "Even if they do take you as a hostage, how do you know they'll let you go once they're away from here?"

"You would have my word on it, for one thing," Cameron said evenly.

"Your word as who—Raefer Montgomery or Alexander Cameron?" She flashed hot eyes in his direction. "And your word as what—a spy or a murderer?"

"I don't know anything about any murders he may or may not have committed," Damien said truthfully, "but I do know he could commit three here and now and no one would be any the wiser for weeks . . . months."

"You want us to trust him? Even though he is neither the friend nor the *gentleman* you thought him to be?"

"A man can change his name and his appearance, but he cannot change who he is inside. If he says he will let us go free in exchange for a few days' worth of silence, I have to damned well believe he will let us go free."

She studied each of the three hostile faces, settling on Cameron. He in turn was watching the subtle changes in her expression with a thoughtful look that combined anger, impatience, and the conviction that even if they could frighten a promise of silence out of her, it would last only as long as it took her to find the nearest garrison of militia.

"Iain . . . how long do you estimate it will take us to reach the border?"

The younger man shrugged. "Four nights. Happens less, happens mair, dependin' on how hard we push the horses an' how thick the patrols might be."

"How thick were they when you came south?"

"Thick as a sheep's coat against the shears."

"What of the roads? Are they passable?"

"Roads? Aye, the militia keep them well used." He looked puzzled and glanced askance at Aluinn, whose smoky-gray eyes were intent upon Cameron's face—as if he knew what the other man was thinking and didn't believe it himself. "Wade's roads are passable, aye, if ye have a cravin' tae see a hangman's gibbet up close."

"Or if we wanted to travel by coach," Cameron said quietly.

"By *coach*? Are ye daft? Why would we be after doin' such a clarty thing?"

Aluinn offered the answer with a sigh. "Because three men—or four—on horseback, riding north, staying well off the main tracks and traveling mostly by night, would draw far more attention if they were stopped by a patrol of lobsterbacks than would a fine English coach carrying an English gentleman, his wife, and servants ... traveling in broad daylight, of course, in plain view of anyone with eyes to see them. Have I about interpreted the gleam in your eye correctly, Alex?"

"You usually do," Cameron acknowledged with a nod.

"But would it work? A coach will add anywhere from a week to ten days—assuming the weather cooperates."

"I am still open to alternatives. But while you are trying to think of some, keep this in mind: Damien's unscheduled absence would be certain to raise a question or two, whereas the newly wed Mrs. Montgomery has a very good reason to disappear for a several weeks during her ... impassioned honeymoon trip."

Damien stiffened. "You cannot seriously be suggesting that *Catherine* accompany you?"

"Accompany him?" she asked. "Accompany him where?"

"You could consider it a vacation," Cameron said dryly, tapping ash from his cigar. "Scotland is beautiful in July."

"Scotland! You *are* out of your mind! I'm not going to Scotland. I'm not going anywhere—especially with you! Tell him, Damien. Tell this madman he's insane."

Damien was at a loss for words. He was also fighting very hard to control the overwhelming desire to shake his sister until her bones rattled. Things were happening too quickly. The duel ... the marriage. . . . Events had blown out of everyone's control before either wit or prudence could arrive at a logical, rational way to stop them. Was there a way to stop them now? Should he just blurt out the truth? What would Catherine do if she knew he had been working for and with the Jacobites for several years? He had come close to telling her—telling them all—so many times over the past few months, and perhaps he should have. He was certainly not alone in his disaffection for the Hanover government; many Englishmen were working both secretly and openly to hasten a change in the reigning powers. But to reveal his true intentions would have meant forsaking family and friends, abandoning his contacts in London, cutting his fellow dissidents off from vital sources of information that had taken months, years, to establish. No, he could not have done it then. He could not do it now, even though his own sister had become an unwitting pawn in a very dangerous game.

"Damien?" She was staring up at him, frowning. "*Tell* him."

"I cannot allow it," he said lamely. "You will have to think of another way."

"There is no other way, short of binding her and gagging her and keeping her somewhere under lock and key for a week," Cameron replied quietly. "If there was, don't you think *I* would be the first to jump at it?"

"But . . . she's my sister."

"And I promise you, she will be treated exactly as if she were mine. Two weeks, three at the most, and she'll be home again, safe and sound." He paused and smiled tightly. "With her 'husband's' death certificate clutched firmly in hand, along with a sweet enough financial settlement to remove any tarnish her reputation may have gathered over the whole affair."

"You could give me every last gold sovereign in the *world* and it would not be enough to buy my silence," Catherine insisted. "Damien, tell him. Tell him it isn't enough."

She waited for his outraged protest, but when it became horrifyingly apparent there was not going to be one, she stared at him again, her poise faltering under a wave of faintness.

"Damien?" Her voice was a mere whisper. "Surely you're not thinking of agreeing to this . . . this madness?"

"You haven't given him much of a choice."

"Oh, but—" She whirled again to face Cameron, but found nothing in the cold black eyes that remotely resembled any emotion she could appeal to. A second wave of light-headedness swept through her, one that threatened to undermine what little composure she had left.

Cameron saw it and addressed Damien. "You have my word. No one will touch a hair on your sister's head as long as she behaves herself and is willing to cooperate."

"On your life, Alex," he said, so softly Catherine could barely hear him over the pounding of her heart in her ears. "Swear it on your life."

"You have my word" was the quiet response.

"And . . . if I still refuse?" Catherine gasped.

"If ye refuse," Iain said impatiently, "it'll be a quick skelp on the heid an' a shallow grave by the roadside."

Damien's tolerance shattered on an explosive curse. He thrust Catherine to one side and clawed his hands into the front of Iain's shirt with enough force to split the seams. The sound of the cloth tearing was followed instantly by the sound of a fist crunching into a jawbone. Aluinn sprang forward to pull them apart, but not before Damien landed two more solid punches, one of them smashing into and breaking the younger man's nose.

"Let me go!" He wrenched his arms out of Aluinn's grasp. "He went too far, goddammit! Too far!"

Iain, having staggered back against the wall, dragged his hand across his upper lip and stared at the slick red smear, the rest of which was sheeting down his chin and throat. He roared like an enraged bull and launched himself across the room, a dirk clutched purposefully in his outstretched fist. Aluinn saw the knife, and it was all he could do to shove Damien roughly out of the way and pivot clear himself.

"Iain!" Cameron's shout halted the boy. "Put that thing away!"

"I dinna trust him," Iain spat. "I told ye afore no' tae trust him, but ye wouldna listen."

"I said, *put the knife away!*"

"Aye." He wiped more blood off his face. "I'll put it away . . . clear through his guts, I'll put it away!"

Iain hurled himself at Damien again, but Cameron was there. With an almost effortless grace he caught the out-thrust wrist and snapped the knife free. The boy screamed with pain and hooked his left fist toward his cousin's face, and again Cameron intercepted the punch, pulling the already bloodied jaw into a forceful meeting with his own fist. Iain hung there a moment, his eyes rolling, his body rippling with the stunning effects of the blow. He crumpled slowly, slumping with Cameron's help into a dazed heap on the floor.

The Highlander straightened, clearly disgusted with this new turn of events. He stared at the blood smeared on his hand, then gazed coldly and meaningfully at Damien.

Catherine, fearing her brother was about to suffer some of the same violent treatment, dashed to his side and placed herself between him and Cameron.

"Don't touch him! I'll do it. I'll do whatever you want me to do . . . only let Damien go. Right now, right this minute. Let him walk out that door and ride away."

"Catherine!" It was Damien's turn to react with horror as he gripped her by the shoulders. She shook off his intentions and continued to confront Cameron.

"I want to *see* him ride away, and if you refuse or if anyone tries to follow him, then . . . then you will have a good deal more blood on your hands, because you *will* have to kill us to keep us quiet."

"Catherine!" Damien spun her around to face him. "Do you realize what you are saying? What you are agreeing to do?"

"I am agreeing to be their hostage," she said calmly. "And I am agreeing to believe their promise that we will all live through this thing."

"But, Kitty—"

"Damien, *please*. I won't be able to go through with it

if you force me to think too long or too hard on the consequences. In fact, I don't want to think about it at all. I intend to treat it like a holiday, like the one we took in *Plymouth* that summer when neither one of us wanted to go but Father insisted. *Do you remember?*"

"Catherine, this isn't a game—"

Her eyes widened and the brightness in them was almost piercing.

Game. Dear God, that was what she was trying to tell him. They had played a game on the crumbling walls of a castle near Plymouth, something to do with knights rescuing a lost princess from her wicked uncle, the king. Damien had pretended to ride away to collect the ransom to pay off the Black Prince, but instead had circled around the castle walls and stormed her imaginary captors by surprise.

Was that what she was asking him to do now? To agree to their terms and ride away . . . straight to the garrison in Wakefield to bring back help? Of course it was, and the conspiratorial glitter in her eyes almost made him groan out loud.

"Kitty, I don't know . . ."

"I will be all right," she insisted. "Everything will be all right. Please, just go while you have the chance, before this *gentleman*"—she cast a scorching glance in Alexander Cameron's direction—"decides to change his mind."

"But—"

"Damien, you only make it harder by delaying. Please, go now."

He drew her into his arms and held her tight. He had no choice but to do exactly what she was ordering him to do—to go, to ride away before any of them changed their minds. His gaze locked with Cameron's over the top of her head.

The dark eyes acknowledged the unspoken threat, then turned to Aluinn. "There are two coachmen out in the stable. Tell them you have been hired to relieve them of their duties and they will be returning with Mr. Ashbrooke to Derby."

He saw Catherine's head turn toward him and he smiled wryly. "Will that help satisfy your concerns, madam, for your brother's safe departure?"

"My only satisfaction, sir, will come on the day I see you walk up the steps to the gibbet."

8

Deirdre was stretched out on the bed, her eyes closed, her head lolled to one side, and for a terrible, heart-stopping moment, Catherine thought she *was* dead.

"Deirdre?" She leaned over the prone figure and touched a hand gingerly to the maid's cheek. There was a flutter of movement behind the closed eyelids and a soft groan escaped the pale lips.

"Thank God," Catherine murmured, and focused her concern on the swollen, purpling bruise high on Deirdre's cheekbone. The skin was cut, and she remembered seeing a flash of gold on Aluinn MacKail's finger.

"The beast," she hissed. "All three of them deserve whatever fate awaits them. Oh, Deirdre, wake up. Wake up! I can't bear any of this alone."

She straightened at the sound of a heavy footstep in the outer hall. The door, with its shattered latch, swung open easily at a nudge from MacKail's elbow and he entered balancing a tray laden with steaming meat pasties, bread, and cheese.

"You can take that right back where it came from," Catherine announced archly. "We want no more samples of your hospitality this night."

Ignoring Catherine's command, he deposited the tray on the nightstand and checked again for the pulsebeat throbbing gently in Deirdre's throat.

"I did not mean to hit her. It *was* an accident."

"Tell that to Deirdre when she wakens. *If* she ever wakens."

The soft gray eyes lifted and held Catherine's for a

brief moment before he turned away and, wordlessly, left the room. She followed, slamming the broken door shut behind him, and after a few seconds of thought dragged the chair over and propped it firmly against the broken latch. Satisfied the makeshift lock would discourage any more unannounced visitors, she backed away and glared bravely at the warped planks of the floor, as if she could see clear through them to the room below.

Fools! Dolts! Did they honestly think Damien would simply ride away and abandon her to their clutches? He had understood perfectly the oblique reference to their summer in Plymouth and was probably even now spilling his story to the garrison commander in Wakefield. An hour, no more, and the cottage and the surrounding woods would be swarming with soldiers. Cameron and his fellow renegades would have nowhere to run, nowhere to hide. They would . . .

They would what?

Catherine's heart thudded dully in her ears as she stared at the door.

They would undoubtedly try to use her and Deirdre as hostages, that was what they would do. They would hold a gun or a knife to her head and use the threat of instant death to buy a safe passage out of the trap. Unless . . .

Her gaze flew to the window.

. . . unless she and Deirdre could somehow sneak clear of the cottage without their gaolers knowing it. They had been on the verge of escaping when Damien had interrupted them. They could still do it now.

"Deirdre!" She leaned over and shook the girl's shoulder. "Deirdre, wake up. Wake *up*."

She patted the maid's face—slapped it rather hard, truth be known—and rubbed her wrists. She ran to the washstand and soaked a towel in cool water, then draped it across the pale brow. A groan was the only result, that and a slight shifting of head and shoulders as Deirdre tried to avoid the cold, dripping wetness of the compress.

It was unthinkable to leave an unconscious woman to

the mercy of brigands and criminals, and Catherine rebuked herself for even entertaining the thought. On the other hand, if she could get away and find help, and if help arrived soon enough, she could insist that someone shinny up the tree and remove Deirdre before the trap was sprung.

"Deirdre ... wake up," she cried urgently. "Please wake up."

The unfocused brown eyes opened briefly, but the effort proved too much and she slipped into unconsciousness once again. There was nothing more Catherine could do. Even if she could have roused the maid, she doubted if Deirdre would have the strength to make the descent from the window.

... Simple as climbing down a ladder ...

Chewing her lower lip, Catherine approached the window and contemplated the darkness outside. The moon hung swollen and glistening above the crust of trees, its rays bathing the open ground in a blue-white light, almost as bright as sunlight. The branches of the oak were etched against the light like the bones of a skeleton, ancient and gnarled; there were few leaves or shoots of new growth at window level to hamper her on the way down.

She gathered the folds of her skirt and tucked the hem into her waistband. On a further thought, she removed two of the bulkiest layers of petticoat, reducing the volume of material she would have to control, not for a moment stopping to actually think about what she was preparing to do. Nor did she spare a thought for the repercussions if she was caught in the act of trying to escape.

A last glance over her shoulder and a quick, silent word of prayer found her balanced on the sill, then on the outer ledge. From somewhere she summoned the courage to lean forward, to grasp the scabbed branch and swing herself free of the cottage. The branch was thick and she felt reasonably secure after the initial lurch of fear passed. Still, she kept her eyes closed until her heartbeat returned to some form of normalcy, and she tried not to think of the ground so many dizzying feet below.

In the end it was the image of what she must look like, clinging like a terrified monkey to a vine, that stirred her hands and feet into motion. She began a slow and careful slide along the branch, lowering herself footstep by scraping footstep, until she arrived, panting and considerably damper across the brow, at the junction of the main trunk. There, to her incalculable relief, her slippered toes found more secure holds—it was indeed like lowering herself down the rungs of a ladder—and with an irrepressible sigh of thanks, she found herself standing on solid ground.

She did not linger to celebrate her victory. The stable was still fifty broad paces or more across the moonlit yard, and she experienced another twinge of panic as she envisioned Alexander Cameron passing by a window, happening to glance out, and seeing a fleet-footed shadow streaking across the open space. But there was no way to avoid the risk. She could not stay fastened to the tree, and she would not get far on foot. The edge of the forest was at least a half mile away, and she had no alternative but to try to steal a horse.

Swallowing her fear, she dashed across the yard and flattened herself into the shadows of the crooked, moldering barn. Thankfully the doors were not in the direct wash of moonlight; she would be able to get inside without being seen from the inn. Flushed and fighting for every breath, she cursed her lack of foresight for not removing, or at least loosening, the laces of her stiff pasteboard stomacher; her gasps were nearly as loud as the rusty groan of the hinges as she cautiously worked one heavy door open wide enough to slip inside.

It was utterly dark and smelled thickly of horse. She inched along the wall, stumbling almost right away over a stave that bent her toe and made her cry out sharply with the pain. She bent over to retrieve it and took a few costly seconds to allow her eyes to adjust to the heavy gloom. Again, luck was on her side, for the roof was so rotted in places that it let in slivers of moonlight, enough for her to see there were six rudimentary stalls built of fieldstone and timber. The ceiling overhead was a hanging garden of leather reins and harnesses. The Ashbrooke carriage had been rolled inside, out of sight, and stood like a silent black shadow in the middle of the barn.

Catherine crept to the closest stall and pulled up with another cry as the velvet snout of Cameron's stallion loomed out of the darkness and shrilled an angry challenge. Stumbling away, she made a wide berth around the front of the stall and ran to the next, where one of the matched bays was tethered. She slipped the rope latch off the post, then on a further thought ran quickly to each of the other stalls—excluding that of the black demon—and opened them as well, taking precious seconds more to unfasten halter knots and set the animals free.

She was returning to the bay when a lanky shadow detached itself from the barn door.

"An' just what the hell d'ye think ye're doin'?" Iain Cameron's voice was pure belligerence and sent Catherine shrinking back against the stall door. "Surely ye werena thinkin' o' ridin' out in the middle o' the night wi'out so much as a fare-thee-well?"

She heard a coarse chuckle as he moved forward. "Caught ye red-handed, did I now?"

"Stay back," she warned. "Stay away from me."

"Or ye'll do what? Scream? Aye, ye could scream an' bring ma cousin out here on the run, but could ye explain any better tae him how ye came tae be here in the fairst place? Or why? You an' me, now . . . we should be able tae come tae some mair . . . pleasurable arrangements. Ye're supposed tae be on yer honeymoon anyway, are ye no'?"

"Don't . . . come any closer."

"Oh . . . I plan tae come a mout closer, Mistress High an' Mighty. I plan tae come so close yer thighs'll squeak wi' happiness—"

Catherine swung her arm up and out, wielding the

stave in the direction of his head. Not as quick with his
reflexes as he might have been before the meeting with
Alexander Cameron's fist, Iain saw the stave coming at
his face but was too late to duck and avoid it completely.
The blow knocked him sideways, and he staggered against
the wall. It stunned him long enough for Catherine to run
to the bay, untether it, and pull herself up onto its back.
Iain shouted and lunged after her as she bolted past, but the
noise only startled the other animals into pushing out of
their stalls and thundering toward the open doors.

Catherine did not look back. She bent low over the
neck of the bay and fought to keep her balance as she
urged him to a gallop along the road. Her last clear image
was of the door to the inn bursting open, spilling harsh
yellow light and two running figures into the courtyard.

Pleading for more speed, Catherine held on for dear
life, her hands twined around fistfuls of the brown, wiry
mane that whipped and stung her face with each racing
stride. Fear scalded the back of her throat, and the cold
wind brought tears to her eyes. Her hair streamed out
behind her in long yellow ribbons; her skirt was peeled
back above her knees and snapped out in velvet folds
behind her. She knew the moon was still her immediate
enemy, and she had to decide quickly whether to remain
on the open road or try to weave her way through the bor-
dering blackness of the forest.

A sense of impending danger made her fight the wind
and motion to glance back over her shoulder. The horse
and rider chasing her were plainly visible—as visible as
she no doubt was to him—and she realized her mistake in
not freeing Cameron's stallion.

Gouging her heels cruelly into the bay's flanks, she
ignored the dangers of hidden foxholes and overgrown
roots, and steered the terrified animal off the road. The
trees closest to the road were widely spaced and allowed
enough moonlight to filter through the branches overhead
to guide their way safely, but deeper into the wood she

had no choice but to sacrifice speed for caution. Low-hung branches slapped her and snatched at her hair. The land dipped and twisted, and for long stretches at a time the light was so dim she could only pray and trust the horse's instincts. They plunged across a shallow stream, sending gouts of water glistening off each pounding hoof, then tore through a dense sea of ferns and saplings, scattering any number of sleeping creatures into the night.

The angry hoofbeats behind them were gaining, and Catherine urged the bay to greater speed. She lost her sense of direction and cut a wide circle back the way they came, no longer able to distinguish trees from shadows. They found the stream again, only this time the land took a sharp dip into a narrow gorge, and the bay screamed as it lost its footing on the crumbled embankment. Catherine heard a loud *crack*, and the world slid sideways. Her hands lost their grip on the reins and she was flung into space, spinning through the blackness as the ground rushed up to meet her. Her own scream was cut short as she slammed into a bed of moss, the angle so steep and slippery that she skidded again, tumbling with the momentum of the fall until a final spin sent her over a lip of hard stone and into the icy, rushing water.

The water was only waist deep, but the current was strong and swept her beneath the surface before she was able to find her footing. She grabbed for a handhold, but the bottom was covered with inches of slime, the sides mud and loose stones. She managed to halt her forward motion long enough to thrust her head above water, drawing no more than a scant breath of air before she was pulled under again. Her skirt quickly twisted around her ankles like a corkscrew, and her body was dragged over stones and rocks, bouncing painfully from one side of the stream to the other. She surfaced again in time to see a huge, jagged boulder rushing up to meet her, and just as she braced herself for the impact, a rough pair of hands caught her under the arms and hauled her clear of the current.

Coughing, choking to catch a clear breath of air, she

swung her arms in a desperate attempt to free herself as Alex Cameron pulled her up onto the bank. Her hair was plastered over her face, blinding her, but she imagined she could see his dark, satanic features leering down at her, imagined his fists bunched and raised to carry through the threat he had issued back at the inn.

She screamed hysterically and lashed out, managing to land a solid blow to his jaw. Without hesitation he struck back, the flat of his hand stinging smartly across her cheek. The shock of it startled her, stunned her, cleared her head enough that she allowed him to lift her the rest of the way onto the embankment and carry her back to where her horse lay thrashing and screeching in agony.

One of his forelegs was broken, snapped like a twig. The bones were gleaming through the torn skin and tendons, and each writhing movement produced a scream and a spray of warm blood. Cursing profusely, Cameron knelt beside the suffering animal and unsheathed a knife from the top of his boot. He made two swift, deep slashes in the straining throat, then remained on his knees, stroking the horse's sweat-flecked coat until the legs had shivered to a lifeless halt.

Angry enough at that moment to have willingly used the same knife on Catherine, he did not trust himself to speak or to look her directly in the eye. Instead, he jerked her up onto her feet and half-carried, half-dragged her to where Shadow stood nervously prancing from one foot to the other, his fine, chiseled head held high in distress.

"Easy," Cameron said. "I won't let her ruin you too."

He slung Catherine's soaked and shivering body across the stallion's bare back, then swung himself up behind her, guiding the horse slowly and carefully back through the forest toward the road. Catherine, faint from nausea, sick at heart over the bay, and still coughing up water, was too weak to do more than collapse against the wall of the Highlander's chest.

Back at the inn Aluinn MacKail was waiting anxiously in the yard. "Is she all right? Where is her horse?"

"She's fine; the horse is dead," Cameron said bluntly. "And it's unfortunate it didn't end up the other way around."

"What did she think she was doing?"

"I have no idea." He jumped to the ground, hauling Catherine after him. "But I'm damned well going to find out. Where is Iain?"

"Running down the other horses."

"When he finds them, tell him to get them in harness; we'll be leaving within the hour."

He scooped Catherine into his arms and carried her into the tavern. He did not take her to her room, but to the one next to it where she had seen him meeting with his two companions. He kicked open the door and flung her down on the bed, glaring at her for a full minute before he turned and slammed the door shut behind them.

"Well?" He planted his feet wide apart and crossed his arms over his chest. "I presume you have some explanation that will convince me not to wrap my hands around your throat and throttle the life out of you."

Catherine pushed herself upright, her lips blue and trembling. "G-go to h-hell."

She tried to brush back the tangled mass of hair from her face and shoulders, but there was too much of it, thick and wet, clinging to her skin.

"Hell will most likely be my final destination, madam, but in the meantime it happens to be Scotland, and I will only warn you once—"

"*Warn* me? A spy, a m-murderer, a traitor to king and country, and . . . and *you* dare to warn *me*?"

His gaze flicked briefly to the torn gap in the front of her bodice. The pure whiteness of her skin was marred by an angry red scratch, and he suspected it was not the only blemish she had earned through her recklessness. "You could have gotten yourself killed tonight."

"Then I would have saved you the trouble, wouldn't I?"

The dark eyes narrowed. "As much as I feel that the inclination could change over the course of the next few days, I am not in the habit of killing women . . . or *children*, as the case may be."

"N-no. You only kidnap them and amuse yourself by frightening them half to death."

"Madam, if I truly wanted to frighten you—"

"You would do what? Run my fiancé through with your sword? Beat my maid unconscious? Threaten to kill my brother if I object to being taken hostage against my will?"

Cameron's lips flattened against a curse. "Mistress Ashbrooke . . . you are a bold, brazen, overpampered piece of irresponsible foolishness, suffering under the delusion that all of mankind was placed on this earth for the sole purpose of catering to your every whim. I imagine you use people as it pleases you, for as long as it pleases you, then discard them like so much rubbish when they are no longer useful. I doubt very much whether you have ever gone hungry a day in your life, or know the meaning of the word fear—*real* fear, the kind that gnaws at your belly and leaves you too weak and shaken to even cry. But if you want to find out how that feels—" He leaned ominously closer. "Keep pushing me into a corner."

His patronizing tone infuriated her, but something in his eyes made her wary of the fine balance he maintained between savagery and civility. His hair was blown wildly around his face; his brows were a straight black slash that knew how to express only two emotions: anger and disdain. He was too tall and too thick with muscle. His jaw was too square, his mouth too full, and his eyes . . . his eyes were too insolent by far.

She clasped her hands around her upper arms and shivered. "You have delivered your lecture, sir. Was there anything else?"

He scowled and turned toward the door. "You had best get out of those wet clothes. The last thing I need on my hands is a child with pneumonia."

"I am quite through taking orders from you," she said through chattering teeth.

He stopped with his hand on the latch and blew out a soft, disbelieving breath. "Either you take those wet things off now, or I'll rip them off for you."

"You wouldn't dare."

She realized her mistake at once as the door slammed shut again and he strode back to the bed. She lunged sideways to avoid him, but his hands were there reaching for her, hauling her onto her feet. She balled her fists and struck his chest, but he was not deterred in the least. He spun her around and held her bent over one arm while he stripped off her jacket, then plucked and tore at the fastenings of her bodice. When it was loose, the sleeves were peeled roughly from her arms and the ruined velvet discarded on the floor. The lacing of her corset and stomacher succumbed to a perfunctory series of tugs and snaps, and despite the indignity of her position and the shocking extent of his audacity, her ribs expanded gratefully as the last winding was freed and the stiffened buckram tossed aside.

The sodden length of her skirt joined the growing heap of garments on the floor, as did the solitary petticoat she wore beneath. She was appallingly aware of the hardness of his thighs where they pressed against her, but the indignity paled in comparison to the one she experienced when he ran his hands down her legs to remove her garters and stockings.

She gasped as she was turned again, and it was worse— much worse—having to face him while the outrage continued. She could feel the rasping heat of his breath on her skin, see the blazing animal lust in his eyes. He was going to rape her! He was going to strip her, rape her, then kill her as coldly and remorselessly as he would kill a troublesome flea!

"Stop," she cried weakly. "Please!"

His hands were on the drawstring of her shimmy, the last vestige of modesty in a scandalously immodest situation. The silk was wet and completely transparent, molded to her breasts, her waist, her thighs like a thin film of oil.

With a seemingly indifferent twist of his fingers, the string was released, the silk was brushed from her body, and her flesh was exposed to the cruel mockery in the dark midnight eyes.

In the next instant he was tearing the quilted coverlet off the bed. He flung it around her shoulders and started rubbing, so vigorously that she almost forgot her nakedness. When he had chafed some warmth and color back into her chilled flesh, he bundled her into the quilt and plunked her into the chair.

He returned to the side of the bed and stripped off his own jacket, then lowered his hands to the fastenings of his breeches.

"Wh-what are you doing?" she gasped.

"I'm changing into dry clothes. You can watch if you like."

She averted her head at once and stared wide-eyed at the blank wall. It was, however, a little like watching the reflection of someone in the surface of a pond or in a mirror, for the lamp was behind him and his every movement, as he peeled off the wet breeches, was played out in shadow.

She closed her eyes. "What are you going to do with me now?"

"What do you suggest I do? What would *you* do with a tiresome, officious nuisance of a woman who is the first to question a man's word of honor, yet the last to keep her own?"

Catherine started to turn, to challenge the accusation, but caught a glimpse of hard-thewed flesh and jerked back. "I hardly consider myself bound by honor to a murderer and a spy."

He sighed and shook his head. "Then may I ask by what distorted logic you suppose a murderer and a spy would be expected to honor *his* guarantee?"

Her hands tightened around the edges of the quilt. How long had it been since Damien rode away? Surely he had reached Wakefield by now. Surely he had roused the guard and they were on their way to rescue her this very minute. She vaguely recalled Cameron giving the order to harness the horses; she had to stall them long enough for the soldiers to arrive.

"Damien knows where you are taking me," she said, moistening her lips. "If you kill me—or abuse me in any way—he will follow you. He will hunt you down and see that you die a truly horrible death."

"So you have already said. I gather you have never been to the Highlands, have you? A man can lose himself in the mountains and glens and never be seen by another living soul if it pleases him."

"Is that why you ran away to France to hide? Is that why you have spent the last fifteen years in exile?"

The shadow thrown by the lamp moved and he was suddenly by her side again, leaning forward, his face mere inches from hers. "In the first place, madam, I did not *run*. I was *sent* to France by my older brother, who happens to be the Chief of Clan Cameron. One does not disobey a clan chief. If it had been my choice to make, however, I most certainly would have gone up into the mountains, but then I might not have become so civilized. For that you have my brother Donald to thank . . . if and when you ever meet him."

"*Thankfully,* I will not have that pleasure, for I have no intentions of going anywhere with you, Mr. Cameron, despite whatever foolish promises I may have made. If you are desirous of my meeting any more members of your family, I daresay the only way you will accomplish it is to bind and gag me and drag me behind the coach—which would draw rather more attention to your pilgrimage than you would want."

Cameron's fingers curled around the arms of the chair, although the urge to throttle was slowly and unexpectedly giving way to the urge to smile. He had called her bold and brazen, but he was thinking now that the characterization was too mild. She was sitting naked, with only a blanket between her and ruin, yet she dared to defy him with those huge violet eyes and that soft pout of a mouth—both of which were sorely undermining *his* efforts to ignore the fact that she was sitting there naked in front of him with only a thin layer of blanket protecting *him* from ruin.

"I am not in the mood for any more games," he warned softly.

"Your threats are beginning to sound very much like the bluff of a desperate man, Mr. Cameron. I believe my brother was right. I do not believe you could kill me, and since you have, by your own admission, few alternatives remaining, I would recommend that you mount your horses and ride as fast and as far away as they will carry you."

The smile that had been battling with his better judgment won and spread meaningfully across the rugged face, revealing a dimple in one cheek that seemed entirely incongruous with his nature.

"I think I have at least one other alternative," he mused, moving his hand from the arm of the chair to the edge of the quilt. Catherine followed the movement, shocked to see how far the blanket had slipped off her shoulder and how much bare white flesh lay open to his gaze.

"A wife," he murmured, "would be far more obliging to her husband's wishes if she knew the exact price she would have to pay for her disobedience."

The shiver that stripped her of breath was not entirely due to the long, square-tipped finger that traced a feather-light path along the edge of the quilt. Her eyes widened, then widened further as she watched him lower his mouth to the curve of her shoulder. She jerked to one side and jumped to her feet, but the quilt hampered her movements and she found herself pressed up against the wall, his big body crowding her into the shadows.

"Don't you dare touch me," she gasped. "I'll scream."

"Scream away, dear wife. Who will hear you?"

"The soldiers. The soldiers who are undoubtedly surrounding this wretched place this very minute!"

His dark eyes studied the confident set to her mouth, glinting with comprehension after a moment. "Ahh. You think Damien has gone to fetch help."

"I don't think it, I know it. He would never just ride away and leave me here with you. He would have ridden straight to the garrison in Wakefield!"

"Where he would find these soldiers you are so confident are lurking in the woods as we speak?" He tipped his head up and laughed softly. "My dear Mrs. Montgomery . . . do you really think we would be here if there was a full garrison of English lobsterbacks less than an hour away?"

Shallow, rapid breaths caused her breasts to rise and fall, unwittingly brushing the already oversensitized peaks of her nipples against his chest each time they did so. Her eyes searched his face, but found nothing to support another charge that he was bluffing.

"We chose this particular inn specifically because the entire regiment is off training in the hedgerows more than half a day's ride from here. By the time your brother discovers this and decides where else he might apply for help, and by the time he could bring that help back here . . . why, we wouldn't have to leave here until midmorning and we'd still be long gone before he arrived."

He said this with his mouth a mere inch from hers and his dark eyes filling her entire field of vision. "Y-you promised you wouldn't touch me. You . . . you gave your w-word."

"I gave my word not to lay a hand on you . . . *if* you behaved."

Catherine was too stunned by the quiet vehemence in his voice to move, much less breathe, as he stepped slightly back and started unfastening the front of his shirt. She felt her skin shrink and tingle with a thousand pinpricks of numbing disbelief as inch by inch the vast expanse of bronzed muscle was bared before her. Her mouth went dry, her legs began to tremble. Her belly flooded with a molten heat unlike anything she had ever felt before as she remembered the kiss on the terrace and

how powerless she had been to stop him from taking
what he wanted, to stop herself from giving him even
more than he asked for.

"Please," she whispered. "Don't do this."

"You know how to stop me," he murmured. His hands
abandoned his shirt, leaving the edges gaping open over
the luxuriant pelt of smooth black hairs. He reached over
to cradle either side of her neck and angle her head up.
Her breath escaped on a harsh groan and she tried to twist
away, but his fingers only raked deeper into her hair,
twining around the tangled thickness to hold her fast. His
lips began exploring the curve of her cheek, the tender
underside of her chin, and she felt the shock ripple the
length of her body and back.

"I'll do anything you want. I'll say anything you
want." Her plea gave way to a great, violent shiver as his
tongue flicked expertly around the dainty curl of her ear.
"I'll . . . I'll go anywhere you want me to go, I swear I
will, and . . . and I won't cause any more trouble."

"Another promise?" he mused. "Worth as much as the
last one? Perhaps I need more than just your word this
time."

The raw edge to his voice made her look up. He was
staring back with an intense stillness that made her understand—possibly for the first time—the gravity of her situation. These were desperate men on a desperate flight to the
border, and they would let nothing, no one, stand in their
way. Moreover, Cameron was right: He was no fop or
dandy, no man given to innocent flirtations or easily
seduced by the absurdities of social custom. He saw what
he wanted and he took it; he had said as much to her
father on the terrace. And she could see quite clearly,
here and now, that he wanted something from her, something hard and physical and breathtaking in its very honesty. Something her body, she was quite sure, would
survive, but perhaps not her soul.

The tears that had been threatening along her lashes
spilled over onto her cheeks and ran in two shiny streaks

to her chin. "I won't cause you any more trouble. I won't try to run away again or betray you in any way. I give you my most solemn word against God, I won't, only"— she closed her eyes and tried to control the quiver in her chin—"please don't do this."

Alexander Cameron was already fighting against an urge so strong it was paralyzing his every thought and emotion. He saw the tears. He watched them collect on her chin and splash onto the milky white half-moon of her breast. It had been so long—too long, he reasoned with the logic of a drowning man—since he had lost himself in the softness of a woman's body. The need was overwhelming, the hunger almost crippling, and he had to force himself to ease away from her, to back away before the smell, the taste, the feel of her undermined him completely.

"You will need clean, dry clothes," he said in a low, hoarse voice. "I'll have your trunk sent up."

He moved back to the bed and retrieved his jacket, waistcoat, and boots. "We will be leaving within the hour. Do not make me come up and get you."

LOCHABER
August 1745

Alexander Cameron reined Shadow to a halt on the rim of a vast amphitheater, the mouth of a chasm that stretched thirty miles to the north to form the Great Glen. The rivers, streams, and cataracts that tumbled down from the formidable reaches filled the basin of the chasm and formed a canal of lochs from Inverness in the north to Fort William in the south. The largest by far was Loch Ness, with waters deep and black and mysterious.

By Alex's reckoning they were an eight-hour journey from Achnacarry—eight hours filled with the most savage yet unquestionably the most spectacular terrain they would encounter. From where he stood he could see the proud splendor of Aonach Mor rising like a shark's tooth against the clear blue vault of the sky. To the south and west were the Gray Corries, gnarled and ominous with shadow; over his left shoulder was the jutting majesty of Ben Nevis, the tallest peak in Britain. Directly below where he stood was a gorge, sparkling with the swift-flowing waters of the River Spean, and beyond, the jagged crests and fertile glens that were the ancient landholding of Lochaber. These tall, mystic tracts of mountain were the heart of the Highlands. To Alex, they were home.

Their progress so far, as Iain had predicted, had been slow and dusty over the red sandstone military roads. Traveling by coach with two sullen women had definitely hampered them; on horseback the trio could have covered the distance in a fraction of the time. Weighing heavily on the other end of the scale, however, was the fact that they had been stopped by at least a dozen patrols

of soldiers who, after a cursory inspection of the Ashbrooke coat of arms and a courteous introduction to
"Lord and Lady Grayston," had been more concerned
with warning them about the dissident Jacobite rebels in
the area than verifying their identities.

"We could bring half the French army into Scotland
under the petticoats of a well-turned ankle," Aluinn had
remarked after one such delay when the soldiers had
actually ridden escort for several miles. "And I confess, I
am glad we have those ankles along. These troops are so
jittery they're ready to shoot anything that moves."

The tension and suspicion they had met while crossing
through the Lowlands had been disturbing as well. Hospitality—an inbred tradition to Caledonians—had been
given grudgingly and guardedly. The Lowlanders were
content with the Hanover government. Their pastures
were lush and green, stretching for miles, filled with
herds of fat, waddling cattle. The cities were prosperous,
the towns crowded with English merchants who spread
their money like lard, and to say a word against King
George was to spit in the hand of affluence. Clan ties had
long since become lax in these border territories, loyalties strained and scattered. A man could better himself
on wits and ambition without the support or protection of
the chiefs and lairds, and being less dependent on heredi-
tary laws they were less willing to commit themselves to
a cause that would see that independence taken away.

Looming above these Lowland pastures, beckoning on
the horizon like ancient, twisted hands, were the mist-
ridden peaks of the Grampian Mountains. They formed a
wall of hostile, impenetrable rock that stood as a clear
division between the Highlands and Lowlands. Within
these forbidding glens and corries, their inhabitants de-
pended upon strict codes of subservience to the clan for
survival. Territories were divided and claimed by power of
the sword, disputed by centuries-old blood feuds, guarded
and protected in some cases by whole private armies. There
were laws—of survival and retribution. The chief's word

was absolute; the Highlander's pride in himself, his clan, his heritage, was his mainstay. An insult to the humblest of tenants was answered by an armed raiding party. A man from one clan found straying on land belonging to another could be hanged without benefit of trial or defense. The history of the Highlands was steeped in bloodshed and violence; it was a land of dark gods and druids, of legends and superstition, where a man was either born to wealth and prominence or born to serve. It was Alexander Cameron's birthright, and as he stood on the crest of the sweeping vista that stretched out before him, his blood sang and his body throbbed with pride.

"Incredible, isn't it?" Aluinn asked softly by his side. He, too, was staring awestruck at the graduating shades of purple and blue and darkest-black chasms that marked the vastness of Lochaber. "All the memories come back on a single whiff of mountain heather."

Cameron smiled and dismounted, then patted Shadow on the rump, setting him free to graze on the sweet deer grass. "I've been seeing faces in my mind's eye that I haven't been able to recall for years. Do you remember old MacIan of Corriarrick?"

"Ruadh MacIan? Who could forget? Arms as thick as tree trunks and hair so red it hurt your eyes." He grinned suddenly. "I wonder if he ever got around to marrying Elspeth MacDonald. He used to turn as red as his hair when he was anywhere near her."

Cameron's eyes crinkled with fond remembrances as he studied the towering cliffs on either side of the amphitheater. There were curls of hazy mist shrouding the summits, and in the foreground a solitary eagle hovered, the sunlight dancing off its wings like liquid silver as it carved a slow, watchful circle on the wind currents.

"What do you suppose we will find when we reach Achnacarry?"

Aluinn glanced over. "According to Iain, nothing much has changed. The war tower still stands, the fruit gardens still bloom, the roses and yews are thriving.

Lochiel has planted a new avenue of elms—probably at Maura's suggestion—to make the approach to the castle less forbidding."

Alex sighed. "That wasn't exactly what I meant."

"I know what you meant. What do you want me to say? That nothing has changed? The curse of all exiles is to dream of a homecoming where everything has remained frozen in time, precisely as they remembered it. But it's been fifteen years. The buildings are older, the people are older. The children are grown, with wives and families of their own; the burial grounds undoubtedly have more cairns than we'd care to see." He hesitated and crooked his head in the direction of the coach. "And speaking of changes, how are you proposing to explain the presence of Lady Grayston?"

Alex followed his gaze. The coach had drawn to a halt several yards away, the door was open, and the head and shoulders of Catherine Ashbrooke were emerging into the sunlight. Alex had avoided any unnecessary contact with his "wife" over the past ten days and nights, an arrangement that had been met with icy approval. It was far easier to deal with her cool hostility than it was to try his patience with forced conversation. It was easier, in fact, just to watch her—something he found himself doing far more frequently than was advisable, or so his conscience warned him. But she was a beauty, no denying. Her hair shone in the sunlight like pure gold, her skin glowed with a refreshing radiance foreign to the powdered, painted faces he had been accustomed to seeing in his travels. Her eyes were bright and keen and noticed every little detail of her surroundings despite her feigned indifference. It would have taken a heart colder even than his to be able to ignore her completely.

Even so, he had been pondering the question of what to do with her ever since they had left Wakefield.

"I suppose I could always tell them a version of the truth—that she is the sister of a friend who was willing to pose as my wife in order to ensure us a safe passage home."

Aluinn looked skeptical. "Lochiel has been anxious to see you married off for years now. Even a hint that the vows were legal, regardless of the circumstances, and he will be converting half the castle into a nursery."

"You have a better idea?"

MacKail pursed his lips thoughtfully. "You could live up to the image she has of you—already well-deserved, I might add—and tell Donald you have brought him a fine English prize to hold for ransom."

"You're enjoying this, aren't you?" Alex asked dryly.

"It has its moments."

"Then I hope you won't be too disappointed when I tell you I plan to make a brief detour south once we have crossed the Spean."

Aluinn sobered instantly. "You're going to take her to Fort William?"

"It should not be too difficult to arrange passage for her on a military supply ship, especially since her uncle is a high-ranking officer in the English army."

"And I suppose you think you will be able to just walk through the gates, brandish an effete accent, and walk out again?"

Alexander turned away, squinting against the glare of the sun.

"I thought we agreed not to take any unnecessary risks," Aluinn reminded him quietly.

"You would rather I risk my freedom by taking her all the way to Achnacarry?"

The attempted humor fell flat as the soft gray eyes darkened with concern. "I would rather you had never thought of this harebrained scheme in the first place."

"If it was so harebrained, why didn't you object more strenuously at the outset?"

Aluinn sighed. "Because at the time Iain seemed just a little too eager to dig three graves. Have you told her yet?"

"No. I was planning to brighten her day now."

Aluinn looked down and stubbed at a mound of dirt with his toe. "You know . . . you could do a lot worse for yourself." He paused and grinned slyly. "And the castle does have a lot of spare room."

Before Alex could answer, MacKail was wisely out of range, already on his way back to the coach. He was still chuckling softly under his breath as he passed by Catherine and Deirdre, both of whom treated him to such a cold stare, he looked down to see if he had trod in something unpleasant.

Catherine looked away disdainfully and followed Deirdre into the shade of a tree. She had found the past ten days to be an excruciating test of endurance. While it was true the three fugitives had been remarkably well-mannered, she could not help but feel it was only a matter of time before their true bestial natures emerged again. Despite her own outwardly good behavior, the promise extracted by the Scottish renegade rankled and abraded her senses at every turn. At each stop they made—each inn, each village, each lowly cow shed they paused at to beg a cup of water—she yearned to scream for help at the top of her lungs. Each time they were stopped and questioned by the militia she grew faint with desperation, hoping against hope they could see the cold steel of the pistol concealed beneath Cameron's jacket and interpret the silent plea in her eyes. Each time she caught a glimpse of scarlet her heart raced and her blood pounded, for she knew it must be Hamilton Garner come to rescue her.

She was thinking about Hamilton as she turned to study her nemesis, about the pleasure she would have watching him slash Cameron's face to ribbons. He stood on the knoll, his big body outlined against the stark blue of the sky. He was hatless, and the metallic black waves of his hair were gathered loosely at the nape of his neck, leaving only a few errant curls to brush forward over his brow and temples. He wore a chocolate-brown jacket and buff breeches, the latter indecently tight where the cloth was stretched to fit the muscles of his thighs. His shirt was snowy white linen, his waistcoat was cream-colored satin embroidered with bright sprigs of green-and-gold leaves.

It was no wonder men and women alike were duped into believing he was someone he was not. He gave the appearance of refinement and elegance, and he certainly spoke with more authority than one would credit a Highland sheep farmer. The faint lilt in his voice was easily mistaken for a Continental accent, and his mannerisms supported the fact that he had been educated in Europe. He was obviously accustomed to expensive clothes and a luxurious lifestyle; what could possibly be inspiring him to trade the comfortable vicissitudes of Raefer Montgomery for a damp stone cottage and sheepskin cloaks?

He certainly had not given the impression he was a fanatical Jacobite, so she suspected it was not politics bringing him home. Money? Were spies well paid? And with regard to money—there was a reward of ten thousand crowns on his head, the fortune of ten lifetimes to most of the Highland rabble they had encountered thus far, some of whom had stared at him as if he were the devil reincarnate. Was he not afraid someone might recognize him without her assistance and alert the local constabulary?

With a small start she realized the dark eyes were upon her. He was frowning slightly, no doubt curious to know why he was earning such a prolonged scrutiny.

Catherine lowered her lashes quickly, but not soon enough to discourage him from joining her in the shade.

"A lovely afternoon," he commented casually. "Perfect for a bit of a stroll. The hill we are coming to is rather steep, and the road does not appear to be in the best condition to accept the coach. It would probably be safer to have Iain drive it down ahead and we will join him at the bottom."

"As you like," she said primly and picked at the lace ruff on her sleeve. When he did not move away at once, she felt annoyingly obliged to look up. "Is it permitted for me to ask where we are?"

"We have been in MacDonald territory since noon yesterday."

"That does not tell me a great deal."

"I had no idea you were interested in geography."

She mimicked his gently mocking smile. "I am merely curious to gain some bearings. Other than being vaguely aware of crossing the border from England *three days ago*, I have not seen anything that could possibly be construed as a landmark since."

Her tone was so accusing and the implication so blatant, he kept his intent to tell her about Fort William on his tongue and arched an eyebrow instead. "You aren't impressed by our mountains?"

"I have seen mountains before."

"No doubt you have seen fine English hills," he agreed and startled her again by reaching his hand out in an invitation. When she quickly clasped her own behind her back, his grin broadened, allowing the barest glimpse of the dimple she had marked once before. "You wanted to see a landmark, didn't you? I am merely offering to present you a better view."

Catherine followed his glance to the top of the knoll. It looked harmless enough, and with a sigh she ignored his extended hand and walked up the shallow incline. As she climbed it the crust of the bluish mountains that dominated the skyline seemed to move farther away, as if sliding independently from the ground she walked on. The mountains themselves grew and expanded until they spread to dominate the entire horizon, whereas the top of the knoll simply ended in a void of space and cool air, a ledge of rock marking the rim of a cliff that fell several hundred feet straight down. Cameron was a pace behind, and as she reached the top of the hill he moved up alongside her. This time she offered no objections to the hand he slipped under her elbow, steadying her against the lure of the sheer precipice that dropped off a mere few feet from where they stood.

At its base sprawled a valley, so far below them that

the road was reduced to a thin ribbon rippling across the green-carpeted floor. Sweeping up on either side, the walls of the two closest mountains were split and broken by fissures piled randomly with rocks, and even though it was a bright, crisp day, the battlements were hazed and gloomy, as if there were places where even the sun was denied entry.

Loath as she was to admit it, there had been other vistas like this that had quite taken her breath away. Sweeping russet meadows; winding silver slashes of rivers and streams; the steep and craggy peaks that lost their summits in the shrouds of opaque mists before falling black and sheer into the inky waters of a loch. There was beauty in the iridescent green of the thunderclouds that gathered at night, and there was brutality in the peaceful majesty of the glens. Only yesterday they had traveled through a valley so still and tranquil it might have been painted on canvas. It was called Glencoe, MacKail had told her, home of the MacDonalds and scene of one of the most treacherous massacres in Scotland's history. Beauty and ugliness, prosperity and awesome desolation; the mood of the land was as changing and enigmatic as that of the man who stood by her side.

Catherine turned her head and leaned slightly forward, the better to identify the muted rushing sound to the left of the knoll. She saw a thin, whisper-sheer cascade of water tumbling over the broken lip of the precipice, spraying a transparent, rainbow-hued mist onto the rocks below.

"It is beautiful," she admitted.

"Beautiful, indeed," he agreed softly.

Something in his voice suggested his comment was not directed entirely to the view, and as she settled slowly back she became disturbingly aware that his hand no longer cradled her elbow but was curved firmly around the indent of her waist.

She had not realized she had moved closer to his side or that she had insinuated herself into the protective circle of his arm, but Cameron was very much aware of both indiscretions. The sunlight was playing with the breeze-blown wisps of her hair, scattering them like threads of spun silk against the dark brown of his jacket. Her violet eyes had absorbed the color of the sky and shimmered with flecks of vibrant blue. She smelled of wildflowers, dewy and fresh, and the effect was intoxicating. It reacted on his senses like a deep drink of sweet wine.

The sudden, awkward silence sent a shiver racing over the surface of her skin, and she extricated herself from his embrace with what she hoped was a subtle step sideways.

"Are we anywhere near this Archberry you keep talking about?"

"Achnacarry. About half a day's hard ride, perhaps a little more."

"Half a day," she repeated wistfully. "And then you will be sending me home?"

The longing in her voice irritated him, and he glanced at the mountain on the left. Fort William was just on the other side, with its fine harbor and stout military ships. "As soon as I think it is safe, yes."

"Safe? I fail to see where I could be any further threat to you or your furtive little mission. We are safely across the border. The farmers we have seen haven't spoken enough intelligible English for me to betray you even if I tried—which I haven't."

"You have been very well-behaved," he agreed.

"I have done exactly what you asked of me. I have cooperated and been civil to the point of nausea each time we were stopped by strangers. Frankly, I don't know what else you want from me, and I think it is vile and unconscionable to keep tormenting me this way."

"What way is that, Mistress Ashbrooke? Have we not stayed in the finest inns, with the hottest baths and the tastiest foods?"

"Food and hot water do not compensate for boorish company."

"Boorish?" Alex cast a frown over his shoulder, assessing the rich black and gold livery worn by Aluinn and Iain, the polished gleam to the carriage, the curried smartness of the new team of horses.

"Your cousin," she said succinctly. "He stares at me constantly. Glowers at me, actually, as if he would dearly like to do me harm."

"You did club him rather soundly over the head," he reminded her. "As for him staring, you are a very lovely woman, I would be more concerned if he didn't stare."

Catherine's cheeks warmed at the unexpected compliment. "He has threatened me. I've heard him."

"You understand Gaelic?"

"I know when a man is threatening me. And I can guess what manner of threat he is promising. Why, he tried to accost me once, in the stables, and if not for the good stout pike providence saw fit to provide, I might well have been . . ."

He smiled politely and searched out a cigar from his pocket. "Yes? You might have been . . . ?"

". . . violated," she concluded lamely, remembering how close she had come to suffering that very fate at the hands of Alexander Cameron.

He watched the color deepen in her cheeks—all the while wondering if the rest of her body flushed such a gloriously warm shade—then cleared his throat and pointed to where Deirdre had set out a blanket for lunch. "You should have something to eat before we make the walk down into the valley."

"I'm not very hungry."

"You hardly ate anything for breakfast." He blew out a gust of smoke and snuffed the match beneath his boot as he hooked a hand under her elbow again. "I would sooner not have to deal with a woman fainting on me from starvation, thank you very much."

"I have no intentions of fainting," she said, resisting his attempt to guide her back down the slope. "I have never fainted before in my life, for that matter. And do let me go. I am not a child to be led about by a string."

"Believe me, I realized at Wakefield you were not a child, but I do wish you would stop acting like one."

Catherine was so shocked by the blatant reference to what had happened at the inn that she allowed herself to be led to the picnic blanket and to be seated on a conveniently low, flat rock. Deirdre hurried over with the last of the provisions—a wicker basket and cutlery—but at a glance from Cameron, she deposited them on the blanket and returned to the coach.

The Highlander, meanwhile, stripped off his jacket, folded it carefully, and set it beside him on the grass.

"What do you think you are doing?"

"Eating lunch," he said. "I suddenly find myself with quite an appetite. Will you serve, or shall I?"

She considered elaborating on precisely where he could put the greasy leg of mutton that poked out of its wrapper, but instead snapped open a linen napkin, selected the cleanest knife from the small tray, and transferred a thin slice of meat and some cheese to her plate. Without a thought to Cameron or his empty plate, she broke off a piece of cheese and began to eat.

He grinned hugely, the cigar clamped between his teeth. "Why, Mistress Ashbrooke, how uncivil of you. And all this time you have been condemning me for my bad manners."

She threw the piece of cheese aside and glared directly into the laughing midnight eyes. Bristling at his arrogance, she reached into the basket, stabbed grimly at two slabs of meat, and thrust the plate in front of him.

"Thank you."

Seething, she watched as he propped his cigar on the grass and tasted the mutton.

"Delicious. You should try it."

"I find it difficult to breathe, let alone enjoy the taste of food with the air tainted so. Dare I ask what is rolled into those miserably foul things you smoke?"

"Foul? Never let a Virginia colonist hear you say

that." He took a long, last draw on the cigar and stubbed it out in the grass. "Better?"

"It would suit me better if we could drop this ridiculous charade once and for all. You have kidnapped me, compromised me, ruined my reputation almost beyond repair, yet you expect me to sit and share a cordial meal. You expect me to answer all of your wretched questions the instant you ask them, yet you haven't the decency to give an honest reply to anything I have asked thus far."

He lounged back on one elbow, enjoying the way the sunlight was exploding in tiny sparks in her eyes. "Very well, ask away. I will answer anything you like—providing I am accorded equal time and liberty."

Catherine tapped her fingertips on the stem of her fork, wary of a verbal trap. "Did you really murder someone? Is there really a reward posted for your capture?"

If he was surprised or caught off guard by the bluntness of the question, it did not show. "Why? Were you hoping to turn me over to the authorities and collect it?"

"There, you see?" She threw down the fork in exasperation. "You always answer a question with another question."

"Do I?" He made an effort to contain a smile. "I suppose I do. Sorry. Force of habit, I guess." His eyes wandered from hers for a moment, distracted by a movement from the coach. "What was it you asked? Ah, yes: Did I really murder a man? The direct answer would be yes, I killed two men fifteen years ago, but I do not believe I *murdered* either one of them. And to be perfectly honest there have been a great many more over the years that haven't earned half so much attention, though they could be considered a more criminal waste."

Catherine stiffened. "You have killed too many men to keep count?"

"It is difficult in the heat of battle to accurately judge how many of your cartridges strike home."

"Battles? You were a soldier?"

"For a while. I have been a little bit of everything for a

while. My turn. How long were you engaged to your hot-headed Lieutenant Garner? I only ask because the news seemed to be as much of a surprise to him as to the other members of your family."

Two bright splotches of crimson stained Catherine's cheeks in response to his sarcasm. "If anyone looked surprised it was because we had not intended to blurt the news out quite so . . ."

"Unexpectedly?"

"*Melodramatically.* And certainly not over a spectacle such as a duel."

"Then you *are* in love with him?"

"What possible business is that of yours?"

"A question with a question, madam?"

She ground her teeth together. "Am I in love with Hamilton? If you must know . . . yes. Desperately. And if you think he will let this incident go unavenged——"

"Desperately, you say? How does one love someone *desperately*?"

"With one's whole heart and soul," she replied tartly. "And to understand that, you would have to *have* a heart, naturally. *My* turn: If you have stayed away from your precious Archberry for the past fifteen years, why come back now?"

"It is my home. Why shouldn't I come back?"

"But why now? Why come back to Scotland in the midst of so much upheaval? You don't believe in the Stuart cause, yet you risk your life to spy for them. You don't even believe the Pretender has a chance of winning back the throne—I heard you say as much at Rosewood—yet you are carrying information home about troop strength and military deployment. Not the kind of news one gathers if one does not believe a war is imminent."

"Perhaps not. But then neither is the latest Paris fashion relevant to putting bread and meat on the table when your people are starving and their homes are being burned over their heads."

"Then you admit you *do* believe in the Stuart cause?"

Cameron pursed his lips and started to reach for another cigar. He saw the look on Catherine's face and dismissed the impulse with a sigh. "I believe the Scots do not know the meaning of the word *compromise*. Simply put, King James is a Scot. He is the monarch to whom all of Scotland pledged allegiance before the English decided they did not like his religion or his manners. A rather shoddy way to treat a king, wouldn't you say? To banish him and invite his cousin and her foreign born husband to fill the vacancy on the throne?"

"It was perfectly legal."

"It certainly was . . . after the English Parliament passed the Act of Succession to make it so. But suppose they made a law declaring that all blonde-haired, blue-eyed vixens must remain in a convent until the age of thirty-five? It would be legal to lock you away, but would it be morally right?"

"That is an outrageous example," she said, scoffing.

"No more outrageous than dictating to a man how he must pray to his god."

"We are speaking of kings, not gods."

"Granted, but whatever happened to the divine right of kings, whose ancestors were supposedly descended from gods? I'm not saying all monarchs are holy, but do we have the right to chop off their heads or banish them to perdition whenever one comes along who does not meet our approval? There have been kings through the ages—murderers, thieves, rapists—guilty of far worse crimes than James Francis Stuart, and I'm afraid in that sense I have to agree with the Jacobite standpoint insofar as an oath of allegiance to one king cannot arbitrarily be redirected to another just because you don't like the first one. The Scots have pledged their loyalty to King James, and it is a matter of honor and pride that they uphold it."

"As simple as that?"

"War is never simple, nor are the reasons for it."

"Then you believe there *will* be a war?"

"If certain irritants have their way I can see trouble ahead, yes."

"But not all of Scotland is united behind the Stuarts."

"Not all of England is especially pleased with the Hanovers."

She scowled at his quick tongue and wondered again at the smile lurking behind his eyes. "They dislike and mistrust papists, however. You will never see England accept another Catholic king, divine right or no."

"My, what religious tolerance you have, dear lady. Do Catholics have horns and forked tails?"

"If you are anything by which to judge, I should say yes."

"But I am not Catholic, nor is my family or clan."

"So you are saying you *won't* fight for a Stuart restoration?"

He sighed good-naturedly. "Religion is not the only issue here. There is also the little matter of summarily declaring Scotland to be part of a union with England; of stripping her own Parliament of any real powers; of placing English mayors in her cities and building English forts garrisoned with English troops to police us. They have stolen our land, taken over our merchant trade, and seek to dictate what we may grow and sell and buy. They lure settlers away to work their colonies, only to have them slapped in irons and indentured to blue-blooded, upstanding English colonists. We are a stubborn lot, we Scots. We tend not to take well to slavery or to having someone else govern our destiny."

"Even so, the Highlands attempted an uprising thirty years ago and it failed miserably. What makes anyone think another one can succeed now? You don't believe it. That night at the inn you said something about a world full of righteous fools chasing each other around in circles and you wanted no part of it."

Alex laughed outright; he couldn't help it. And under different circumstances Catherine might have enjoyed the deep, lusty sound as well as the complete change it made in his appearance. The dimple reappeared and the lines across his forehead vanished. His eyes sparkled and a hint of ruddiness crept up beneath his tan, drawing attention to the length of his lashes, the glossy thickness of his hair, even the roguish shadow of stubble on his jaw.

Conversely, of course, it drew the curious stares of both Aluinn MacKail and Deirdre O'Shea, which made Catherine fidget uncomfortably on her rock.

"By God " He brought his mirth under control with an effort. "A woman who actually listens and thinks and reasons."

"Just because women wear skirts and pin their hair in curls, it does not follow that we are deaf, dumb, or blind."

"I promise never to make such an assumption again," he said, wiping at the dampness around his eyes. "Not around a Highlander, at any rate. Some of the men can fix themselves up as pretty as the women."

Catherine had to look away and pinch her lips to keep her own smile from completely destroying her credibility. When she had the urge under control again, she looked back and frowned. "You still haven't answered me. Will your family fight in a war if it comes to that?"

"In all honesty, I do not know. One of my brothers—Archibald—is a physician, dedicated to saving lives, not taking them, but his temper is as unstable as the *uisque baugh* he brews. Another—John—has openly declared all along that he will not declare either way. The eldest, Donald, is the clan chief, The Cameron of Lochiel, and it will be his decision that will affect the way a thousand clansmen behave over the next few months. So far he has been a strong advocate for peace, and so long as he stands fast, the Highlands will remain quiet."

"He carries that much influence?"

"Influence, good judgment, common sense. A third of the Highland clans look to Lochiel for guidance. An equal number of cooler heads in England look to him for sanity. He knows a rebellion now would be ill-fated and probably disastrous to Scotland in the long run. But he is also a man of intense honor and pride. I think if his loyalties were challenged point-blank, all of the good, sane intentions of the world would not save him . . . or his enemies."

For a brief moment Catherine was allowed to see yet another side of Alexander Cameron. This one did, indeed, appear to have a conscience, as well as affection, love, and concern for a family he had been forced to leave behind fifteen years ago. Was that why he was returning now, despite the dreadful risks? Having never experienced family ties that could be so strong and binding, Catherine could not understand how they could reach out and beckon to a man years and continents away. Moreover, she did not necessarily want to believe that a sentiment so basic and lacking in ulterior motives could be responsible for Alexander Cameron's journey. It would make him more human and less the monster she had willed him to be.

The sun was warm, and the black hair at Cameron's temples glistened with tiny beads of moisture. The saber slash was all but healed. In a week or two there would be nothing to mark the wound but a thin white line cutting through the tan. The fine linen of his shirt was almost transparent, affording a breathtaking reminder of the hard, sinuous muscles in his arms and across the breadth of his chest. He possessed the deadly grace and power of a panther, and Catherine was just as wary of the danger as if she were sitting in the open wilds. He would fight. Despite his reservations and his cautions and his logical arguments, she did not think he was a man who would stand by and watch others throw themselves onto the swords of their enemies.

An image of a violent, bloody battlefield flashed before her without warning. Acres of green piled with bloody corpses, echoing with the sounds of screaming and dying men. In the midst of it all, a tall, black-haired warrior, his back toward her, was laughing out a curse as a dozen scarlet-clad soldiers slashed at him with bright, gleaming swords. . . .

The image was so real that Catherine gasped aloud and dropped the knife she had been holding. Cameron turned at the sound and his eyes went to her hand, where a dark red bead of blood was swelling on her fingertip.

"I . . . I cut myself," she stammered, and reached hastily for her napkin.

The image of the battlefield faded away against the backdrop of the azure blue sky, but a haunting chill persisted, and she could not help but wonder if she had somehow glanced through a curtain and seen the past— or if it was something the future held in store.

10

"I'll carry those for you."

Deirdre looked up at the sound of the voice. Aluinn MacKail had come up behind her and stopped a few feet away. During the past ten days she had scarcely glanced in his direction, much less acknowledged any of his embarrassed, apologetic smiles. Several times he had attempted to engage her in conversation, but she had always presented a cold shoulder and walked away without uttering a single word. Each time the coach stopped she simply glared a warning that he should not even dream of offering her assistance to step down, and when it was necessary for her, as a servant, to remain with the other "servants" in the Earl of Grayston's entourage, she gave both Iain Cameron and Aluinn MacKail the full benefit of her seven years of watching Catherine Ashbrooke handle insolent underlings. She affected a stare as cold and remote as a mountain glacier.

For Aluinn it was a distinctly new sensation. He possessed a certain careless charm that most women found irresistible, and he had never been reluctant in the past to capitalize on it. Catherine's first impression of him as a scholar and philosopher was not entirely off the mark, for he could speak six languages fluently and was not averse to composing lines of poetry when a beautiful day or a ravishing woman inspired him. He was no less dangerous than Alexander Cameron, possibly even more so because of his deceptively soft-spoken manner. Where Cameron was seen instantly as a powerful adversary and potential danger, Aluinn was apt to disarm an opponent with a rueful smile seconds before cutting him to ribbons with his saber.

Raised as foster brothers since infancy, he and Alex were not equals in the finest sense of the word. Alex was the son of the clan chief; Aluinn was the son of a tenant crofter. They had been weaned on the same breast milk, however, and raised as playmates and companions until it was time to share the same tutors, attend the same schools, vie for the same pretty lasses as they vaulted through adolescence. When Alex had been sent into exile, Aluinn had neither balked at nor questioned the need to accompany him throughout the fifteen long years of wandering. They were bound together by obligation, loyalty, and friendship, and either would have given his life for the other without hesitation.

Deirdre knew none of this, of course. She viewed the pair as Catherine did: as criminals. Worse for Aluinn, she saw him as a lowly worm who had raised his fist and struck a woman unconscious. The bruise on her cheek may have faded, but the anger of the Irish gamekeeper's daughter was as livid as ever.

"It is over a mile to the bottom of the hill," he explained, his handsome, boyish face reddening slightly under her steady glare. "You might find your case a little heavy by the time you get down there."

Deirdre clutched the portmanteau tighter in her hands. It was never far from her side, certainly never out of her sight whenever any of the three brigands was nearby.

"I am quite capable of walking the distance unassisted. Now, if you'll excuse me—"

She started to brush past, but his hand shot out and grasped her by the arm. "Look . . . I can understand why you are angry, and believe me, I have been angry with myself ever since . . . well, ever since it happened. I didn't mean to hit you. I have never hit a woman before in my life."

Her fawn-brown eyes glittered with contempt, and he cursed under his breath. "All right, you win. I'm a cad. A blackguard. A bounder. You're absolutely right. I beat women every morning before my tea and toast. If it will make you feel any better you can take a swing at me. Right here—" He turned his head and angled his cheek toward her. "Go ahead. Your best shot."

There was less than a moment's hesitation on Deirdre's part before she swung hard and sharp, catching his smooth-shaven cheek with the flat of her hand. The slap startled him—stunned him more likely, since he had not expected her to take him up on the invitation. Throwing charm in the face of a woman's temper had never failed him before, and he found himself gaping after the slender figure as she stormed away, his vanity stinging almost as badly as his cheek.

"Makin' friends, are ye?" Iain chuckled as he walked by. "Waste o' time tae sweet-talk a lass like tha'. She'd take tae ye better if ye just threw her on the ground an' jumped atween her thighs. I warrant they've spread plenty o' times afore now."

Aluinn's frown darkened at the younger man's crudeness, but his retort was cut abruptly short by the sight of riders approaching along the road.

"Alex! Company!"

Cameron was beside the coach in a few long strides, his eyes narrowed against the shimmer of heat rising off the sun-baked road.

"They have the look o' the Watch about them," Iain muttered, already swinging his lanky frame up into the driver's box. He passed a long-barreled musket down to Aluinn, who checked the charge of powder before sliding it beneath the canopy on the boot of the coach. Alex whistled softly for Shadow and retrieved his own brace of steel-handled dags out of the leather saddle pouch.

"We'll try to talk our way through it first," he said grimly, cocking each pistol and checking the priming pans. "The two of you stay near the coach and don't make any unnecessary moves unless you see a signal from me."

Catherine was standing with Deirdre when Alex returned to her side, her eyes widening when she saw the guns.

"Who are they? I thought we were relatively safe now."

"Those are Argyle militia. The Black Watch. Aptly named since they are comprised mainly of thieves and cutthroats, castoffs who enjoy terrorizing local farmers for a few coins here and there." He ordered Deirdre back to the coach, saying, "I want you to stay out of sight. Keep your eyes on Aluinn, and if anything happens get on the floor of the coach and stay put until it's clear. Catherine, I'm sorry, but you will have to stay with me. Chances are they have already seen you anyway"—he nodded at the blaze of yellow and green stripes in her skirt—"and any sudden dash for the coach will only make the bastards more curious than they are by nature. Follow my lead and act as normal as possible . . . but if I tell you to run, make for those trees and for Christ's sake, keep your head down."

She was staring at him. "Argyle. Isn't that the name of the man who has posted the reward for your capture?"

"Indeed, it is. And yes, our impending visitors would undoubtedly sell their firstborn sons for the honor of presenting my head to the Duke of Argyle. I have no intentions of letting that happen, however. It's much too nice a day to die."

She still did not move, and Alex put a hand on her wrist to pull her back down onto the blanket. "Just relax. We're having a picnic, remember?"

"How do you know who they are? How do you know they are from Argyle?"

"The tartan."

Catherine squinted to see along the sandstone road. She could barely distinguish the drab red coloring of their jackets, much less determine the pattern on the short woolen skirts they wore. But they were soldiers and they represented the law; there were also eight of them against the three renegades, odds that brought a blush of excitement to her cheeks. Cameron was so close to his final destination, this might be her last chance to stop him.

"I wouldn't even think about it if I were you," he advised quietly as he concealed his pistols beneath the folds of his jacket. "Whatever else they might be, Watchmen are not known for their kindness or their gratitude. They might thank you for turning us over, but they would repay you by raping you raw and stealing everything of value you have in your trunks. Even then, if they thought you were worth something they would keep right on amusing themselves with you until someone showed up with a ransom. The choice is yours, of course. You can trust them, or you can trust me."

Hoofbeats, distant but steadily advancing, came toward the knoll. Catherine could see them much more clearly now. Their bonnets were blue, their waistcoats and jackets red with buff facings and white buttons. Dark-green-and-blue lengths of plaid were draped over burly, stooped shoulders, the colors and patterns matched with the pleated tartan they wore belted about their waists. Across each barrel chest was a crossbelt and sword. A brace of claw-butted pistols were sheathed in each man's belt, and a long-snouted musket was slung across each saddle.

"Catherine—" The warmth in Cameron's voice dragged her attention away from the advancing soldiers. "If you looked any more relaxed you would frighten away the devil himself."

"Why should I trust you?" she asked slowly. "Why should I even believe you?"

He shrugged and leaned back on one elbow. "Maybe you shouldn't. Maybe those eight men are your salvation. Heaven only knows we have beaten you every day, tied you hand and foot every night, starved you, mistreated you in every way imaginable. Why, indeed, should you trust us now?"

His sarcasm stung, and she felt tears stinging her eyes. "What if they recognize you?"

"It has been fifteen years," he reminded her softly.

How could anyone forget him, she wondered, having felt the power of those accursed eyes? She said nothing, glancing instead at the coach where Deirdre stood partially shielded behind Aluinn MacKail. The Highlander had donned his black and gold frock coat, as had Iain Cameron, and both had pulled the wide-brimmed hats low over their foreheads to throw shadows over their features—shadows the younger man needed most of all to hide the bruises from his broken nose.

"They look about as much like servants as I do," she bristled.

Cameron was pensive for a moment, then curved his lips in a faint smile. "I shall trust your judgment in that, but since we are a little pressed for alternatives, I guess we will just have to make sure the Watchmen have something else to look at. Put your arms around my neck."

"What?"

"I said—" He curled a muscular arm around her waist and brought her down beside him on the blanket. "Put your arms around my neck. I am going to kiss you, Mistress Ashbrooke, and the effect would be far more convincing if you appeared to be enjoying it."

"You will do no such th—"

His mouth moved swiftly to cover hers and smother the protest at the same time that his body shifted to pin her firmly beneath him. Her skirts flew up in a splash of lace petticoats, but the absolute authority of the hand that was suddenly pressing over her windpipe quickly brought her efforts to dislodge him to a standstill. Having won her attention, his lips slanted purposefully over hers. His tongue thrust insolently past the barrier of her teeth and lashed boldly around the recesses of her mouth. She was forced to submit, she had no choice, yet the temper she had so painstakingly held in check over the past few days snapped like an overdrawn bowstring, and she was determined he was *not* going to amuse himself again at her expense.

With a devious little gasp she parted her lips wider and pretended to melt beneath his lusty ministrations. She ran her hands up and around his shoulders, deliberately raking her fingers into the thick, glossy waves of his hair. She began kissing him back, her efforts matching his thrust for thrust, her lips as energetically demanding as his.

She expected him to flinch warily back and was not entirely disappointed, but his retreat was effectively—and painfully—sabotaged by the sharp points of her fingernails digging into his scalp. Her teeth bit down with malicious relish on the meat of his tongue, and she could have laughed aloud at the sound of the strangled cry that broke from his throat!

Her smugness was short-lived, however, for in the next instant his hand slid down the arch of her neck and brazenly cupped itself around the swell of her breast. It had become her custom—since it was hot in the coach and no one of importance was likely to be seeing her, whether at her best or her worst—to forgo the discomfort of lacing herself into a tight corset or stomacher. Thus there was very little protection between her flesh and the palm of his hand, and shocked by the intrusion, she renewed her efforts to twist away. He *did* laugh, for his weight was solidly above her and her squirming only mimicked the frantic urgency of rushing pelvic thrusts.

A warning cough from the vicinity of the coach forced an abrupt end to the contest as Alexander ended the assault on her mouth and turned to glance at the road, a hand raised to shield his eyes from the noon sun. The eight horsemen had reined to a halt nearby; two were in the act of dismounting.

"Good God!" Cameron feigned surprise in his best upper-crust London accent. "Where the deuce did you fellows come from?"

The tallest and burliest of the pair had his eyes fastened on the slim length of Catherine's calf where it was exposed by the mussed petticoat. "We was aboot tae ask ye the same thing. Isna verra often we see such a fine coach on these roads."

Alexander stood and extended a hand to assist Catherine to her feet. She was slower to catch hold of her wits. Her lips were throbbing from the roughness of his assault, her breasts tingled as if all the skin had suddenly shrunk away. She could feel the hot eyes of the Highlanders on her, and when her hand fluttered to her throat she discovered why. Sometime during his groping Cameron had loosened the laces of her bodice and, without the support and modesty of buckram underpinnings, had exposed more soft white flesh than would have been acceptable in a brothel. The two Watchmen stared. Even the men on horseback craned forward, their mouths agape.

"Sergeant," Alex said, calmly capturing Catherine's hand before she could repair his mischief. "Permit me to offer introductions. The name is Grayston. Winthrop Howell Grayston, esquire, at your service. And this fetchingly disheveled creature is my wife, Lady Grayston. We were trying to snatch a bit of a rest before we tackled this nuisance of a hillock. What were you saying about these roads? They certainly are dreadful, I must agree. I say . . . you wouldn't happen to know of an easier way down, er . . . Sergeant—"

"Campbell. Robert Campbell, an' this mon is Corporal Denune. I mout be askin' where ye're bound."

"Fort William," Alex supplied readily. "We were in Glasgow, y'know, on business, and thought we might like to see some of the countryside. Would have gone by sea, but dear Lesley gets so noxiously ill on ships of any kind, don't you, my dearest?"

The unsubtle pressure on her wrist forced a pinched smile to her lips.

"Been safer, nonetheless," the sergeant grunted. "These glens are crawlin' wi' rebels."

"Rebels? Here? But we're less than ten miles from the fort."

"Aye, an' scarce ten minutes ride f'ae the borther o' bastard Cameron land. Be north o' here—" He thrust a filthy finger over his shoulder and spat messily onto the grass. "Lochaber. Worst o' the lot, them. Just as like tae kill ye as let ye pass."

"Good heavens! They wouldn't provoke an attack on us, would they?"

"Might. Dung farmers, the lot o' them. Murtherin' sods wha'd steal ye blind an' take yer lives f'ae the pleasure o' drawin' bluid."

The sergeant's eyes were small and ferretlike, and when they flickered over Catherine she was hard-pressed to restrain a shudder of revulsion. She did not like the looks of any of these Watchmen. They were unshaven and unwashed. Their tunics were crusted with filth, their hair shiny with grease, their hands as black and callused as the bark on a tree. She thought of Cameron's warning and did not even care to contemplate the horror of feeling those hands, those coarse, pest-ridden bodies pulling and tearing at her.

"Thieves and rebels," Alex was saying, dabbing a finely worked lace handkerchief across his brow. "I daresay the conditions in this country worsen by the hour. London, my sweet, definitely beckons us home."

The sergeant agreed with a slow nod of his head. "Ye've heard the rumors, then?"

"Rumors?"

"Aye. There were a battle at sea, atween the French an' English. The Stuart pup were on board one o' the ships an' managed tae slip away in a storm. Rumor says he's tryin' tae land somewheres in the Hebrides. Rumor says he's expectin' tae be met by a grand Heeland army. Faugh! Only army he'll find is maggots. Maggots an' dung farmers who'd attack their own mithers f'ae a handful o' coppers."

"A battle at sea, you say?" Alex had grown very still. "When was this supposed to have taken place?"

"Did take place. Two weeks gone. Only supposin' tae be done is whither or no' the daft Stuart pup could swim." He guffawed loudly and poked his companion in the ribs. The corporal responded with a vaguely sinister smile, for his attention was distracted, divided between the deep *V* of Catherine's bodice and the rich-looking coach with its full boot of luggage.

"What kind o' blatherin' fool," he grumbled in Gaelic, "comes all the way from Glasgow wi'out an escort?"

Both men glanced at Cameron's face to see if he understood, but Alex was dusting his sleeve with the lace handkerchief, frowning over a speck of soil.

"Aye," said the sergeant in English. "Well then, we'd best be biddin' ye good day. Mind what I said an' watch yer backs. Have ye a few stout weepons tae protect yersel's wi'?"

"Weapons? Goodness . . . I believe the driver may have a fowling piece of some sort. Yes, I'm sure he does. It seems to me he tried to shoot a grouse with it the other day, but missed. I prefer the bow and arrow for hunting, myself. Gentleman's weapon, what? Builds strength in the upper torso."

The sergeant smiled wanly as Cameron flexed a biceps by way of illustration. Even Catherine stared in amazement; he had transformed himself so convincingly into a buffoon, the two Highlanders were openly contemptuous as they exchanged another muttered observation in Gaelic.

"Is there a problem, Sergeant?"

"Problem?" The Watchman grinned through teeth that were chipped and coated with green rot. "Nae problem, yer lairdship. We was just thinkin' . . . the lady mout feel better if we was tae keep ye company the rest o' the way tae the fort. Rough country here tae there. We wouldna want tae fret about ye out here on yer own."

Catherine was increasingly conscious of the lurid

whispers being passed between the men on horseback. They were alternating their stares between herself and Deirdre, gesturing among themselves as if they were already casting lots to see who would be the first in line. Some were making ready to dismount, others were sidling their animals closer to the coach and reaching down to unhamper their swords and muskets.

Cameron seemed blithely unaware of the danger.

"That's very thoughtful of you, old sport, but we couldn't possibly take you away from your duties."

The sergeant clamped a fat, stubby hand around the butt of the pistol tucked in his belt. "Still an' all, we'll stay. The men could do wi' a wee rest . . . an' mayhap a share o' what the lassies have tae offer."

"The lunch?" Alex half-turned to frown down at the picnic basket. "I'm afraid there isn't much left, but of course you are more than welcome to—"

"We werena speakin' o' the victuals, ye daft bastard." The sergeant laughed and drew his gun out of his belt. It flew out of his hand in the next instant, blown into the air by the impact of a lead ball plowing through the hairy wrist. A second explosive retort had one of the Watchmen nearest the coach screaming and slumping out of the saddle, and with both guns empty, Aluinn MacKail flung them aside and drew his sword from beneath the canopied boot.

In a blur of motion Alex spun Catherine around and away from the soldiers, propelling her toward the trees with such force that she stumbled and fell. He dove for his own guns and rolled onto his feet again, his shots tearing out the side of the corporal's throat just as he was shouting the order to attack.

Iain Cameron dropped to one knee and shrugged his guns free of the feed bag he had been holding. Of the two shots he fired, one caught an Argyleman high in the shoulder, jerking him back in his saddle and causing him to lose his grip on his musket—which Aluinn was there to catch. The second went wild, the lead ball ricocheting off a boulder before it spat into the dry earth only inches from where Alex had snatched up the corporal's musket and was taking aim at a charging Highlander.

A piercing shriek from Deirdre warned Aluinn as a broadsword came slashing in an arc toward his head. The steel missed his neck and shoulder, slicing harmlessly through a layer of gold braid on his sleeve, but Aluinn was hit solidly by the horse's swinging rump. He lost his grip on the musket and crashed painfully into the spoked wheel of the coach. Deirdre flung herself out of the coach as the soldier wheeled his horse around for another attack, but before she could reach the musket Aluinn had dropped, the Watchman was reeling out of the saddle, his hands clutched over the eruption of blood and tissue from his chest.

Alex lowered the smoking Brown Bess and reversed the barrel for the stock as a horseman came swiftly at him. Using it as a club, he smashed the broadsword out of the rider's hands and sent the terrified horse swerving toward the coach. Still off balance and slightly dazed, MacKail saw the horse and rider coming straight for him, at the same time that he saw Deirdre step clear of the boot and raise the heavy musket to fire. The recoil sent her staggering back in a choking fog of smoke, and Aluinn shouted a warning. Another soldier was charging in from the opposite direction, leaning over his saddle, his arm hooked, his hand reaching for Deirdre's throat. Aluinn launched himself at the horse and managed to grab a fistful of the rider's kilt. His weight dragged the Watchman out of the saddle and they went down hard together, grappling even before they hit the ground, a cocked pistol sandwiched between them.

Alex dispatched the last of the attacking troop with a mercifully swift and clean stroke of his sword. He was pulling the blade free from the man's gut when the sergeant, his bloodied and shattered hand cradled against his chest, lunged for Cameron's back. The tip of his sword arced past the broad shoulder, nicking an earlobe.

Alex spun and reached into the top of his leather boot, and with the flick of a wrist sent his dirk flashing through the air to embed itself in the base of the sergeant's throat.

The ferret eyes widened and the hairy fingers clawed at the white-boned hilt of the knife where it protruded from his severed windpipe. He staggered back several paces before his foot tangled in the corner of the picnic blanket and he toppled sideways onto the ground, landing squarely on Catherine's feet and ankles. She screamed and tried to free herself as a spray of blood splattered the length of her skirt, but he was too heavy, and she screamed all the louder, covering her ears now against the sickening hiss and gurgle of air escaping the hole in his throat.

Alex quickly lifted her clear of the twitching body. She buried her face against his shoulder and clung to him, refusing to let go even after he had carried her well away from the carnage and set her down safely by the stream.

"You're all right," he assured her, his hand skimming her calves, her ankles, her knees in search of any broken or wrenched bones. "Catherine . . . you're all right now. It's over."

She gazed blankly up into his face, saw the blood dripping from his cut earlobe, and emitted a tiny, airless gasp. Her eyes rolled back and her lashes fluttered closed; she collapsed in a soft, limp, warm bundle in his arms.

He swore under his breath and deposited her gently on the bank of the stream. A shout and the sound of running footsteps had him standing and bracing himself again, only to see Iain rushing up behind him.

"I couldna stop him! He were out o' range afore I could reload an' fire!"

Alex straightened and stared hard after the rider galloping away in the distance. He glanced at Shadow and knew the stallion could catch the escaping militiaman, but the pursuit would take time—time better spent on removing themselves from the scene.

"He will be long gone before anyone can reach him. Aluinn . . . Where the hell is Aluinn?"

There were two bodies tangled together in the red dust of the road, both of them liberally smeared with blood, only one of the them showing any signs of life. MacKail was struggling, with Deirdre's help, to push himself to his knees as Alex and Iain ran up. His hand was clamped protectively over a wound low on his shoulder; his face was streaming sweat, and his teeth were clenched against the pain. Alex helped lower him onto the step of the coach, then quickly determined where the shot had entered and exited the bloodied flesh. Deirdre, standing pale and shaken to one side, began tearing long strips of cotton from her petticoat to fold and wad in place over the torn flesh. The wadding became soaked almost at once, despite the pressure Alex applied, and she chewed her lip worriedly.

"He'll need a doctor—and soon—to stop it proper."

Alex turned his head and shouted. "Iain—collect the guns and all the spare shot and powder you can find; we may need it. Unsaddle the horses and set them free, then unload those trunks from the boot. In fact, dump everything we haven't a use for except blankets and water."

"The coach will slow you down," Aluinn gasped. "Take the women and the horses and get the hell out of here."

"And leave you to play the hero? Not bloody likely, my friend. And besides," he added grimly, "you're not the only casualty."

Deirdre looked up and her face drained to a sickly gray. "Mistress Catherine?"

"For someone who insists she has never fainted before in her life, she is giving a good imitation of it over by the stream."

"I must see to her," Deirdre cried, jumping to her feet.

"No," Alex ordered, taking her by the wrist. "I'll see to her. You stay here with Aluinn and keep pressure on these bandages."

"Alex—" Aluinn grabbed a fistful of Alex's sleeve. "Alex, wait. Something . . . something's not right."

"What do you mean *not right*? What else could possibly be wrong?"

Aluinn shook his head to clear it and to try to hold back the nausea. "I don't know. Something . . ."

Alex's attention was absolute. "What is it?"

The blurred gray eyes looked up at him. "For a man we have both seen shoot at flying sparrows for practice . . . Iain missed two clear shots at point-blank range."

It took a moment for Alex to grasp Aluinn's meaning. "Everything happened so fast, maybe he wasn't—"

"It happened fast," MacKail agreed. "Too damned fast to calmly hang back and reload."

"What are you saying? Spit it out, man."

"I'm saying the shot that passed through my shoulder came from his musket."

"He might have been aiming for the man you were fighting."

"Then his timing is as rotten as his aim, because I was hit a few seconds after I had already dispatched the Argyleman and was shaking his blood off my hands."

Alex's jaw tightened. He knew Aluinn hadn't liked or trusted the boy from the outset. He'd been too outspoken and cocky—traits Alex had credited to his youth. This was a far more serious charge, one that Aluinn would not make lightly despite personal differences.

A rustle of black gabardine reminded both men that there was another possible witness, and Deirdre glanced from one questioning stare to the other.

"I . . . I don't know. It all happened so fast."

"Think," Aluinn urged gently. "It could be very important."

She frowned, but a careful search of her memory over those panic-stricken moments progressed no further than a small gasp as she saw the dull gleam of a musket being raised and pointed squarely at Alex's back.

* * *

"Ye're a wee bit too obsairvant f'ae ma likin', MacKail," Iain said matter-of-factly. "Ye've been like a fly on ma neck since we fairst met up togither."

"Would you care to explain just what the hell you think you're doing?" Alex's voice was a sheet of ice. "And it better be damned good, mister."

"Fairst things fairst. The dirk in yer boot, MacKail . . . kick it over here along wi' the one in yer belt. No sudden moves now, or ye'll have the lassie's head in yer lap quicker than ye'd hoped."

He aimed the musket at Deirdre, but Alex stepped to one side, keeping himself in front of the terrified maid. "I am assuming your quarrel is with us, boy. Let the women go and we'll discuss it."

Iain grinned coldly. "I'm no' a *boy*, Cameron of Loch Eil. An' ye were right; ma aim was poor the fairst time around—too much dust an' all—but easily fixed."

"Why?" Alex demanded. "What do you hope to gain by killing us?"

"Oh, I dinna plan tae kill *you*, Alexander Cameron Dead, ye're only worth half as much tae me."

"The reward?" Aluinn spat. "You're doing this for the money? You're turning in your own kinsman for a few miserable gold coins?"

"Ten thousan' gold sovereigns are no' miserable. An' it's *twenty*, it might please ye tae know, if Malcolm Campbell has the pleasure o' drawin' the blade himsel'. As f'ae the *Camshroinaich Dubh* bein' a kinsman o' mine—" His grin turned sly and evil. "Unless he's the bastard scion o' a Campbell, like as I am, then we're no kith or kin."

"Campbell?"

"Aye. Gordon Ross Campbell o' Dundoon, at yer sairvice. Enough like the real Iain Cameron o' Glengarron tae be mistaken f'ae brithers, so we found out. Enough ye didna even suspect the change."

Alex's face remained impassive except for the tiny vein that throbbed to life in his temple. He was getting old. Or sloppy. He had accepted the boy at his word because they had been expecting him and because he'd carried personal letters from Donald. He had never questioned the possibility that the letters might have been intercepted and the courier substituted. He had just been so damned anxious to go home . . .

"How did you know where to find me, or that I was expecting my brother to send someone to France?"

"We knew it were only a matter o' time afore Lochiel sent f'ae the grand *Camshroinaich Dubh*. We're no' wi'out our own spies at Achnacarry, an' when young Glengarron left the castle, bristlin' with importance, he an' his men were followed, stopped, an' taken tae Inverary. He were stubborn, o' course. He didna want tae tell us where he was supposed tae meet ye, but—" Gordon Ross Campbell shrugged his shoulders. "He did, by the by."

With an effort Alex controlled a hot surge of rage. "You played your part well. But if your plan was to take us to Inverary, why haven't you made your move before now? You've had plenty of opportunities."

"I'm no' fool enough tae try tae take the *Camshroinaich Dubh* by masel'," he admitted with a lift of his eyebrow. "There are twenty men waitin' across the Spean f'ae that very reason."

"This"—Alex waved a hand to indicate the bodies—"wasn't part of it?"

"Never saw them afore," Iain said easily. "Clumsy bastards. Greedy too, an' I didna fancy sharin' ought wi' the likes o' them. Now—" The barrel of the musket moved. "Enough talk. Ye've as glib a tongue as an adder when it suits ye, an' I've nae more time tae waste listenin' tae ye."

"Let the women go," Alex said, tensing. He kept his gaze leveled on Campbell, willing himself not to look past the younger man's shoulder. "They have no part in this; they couldn't care less what happens to me . . . or to you, for that matter."

"Let them go? Aye, this drab doxy maybe. She seems mair trouble than she's worth. But the ither one? Ach! The *wife* o' Alexander Cameron?" He paused and smacked his lips with anticipation. "Can ye imagine what the Duke will make o' that? Besides the extra bit o' coin she'll bring, I can see the pleasure she'll gi' when he fills her wi' a Campbell bastard an' sends her home tae Achnacarry. I can just see the look on Lochiel's face when—"

Behind him Catherine released her breath on a gust as she swung the heavy stock of the musket, using every last scrap of strength she possessed. She had recovered from her fainting spell and walked back from the stream, too dazed at first to see the weapon in Campbell's hands or to realize what was taking place. She had even started to call out, thinking no one had noticed her or cared that she had been abandoned, but the cry had frozen on her lips when she saw Deirdre's frantic warning, delivered from behind the shield of Cameron's broad back.

Deirdre had tried to wave her away, and for the longest moment Catherine had been tempted. But then, the next thing she knew, she was bending over and prying a musket from the still-warm fingers of a dead militiaman. The gun was empty, but there was no time to reload it even if she could have found the powder and shot to do so. And with her heart lodged firmly in her throat she had crept up behind Campbell's back, the musket raised, her arms quivering with the strain. Deirdre had watched in horror. Only Alexander Cameron had remained composed enough to keep the young Judas distracted with talk.

Even so, Gordon Ross Campbell flinched at the last moment, some instinct warning him of the danger at his back. His finger jerked the trigger of the musket just as the flat of the walnut stock caught him high on the cheek and tore open a strip of flesh from the corner of his eye to his ear. Alex had already started forward. He grabbed the barrel of the musket and shoved it aside a fraction of a second before it discharged harmlessly into the air, then wrenched it out of Campbell's hand and pulled the younger man into a bone-crunching reunion with his clenched fist. A second devastating blow lifted Campbell off his feet and propelled him into the side of the coach, the impact dazing him long enough for a third punch to crack his teeth off at the gumline.

In no time Campbell's face was awash in blood, his nose again crushed to a misshapen mass of cartilage and tissue. He raised his hands in an attempt to fend off the subsequent blows, but he barely had the strength or sensibility to saw his fists back and forth with each hammer-like punch that came from the left, the right, the left . . .

He staggered and fell, but Cameron was there to haul him upright again, to turn him around, to prop him upright for another barrage of blows.

Catherine had thought the horror could not intensify beyond the slaughter she had witnessed only minutes ago, but seeing the cold killing fury in Cameron's eyes, watching him slowly, deliberately beat the life out of another human being was too much to bear. She ran forward and threw herself at his uplifted arm, closing her hands around his bloodied fist to keep him from striking again.

"Stop it! Stop! You're killing him!"

"He deserves killing," Alex snarled. "Get out of my way."

"I won't get out of your way! I won't let you murder him! Look! Look at what you've done! Isn't it enough?"

Alex curled his lips back in another snarl, and he would have flung her aside without a qualm if not for the tears that flooded her eyes. It startled him, because the pity was not directed at Gordon Ross Campbell, but at him, for what she saw as his loss of humanity.

"Please," she begged, her fingers digging into his flesh. "Please, Alex, let him go. He isn't worth it."

He lowered his fist slowly, releasing his grip on Campbell's shirt at the same time. The boy's legs buckled beneath him and he slumped down against the wheel of the coach, blood spraying from his mouth on each labored breath.

Catherine collapsed against Alex's chest, too weak with relief to think about what she was doing as she wrapped her arms around him and buried her head in his shoulder.

Deirdre, having not dared to move or breathe during the display of explosive violence, crumpled to her knees beside Aluinn MacKail, covered her face with her hands, and wept.

"I thought I told you to keep your head down and run."

Catherine stirred reluctantly and lifted her cheek away from the comfort of Cameron's shoulder. The terrible flush of rage had faded from his face, and his eyes . . . his eyes were darker and deeper than any ocean she could imagine. Deeper, warmer, safer . . .

Alex was all too aware of her vulnerability at that moment, aware also of his body's response to it. Her loneliness and uncertainty were etched as clearly on each feature as if painted there by an artist's brush, and he longed to draw her back into his arms and reassure her that as long as she stayed there nothing would ever harm her or frighten her again. Only once before had he felt so strong a need to protect someone, but that one time he had failed so badly to honor his promise that the memory of it hardened his heart and made him ease Catherine gently to arm's length.

"We haven't much time," he explained, avoiding her gaze. "Why don't you and Deirdre go to the stream and fill the water cans while I see to the coach."

Against her will she glanced down at Campbell's sprawled body. "What about him? Wh-what about . . . them?" she added, including the other bodies steaming in the sun.

"Campbell can choke on his own blood for all I care. As for the others . . . when their comrade brings back help from the fort, perhaps they'll stop long enough to bury them. With luck, that should buy us a little extra time."

Catherine shuddered at the coldness in his voice. She offered no resistance as Deirdre led her away, though she looked back over her shoulder once before they were swallowed into the shade of the trees.

"You were a little rough on her, don't you think?" Aluinn observed. "Especially after what she's just been through."

"She's tougher than she thinks. She'll survive."

"What about you? Exactly how tough do you think you have to be? Annie is dead, Alex. You can't bring her back, and you can't keep punishing yourself for something that happened half a lifetime ago."

Resentment darkened Alex's complexion as he started unstrapping the trunks from the boot of the coach. "What the hell does any of this have to do with Annie?"

"You tell me. You're the one who keeps breathing life back into her ghost every time you start feeling yourself turning human. It isn't fair, Alex. Not to her, not to you."

"I loved her, Aluinn. And because I loved her, she died."

"I doubt Annie would have seen it that way."

The two heavy trunks crashed on the ground, one after the other. "Am I supposed to forget what happened? Or forget she ever existed?"

"Of course not—"

"Or should I ignore the fact that one of the animals who killed her is still sending his puny assassins after me to make sure I know *he* is still alive and well?"

"Is that why you have come back? To finish what you started with Malcolm Campbell fifteen years ago?"

Alex glared down at Gordon Ross Campbell. "The God's truth—whether you choose to believe it or not—is that I bled Malcolm Campbell out of my system long ago. He bought his passage to hell fifteen years ago; my hastening him on the way won't make the flames any hotter." He paused and examined the scraped skin of his knuckles. "Mind you, I'm not saying I wouldn't oblige the bastard if he crawled out of his rat hole long enough for me to catch a whiff of him, but as for my going out and actively hunting him down . . . no. That isn't why I've come back."

"You may catch more than just a whiff," Aluinn sighed, "if what Iain—I mean, Campbell—said is true. That there are twenty men waiting in ambush for us on the other side of the Spean." He turned a grim eye on the bodies. "I guess this more or less cancels any detour to Fort William?"

Alex cursed freely by way of an answer and fetched a pouch containing powder and shot from beneath the driver's seat of the coach. He collected the muskets and pistols from the scattered bodies and handed the best of the lot to Aluinn while he threw the others over the edge of the precipice.

When he returned, Aluinn was leaning against the door, his face gray and shiny with sweat, his last reserves of strength drained from the effort of reloading and priming the guns.

"We will have to risk all of us riding the coach down into the glen," Alex decided as the two women came back from the stream. He saw Catherine eye the discarded trunks, but she said nothing. She was still so pale, there were fine blue lines visible beneath the smooth porcelain surface of her skin. "We will take it as slowly as we dare, but I have to warn you, it will not get any easier when we reach the bottom."

"Are you worried about the man who got away?" Deirdre asked.

Alex hesitated, debating whether or not to elaborate on the potential dangers they faced, not only from the Watchman, but from Gordon Ross's men. A glance into the maid's expressive brown eyes reminded him that she had been present when Campbell had told him about the trap;

they also made clear that there would be no need to frighten Catherine any more than was absolutely necessary.

He acknowledged her unspoken request with a slight nod. "He is probably halfway to Fort William by now and debating how large a troop to return with."

"Help me up into the driver's box," Aluinn said, setting his teeth against the pain as he tried to pull himself to his feet. "You'll need someone with you to ride the brake."

"Surely *dead* weight will be of no help whatsoever," Deirdre said calmly. She squared her shoulders and reinforced her silent pact with Cameron. "I am not unfamiliar with driving a team, Mr. Cameron, and I think your strength would be put to better use holding the brake."

One look at Aluinn's waxen face told Alex he had few options. "Very well, Mistress O'Shea. If you are willing to take the reins, I will do my best to keep us from spilling over."

"Indeed, sir, I would be more than willing to do whatever I can to speed my mistress and myself away from this accursed country and away from the likes of you." She looked Alex directly in the eye. "You, sir, ride with death on your shoulder, and it does not make for pleasant company."

II

The descent from the bluff was hair-raising and slow. As the wheels slipped and skidded on the steep, broken sandstone road, the passengers were forced to cling to the seats and brace themselves as best they could while being tossed and tilted from one side of the coach to the other. Catherine had the gruesome task of trying to keep Aluinn MacKail as steady as possible. Cameron had strapped thick pads of cloth over his wounds and belted them tightly to staunch the flow of blood, but there was no help for the pain caused by the constant jolting. MacKail lapsed into a state of semiconsciousness almost immediately, adding to Catherine's anxiety. She had never had a man die in her arms, never been witness to the dreadful deterioration she saw as his complexion changed from simply pale to an ominous, ashen gray.

She could hear Cameron's husky baritone overhead, alternately shouting words of encouragement at Deirdre and barking orders at the horses. The maid was obviously terrified, for the voice she used to respond was shrill and brittle, as cutting on Catherine's nerves as broken glass.

When they arrived in the basin of the valley, Cameron stopped only long enough to check on MacKail—he was fully unconscious by then—and to allow Deirdre to relinquish the reins and join Catherine inside. Cameron whipped the horses into high speed, veering east off the main course and traversing the grassy floor of the glen.

Aluinn's worsening condition was Alex's foremost concern. He had lost more blood than Alex thought was possible for a body to lose and still maintain a heartbeat.

Taking the High Bridge that spanned the River Spean would have seen them on Cameron land within the hour, but if Campbell's men were waiting and watching, they would have to circle far to the east and cross the river where it met the tributaries to Loch Lochy—a ten-to-twenty-mile detour over trails that were not meant for elegantly spoked carriage wheels. The condition of the coach itself was his next priority. At the bottom of the steep grade he had noticed a crack in the rear axle. They carried no spare parts, and if the crack deepened or broke through entirely, they would be in even worse straits.

The hours wore on with Alex calling infrequent halts to rest and water the flagging horses. They appeared to be suffering as much as their human counterparts; their glossy brown coats were crusted in a salty foam, their flanks quivered, and their mouths were worried raw around the bits. Only Shadow seemed unaffected. He cantered easily behind the coach, his coal-black head held high, his tail arched in a silken fan.

"You are ruining these poor animals," Catherine murmured dispiritedly as she watched Alex water the loudly blowing team. "They were not intended to pull this coach ten hours, much less ten days without rest. Must you drive them so hard?"

Alex stroked each velvet snout as he let them drink sparingly from a canvas bucket. She was right, of course. He was pushing the horses too hard. He was pushing everyone too hard. But the only alternative creased the frown deeper into his forehead as he contemplated the eerie stillness of the forest that was now closing them in on all sides. They had been climbing over or winding their way around high hillocks for the past hour, and the shadows were thickening, the air becoming heavier with mist.

"We only have about an hour or so of daylight left. Maybe it would be best for me to take Shadow and ride on ahead to find out exactly how far it is to the river. Do you think you could manage here on your own for a while?"

"On my own?" She looked up with a start, never thinking he would take her criticism of the horses seriously.

"It wouldn't be for long. Just until I find the river."

"Find it? You mean you don't know where it is? You don't know where *we* are?" She clasped her hands together and drew a steadying breath. "Are you trying to tell me we are lost?"

"Temporarily misplaced. It has, after all, been a long time since I hunted in those woods."

The indignation and contempt he expected to see flash across her features did not appear. Instead, she seemed to take the admission calmly, almost with a touch of wry humor.

"You cannot find your way out of a forest, yet you have the nerve to call yourself a spy?"

"The term was affixed by you, not me."

"What else would you call a man who poses as someone he is not just to gain information for the enemy?"

"You still think of me as your enemy?"

She trod lightly around the question. "I certainly do not consider you a friend."

The corner of Cameron's mouth pulled into a grin, and his admiration for her spirit soared a few degrees higher. "Come on, you must admit your situation has been enlivened considerably since we met. Think of the experiences you will have to tell your grandchildren."

"Being frightened half to death every other minute of the day," she recounted dryly, "being involved in a confrontation with armed soldiers and nearly being killed . . . not exactly bedtime stories. A further presumption is to suggest I will even live long enough to have *children*."

"Madam: sheer obstinacy on your part will no doubt ensure you live to a very ripe old age."

Catherine did not share his optimism. "If you have no idea where we are, pray tell how do you presume to know where to look for the river?"

He whistled for Shadow, and when the stallion danced up beside him he swung his broad frame into the saddle.

"If I am not back within the hour, you will know I presumed wrong."

"You're just leaving me . . . us . . . all alone?"

Alex studied her and felt his heart give a peculiar thud against his breastbone. Her hair was half out of its steel pins and trailed carelessly over her shoulders like spilled gold. Her skin was pale, but against the deep green of the forest and blue-white hint of mist, she looked luminous, radiant, all eyes and soft, pouting mouth. Her skirt was torn, stained with blood and mud, and he was unable to stop himself from comparing the bedraggled waif who stood before him now with the haughty, imperious vixen who had commanded him to vacate her father's forest before she had him arrested for poaching.

And instead of answering her question, he leaned over and cupped his hand under her chin, tilting her mouth up to his. He kissed her deeply, thoroughly, and when he released her, the confusion shimmering in her eyes was not there solely because he was leaving.

"I won't be long," he promised.

"On your honor?" she gasped.

The faint, distant grin returned. "On my honor."

He urged the stallion to a quick trot and within moments had vanished around a bend in the overgrown track. Catherine remained where she was, listening to the sounds of the fading hoofbeats until they had blended into the rustling of the wind overhead and the sounds of the forest breathing around her. She raised her hand and pressed her fingertips to her lips, imagining they were still warm from his caress. Her whole body, in fact, felt warm, her blood stirred by a confused array of emotions.

On the one hand she was coming to appreciate his strength, his confidence, the self-assuredness that had at first made him seem arrogant and cynical. Conversely, the more she came to know him, the more reasons there were to guard against his intruding any more upon her life. He was dangerous and unpredictable. He seemed able to quickly rationalize the charge of spying; had he just as easily dismissed in his own mind the fact that he had kidnapped her and forced her to accompany him to Scotland against her will? That he was capable of taking another life was no longer a question in her mind . . . but was he a murderer? He may well have beaten Gordon Ross Campbell to death in the heat of the moment had she not stepped between them . . . but wouldn't any man in his position do the same? Betrayal, deceit, and the specter of death at the hands of the Black Watch had set everyone's blood running hot and fast. Good heavens, she might well have killed Campbell herself had the musket been loaded.

Catherine sighed and gave the empty forest path a final glance before she returned to the coach. He had said they were on Cameron land now and there wasn't anything to fear from the militia, but her skin prickled nonetheless at the encroaching shadows.

"Mistress Catherine?"

Deirdre's whisper brought Catherine whirling around with a sharp gasp.

"Oh. I'm sorry, mistress, but I fear Mr. MacKail is taking a turn for the worse. His brow is growing warmer by the hour, and there is no more water in the bucket to bathe him. Do you suppose we might be near a brook or a stream?"

Catherine scanned the fearsome woods once again, convinced there was an army of filthy, bearded faces peering out from behind the sea of ferns. Despite the lack of any real breeze, twigs were snapping, birds were arguing, branches were shaking all around them. The thought of leaving the relative safety of the trail to forage for water was as appealing as the notion of picnicking in a crypt.

How could Cameron have left them like this? His best—and probably only—friend in the world was slowly bleeding to death. Didn't the Highlander care?

Furthermore, she had seen no fences or hedgerows, no posts to mark the edge of Cameron land. What if someone *had* followed them into the forest? Two English-speaking women in a fancy English coach, lost in the heart of mountains that were supposedly overrun with blood-thirsty Jacobite rebels . . .

"Sweet merciful heaven," she muttered. "Could he not even have checked the water supply before he deserted us?"

Deirdre poked her head out of the coach window. "Deserted us? Mr. Cameron has deserted us?"

"He as much as admitted we are hopelessly lost. He *thinks* he can find the river, which he *thinks* will lead us to safety."

"Oh." Deirdre sank back onto her seat. "Well then, we must believe him, mustn't we? In the meantime I do not mind going and looking for water if you would prefer to remain here with Mr. MacKail."

Catherine declined the advice and the offer with a scowl. She would scream if she had to sit inside that stuffy coach a minute longer than necessary, gagging on the cloying stench of blood and sweat.

"No. I'll go. There must be a spring nearby; I can hear it."

Deirdre handed her the canvas bucket. She also handed her one of the loaded Highland dags Cameron had appropriated from the dead Watchmen, and Catherine bit her lip so hard she tasted the rusty taint of blood.

"Perhaps you'll see a hare, or a quail," Deirdre said lightly. "I'm ever so hungry."

Catherine smiled wanly at the maid's attempts to lessen her fears. "I shan't be long. If that wretched bounder returns in the meantime, tell him we should like a fire. I shall try to find some marigold or purslane for tea; something hot would do us all a world of good."

She set off in a direct line due west from the coach and followed the slope upward, picking her way carefully through the tangled growth of saplings. She stopped every few paces to look over her shoulder at the coach, reassuring herself that no mysterious hand had lifted it off the road and banished her to the horror of her fantasies. She also tried to listen for the source of the running water, which she could hear quite clearly the higher she climbed. Cameron had not seemed overly concerned about their water supply—probably with good reason, for these hills seemed to be riddled with creeks and natural springs.

Higher she climbed, and the stillness of the woods enfolded her like a shroud. As chilly as the air was becoming, she could feel dampness across her brow and steaming between her breasts. This time when she stopped to catch her breath, she could no longer see the coach, which was hidden behind a wall of mist-soaked green. She was tempted to turn around and scurry back down, but a distinctly liquid *blip* drew her attention to the right. She tramped quickly through the last knee-deep wall of ferns, and there it was: a tiny crack between two boulders from which spouted a thin, clear ribbon of water. Resembling a man-made fountain, the water collected in a shallow basin worn into the granite before spilling over the edge and running off and soaking into the black, spongy earth.

Catherine knelt wearily beside the small pool and set the gun and bucket on the moss. She cupped her hands and splashed some of the cool water on her face and throat, letting it run down the front of her bodice. She pushed back the soiled and limp lace of her cuffs and washed the grime from her hands and arms, then debated peeling down her stockings and soaking her aching feet. It was her conscience that gently reminded her of the weak and feverish man waiting below, but it was her heart that ground to a thudding, horrified halt as she turned to retrieve the bucket.

A pair of coarsely shod feet stood mere inches from her outstretched fingers. Above the feet were thick-hewn calves clad in diamond-patterned wool stockings that ended just below the bony knee. There was a span of a hand's width before the hairy, muscular thighs were concealed beneath the folds of a tartan kilt. A voluminous garment, it was wrapped about the man's waist and girted in pleats, with several yards left at the end to fling up and over the shoulder. Beneath the draped tartan was a sleeveless leather jerkin, which seemed at once too small and tight to fit the boldly muscular arms where they were crossed over the burly chest. Higher still, a beard as black as coal, as grizzled as frayed wire, framed a face more harsh and forbidding than a chunk of ice-clad rock. Surmounting the nest of hair that crowned his head was a woolen bonnet incongruously tilted at a jaunty angle, a bit of weed tucked in the cockade.

Catherine's hands flew to her mouth and a scream rose in her throat. It was a rebel! She had not been imagining the phony birdcalls or the feeling that she had been watched every step of the way from the road! And watched by—her shocked, frozen gaze locked on the woods behind the rebel's shoulder—the four ... five ... six more Highlanders who were melting slowly out of the trees.

For the second time that day, the second time in her young life, Catherine Augustine Ashbrooke slumped over in a dead faint.

When Alex had ridden away from the coach, his mind had not been on the forest or on the possible dangers that could be concealed behind the thick walls of greenery. Instead, his thoughts remained back on the road, and more specifically on the pair of violet eyes that had watched him until he had ridden out of sight.

It was no wonder he did not see the score of armed men crouched on either side of the track until Shadow had passed into their midst. When he did notice a flicker of movement, it was already far too late. A gleaming circle of muskets had moved swiftly to block the road ahead of and behind him, and more than one eager thumb reacted instantly to cock their weapons as he tried to reach for his own pistol.

"I wouldna do that, i'an' I were ye," a harsh voice grated from the shadows.

Alex traced the source and saw a giant of a Highlander leaning casually against a gnarled tree trunk. The tree was fully grown and wide as a barrel, but the breadth of the man's shoulders dwarfed it by comparison. He stood well above six feet, his height aggrandized by a lion's mane of straw-colored hair that, combined with the magnificent froth of a beard, flowed around his brawny shoulders like a regal mantle. His eyes were small and hawklike, missing nothing as they shrewdly assessed the worth of both man and beast.

Alex was careful to keep his hands in plain sight and, after his initial reaction, made no more sudden moves. Shadow stood as still as a black marble statue, his ears pricked forward, his flesh shivering as he awaited a command.

"Ye seem tae have strayed a ways from home, Sassenach," the Highlander spat. His gaze raked derisively over the rich brown velvet frock coat, the ruffled linen shirt, the expensively worked satin waistcoat and fitted breeches. "Ye look as though ye mout have a coin or two tae spare f'ae the insult. But were ye no' warned against ridin' in these hills alone?"

"The only warning I received," Alex replied calmly, "was to guard my back against a rebel ambush. I was told a particularly amateurish clan raids these hills, a godless coven by the name of Cameron."

The distinctly metallic rasp of several more hammers locking into full cock brought the huge Highlander's hand up in a staying gesture. "Ye've a strange lackin' in common sense, Sassenach. Ye should ha' heeded the advice ye were given."

Moving cautiously, deliberately, Alex swung a leg over the cantle of his saddle and dismounted. "I rarely heed advice I don't ask for, and certainly not from any bastard named Campbell."

The Highlander straightened from the tree. His eyes flicked along Alex's clothing again, this time alerted to the stains of dried blood.

"Who are ye, Sassenach? An' what quarrel do ye have wi' the Campbells?"

Alex smoothed a hand along Shadow's muzzle to set him at ease. "If you don't know the answer to either of those questions, Struan MacSorley, you deserve to spend the rest of your miserable life digging acorns in the forest."

The gigantic Scot took an ominous step forward. "Ye've a tongue like a wasp as well. The sound o' it brings tae mind a wee surly pup I were fond o' thrashin' now an' then f'ae bein' too damned big f'ae his breeks. He used tae give as good as he got, but that were a long time ago, an' I hear tell he's grown soft an' sweet-smellin' now. An' pretty as a wee lassie."

Alex advanced another step. "Not too soft to bring a sour-breathed Lochaber boar to his knees . . . and whistle a merry tune while doing it."

"Mayhap I'll let him try," MacSorley said on a grin. In the next breath he had spread his arms wide and clamped them around Alex's shoulders, pulling the willing man into a fearsome bear hug. "Alasdair! Alasdair, by the Christ, it's bonnie tae see ye! Where the devil have ye been? Lochiel's half mad wi' worry. He has our lads scourin' every glen an' glade from Loch Lochy tae Glencoe!"

"We met some trouble on the road near the Spean. We were planning to come straight through, but . . . it's a long story, and I've left a wounded man and two women a ways back along the road."

The bushy eyebrows crushed together and the death grip relaxed. "God's truth, why did ye no' say so instead o' standin' here blatherin' like a fishwife? Who's the wounded mon?"

"Aluinn MacKail. He took a shot in the chest—"

"Angus! Fetch up the ponies, then take three men an'

ride on ahead tae Achnacarry; let them know we've a wounded mon. Madach—keep half the men here wi' ye, the rest'll come wi' me. An' f'ae pity's sake, shy those guns awa' afore the *Camshroinaich Dubh* takes it in his heid as an insult an' scatters the lot o' ye across the road!" He paused and peered closely at Alex. "Two *lassies*, did ye say?"

"A *very* long story," Alex murmured. He mounted Shadow again as a shaggy-haired garron was led up to MacSorley. "But what news from Achnacarry? Other than my brother's lack of faith in me, is everyone well? Is it true what I've heard—*has* there been a landing in the Hebrides?"

"Aye, laddie." MacSorley nodded somberly. "Wee Bonnie Tearlach has come home, or so he says."

Alex wheeled Shadow around and rode in silence, alarmed by the confirmation that Prince Charles had returned to Scotland. There was no time to ponder the consequences, however. Around the next bend in the road they came upon the coach and only two of its three passengers. The whereabouts of the third were marked by a long, ear-piercing scream.

The tartan-clad Highlander bent over quickly, almost, but not quite, catching Catherine before she struck the ground.

He swore in Gaelic, then swore again as he heard footsteps pounding up the hill behind him.

"The lassie's fainted," he said, swinging around. "I ne'er touched her, she just fainted."

Alex hurried forward and went down on one knee. "I wouldn't worry, she's becoming quite proficient at it. Catherine?" He stroked her cheek and chafed a limp wrist. "Catherine, can you hear me? You are all right. You are among friends. Catherine . . ."

Her head lolled and she came swimming back to consciousness. Her eyelids slitted open, but it took her a moment or two to focus, to recognize the handsome features of the man leaning over her. Her eyes widened, and her lips parted. A gasp found her flinging herself up and into his arms.

"Alex! Oh, Alex, you came back!"

"Of course I came back," he said gently. "Didn't I promise you I would?"

"Oh, yes, but—" She stopped and gaped over his shoulder at the dozen or more bearded rebels standing around, staring at them. "Alex! Alex, have they caught you too?"

"Caught me?" He looked puzzled a moment, then smiled. "These are Cameron men, Catherine. My brother's men. They have been looking for us for a couple of days now. Are you feeling stronger? Do you think you can stand?"

Suddenly aware of how tightly and how closely she was holding him, she demurred. "Yes. Yes, of course I can stand."

Keeping a protective arm around her waist, Cameron helped her to her feet. She stumbled slightly and leaned unabashedly against him, still unsure as to what to make of his so-called friends. They hardly seemed any cleaner or less dangerous than the kilted soldiers they had met earlier in the day.

"Are you absolutely certain they are who they say they are?" she asked in a whisper. "After all, you did think Iain was your cousin."

Alex scowled. "Yes, I can see you are feeling better. If so, we had best get moving while there is still some day-light left."

"Are we near the river? Did you find it?"

"It's just over the crest of the next hill. Don't worry, you are perfectly safe now. The coach will get you to Achna-carry in a couple of hours. I am going to go on ahead with some of the men, but you will be well-protected. I'll leave—"

"No!" Catherine had kept her voice low up to then, but the shock of hearing that he planned to leave her

alone again brought such a shrill cry to her lips that some of the clansmen reached instinctively for their pistols. "*No!* No, you are *not* going to leave me with *anyone*! I do not *know* these men, I have no reason to *trust* these men. Furthermore, I am tired of being told what to do and where to go! I am not part of the baggage, damn you. I am your *wife*!"

Such a silence descended on the forest, it seemed as if the mist itself had stopped curling around the trees to pause and listen. Alex gripped Catherine's wrist, but the warning came too late. She blundered forward, unmindful of the hard, riveting stares that followed her every word.

"I am your *wife*, as you keep reminding me. However it may have happened or for however long I am forced to endure the indignity, *I am your wife!* Not a servant, not a child, and not just when it is convenient for you to throw it in my face!"

More stunned expressions rippled through the clansmen. Many spoke only Gaelic, but already those who understood the *Sassenach* tongue were hissing a translation of her fiery tirade.

The muscles in Alex's jaw worked furiously, and his midnight eyes bored into Catherine's with a lethal mixture of incredulity and fury. Slowly, with an even deeper chill of foreboding, she realized what she had done. Until that very instant she had not seriously troubled herself as to how he planned to explain her presence to his family. She had never once considered their vows as legal or binding, nor had he. But now . . . now she had verbally consummated their union in front of a score of his own clansmen.

"I'm sorry," she gasped, her fingertips pressing over her lips. "I didn't know what I was saying. I didn't think. Perhaps if I explain—"

"You have done quite enough explaining for the time being," he said coldly.

"But you must do something! You cannot let them believe—"

"At the moment, what they believe is of no consequence. What I believe, however, is that you should keep your mouth firmly shut from here on in." The anger in his voice matched the threat of violence in his hand as he clamped it painfully around her upper arm. "And you are absolutely right: I don't dare leave you alone. Struan"—he turned to the burly Highlander—"have you an extra horse?"

MacSorley appeared to still be in shock. "Eh? Oh, aye. Aye. One o' the lads can spare a pony."

"I . . . I think I would prefer to remain with the coach," Catherine said, trying to pull away from the iron grip. "I think I would prefer to stay with Deirdre."

"You are coming with me, dear *wife*," Alex insisted. "But if you wish to argue the matter further, I would be more than willing to demonstrate how a Highlander disciplines a spouse who dares to speak out of turn."

Catherine opened her mouth, but snapped it closed again without making a sound, wisely deciding not to challenge the promissory glitter in his dark eyes.

As for Alex, he almost wished she would defy him. One more day—one more *hour* and he would have had her safely across the High Bridge and on the road to Fort William. Damn the Argyle men. Damn Gordon Ross Campbell. And damn whatever demon had made him dance with Catherine Ashbrooke under a starlit sky!

12

Catherine rode the remaining miles to Achnacarry in utter despair. Since Cameron had turned his back on her on the hillside, he had not spared a glance or a word in her direction. She could feel his anger crackling in the air between them, and while she was prepared to accept the blame for her ill-timed slip of the tongue, it was unfair and unreasonable for him to treat her as if she had deliberately and spitefully set out to entrap him.

Far from being comforted by the presence of an armed escort, she found herself growing more and more leery of what lay ahead. Having never dreamed the charade would last this long or take her so far into the heart of the Highlands, she had not dared to imagine what his precious home might look like or what kind of a reception she could hope to receive. Visions of caves with firelit ceilings and great hanging stalactites spun wearily through her head. Cameron had referred to his home as a castle, but so far most of the structures she had seen peppering the land were nothing more than cramped, rancid-smelling stone cottages. Once or twice she had glimpsed the distant silhouette of battlements against a wind-blown sky, but the impression had been bleak and forbidding and brought to mind her father's tales of thick-tongued savages who wore stinking fur robes and made their homes in mountain lairs. Ancient stone keeps, dungeons, ramparts guarded by gargoyles and grotesques . . . would this Achnacarry be such a place? Would its inhabitants stare at her and sneer contemptuously behind her back as did these silent, belligerent outriders?

She was exhausted, confused, and frightened. She had
not had a decent bath or a familiar meal since crossing
the border into Scotland. The soiled, stained gown she
wore was the only garment she possessed now that
Cameron had seen fit to abandon her trunks. She did not
even have a cloak or shawl to ward off the evening
dampness. One of the clansmen had grudgingly provided
her with a coarse length of wool tartan to wrap around
her head and shoulders like a bedraggled peasant. Her
fingers stung from the unaccustomed abuse of handling
the stiff leather reins without gloves. Her hair was a
yellow tangle, her nose red and dripping, her eyes
swollen almost shut from the tears and filth and despair;
her body ached in places too pampered to have contemplated the possibility of bruising.

The sun had long since vanished behind the crust of
blue-black mountains. The road they were following
skirted the banks of a loch, plunging and twisting around
the shoreline like a coiling snake, so thick with mist in
places it seemed as if they were riding into an opaque wall.
The air smelled wet and oddly sweet, as if there was a
forest of fruit trees hiding behind the fog, and sure enough,
when they rounded a bend in the road and climbed high
enough to surmount the mist, she saw apple trees and two
tall columns of elms flanking either side of the road. At the
end of this regal promenade was Achnacarry Castle.

Perched on an isthmus of land between two deep, inky
lochs, the buff-colored masonry stood tall and stark
against the last dying shades of twilight. The walls rose
sheer from the edge of a bluff, the cold stone facings presenting a monstrous and deadly fortification nestled in a
setting that was a perfect gem of tranquillity. The castle
itself consisted of huge square war towers capped by
rust-hued turrets. Long ranges of rooms, each carefully
designed and fitted one upon the other in tiers, were but-
tressed to the walls to form the upper stories, and sur-

rounding the whole were tall, saw-toothed battlements, where sentries could see for miles in all directions.

Catherine was suitably awestruck. Achnacarry Castle could easily have absorbed four Rosewood Halls within its walls and afforded living space for a small town should the need for such a defense arise.

The castle was approached along a well-packed road of earth and crushed stone called the dark mile, she would later learn, because of the heavy shadows thrown by the twin rows of elms. The breastworks became even more impressive the closer they came, rising in places to a height of well over eighty feet. The entrance was marked by two bright streaks of lantern light. Sandwiched between enormous square barbican towers, the black oak gates opened to a width equal to that of a large carriage and were protected by a portcullis—a massive grille of iron spikes that could be dropped into place to seal the entryway at a moment's notice. Between the port and gate the walls were slit at intervals, wide enough for men with muskets to question any uninvited guests. It was also planked underfoot, so that the arrival of so many men and horses echoed loudly throughout the inner courtyards.

Inside the walls there were two baileys fashioned in the style of Norman strongholds. A long range of lighted windows spanned the two like a bridge, with a vaulted stone undercroft forming a covered walkway beneath. The "bridge" housed a long gallery and connected the two main wings of the castle. Stables occupied one full length of the outer courtyard, alongside the blockhouses, pens, smithy, and salt house. Here also were the servants' quarters and the guardhouse, and one of two huge outbuildings that contained a kitchen and laundry. There were lights in nearly every window, and at the echo of their horses' hooves the glare was bisected by curious heads filling the spaces, craning to identify the visitors.

The second courtyard was measurably smaller, with a large stone well occupying its center. Here was the principal entrance to the main living quarters as well as the chapel, smokehouse, and family kitchen. Catherine could hear the excited murmur of voices before she had fully cleared the archway and was not surprised to see several dozen men and women rushing out of doors to greet the late-night guests. The men all seemed to be bigger than life—tall and broad-chested, draped in swathes of tartan dyed in crimsons, greens, and blues. Some of them carried torches and lanterns, and soon the misty air was hazed further with smoke and stained yellow by the flickering flames.

Catherine had read stories about the Christians being led to the lions in the days of the Roman Empire—she was beginning to understand something of what they felt. Cameron had treated her with blatant hostility on the long ride through the mountains, but now, as he dismounted and was engulfed in a sea of waving arms and hearty handclasps, he was all smiles and laughter. Hugged by men and women alike, he was passed willingly from one deliriously happy group to the next until he found himself standing before the main entrance.

There, a tall, elegantly lean man stood patiently in the spill of light from the open doors. Although his features were less angular than Alexander's and his coloring a fair contrast to his brother's rugged darkness, there was no mistaking the family resemblance. There was also no mistaking his rank and station. He wore plaid woolen breeches patterned in crimson and black and a frock coat of hunting green, the cuffs and collar thick with lace, heavily embroidered in gold thread. Without hearing an introduction Catherine surmised he was Donald Cameron, The Cameron of Lochiel, and realizing this she experienced a small shudder of relief. He did not look like a mountain savage, nor did he look like the type of man who would hold her prisoner in a cave and ransom her as a hostage. He looked reasonable, rational, and totally civilized in the midst of a world she had begun to believe was plunged in utter madness.

Slowly the swelling crowd fell silent and turned, one by one, to witness the reunion of the two brothers. For a long moment neither man moved, their expressions mirrored in the slight, crooked smiles and shining eyes.

"So then. Ye've come home, have ye, Alexander Cameron," the laird said finally. "By all that's holy, we've missed yer comely face nigh these long years."

"Not nearly as much as I have missed yours," Alex said quietly.

The two men came together and embraced, triggering another eruption of cheers and laughter. When the noise again subsided, Donald Cameron raised his voice and addressed the crowd in Gaelic, an obvious invitation to bring forth ale and wine to help celebrate the prodigal's homecoming. Alex, meanwhile, had turned his attention to the slender, dark-haired woman who was standing quietly by Lochiel's side.

"Maura. You are still the most beautiful woman in all of Scotland."

Lady Cameron laughed and wept openly as Alex swept her into his arms and spun her in a happy circle. Two gangly, awkward youths were beckoned forward in turn and introduced to their infamous uncle, but before any further formalities could be observed, a voracious roar reduced the crowd to quivering silence again. A shorter, rounder version of Donald Cameron exploded through the doorway and smothered Alex in a hearty, shoulder-thumping embrace.

"Alasdair! Alasdair, be damned if ye're no' the sicht f'ae sore eyes! Stand tae the light an' gie us a better look! By the Christ . . . he's grown tae the image of auld Ewen! Donald—if he isna Ewen Cameron born again, I'll set masel' doun here an' now an' eat ma own liver!"

"Ye've nae call tae waste the effort, Archibald Cameron," declared a cackle of a voice behind them. "Yer liver's well enough along eatin' itsel'."

The portly physician was elbowed aside by his wife— a short firebrand of a woman who barely reached the

height of Alex's chest but whose hug very nearly lifted
him off his feet.

"A fine welcome home," she scolded, glaring up at
him through bright, twinkling eyes. "Though ye dinna
deserve it, ye askit me. A glib-glabbet, educated man, an'
what do ye send home but a miserable wee scratchet note
once or twice the year. Ungrateful swine, that's what ye
are. If it were up tae me, I'd send ye packin' back tae
France again, no never mind."

"Jeannie." Alex laughed. "I'm glad to see you haven't
changed a bit. Still the sharpest tongue in Lochaber."

"Sharp enough tae cut ye doun a step or two," she
warned, thrusting a finger up under his nose. In response
to the threat he gathered her into his arms and twirled her
so hard and fast her velvet skirts belled up and over her
thrashing, pantalooned legs. "Enough! Enough, ye daft
fool! Put me doun afore I'm up tae seein' ma supper
again, poor as it were the fairst time around."

Alex set her aside and turned to Archibald again. "You
know we met with some trouble on the road?"

"Aye, so Angus told us. Everythin's ready an' waitin'.
How bad off is the lad?"

"Bad enough even before we had to rattle about in a
coach for six hours. He has lost a great deal of blood—"

"A coach?" Archibald interrupted. "Were ye after
tellin' the whole world ye were on yer way home?"

"It seems the whole world knew already," Alex said
grimly. He started to briefly recount the treachery surrounding Gordon Ross Campbell, but was halted by
another subtle swelling of whispers and speculation that
centered around the tartan-wrapped figure still seated on
her horse in the middle of the courtyard.

Catherine, for her part, had been quite content to
remain forgotten. She was petrified at the very idea of
dismounting, for that would mean she was *here*. She was
in the Highland stronghold of the man generally considered to be the leader of the Jacobite faction in Scotland.
As reasonable, rational, and civilized as Alexander's

brother appeared to be, he was still in command of the loyalties and swords of a thousand or so clansmen who were blatantly less refined. Some of those men had been in the escort and were milling in the crowd now, telling their own version of what had happened in the mountains. And some of those whispers reached the ears of Archibald Cameron, who held up a hand and exclaimed in a voice loud enough to startle the devil, "A wife? Saints presairve us, ye've come home wi' a wife?"

Without waiting for an answer or an explanation, the doctor pushed his way through the crowd, his Gaelic greeting as broad as the grin that beamed on his face. Catherine did not understand a word of what he was saying; she only saw the short, stubby hands reaching up to snatch her out of the saddle.

"Don't touch me!" she cried, flinching back. "Don't you dare touch me!"

The doctor's wiry chestnut eyebrows flew upward at the sound of the cultured English accent, and he did, indeed, come to an abrupt halt.

An angry, defensive flush rose in Alex's face as one by one the startled and disbelieving stares focused on him. Aluinn's words of warning flashed through his head a heartbeat ahead of Jeannie Cameron's less-than-subtle gasp of shock.

"English? *Ye've brung a* Sassenach *wife home tae Achnacarry?*"

Whether it was an instinctive reaction to the contempt in his sister-in-law's voice or an equally instinctive reaction to the notion that his choice of wives should have been approved by them first, Alex walked slowly back through the parted crowd to where Catherine sat trembling with fresh shivers of apprehension. His eyes were colder and bleaker than anything she had ever seen before, the warning in them explicit and clear: *Say nothing. Do nothing. Just go along with it for now.*

Without a word he reached up and clasped his hands around her waist, lifting her down from the saddle. He escorted her back through the grim silence, his arm rigid with forced politeness, his smile a mere flattening of the lips.

"Catherine, may I present my brother Donald, The Cameron of Lochiel. Donald, my . . . wife, Catherine."

Catherine was all too aware of everyone staring at her and of the collective breath that was being held as they all waited to see how the Chief of Clan Cameron would react to having a *Sassenach* in the family.

The keen blue eyes of the laird studied her intently, seeming to see her fear and nervousness, and regardless of how he felt about the matter personally, he raised one of her cold and chafed hands to his lips and brushed it with a smile.

"A rare privilege and an honor indeed, Catherine," he said warmly. "Ye've nae idea how long we've waited tae see our wee brither happily wed. But then, wi' a lassie as lovely as yersel', how could he have resisted?"

Catherine felt herself shrinking into a deeper sense of mortification, for she was hardly lovely at that precise moment, and if he was mocking her he was even more cruel and unconscionable than his renegade brother.

Lady Maura Cameron did not wait for a formal introduction, but stepped forward and took Catherine's hands in hers.

"You must excuse our manners, dear," she said. "We have all been anxiously awaiting Alexander's arrival and, well, naturally we should have suspected he would not be able to resist doing it with a flourish. But we are all so happy he brought you home to us. Welcome to Achnacarry."

Archibald had rejoined the group and was presented along with his wife, Jeannie, who murmured a civil enough greeting under Lochiel's warning eye. Sons, daughters, aunts, and uncles started to push forward, their curiosity getting the best of them, but Lady Maura stopped the crush, slipping her arm around Catherine's waist and urging her into the warmth of the castle.

"That is enough for now," she declared, her own cultured accent hinting at an English education. "Can you not see the poor child is cold and hungry? Jeannie—to the kitchen with you and see if there is some broth left from supper. Archibald—hadn't you best finish your preparations in the surgery before you start celebrating? Aluinn MacKail will not want a foggy eye and an unsteady hand attending him. Donald—"

"Aye, love. Aye, ye're right. There will be plenty o' time on the morrow f'ae greetings an' the like." He took Alex's arm and steered him to the door. "Yer old rooms in the west tower have been shaken out an' made fit f'ae a king . . . although . . . ye might be wantin' something more . . . comfortable now."

"The tower is fine," Alex said firmly.

"I'll have plenty of hot water sent up," Maura said, giving Catherine a little squeeze for encouragement. "A long bath and a change of clothes can work wonders on the spirit."

"I . . . I h-have no other clothes with me," Catherine stammered, glancing back at Alex even as she was being bustled away. "We were forced to abandon my trunks."

Lady Cameron smiled. "In a household the size of this one we should have no trouble outfitting you until our seamstresses can make up for your loss. We have a storeroom full of silk and brocade and the latest patterns straight from France."

"I . . . I couldn't possibly impose."

"Nonsense. You are family now. What is ours is yours."

Any further protests were forgotten as Catherine's eyes adjusted to the brighter lights inside the entryway and she found herself being led along a richly paneled hallway hung with tapestries and paintings that depicted several centuries of Cameron pride. The vaulted ceiling rose three full stories, with every square panel of polished wood displaying the family history in pictures, woven and painted. At the end of the long corridor was a wall of glass windows that soared as high as the ceiling and offered a breathtaking view of the loch and surrounding mountains.

Conscious only of putting one foot in front of the other, Catherine followed Lady Maura as if in a daze, her head turning to the left to stare in awe at a vast array of swords, axes, and medieval armor, then to the right to admire the artifacts and treasures that filled the twelve-foot-high niches in the walls. The floor was covered in oak strips, sanded and polished to such a high gloss it reflected the arms and armor, the colored standards and family crests. The great hall was aptly named, for she had seen no other like it.

Once up the stairs she was taken along a second hallway not quite so impressive in decoration but equally rich in paneling and smaller tapestries. She passed several minor passageways and entrances to stairwells and was afforded brief glimpses through open doors into the library, receiving room, and dayroom. They were all proportionately large and well-furnished, and Catherine was struck again by the incredible size and substance of Achnacarry.

When they turned down the long gallery that bridged the two outer courtyards, Catherine drew to an abrupt halt. Between the many multipaned windows were hung life-size oil paintings of the Cameron men and women and, beneath each, clusters of miniatures representing members of that particular figure's immediate family. It was an amazingly well-documented chronicle of the Cameron clan, and it caught Catherine's attention despite her weariness.

Maura raised the candle she was carrying and aimed the brighter light at the series of portraits that were holding Catherine's gaze the longest.

"The large one is of John Cameron—Donald and Alex's father. He lives at present in Italy, with the court of King James."

Catherine recognized familial traits in the strong jaw

and ironlike gleam in the brooding eyes. She vaguely recalled Alex mentioning that his father, a staunch Jacobite who had been attainted after the 1715 rebellion, had chosen to share the exile of his Stuart monarch rather than swear an oath of allegiance to the Hanover king.

"Donald keeps in constant touch, naturally, and the clan makes a fine distinction between Old Lochiel and Young Lochiel, but . . . he's a proud and stubborn old Scot, our father-in-law. He vows he will not come home until a Scottish king sits upon the throne again. He refuses any money Donald sends and lives in Italy like a common courtier rather than the Chief of Clan Cameron. You would like him, I think. His sons share a good many of his qualities."

Catherine studied the noble features more closely and agreed they were as strong and uncompromising as his sons'. His cornflower-blue eyes and chestnut hair had been passed down to Donald and Archibald, while his massive shoulders and powerful presence were more dominant in Alexander. There was a miniature of a fourth son in the cluster beneath the portrait, one who shared the fair coloring but whose features were thinner and sharper, almost unpleasant.

"John Cameron of Fassefern," Maura explained. "He should be here by tomorrow; you will meet him then. He is . . . somewhat less committed in his politics."

"A bald disgrace, ye mean," Jeannie declared, coming up behind them. Ambling along beside her was a petite, white-haired woman introduced simply as Auntie Rose.

"The Camerons are a very old clan," Maura continued, ignoring the interruption. "The very first Cameron of Loch Eil was slain by Macbeth in 1020, but he fought so bravely and so well to defend his land that the king honored him and pronounced him 'the fiercest of the fierce'—a motto the clan adopted and has kept ever since."

Catherine's gaze wandered to another canvas, and she felt the blood react oddly in her veins. The intensity in the blue-black eyes sent a shiver along her spine and gave her a chilling sense that the man in the portrait was alive and breathing and poised to leap down off the wall.

"Sir Ewen Cameron," Maura explained. "Your husband's grandfather."

"Grandfather? But I thought—"

Maura raised the candle higher. "There is an incredible resemblance, isn't there? Even as a boy Alexander was mistaken for the son rather than the grandson, a fact the old rascal never denied in the company of beautiful young women. They are the only two of many generations of Camerons to possess the black hair and eyes—a legacy from the dark gods, or so the legend goes."

The silky hairs across the nape of Catherine's neck rippled to attention. "The dark gods?"

"Druids," Maura said, smiling. "They either charm you or curse your life at birth; they watch over you with a keen eye or laugh cruelly at each mistaken step. They certainly watched over Ewen. He was brash and arrogant, brave to the point of lunacy. He was the only Highland laird who dared to refuse to submit to Cromwell's rule after King Charles was defeated back in 1649. He refused to take an oath of allegiance to a 'white-collared, cattle-lifting prelate' and even sent a demand to the new Parliament for remunerations, accusing the so-called New Model Army of destroying some of his fields and carrying away valuable livestock without paying for it."

"What did Cromwell do?" Catherine asked, having heard stories about the English reformer's swift and harsh justice for all rebels.

"He paid it. He also issued strict orders to his generals to stay clear of Cameron land."

Catherine studied the darkly handsome face again while Maura added softly, "They were inseparable, Ewen and Alex. I am surprised he has not told you all about the old warrior."

"To be honest—" Catherine set her jaw and turned to face Lady Cameron, the need to terminate the entire farce once and for all burning at the back of her throat. "To be *perfectly* honest—" The soft brown eyes were waiting expectantly, and her resolve faltered. "We have not known each other very long; he has not told me very much about anything. In fact, I had no idea what to expect when we arrived and, well, frankly . . . I had imagined all manner of . . . of . . ."

"Naked, bearded mountain men?" Maura's laugh was directed more at herself than at Catherine, at some memory from her past. "I spent eight years in London attending school. I know all too well the image most Englishmen have of Scotland and her people, and in some instances it is well-deserved. We are a proud and touchy breed, especially here in the Highlands where a man will draw his sword rather than shrug aside an insult. There are blood feuds that have been carrying on for centuries, some so long no one remembers the original cause of the dispute."

"Like the Campbells and the Camerons?"

Maura drew back and for a moment looked as if she might drop the candle. It surely wavered in her hand, dripping hot wax over her fingers, but she did not seem to notice.

"I'm sorry. Did I say something wrong? I only asked because it was Campbell men who attacked us on the road today and a Campbell who seems bent on seeing Alexander hanged for murder."

This time Maura blanched. Her gaze flicked past Catherine's shoulder to the other two women, and she indicated by a firm shake of her head that they were not to say anything.

"Lady Cameron, I—"

"No. No, you have not said anything wrong, dear. I was just not prepared. But of course, if Alexander has not told you anything about the family, you could not possibly be expected to . . . to know that I am a Campbell. Or that the Duke of Argyle is my uncle."

An image of the coarse, foul-breathed sergeant flashed

through Catherine's mind, and she found it difficult if not impossible to believe there could be a blood connection between him and the delicate, gracious woman who stood before her. Even more disconcerting was the realization that one of Maura's relatives had fixed the price on Alexander Cameron's head, and that he had been directly responsible for the treachery of Gordon Ross Campbell.

There was simply too much going on that she did not understand, too many complexities she did not *want* to understand, and her sense of isolation, her exhaustion, her aching weariness came reeling down upon her with a vengeance and she raised a trembling hand to her temple.

"Ye think tha's a shock, hen?" Auntie Rose muttered, her accent thick as soup. "Anyone tald me fifteen years back oor Alasdair would ha' taken himsel' anither wife, I would ha' called the bastard a liar an' sent him tae the devil masel'. I still canna believe it. He kissed the dirk f'ae wee Annie MacSorley an' swore he'd take nae ither, an' I canna believe he didna keep the oath."

Maura hushed the old woman in Gaelic, ignoring courtesy for the sake of expedience, but the damage was already done. Auntie Rose had said *another* wife, meaning ... Alexander Cameron had been married before?

Catherine stared at Maura, then the elderly aunt. Rose was flushed and still muttering to herself, and it occurred to Catherine then to wonder if part of the animosity she had sensed in the courtyard was not so much because Alexander Cameron had returned with an English wife, it was that he had returned with any wife at all.

13

Catherine slept eighteen hours straight through, waking at four o'clock the next afternoon without the slightest desire to rise from the heavenly comfort of the feather mattress. She lay in a huge catafalque bed and studied her surroundings with a slumberous eye, feeling at first she must still be asleep, immersed in a dream where she was playing the role of a medieval princess. The walls of her bedchamber certainly gave the impression of an ancient castle tower. They were built of naked stone blocks, devoid of even the thinnest layer of plaster or paint to seal the cracks in the mortar. There were no curtains, no tapestries, no rugs of any size or thickness on the rough plank flooring to alleviate the starkness. The tower was part of the breastworks of the original keep, dating back God only knew how many centuries, and the only source of air or light in the ten-foot-thick walls was a long, thin window corbelled out from the outer face of the stonework. The embrasure was deep enough to stand in, the window itself elaborately molded with carved stone tracery. No glass had been fitted to the panes, but there were heavy wooden shutters that closed from the inside and an inches-thick wool tapestry that could be lowered over the opening to keep out the winter winds.

Apart from the antiquated bed—a monstrous thing at least twice the size of her own at Rosewood Hall—the only other furnishings in the spartan chamber were a large armoire and dresser, a pair of boxlike dressing

tables, and two deep, high-backed wing chairs. There
was no fireplace, no immediate source of heat other than
a small portable iron brazier that Maura had sent to the
room during the night.

The chamber next to hers, however, was the fireroom,
appropriately named for the predominance of a wall-to-
wall, floor-to-ceiling fireplace that supplied heat for the
three rooms located in the tower. A brass and ebony
bathtub was the only permanent fixture of the fireroom,
and it was there that Catherine had scrubbed away the
aches and pains, the weariness, the horror of the day's
events. She had soaked until the steam and heat had made
her light-headed, and then she had consumed an enormous
meal of hot beef broth, fresh baked bread, roasted meat,
and thick yellow cheese. Stuffed, warmed, and clean, she
had fallen into bed and was asleep before Maura and Rose
could even draw the quilts over her.

Now she stretched and wriggled her toes, groaning
inwardly at the luxury of snowy-white sheets and a soft,
dry bed. It was the first time she had felt safe or comfortable since leaving Derbyshire, and the mere thought of
stepping down onto the bare plank flooring drove her
deeper into the nest of blankets.

"These were Sir Ewen's rooms," Maura had explained.
"He preferred the old ways, as he liked to call it, acknowledging his roots, not giving over to the luxury and corruption of modern conveniences. He claimed it kept a man
honest having to empty his own chamber pot in the
morning. When he died Alexander moved his belongings
in here and took the tower rooms as his own. He said he
could look out the window in the evenings and see the old
gaisgach liath—the gray warrior—riding through the
mists over the loch."

Catherine wrinkled her nose disdainfully. She hadn't
been impressed by either the sentiment or the view. She
was not particularly fond of heights, and the tower seemed
to be perched at the very edge of the spur of land. As to the

jagged, mist-shrouded peaks that lay beyond, she had had enough of mountains and landscapes and breathtaking tableaux to last a lifetime, thank you very much.

What she did want, and what she would probably not be able to get enough of over the next few days, was another bath. She had no idea how long she would be kept prisoner in this castle keep, or if the return journey to Derby would be as primitive or as miserable as the trek here, but she intended to make use of every opportunity for comfort while she had it. She could still feel a crawling sensation where the blood of their attackers had splashed on her skin. Worse still were the prickly suggestions that her scalp was not entirely free of guests.

A sudden spate of vigorous scratching sent her hopping out of the bed. She was wearing a loose cambric nightdress laced modestly high at the throat and fitted snugly to her wrists with a profusion of satin ribbons. A heavy woolen robe had been draped over the foot of the bed for her use, and she was just tying the belt around her waist when she heard the door to the chamber rasp open.

Standing in the entryway was a young woman Catherine had not seen before and certainly would have remembered had they been introduced. Tall and slender, she had the complexion of someone accustomed to sun and wind and fresh country air. Her long hair was lush with natural waves, a fiery titian red with streaks of sun-bleached gold. Her eyes were large and almond-shaped, of no distinct color but rather a shifting blend of green and gold and brown. She stood with one hand on her hip, a stance that had apparently been cultivated to best display the astonishing fullness of her breasts.

"So. It's true, then," the newcomer mused in broad Scots. "Alasdair has come hame wi' a new bride."

Catherine could think of no immediate response as the girl came slowly into the room—undulated was a more apt description of the way her hips swayed side to side beneath the butternut homespun of her skirt. She smiled, her tiger eyes sparkling as she scanned the shapeless folds of the wool robe.

"No' much tae look at, are ye? Just a wee snip o' a thing. Must be the English weather grows 'em small. Ma name's Lauren, tae save ye askin'. Lauren Cameron, cousin tae yer husban' Alasdair. I ken that makes us cousins as well . . . by marriage."

"I'm . . . pleased to meet you," Catherine murmured hesitantly.

"Mmm." The girl approached the foot of the bed and seemed amused to see only one side of the bedding rumpled. "Ye spent yer fairst night at Achnacarry alone?"

Catherine lowered her lashes. "I imagine my . . . Alexander had a great deal to discuss with his brothers."

Lauren nodded. "Aye, so they must've. I ken he kept company wi' Lochiel till well past midnight, an' then later, when the coach arrived, he stayed wi' Archie an' helped sew up the holes in Aluinn MacKail's chest. Still an' all, ye think he might ha' found time f'ae a wee *visit*. The ghost o' the auld Dark Cameron could have come an' snatched ye awa' durin' the night."

"Mr. MacKail . . . he is still alive, then?"

"O' course he's alive. He's a Cameron, is he no'? The ither side o' the hedge, so tae speak, but still a Cameron, an' no' likely tae give a Campbell the satisfaction o' killin' him so easy." She swayed her hips again and ran her fingers down one of the carved bedposts. "He an' I might ha' wed had he stayed in Scotland. Or mayhap Alasdair an' I. Camerons usually wed their own kind, so they do."

At long last Catherine felt more familiar ground beneath her, recognizing the green eyes of jealousy when she saw them. And while it shouldn't have bothered her in the least, knowing she had no claim on Cameron's affections—knowing she *wanted* no claim—it was mildly surprising to feel the warm flush of resentment rising in her cheeks.

"Talk last night was all about ye an' Alasdair," Lauren continued. "Nary a one thought the *Camshroinaich Dubh* would marry again." The hooded eyes narrowed slyly. "Ye did know he was married afore, did ye no'?"

If I didn't, you certainly would have corrected the oversight. "Yes, I knew. To . . . Annie MacSorley," she added, putting Auntie Rose's slip last night to good use.

"Aye, wee Annie. The fairest, sweetest lass in all o' Lochaber. Mind, they were only handfasted, but they acted like man an' wife . . . if ye ken what I mean."

"Handfasted?"

"Aye. Spoke their vows wi' only the stars above an' the heather aneath them as witness. They would ha' gone tae the altar proper, but . . . well . . . Annie died then, did she no'?"

Catherine picked up a brush and began running it through her hair, fighting to keep her voice cool, her questions casual. "MacSorley? Wasn't that the name of the tall blond man who rode in with us last night?"

"Aye, Struan MacSorley. Annie's brither." The feathery red lashes lifted as she glanced sidelong at Catherine. "Now, there's a man would never leave his wife's bed wantin' f'ae company. Big as a bull, accordin' tae Mary MacFarlane, an' able tae ride his woman all the blessed night long."

The brush came to an abrupt and startled standstill.

"I doubt he'd take a *Sassenach*, though. I doubt any but Alasdair would dare such a thing. Then again, he always was the one tae go against what was expected. It's the Dark One's legacy, I warrant. There's a rumor says one o' Sir Ewen's wives carried the taint o' English bluid in her."

Drawing on a dozen generations of that same tainted blood, Catherine's smile was frosted with apathy. "Well, I truly have enjoyed your company, and your quaint anecdotes, Mistress Cameron, but I mustn't keep you from your chores any longer. Since you seem so interested in my bed, may I assume you have come to change the linens?"

Lauren's eyes sparkled with tiny green flecks. "In truth, I might ha' thought yer own lass would ha' done it by now . . . ach, but I forgot. She's away tendin' tae someone else's bed, is she no'?"

"Someone else?"

"Aye. She's been fawnin' over MacKail all mornin' long, fetchin' this, fetchin' that, bathin' his brow . . . an' Lord knows what else."

Catherine's patience slipped another notch. "Well, I need her here. Where is Mr. MacKail's room?"

"North court. Ye'll never find it, but happens I'm goin' that way, though, an' I'd be pleased tae tell her ye need yer hands washed an' yer hair fixed, if ye like."

"You're too kind," Catherine said stiffly.

Lauren paused on her way out the door, her glance traveling back to the tousled bedding. "Mayhap I'll send someone back f'ae the linens . . . when they've had some use."

Lauren pulled the door closed behind her with a satisfied bang. The nerve of the bitch, thinking her a laundress or a maid come to change the bedding. Aye, maybe one who was *in* the bedding, if she wasn't careful.

If nothing else she had satisfied her curiosity as to what the Englishwoman looked like. Lauren did not particularly consider white skin and pale hair especially beautiful, nor did there seem to be much to the *Sassenach*'s figure beneath the woolen robe. Men liked their women full-breasted and wild as the heather that grew on the moors, not thin and vapid and blushing at every other turn of phrase. What on earth had Alasdair seen in her? Could it be he had gone soft living so long on the Continent?

She frowned thoughtfully as she descended the spiraling stone staircase. He certainly did not look soft. He looked hard and conditioned, his muscles honed to perfection. His conversation with Lochiel last night had been all about war; not once had he mentioned the latest fashions or the newest trends out of Paris. Donald Cameron had been anxious to hear about the political climate in England and Europe, and in turn he had answered Alasdair's questions about Prince Charles, confirming the royal's arrival on the west coast of Scotland on July 25, in the tiny inlet of Loch nan Uamn.

Word had reached Achnacarry that a Cameron had been on board, acting as pilot to navigate the ship through the myriad islands off the Hebrides, and Lochiel had thought at first it was Alasdair. But it had turned out to be a distant cousin, Duncan Cameron, and Lochiel's eyes had turned to the roads and mountain crossings again. He had, in fact, used his concern over Alasdair's pending arrival as an excuse to politely refuse the Prince's request for an audience. A second, more petulant summons had arrived that afternoon, and again Lochiel had declined to answer, all too aware that if he did appear at Arisaig, it would seem he supported the idea of rebellion.

Already aware of Lochiel's moral dilemma and bored by politics in general, Lauren had listened to their voices without really paying heed to the words. Alasdair's voice, deep and melodic, had flowed down her spine like warm syrup and pooled in her loins so that the slightest movement had caused ripples of tingling pleasure throughout her body.

He had avoided discussing his wife for the longest time—almost as if she hadn't existed until a few days ago. But when talk had turned to the events of the day and he described the encounter with the Watchmen, including the near success of Gordon Ross Campbell's plot to lead them into an ambush, Alasdair had given full credit to the *Sassenach* for saving the day.

Now that Lauren had met the woman in person, however, she could plainly see the lie for what it was. Such a pampered, weak-kneed, lily mouse would hardly be capable of lifting a musket, much less swinging it with enough conviction to crack a man's head open. No doubt Alasdair had been trying to protect his own honor by lending some to hers. Heaven only knew why he had married her. Men took wives for all manner of reasons: money, prestige, power. Since Alasdair had been masquerading as an English peer for so many years, it was only reasonable he should acquire the necessary camouflage, including a pale-skinned wife. But God's teeth! He was still a Cameron, and his blood surely ran hot. The purple-eyed bitch hardly looked adequate for his needs; like as not, she squealed and clamped her knees together in sheer fright every time he entered the bedchamber.

A man like Alasdair was exactly the kind of man Lauren had been hungering for since her breasts had grown large enough to warrant slack-mouthed stares. The existence of a wife was an annoyance, but nothing she could not overcome, and the mere thought of seeing Alasdair Cameron standing on the threshold of *her* bedchamber sent a warm, moist shiver through her thighs.

So strong was the image and so distracting the sensation it produced, she rounded a corner in the hallway and ran headlong into a clansman coming the other way.

"Whoa there, lassie, where's the hurry? Have ye a bee up yer kirtle tae put ye in such a rush?"

Lauren smiled and smoothed her skirts as she looked up at the coarsely handsome features of Lochiel's captain of the guard.

"Why, Struan MacSorley, kiss me stupid if ye werena in ma thoughts not five minutes gone by."

"I'll kiss ye daft ten ways tae Sunday," he said, grinning as his gaze dipped appreciatively to the deep cleft between her breasts. "Ye just tell me where an' when."

"I can think o' at least one place ye could put yer lips

tae good use," she teased, stepping closer and pillowing her breasts against his broad chest. Her hand pressed boldly over his thigh and she felt the immediate response stirring lustily against her belly. "Mind, I wouldna want tae be the cause o' breakin' Mary MacFarlane's heart. It *is* her bed ye warm at night, is it no'?"

"I've nae claim on Mary," he said thickly. "An' she's nae claim on me."

"What o' the bairn ye've put in her belly?"

"It were put there long afore I ever spread ma kilt aneath her." MacSorley's big hands went around Lauren's waist to pull her closer. "But if ye're envious o' her condition, I'd be only too happy tae oblige."

"Envious o' a hedge-born brat?" She squirmed half-heartedly to break loose. "Thank ye, but no. I've better things planned f'ae ma future."

MacSorley took a last lingering look down the front of her bodice before he released her. "If ye grow weary o' the party tonight," he said huskily, "ye ken which room is mine?"

"Aye. The one with the well-worn path tae the door."

"Makes it easier tae find in the dark," he agreed blithely. "Just dinna go knockin' if ye find the latch bolted. Unless ye fancy sharin' a romp f'ae three, that is."

"I never share," she purred, dragging her hand across the bulge in his loins. "An' I've never met the man who'd want tae share once I've taken him in hand."

With a flash of her amber eyes Lauren brushed past him and continued along the gallery. She could feel him watching her all the way to the far end of the hall, and the knowledge of the condition she had left him in fixed a contemptuous smile firmly on her face. He was handsome and virile and eager to take *her* in hand, but he was after all just a bodyguard, and a liaison with Struan Mac-Sorley would get her exactly nowhere at all.

She hated this place. Hated Achnacarry with its oppressive stone walls and mountainous isolation. There was another world out there waiting for her, a world infinitely more suited to her talents and desires. She craved a life of gaiety and bright lights, of exquisite gowns and handsome lovers only too eager to part with their gold and favors.

Orphaned when she was twelve years old, Lauren had been sent to Achnacarry—banished, as she thought of it—to the care of her great-aunt Rose Cameron. Born and raised in Edinburgh, the sudden seclusion had been almost as great a shock to the young girl as her appearance had been to the sedate and orderly Cameron household. Anticipating a shy and refined lass barely out of bibs and aprons, they had been surprised to greet, instead, a developing beauty with a mind and will of her own. Moreover, coming from a distant branch of the family, they were ignorant of the fact that her father had been hanged for a thief and her mother had owned and run one of the most successful brothels in the city. A Cameron was a Cameron, they decreed, regardless of her sly disposition and despite the jealous, bloody fights she provoked almost weekly.

A thin, malicious smile drew out the corners of her mouth as she thought of what fools men were. How truly weak they were in spite of all the brawn and bluster. A few scant inches of moist pink flesh could undermine the best of them, could reduce the most fearsome warrior to a quivering mass of witlessness. In the beginning such power had intrigued and stimulated her. The bolder the conquest, the higher her aspirations and, coincidentally, the greater her own pleasure. She had been even quicker to realize the material benefits of a lusty romp in the haystack, and many an unknowing wife went missing coins and trinkets and precious family heirlooms.

Her nest egg had become quite impressive and would have been more so had a young clansman named MacGregor not fallen prey to his passions while aiding her in an ill-conceived attempt to run away two years ago. When they were caught, not only was his kilt loose and his body rigorously demanding its reward for his romantic ardor, but his saddle was weighed down with the rings, bracelets, gold and silver coins she had extracted from Lochiel's family chest. She had been left with no recourse but to smash a rock against the side of his head and scream for deliverance. Her performance had been flawless and convincing. Her aim had been faultless as well, for the lad never did regain his full senses, and tempers had been roused to such a peak that no one troubled to delay the hanging long enough to hear his defense.

Unfortunately, the nest egg of her own painstakingly gathered coins could not be separated from the pouch of looted goods before it was returned to Lochiel, who in turn blithely locked it away in his strongbox again. There were some who suspected Lauren was not entirely innocent in the theft and alleged kidnapping, some who even encouraged Lochiel to marry her off to some thick-necked Highlander who would then take responsibility for her actions, thereby sealing her fate forever.

For that reason she had become the model of good behavior and constraint, resisting on more than one occasion the blistering temptation to visit Struan MacSorley's room. The lusty blond giant's prowess was near legendary, and she had spent many a restless night wondering how it would feel to have all that brute strength inside her, on top of her, beneath her. But he was not the type of man to keep an affair secret, nor was he the type to dally carelessly with his laird's niece without feeling duty-bound to make an honest woman of her. Lochiel would be only too happy to see his old friend wed again; Struan had been without a wife for nearly three years now.

The dilemma vanished when the first rumors of Alexander Cameron's homecoming began to spread.

She had, naturally, heard all the stories centering around the black-haired, black-eyed renegade known as the *Camshroinaich Dubh*. She had stood for hours in front of the portrait of Sir Ewen Cameron and knew without a doubt that the grandson was exactly the type of man who would suit her needs perfectly. He was a soldier of fortune, a man who had spent half his lifetime in cities like Paris, Rome, Madrid. . . . He had even been to the colonies, for heaven's sake! He would not be content to ramble about the decaying walls of a medieval castle. Bored with the peace and tranquillity, he would soon be lured back to the adventure beyond the borders of Scotland, and when he left this miserable formation of rock and mortar, surely he would have no qualms about taking someone along who shared his hunger for excitement.

In the days and hours prior to his arrival, when the tension had been palpable, Lauren had paced the battlements as often as the guards searching for some sign of activity on the road. Scores of clansmen had been sent out to scour the countryside, and she spent every spare moment ingratiating herself with the Cameron women, running errands, coddling their loathsome brats, sitting through hour after hour of trite conversation, advice, lectures . . .

And then the wait was over. A clansman had galloped into the courtyard shouting the news at the top of his lungs. The *Camshroinaich Dubh* was less than five miles away! He would be at Achnacarry within the hour!

There had been no mention of a wife. The entire family had been stunned to learn not only of her existence, but of her nationality. Alexander Cameron, a man who had almost single-handedly started a war between the Hanoverian Campbells and dozens of enraged and sympathetic Jacobite clans, had come home with a pinch-lipped, stiff-backed *Sassenach* who reeked of Georgian decadence. Her presence at Achnacarry was an insult, a slap in the face to every clansman old enough to remember the arrogance of the English victors after the '15. It was bad enough having to bear the thought of their chief married to a Campbell, but at least Maura was a Scot and a Highlander.

No, this was an insult that could not simply be shrugged away. Besides which, Lauren had her mind set on Alexander Cameron being her means of escape from this place, and by God, he would provide it one way or another. The fact that a man she wanted was married had never been an obstacle before; it certainly would not be one now.

14

"**S**weet merciful heavens, where have you been?" Catherine paced back from the window embrasure as Deirdre came through the doorway. "And how dare you leave me to fend for myself while you chase after that . . . that *criminal*."

"I'm sorry, mistress," Deirdre said contritely. "But I did check on you several times, only to find you were still asleep. And Mr. MacKail is so dreadfully weak. I . . . I cannot help but feel responsible for him somehow."

"Responsible? What utter nonsense! You didn't get him shot." In a bristling temper Catherine paced to the window again and glared back at the girl, but Deirdre looked so worn and weary herself that the anger turned swiftly to concern. "You haven't slept a wink all night, have you?"

The dark brown eyes remained downcast. "I . . . think I did, mistress. Here and there."

Catherine chewed on her lip. "Well? How is he?"

"The doctor had to cauterize the wound to stop it bleeding. He hasn't wakened but the once, in the middle of it all when it would have been far better for him to have remained unconscious. It took both Mr. Cameron and myself to hold him still so the doctor could finish. I hope to never have to see a sight like that again, mistress. Never."

"Will he live?"

Deirdre looked up. "I don't know, mistress. The doctor said he is young enough and strong enough to see it through, but . . ."

"Well, I wouldn't worry too much. I have come to the conclusion these Highland rogues are too mean to die. They will all live forever, if only to see us perish from sheer frustration first."

Deirdre smiled faintly, and seeing the wild blonde tangle of her charge's hair, she pointed to the scuffed portmanteau she had left by the armoire. "I managed to save some things from your baggage before it was taken off the coach. Your hairbrushes, your combs, some bath salts . . ."

"Bath salts? Oh, Deirdre, you are a marvel. I swear the soap they gave me last night was vile enough to scrub pots. I would die for a *real* bath with *real* soap and *real* perfumes. I fear I will never get the smell of blood and dirt off my skin—*not* that anyone cares, of course. Once again it seems we have been shoved into a corner and forgotten."

"I saw Mr. Cameron this morning," Deirdre said as she fetched the portmanteau. "He did say he came by your room to speak with you, but—"

"He was here? In this room?"

"He asked—and very nicely too, I might add—if we had everything we needed."

"He did, did he? A guilty conscience speaking, no doubt. If not for Lady Cameron he likely would have left me sitting out in the courtyard all night long, although . . . I warrant if I had wild red hair and breasts spilling out of my bodice he would have remembered me."

"Mistress?"

Catherine shook her head to dismiss the remark, and Deirdre added, "He also asked me to inform you that the family will be dining at eight. I gather they have planned some sort of celebration to mark his return."

"What, pray, do *I* have to celebrate?"

"He said . . . he expects you to be dressed and ready to accompany him."

"*Dressed?* In what, pray tell? A nightgown and bathrobe?"

Deirdre glanced nervously at her mistress as she walked over to the armoire. She opened one of the doors to reveal several formal gowns hanging alongside shelves filled with neatly folded underthings.

"So." Catherine planted her hands on her hips. "He threw away all my clothes, now he expects me to wear someone else's castoffs? I should sooner go naked."

"An original idea," a husky baritone said from the open doorway. "Although it might play havoc with the digestion of the other guests."

Catherine whirled around and scrambled to clutch the edges of the red wool robe higher to her throat. Alexander Cameron was standing there, leaning casually against the jamb, one of his infernal little cigars clamped between his teeth.

"Deirdre, in the future remind me to lock and bolt the door."

"I have never cared much for locks," Cameron remarked conversationally. "Most of the time when I run across one in my way, I am driven to kick it down just to see what it is I am not supposed to see."

"What do you want?" she demanded. "Why have you disturbed us?"

"Do I disturb you?" His grin broadened and he pushed away from the jamb. He walked into the room and cast a lazy eye in the direction of the bed. "You slept well, I trust? You certainly looked cozy enough—like a little golden kitten all curled up around the pillows."

He came close enough for Catherine to reel from the smell of cigar smoke and raw spirits.

"You have been drinking," she said, wrinkling her nose in distaste.

"I have indeed, madam. Everyone from the smithy to the lowliest gillie has offered to share a toast to my new bride and wish me lifelong bliss and prosperity."

"Added to my hopes that you endure everlasting hell-fire, sir, you should have an interesting future."

"Ah, the sweet sentiments of marital euphoria. It is no

wonder I have avoided the ensnarement for so long." He winked in Deirdre's direction, earning a blush and a curbed smile in response. A scathing glance from Catherine drew a hastily murmured excuse to see to the bathwater and a quick retreat from the room. When the maid was gone, the hot violet of Catherine's contempt was concentrated on Cameron.

"*What* do you *want*?"

"What I want"—he let his eyes rake downward over her body—"and what I can hope to get are obviously two very different things . . . unless, of course, you feel inclined to join me in a few hours of relaxation before we have to prepare for our performance tonight?"

"What performance?" she asked warily.

"Why, that of the loving husband and wife, naturally. The entire household is priming itself for the unholy inquisition; they have been sharpening their teeth all morning on vestal virgins. I trust you will be equal to the task."

Catherine narrowed her eyes. "You are more than simply drunk, sir. You are delirious if you think I have any intentions of continuing this farcical charade. I do not intend to join you in any performance tonight—or any other night, for that matter. I shall remain in my room behind locked doors until such time as you see fit to honor your end of our agreement."

He swayed slightly and frowned to keep his eyes in focus. "Our agreement?"

"You promised to send me home if I cooperated."

"Ah . . . *that* agreement. Yes, well, I shall certainly see what I can do."

"What do you mean, *see what you can do*?"

He stared thoughtfully at the glowing tip of his cigar and shrugged. "These things take time to arrange, you know. It could take weeks—"

"*Weeks!*"

"Months even."

Catherine's jaw dropped open. "But you promised!

You gave Damien your word of honor! You pledged the fate of your soul!"

"I seem to recall some promises and oaths you made that you conveniently elected not to keep."

"Once," she gasped. "I tried to run away once! It was no more and no less than what you would have done had you been in my position. Since then I have done everything you asked—*more* than what you have asked, or have you *conveniently* forgotten about Gordon Ross Campbell?"

"I haven't forgotten," he said lightly. "Self-preservation is a strong instinct in all of us; I'm sure you were glad to discover you could call upon it when it was needed."

Catherine backed up a step, the fury blazing from her eyes like darts of fire. "Haven't you a single shred of common decency in your entire body? How can you expect me to attend something as . . . as frivolous and . . . and as ludicrous as a dinner party after everything I have been through?"

"I have been through exactly the same things, madam, only without the luxury of a bath and twenty-four hours of sleep. And the longer you stand there arguing with me, the less likely it appears I shall get to indulge in either."

Catherine set her teeth on edge. "You can sleep until next year for all I care. I have no intentions of accompanying you anywhere. Not to dinner, not to breakfast . . . not *anywhere*!"

"You were the one who announced before God and man that you were my wife," he reminded her coldly. "You were also the one who insisted on being treated accordingly—*for however long I am forced to endure the indignity*. Those were your exact words, were they not?"

"That was yesterday. I was angry and frightened and . . ."

"Yes?"

She squared her shoulders. "And today I have a terrible headache."

"I'm sure it will feel better when you have something to eat."

"I am not hungry. I do not feel well enough to eat."

He arched the slash of his eyebrow. "If you are ill, then it is my husbandly duty to remain here and offer you what comfort I may."

"I plan to go directly to bed."

His grin turned wolfish. "I have no objections to comforting you there."

"You are bovine and disgusting."

"And you, madam, are coming to dinner with me if I have to strip you and dress you myself—and we both know the consequences if you call my bluff."

She clutched the edges of her robe tighter. "Get out. Get out of my room, get out of my sight at once, or I swear I shall scream the roof down."

"Scream away. The walls are ten feet thick, the floors six. I doubt if anyone but the ghosts will hear you."

"If you force me to go to supper with you," she warned venomously, "I will tell anyone who will listen how you kidnapped me and held me hostage; how you hid behind my skirts so that you and your fellow criminals could sneak back into the country like the true cowards you are."

He folded his arms across his chest and smiled. "Is this before or after I tell them you are an English spy who duped me into marriage so you could come north and send detailed information back to your dragoon lieutenant?"

"No one will believe that for a minute," she countered hotly.

"No? They know me a fair sight better than they know you, and they are already splitting at the seams to know what would have inspired me to marry you. Being compromised and forced to do so at gunpoint would explain a great deal. And if they needed any more proof of your devious nature, I could produce the dozen or so furtive little notes you left behind at every tavern and inn we passed. Notes in which you sought to leave a message in one form or another to help your lieutenant find us."

The blood drained from Catherine's face in a rush. "You knew?"

"Of course I knew. As you said, I likely would have done the same thing in your position."

Her knees faltered and she had to grasp the back of a chair to keep from falling. He said it so casually, so coldly, mocking her even as he shattered whatever hope she may have had that her family would not think she had simply vanished off the face of the earth.

"Why did you not say something?"

"It hardly seemed important. Annoying, perhaps, but not important. And it was a useful diversion. It kept you happy and out from under my skin by letting you believe you were being so very clever."

His arrogance warmed her cheeks, and in a move swift and unexpected she swung her hand up and slapped him squarely across the face. His head remained turned to the side for almost a full minute, and when he finally did turn slowly back to face her, the dull red imprint of her hand was staining his cheek, glowing through the ruddiness of anger.

"By Christ, woman," he said softly, "you have more spirit than I would have credited to you. Far, far more than is healthy or wise to keep throwing at me."

"What would you have me do? Throw it under your feet to be trampled upon and ground into the dirt? Is that how you prefer your women: groveling and spineless, so frightened of your bullying ways that they shrivel and turn to dust before you?"

Cameron flung his cigar aside and wrenched her forward into a crushing embrace. "Since you ask, madam, I like my women with fire and spirit. I like them blonde. I like them slender and willowy and soft in all the right places. I like them with eyes the color of wildflowers and an insolent little pout of a mouth that begs to be kissed—

kissed so thoroughly there isn't the breath or wit left for words."

His mouth, hot and possessive, flavored with the musky sweetness of whisky, came down on hers, forcing her lips apart without any pretense at civility. His breath was fierce where it rasped against her skin, his tongue was bold and demanding as it invaded her mouth, thrusting and probing with a mindless violence that sent shocked reverberations through her body, even to the soles of her foot. One of his hands twisted itself in the tangled mane of her hair, the long fingers ensuring she could not pull away or avoid the relentless plundering. His other hand moved to her waist and started tugging at the ends of her belt, loosening the wool enough to insinuate itself beneath the robe and seek the rounded swell of her breast.

Catherine's smothered cry was ignored, as was the barrier posed by the cambric nightdress. One swift, savage tug tore the ribbon fastenings and his hand was there, holding the cool heaviness of bare flesh, his fingers kneading and shaping the velvet-soft nipple into a hard, rucked peak.

She groaned again and this time her knees did give way, but he was there to support her, deepening his kiss, teasing her flesh until she could scarcely breathe, scarcely think beyond the waves of hot shame that engulfed her.

"Why don't we stop playing games, Catherine," he muttered coarsely, his mouth spreading the flames along the slender arch of her throat. "You want me to honor my promises? So be it. I will honor them . . . starting with the ones I made in your father's study to take you as my lawfully wedded—and bedded—wife."

"No," she gasped. "No—"

"Your lips keep saying no, Catherine, but your body wants more. Much more."

"I want nothing from you," she cried weakly. "Nothing . . ."

He pushed aside the offending layers of wool and cam-

bric, and his lips closed around her breast, suckling it
hard and deep into the heated wetness of his mouth. She
tried to scream, but the breath was not there to do it;
she tried to push against his chest, but her fingers
betrayed her and curled around the silk of his shirt,
clinging to him through wave after wave of dark, throbbing pleasure. Her mind was fighting the conquest, but
her body was reveling in the possession, shuddering with
the raw desire to feel the roving heat of his mouth elsewhere, everywhere, scorching a trail of shocking caresses
over flesh that had never known, never dreamed, such
intimacy was possible.

She heard a sound, a deep, ragged groan, and realized
it came from her own throat. Her eyes fluttered open to
find his darker ones staring down at her, studying her
with an intense stillness she dared not challenge. She
could feel his every muscle tensed and straining; she
could see in his eyes that he wanted her, that he was
fighting the hunger in his own body even as he fought to
deny its existence, and, far from frightening her as it
should have done, it made her feel more like a woman
than she ever had before. A single stroke of his hand had
rendered her past flirtations infantile and meaningless,
her profound insights into passion as lacking in substance
as the breath wasted in uttering them.

Alexander Cameron *was* passion, raw and primitive,
and she knew full well she would be lost to the power of
it the instant his flesh touched hers again.

But he did not touch her again. He lowered his hands
by his side and took a precisely measured step back.

"You will oblige me by dressing for dinner," he said
tautly. "You will accompany me to the party later this
evening, and you will be on your very best behavior or so
help me God"—he waited until the shimmering liquid in
her eyes was blinked free—"I shall assume you have no
further desire to see your England or your precious Lieutenant Garner ever again."

With the tears still bright along her lashes, Catherine

tilted her head defiantly upward. "At the cost of your own soul, Mr. Cameron?"

"I have no soul, madam. It died in my arms fifteen years ago."

She took a deep, shaky breath. "You are indeed a loathsome creature. You have no scruples, no morals, no faith, no conscience . . . not one single redeeming quality that should permit you to walk upright on two legs."

Alex stared a moment, then offered a swooping bow. "A man always appreciates knowing where he stands in a woman's estimation."

"You stand, sir, with one foot on the road to hell, and I do not envy anyone who chooses to stand alongside you."

Alex walked angrily alone to the north tower, though Catherine might have been beside him for the echo of their conversation that kept repeating itself in his head. He had sobered considerably since leaving her chamber, yet there was no help for his blood, which continued to race and pound throughout his body. And no help for the lingering taste and scent of her that clung to his every pore. He had come close—closer than he even cared to think—to simply throwing her across the bed and getting her out of his system once and for all. Was that the answer? Would the physical possession of her body ease this nerve-grating frustration he felt whenever they were in the same room together? Or would it only make matters worse? Those eyes, that mouth . . . she defied him at every turn, baited him to do his worst, and by God, if he did not find some way to get her out of Scotland, out of his life soon, he would . . .

He would what?

He paused on the threshold of MacKail's chamber and let his eyes adjust to the gloom. There was only one candle alight; the glow it shed barely reached beyond the canopied bed. As he walked toward it the answer to his question eluded him, though the frown stayed etched across his brow.

"Problems?"

Alex looked down at the pale figure and was surprised to see Aluinn's gray eyes sharp and clear, as free of congestion as if he had slept for days instead of hours.

"Problems? Not really. Go back to sleep."

"Just how am I supposed to do that with you hovering over me like a carrion crow every time I turn over?"

"All things considered," Alex said dryly, "I should think you would be far too ill to be so witty."

"With Archie dispensing almost as much whisky as laudanum?" Aluinn shifted his weight on the pillows, wincing as he jarred the heavily bandaged shoulder. "He is threatening to have me dancing to the pipes by week's end, and frankly, I have no reason to doubt him."

"Seriously, how are you feeling? How bad was the damage?"

"Seriously? I feel like a mountain dropped on me. As for the arm, Archie seems to think it shouldn't lay me up too long. The shoulder will be stiff for a while, but the strength should come back. Thank God it was the left side and not the right. I would hate to think my days of jousting at windmills are over."

Alex smiled and helped himself to a dram of whisky from the bottle beside the bed.

"No, thanks," Aluinn said to the offered glass. "But you go ahead. Have you caught any sleep yet?"

"Some."

"It doesn't look it. You look, in fact, downright miserable for a man who has come back to the bosom of his family after half a lifetime away."

Alex sighed and raked a hand through his hair. "I am seriously beginning to think we should have stayed away. Or at least come home by sea."

Aluinn grinned and nodded. "Maura was in to see me earlier. She could hardly speak of anything but your lovely new wife. Should I say 'I told you so' here, or should I wait a few minutes?"

"Wait. You'll undoubtedly find more reason to say it."

"There is more?"

"Glengarron. Struan MacSorley is all for forming a raiding party and going after what is left of Gordon Ross Campbell."

"What does Lochiel think?"

"He has sent for Iain's father. It will be up to Old Glengarron which reprisals there should be for young Iain's death, if any. My guess is that Donald will caution him to wait. He may get his chance to kill more Campbells than he ever dreamed."

"That sounds like Lochiel is expecting the clans to rise for Prince Charles."

"I'm afraid my brother is caught with his breeches halfway down. If he pulls them up and buckles on his swordbelt, he keeps his dignity and his self-respect, but he will have to bear the pain of knowing he has accomplished nothing. On the other hand, if he drops them all the way down, he reveals his strengths and weaknesses for all the world to see, and the relief would only be short-lived at best. It is *my* considered opinion that the English want this rebellion almost more than Scotland does, if only to crush us once and for all and stake their claim on our land in a way that can never be questioned again."

"The eternal pessimist."

"The eternal fool, you mean. Was it so wrong to hope we could just come home and blend into the background somewhere?"

"You, my fine legendary friend? The *Camshroinaich Dubh*—the Dark Cameron—fade away with a wife and a brood of drooling children?"

"It was just a thought. And who mentioned wives and children?"

"It was just a thought. If you fade without a whimper, who will be around to fulfill the old prophecy?"

"What old prophecy?"

"The ravens will drink their fill of Campbell blood three times off the top of Clach Mhor," Aluinn quoted. "It seems the Duke of Argyle is a superstitious man and believes, because of you, the ravens have drunk twice already."

"I had almost forgotten that old fishwife's curse."

"So had I until Archie reminded me. Rumor has it the Duke wakes up out of a sound sleep, frothing at the mouth because he swears he has seen you standing over his bed with a dripping *clai'mor* in one hand, Malcolm Campbell's head in the other."

"If he chooses to believe the two-hundred-year-old ravings of a lunatic, who am I to enlighten him?"

"Allow me to enlighten you, in that case. Something else Archie told me: Gordon Ross Campbell is Malcolm Campbell's bastard son."

"His *son*?"

"Sort of changes the perspective a little, doesn't it?"

"It sort of makes me feel as if the curse is on me, not them," Alex muttered. "That makes two men I should have killed when I had the chance, but spared out of a blind sense of Christian charity."

"Two men?"

Alex thought of Hamilton Garner and the corner of his mouth pulled down. "Maybe I'm just getting old and soft. I should have aimed my sword true, used my fists harder . . . and taken my peace of mind when it first tempted me."

Aluinn had no doubt the common factor in all three instances had long blonde hair and violet eyes. "What are you going to do about Catherine?" he asked quietly. "I am loath to dwell on the obvious, but you are going to have to do something one way or the other, and soon."

"I wasn't aware there was an 'other.' "

"Isn't there?"

The silence stretched out, broken only by the faint ticking of a clock somewhere in the shadows.

"You only think you can read my mind, old friend," Alex said. "And this time you're dead wrong."

Aluinn leaned back and half-closed his eyes. The candlelight was not kind to the smears of fatigue under his eyes or the bloodless cast to his lips. "Dead wrong, eh? If you say so."

"I say so." There was another lengthy pause. "Even if it were possible . . ."

"Yes?"

"It could never work."

"Why? Because you are infallible as well as legendary? Because you expect everyone to have the same thickness of armor around their hearts as you do?"

A tic shivered in Alex's cheek. "You don't understand."

"You are right, Alex. I don't understand. For fifteen years you have been killing yourself on the inside, blaming yourself for what happened, and I don't understand."

"Aluinn, for Christ's sake—" The sudden creaking of the door interrupted what he was about to say and he turned, the look on his face so shockingly stripped of all defenses that it sent Deirdre's hand fluttering up to her throat.

"I'm sorry," she said. "I did not mean to intrude."

"No intrusion," Alex said quickly. "Please, come in. I was just about to leave anyway. Aluinn . . . I'll look in on you later; try to get some rest."

"Alex—"

But he had already brushed past Deirdre and vanished into the darkness of the hallway.

"I m-mustn't stay," Deirdre stammered and backed toward the door. "I've left Mistress Catherine in her bath and—"

"Please," Aluinn said wearily, rubbing his temple. "Don't go. Sit with me for just a few minutes. Talking to

Alex these days is like . . . seeing how long you can hold
your hand over a flame without pulling it away."

"I know what you mean. My mistress's temper is as
short as a fuse."

She had agreed so readily, Aluinn looked over and
smiled. "Please, won't you come all the way in?"

"I . . . I really shouldn't. I only came to see if . . . if you
wanted for anything while I was in the kitchen. I was
going to get some broth for Mistress Catherine and . . .
and . . ."

"Actually"—his gaze darted to the nightstand—"I *am*
a little thirsty. There is water in the jug, if you wouldn't
mind."

The glass, she saw, was within easy reach, as was the
pitcher, but she walked to the side of the bed anyway and
poured it for him.

"I confess I am a little surprised you would care one
way or another for my well-being. Pleasantly surprised,
to be sure, but still . . ."

"I was only wanting a chance to . . . to thank you properly for what you did yesterday," she said quietly.

"What *I* did? As I understand it, I should be the one
thanking you for keeping me from bleeding to death."

"It would not have been necessary if you hadn't
thrown yourself after the brute who tried to snatch me off
my feet."

"Well . . ." He remembered and offered up a mock
frown. "I suppose you do deserve a mild scolding at that.
You were supposed to stay inside the coach."

"I am not one to cower with my hands over my head,
just for the sake of a few ruffians. Eight brothers I have,
and not a one able to pull my hair or knock me down in a
fair fight."

"I can believe that," he mused, prodding the faint
bruise on his jaw. "You have a damned fine left hook."

She warmed under his smile, then, remembering the
glass she was holding, offered it to him, uncomfortably
aware of the tremors in her hand. Even worse, the gray

eyes were staring at her hard enough to drain away all the sensation in her fingers.

"Do you want the water or not?"

"I want it," he murmured. He closed his hand around the glass, engulfing her icy fingertips at the same time, and although she tried to balk at the contact he held firm.

"Will you sit with me awhile?"

"I mustn't. Truly. My mistress is waiting for me."

"Just for a few minutes. Please. The last request of a dying man."

She extricated her hand and smoothed the folds of her apron. "You shouldn't joke about such things. They could come true."

Aluinn smiled and took a sip of the cool water. The effort seemed to drain his reserves, and he closed his eyes.

Deirdre found herself holding her breath. With his long, bronzed lashes and sand-colored hair, he was almost beautiful. His tanned skin was smooth and stretched evenly over high Celtic cheekbones. A faint stubble of fair bearding covered the angular jaw and led down to the reddish-gold cloud of hair that exploded across his chest. The muscles beneath were hard, the skin supple, with bands of precisely molded sinew narrowing to a trim waist and flat belly. Below that, below the line of the blanket, it was left to her imagination to surmise what might be seen there, but she had no difficulty envisioning the long legs, steely with muscle, furred with the same fine coppery hairs as his wrists and forearms.

With eight brothers she had indeed thought herself immune to the mysteries of a man's body, but the one lying before her now was so overwhelmingly seductive, it made her mouth dry and her palms damp. She could no longer believe he was evil. Dangerous, perhaps, but not evil. And not a cold-blooded murderer. Not him, and not Alexander Cameron.

"What did you mean when you said he had been killing himself on the inside for the past fifteen years?"

The gray eyes opened slowly.

"I was not eavesdropping deliberately," she said. "But I was fully through the door before I could do anything about it. You needn't tell me if it's a great dark secret, it's just that . . . well, it might help if one or both of you stopped treating everyone as if they were your enemies."

"For the past fifteen years everyone *has* been our enemy. Moreover, Alex is a very private man; he does not find it easy to offer up his trust at the best of times. Neither do you, for that matter."

Deirdre laced her fingers together and studied them. "You have not given anyone any reason to trust you. You have forced my mistress to compromise herself. You have dragged us both across half the length of Britain against our wills. You very nearly were the cause of getting us all killed yesterday, and goodness knows what might happen between here and home again—if we are ever allowed to go home again, that is."

"Alex gave his word, and I have never known him to break it. If he has promised to send you and your mistress home, and if you still want to go, he will see that you get there."

"*If* we still want to go?" she queried softly.

"People change their minds."

"Not my mistress. She has it firm in her mind that Mr. Cameron is a spy and a murderer, and so far he has done nothing to defend himself against either charge."

Aluinn watched the long, delicate fingers twining and untwining. "Tell me something, Deirdre. If you went back to Derby tomorrow, and if Lord Ashbrooke asked you what military preparations you saw and heard while you were traveling through Scotland—would you tell him?"

"Of course I would. It's my duty, both as a loyal servant to my mistress and as a loyal subject to my king."

"King George?"

The brown eyes sparkled. "He is my sovereign."

"Ah, but what if you believed your sovereign to be unjustly exiled in Italy? What if you believed King James

Stuart to be the rightful king of Scotland and England—
and please"—he held up his hand to forestall the protest
forming on her lips—"I do not want to argue politics or
semantics or who is right and who is wrong. I just want
you to offer me a straight and honest answer to the question. If you believed James Stuart to be your king, if your
family had fought and died for that same belief, would
you still look upon Alex and me as spies simply because
we rode through England with our eyes and ears open?"

"Under those circumstances . . ." Her eyes sought his
and she frowned. "Probably not. But loyalty to one king
over another does not explain away a charge of murder."

"No, it doesn't. And there are two murder charges over
Alex's head, neither one worth the spit it would take to
deny them."

"He murdered *two* men?"

"It would have been three but for a small fluke of
nature: The third bastard survived his wounds."

Deirdre's hands fell still. "You sound almost proud of
the deed."

"I am. I only wish I had been with him at the time. I
would have made sure there were no flukes of nature to
get in the way."

A cold, hard edge had crept into his voice, and Deirdre
was not sure she liked it. She was trying to understand,
truly she was, but not only was he admitting the murders,
he was condoning them.

"It happened the week of Donald and Maura's wedding," he explained, his head falling back as he stared up
at the patterns the candlelight threw on the ceiling. "She
is a Campbell. Her father and the Duke of Argyle are
brothers. She met Donald while on a tour of France, and
even though I'm sure they both did their damnedest to
prevent it, they fell hopelessly in love.

"I should say here that the Campbells and the Camerons
have been snapping at each other's hindquarters for generations. Lochaber is a nice rich plum of land the Camp-

bells would dearly love to absorb into their own territories. But since our clan has always been blessed with either warriors or diplomats for chiefs, the glen has remained in Cameron possession.

"At any rate, the wedding took place as planned, here at Achnacarry. As a gesture of goodwill a large party of Campbells was invited—an attempt to calm the troubled waters—including Maura's cousins from Argyle: Dughall, Angus, and Malcolm Campbell."

Aluinn paused, his features darkening as the memories crowded back.

"The ceremony went smoothly. Maura's father, Sir John Campbell of Auchenbreck, had become genuinely fond of Donald by then and was actually supporting the union in hopes of making peace between the two clans. Argyle did not want that, of course, and took it as a personal affront, especially since he had previously chosen Dughall Campbell to be Maura's groom. Have I managed to totally confuse you yet?"

Deirdre unconsciously moved closer to the bed. "Who is this Duke of Argyle? He sounds very important."

"He is unquestionably the most powerful ally the Hanovers have in Scotland. He personally commanded the army that all but finished it for the Jacobites in 1715 at Dunblain. He is power-hungry, land-hungry, and not above a fair amount of cheating, scheming, and backstabbing to get what he wants—namely, the position of Prime Minister of Scotland when and if we come completely under English rule."

"He does not sound like a very nice man."

"He isn't. And wasn't. I expect his displeasure over Maura's defection was communicated to the Campbell brothers, for the tension was so thick in the air that day, it made your ears ring. Yet for a while they seemed to be behaving. They filled their bellies with our food and ale, they sang, they danced, they even flirted with the Cameron women."

Again he paused, as if in the telling he was also reliving the events as they unfolded.

"Alex was in love, as are most healthy seventeen-year-old young cocks. And Annie MacSorley was simply the most beautiful, the sweetest, the most sought-after lass in Lochaber. Half the countryside was in love with her, myself included, but it was Alex who won her heart, completely and absolutely. They were both smitten and as much in love as two people have a right to be. They had been handfasted the previous winter and planned to marry in the church later that summer—" The words backed up in his throat and he faltered. "Perhaps they should not have waited or been so secretive about it. Or perhaps we just should have found some reason to keep Alex away from the wedding, knowing how much he and Dughall Campbell loathed one another. At any rate, the trouble started when Annie and Alex slipped away to steal a few moments of privacy. The Campbell brothers saw them and followed.

"To make an ugly story short, they managed to sneak up on the lovers in the stables. They saw a chance for some crude fun and knocked Alex around just enough to leave him semiconscious. They tied him up and propped him where he could see while they took turns with Annie. One of them—I don't know who—got a little rough and slammed her head against the stone wall. Alex was nearly insane by then and somehow broke free of his bindings. He grabbed a sword and attacked, killing the youngest—Angus—on the first pass. The other two fought back, and . . . frankly, I do not know how he did it, but when the bodies were discovered later that night, Dughall had been gutted stem to stern, and Malcolm . . . well, it would have been a greater mercy at the time for someone to have finished him off. Alex was more dead than alive himself, acting like a wild, wounded animal, not letting anyone near him or Annie. She died in his arms.

"The Campbells naturally claimed the ambush had been deliberate. All of them at the wedding swore that they had seen Annie flirting with the brothers and that she'd lured them into the stables where Alex was waiting to attack."

"Did no one take Mr. Cameron's side?" Deirdre asked in a shocked whisper.

"The entire clan was willing to put their swords with his; we would gladly have taken on the Campbells, the militia, the whole damned government at a nod from Lochiel. Donald agonized for weeks over what to do. Argyle had declared it murder and demanded a warrant be issued for Alex's arrest. There was no possibility of a fair trial. To refuse to surrender him or to call the clan to arms to protect him would have laid the Camerons open to military discipline. Finally, knowing it was the only way to save Alex's life and avoid a bloody clan war, Lochiel sent him to France to be with their father, Old Lochiel."

"But . . . that was so unfair. He wasn't guilty of murdering those men. He was trying to protect his wife."

Aluinn agreed with a wry, weary smile. "And for the first ten years or so he expended most of his energy hating the world, seeking revenge in different bloody battles. He threw himself into every war he could find on the Continent, and when he ran out of enemies to fight there, he took us across the ocean to the colonies, where there were plenty of savages to oblige his thirst for mindless violence."

"You have stayed with him all these years?"

His smile softened. "We were raised like brothers; it seemed the natural thing to do. Mind you, it did become a rather poignant test of friendship when the Duke put a price on his head and we were pressed to dodge assassins everywhere we went. I have a few scars I would prefer not to remember coming by and a nightmare or two that still chase me into a cold sweat. On the whole, though, we have managed to come through it with both feet on the ground."

"The pair of you do seem to be indestructible," Deirdre conceded. "I should think an army of you

Cameron men could conquer the world, never mind England."

"Why, Mistress O'Shea," he murmured. "That sounds suspiciously like a compliment. Does this mean I have almost convinced you we are neither brutes nor beaters of innocent women?"

She lowered her thick, dark lashes. "I never truly thought you were either."

"Never? Not even at the inn in Wakefield?"

"You hadn't ought to have grabbed me. I don't like being grabbed."

"I shall endeavor to remember that." He reached forward and his hand gently cradled the side of her neck. Against her instinctive resistance he drew her to him until her mouth was a breath away from his. He felt a shudder ripple through her, then another. A soft protest parted her lips as his hand shifted and he ran his fingers up into the silky brown waves of her hair. The kiss was long and impassioned, full of honest tenderness, and he was surprised at how sweet she tasted. Sweet and innocent and trusting, like someone who could forgive all faults and transgressions, someone who could offer her heart with no conditions, no pretenses.

He released her slowly, reluctantly, noting that even the pain in his shoulder seemed to have been eased by her touch.

Deirdre brushed her fingertips across her lips and blushed profusely.

"You should not have done that, sir," she whispered.

"There are a good many things I should not have done in my life," he replied sincerely. "That was not one of them. And my name is not sir, it is Aluinn. *Al-oo-in*. You have to wrap your tongue around the middle part a bit; it's the Gaelic word for—"

"For *beautiful*," she said on a rush. "Yes, I know."

The gray eyes gleamed softly as they held hers, and for

the moment the world did not exist beyond the cocoon of pale yellow candlelight that encased them.

"I . . . I must go," she said. "I have been neglecting my mistress terribly."

"Will you come back? Will you come back and sit with me when you can?"

The question dusted her cheeks with roses again and he thought to himself: My God, but she is lovely. Born to a king instead of a gamekeeper, she would have slain half the hearts in Europe.

"Will you?" he asked again.

"If you wish me to, sir," she murmured.

"Aluinn," he reminded her gently. "And I do wish you to. Very much."

15

Wary of the wintry frost that emanated from her mistress, Deirdre worked quickly and diligently to shape Catherine's long golden mass of curls into a reasonably artful presentation. Her task was severely hampered by her subject's frequent need to pace from one end of the room to the other, by an impatient hand flinging finished sets of curls into disorder, by twists and turns that tore the combs and pins out of the maid's hands before she could position them.

The *toilette* at last finished, Catherine stood broodingly silent as Deirdre fetched a borrowed chemise and pantalets, then assisted her into snowy-white stockings and lace garters. She sucked in her tummy grudgingly and braced herself against a bedpost while the heavily boned corset was girded tight around her midsection. Deirdre hauled on the laces, squeezing much of Catherine's natural waistline up into her chest, shaping her torso into a highly prized but hellishly uncomfortable funnel so narrow it could be spanned by two large hands. To contrast the trimness, wire panniers were positioned like baskets over each hip, held in place with satin tapes, and covered by three billowing layers of petticoats. Still gasping from the pressure around her ribs, Catherine rounded on the bed with a curse that made the Irish girl look up in surprise.

"Do you see what she had the nerve, the utter *gall*, to loan me?"

"Beg pardon, mistress? She?"

"That red-haired Scottish virago." Catherine was

momentarily lost under the voluminous folds of silk as the gown was lowered over her head. "She did it deliberately, I know she did. It is six months out of style, and I am certain I saw a gravy stain on the bodice. *Good God!*"

Deirdre joined her mistress in staring at the shocking expanse of pale flesh exposed by the plunging neckline. Very little remained to the imagination, whereas a great deal was left to chance. Her breasts sat like two half-moons, propped and plumped in such a way as to make the viewing of her toes impossible. At the smallest movement of her arms forward or back, her nipples were in peril of springing over the edge of the pale green silk.

Catherine ventured to the mirror and her mouth went slack. She looked like one of the preened and painted courtesans who frequented the royal court and vied for the paid attention of lewd, gout-ridden ministers!

"Will you be wanting a shawl, mistress?" Deirdre asked hopefully.

Catherine was about to reply wholeheartedly in the affirmative, but a movement in the reflection of the mirror caught her eye and her attention was distracted momentarily by the figure who stood quietly in the doorway.

Since their arrival at Achnacarry, Alexander Cameron had elected to retain the English style of clothing—the plain frock coat, dark breeches, stark white shirt and neckcloth. For this, his first dinner at home, he had been provided with a more formal, richly shaded coat of sky-blue velvet, the cuffs of which were turned back almost to the elbow and trimmed with wide gold braid. The coat was left open over a gold-and-royal striped satin waistcoat buttoned high to the throat and seating a dazzling white, multitiered lace jabot that matched the fountainous spill around each wrist. Around his waist he wore a length of scarlet-and-black tartan, pleated into a kilt and held in place by a polished leather belt. The end of the tartan was brought up and draped across one shoulder, pinned to the coat with an enormous silver brooch studded with topazes. His face had been shaved clean of the slightest shadow; his sable hair had been molded into curls at his temples, with the remainder tied back in a neat queue.

For a long moment Catherine almost did not recognize her "husband." Even the most grudging appraisal would deem him magnificent; he looked as if he could stand atop a mountain and command the sun to rise and fall at will.

Yet despite the change in his appearance the eyes remained the same. Black and bold, they studied Catherine's reflection, leaving her with the distinct impression that her own assessment had been too kind.

"You might want to take Deirdre up on her suggestion," he said politely. "The dining hall is apt to be chilly."

"In that case—" Catherine ignored the delicate lace offering Deirdre held out and forced Alex to step aside as she swept past him out the door, "if I turn blue, someone is bound to take pity on me and send me back to my room."

Not a single word was exchanged through the twisting, turning descent from the tower. The only sound along the vaulted stone corridors was their footsteps—his firm and regulated to keep pace with her smaller, softer taps. It was only when they approached the main receiving room, guided there by the sound of laughter and clinking glasses, that Catherine's nerve faltered and she started to hang back.

Cameron's hand was instantly under her elbow, steering her forward.

"Don't worry," he said out of the side of his mouth. "We Camerons have pretty well forsaken the rite of offering sacrifices to the dark gods. I think."

They entered a room full of glittering candlelight and splashes of brightly hued tartan. Almost immediately, at their appearance, all conversation ground to a halt, and one by one the heads swiveled and stared at the couple in the doorway. Catherine felt the first blush of color in her cheeks recede, only to rise again, darker and hotter as she imagined most eyes were on her. The Englishwoman. The *Sassenach*.

Archibald and Donald stood together by the huge marble fireplace, their heads bent in conversation with their brother, John Cameron of Fassefern. Catherine recognized him from the miniature in the gallery and her opinion did not change, for of the four brothers he was the least attractive. Slighter in build, with thin, bony knees, he did not do near justice to the black-and-crimson tartan.

The same could not be said for the women. They were all elegantly gowned in silks and brocades, laying rest to yet another of Catherine's preconceived notions that Highland women would still regard Elizabethan bombazine and Norse braids as the height of fashion. And in spite of her prior reservations, there were several décolletages equally as shocking as her own. Lauren Cameron, for one—Catherine's feline instincts had spotted her at once—dared not bend over so much as an inch else she risked spilling herself into someone's eager hands.

"I hope we have not kept everyone waiting," Alex said, trying not to notice the shine of tears in Donald's eyes when he and Maura crossed the room to greet them. He had made the right choice in wearing the clan tartan; if he needed more proof it was in the bone-crushing grip his brother used to shake his hand.

"Welcome home, brither," Lochiel rasped, his voice thick with emotion. "This is as it should be at long last, by God. The Camerons togither, strong an' united. Let no man, king, or government step between us again!"

A round of passionate "ayes" rose to the ceiling beams. From somewhere two crystal glasses appeared and were thrust full into Alex and Catherine's hands.

Donald raised his in a toast. "The Camerons!"

"The Camerons!" Family and guests responded and as

one tilted their glasses and tossed back the golden liquor in a single swallow.

Catherine, acutely aware of the eyes watching her every move, drained her glass as she had seen the other women do and was feeling quite proud of herself . . . until the liquid fireball plunged down her throat and sucked the air from her lungs with such a vengeance, her knees buckled beneath her. Unable to catch a breath through the flames, she grabbed frantically for Alex's arm and would have fallen had someone not cried out to him to catch her.

"Oh dear!" Maura's face swam before her. "Who gave her the whisky?"

"Wisna me," Jeannie declared at once, looking as innocent as a cat with feathers clinging to its lips.

"The poor child has probably never had anything stronger than canary wine. Someone fetch some water, quickly."

"Here, gie her this." Auntie Rose pushed a glass into Maura's hand. "Ye canna gie her plain water, it'll only bring the *uisque* back up again. A wee dram o' claret, that'll dae it. Just a wee sip tae clear the throat."

"A small sip," Maura cautioned, holding the goblet to Catherine's lips. Thankfully the remedy worked; the sweet red wine doused the embers in her throat and returned some of the sensation to her mouth and tongue.

"My Lord," she gasped. "What was that?"

"Only the finest *uisque baugh* in all the Heelands, lassie," Archibald Cameron boasted proudly. "A man can drink ten pints an' still stand tae piss in the mornin'! Goes off like a cannon when ye mix it wi' the black powder. Tha's how ye test the virtue o' prime *uisque*, if ye didna know. Ye mix it wi' gunpowder, light it, an' if it disna explode, it's no' warth the effort tae swallow it. Aye, an' may God strike me deid, Donal' has lost near a score o' good stillmen over the years—been blown clean tae hell an' gaun wi'out even a footprint left ahind tae tell the tale."

"Footprints me arse," Jeannie scowled. "I'd as like tae mix a wee bit o' powder up yer kilt an' see what the virtue is there."

Lochiel cleared his throat over the laughter and smiled. "Well, now, I believe we are all present, an' I, f'ae one, have the appetite o' ten men."

He raised his hand in a signal to someone out in the hallway, and the seams of Alex's coat suffered another moment of stress as Catherine reacted to what sounded like the screams of a tortured animal. Looking quickly around, she was confronted by the innocent sight of a piper filling his instrument with air. As soon as the bladder was inflated, the raw screeching assumed a clean and distinct wail, one that was no less fearsome in substance but was at least recognizable as music.

"The pipes are inviting us to dinner," Cameron murmured in her ear.

"Inviting? It sounds as if they are trying to frighten us away."

"That was the original intent of the *piob'rachd*—the clan marching song—to throw terror into the hearts and souls of the enemy. Ten pipers playing at the head of a column of clansmen can do as much damage to an adversary's nerves as a battalion of artillery."

Catherine did not doubt it.

"And this is a cheerful tune they're playing," he added.

She looked up and nearly returned his smile. But then Donald was beside her, offering his arm, escorting her out of the receiving room at the head of a solemn procession that followed the piper along the hall and down the short flight of stairs to the great hall. Two long oak tables had been set up to accommodate the family and guests. The smaller of the two was mounted on a foot-high dais that ran the width of the room. The second ran at right angles and stretched the length of the hall, providing seating for the nearly fifty aunts, uncles, cousins, children, and friends who had gathered to celebrate the homecoming.

One by one the deep-chested, long-winded Scots rose to offer toasts or speeches or to recount various historic moments in the clan's past. Many of the speeches were unintelligible to Catherine, for they were delivered in rousing Gaelic with much gesturing and shouting. She had been seated on Donald's right, with Archibald on her other side and John of Fassefern's wife Elspeth opposite her. A short, stout gentleman addressed only as Keppoch sat between Elspeth and Jeannie Cameron, and across from him was Auntie Rose, who never missed an opportunity to exchange winks with the futsy old fox. Lady Maura was seated well along at the far end of the table, with Alex on her right and his brother John to her left. By leaning forward ever so slightly and peering through the tines of a candelabra, Catherine could frame almost all of Alexander's face. A small flick of the eye, however, and she had an exasperatingly unimpaired view of Lauren Cameron, who had somehow managed to win the seat next to Alex.

When the speeches drew to an end, more pipes heralded the arrival of the first course of the meal. The dish was unfamiliar to Catherine, but proved to be a delectably creamy soup of lentils and potatoes playing host to chunks of tender pink salmon. There immediately followed platters of roast duck drowning in a rich butter sauce, potato scones browned and crisped in bacon fat, mutton pies smothered in gravy; puddings, sausages, and crusty pasty shells stuffed with spiced venison. Various wines accompanied each course, and due to the diligence of Dr. Cameron, Catherine never found her glass wanting. By the time she had allowed for a sampling of everything, she was regretting the effort Deirdre had expended lacing her into her corset.

"Ach, so ye like our Heeland victuals, dae ye, lassie?" Keppoch caught her eye and winked. "Aye, I were in London no' long ago an' found the townsfolk too purse-proud tae make but one sauce, an' that they poured on everythin'. The English," he said, expanding his remarks to enlighten everyone at the table, "have a hundred opinions, but only the one sauce. They come up here an' tell us wha' fine silver an' gold they have, such fine glasses, such fine linens. I once't bade ma clansmen tae stand round the table, each wi' a taper in their hands, an' demanded tae be shown a finer lot o' candlesticks in all the land! That's wha' should matter tae a laird—the wealth o' stout lads he has willin' tae walk intae battle ahind him. Nae gold, nae silver. *Men!*" He paused and drilled a sharp eye in Lochiel's direction. "Aye, an' ye may have need o' such wealth afore too long, Donal'. It willna take a kick in the heid f'ae Argyle tae know that wee Alasdair has come home."

Lochiel nodded. "I've already warned The MacDonald an' The MacNachtan tae be on the watch, them bein' on the border o' Campbell land. Nae doubt the Duke will be sniffin' after blood."

"Squint-eyed bastards," Jeannie declared to no one in particular. "High time someone hung the lot o' them."

"Mayhap someone will, hen," said a sage and tipsy Auntie Rose. "Mayhap soon."

"Aye—" Jeannie brightened a moment. "The Prince has called f'ae an army, an' when he gets it, ye'll see, he'll send all the vermin back tae England where they belong."

"Whisht, woman," Archibald commanded. "Hold yer tongue."

"I'll nae hold ma tongue!" she countered indignantly. "There's been far too much holdin' o' tongues already!"

"We will not hold war councils at the dinner table," Maura said firmly. "Nor will we start any arguments."

"I'm no' arguin'," Jeannie insisted. "I'm only statin' fact. Wee Tearlach has summoned the chiefs tae meet wi' him, an' they have tae go. *They have tae go!*" She glared directly at Lochiel and added with a snort, "They canna say they dinna *want* tae go, an' they canna send an auld daft cow tae do their talkin' for them—"

"Jeannie!" Archibald's face was glowing red. "Mind who ye're talkin' to!"

"No," Lochiel sighed. "Let her speak. She'll burst otherwise."

"Aye, I'll speak. F'ae every man, woman, an' bairn who lost kin in the last rebellion, I'll speak. Yer faither wouldna turn his back on a Stuart! Yer faither wouldna question the right or wrong o' it, nor send the poor wee lad cringin' into the ground wi' shame!"

Lochiel pushed his plate away. "My loyalty tae King Jamie has never been questioned, nor has my respect f'ae his son. Have I no' worked all these long years tae find some way tae bring them both home again?"

"Wi' *words*," Jeannie spat. "But ye canna fight the *Sassenach* wi' words!"

"We could if they had yer breath ahind them," Archibald roared. "Now hold yer silence, dragon, afore ye send *me* cringin' tae the ground wi' shame."

"*Me* shame *you*?" Jeannie's eyes bulged with defiance. "*You*, who rode tae Arisaig wi' yer tail tucked up atween yer legs where yer manhood should ha' been? *You*, who told the Prince he wouldna find a home here an' tae go back tae France?"

"I told him the bald truth, woman! I told him we couldna form an army wi' naught but a handful o' rusted *clai'mors* an' a few score matchlocks."

"Bluid an' courage will form an army," Jeannie persisted.

"Aye. The bluid o' Scotland's youth an' the courage o' fools like you!"

Jeannie surged forward in her chair, and for a moment Catherine thought the tiny firebrand was going to fling herself across the table and physically attack her husband. She was already shocked by the very notion of a woman daring to be so outspoken in front of friends and neighbors as well as family. No one else seemed too outraged by the impropriety, however. They sipped their

wine or picked at their sweet cakes as if it were a common-
day occurrence with the doctor and his wife.

"Dinna listen tae any o' this, Donald," John of Fassefern
said, sucking a piece of meat from his teeth. "Ye've made
the wisest decision an' now ye must stand by it. Ye always
said there could be no uprisin' against the Hanover government unless we had solid support from France. The
Prince knew that. He knew it afore he came, yet he came
anyway, wi'out the men he promised, wi'out the guns or
the powder. Since he didna keep his pledge tae the Highland lairds, it stands the Highland lairds shouldna be
bound by a pledge tae him."

"I am bound by ma honor tae King Jamie," Lochiel said
with quiet intensity. "An' if he was tae command me tae
fight, I would—tae the death if need be, an' glad f'ae it."

"Exactly," John said, leaning forward. "But it isna yer
king askin' ye tae risk yer home, yer family, the lives o' a
thousand brave men! It's that wee upstart o' a pup who
had tae sneak out o' Italy wi'out his father's permission,
because he knew full well it wouldna be given. He's
naught but a lad o' four an' twenty. What does he know o'
fightin' an' dyin'? Ask me, he's drunk on the romance an'
the sweet smell o' power!"

"Aye, he's young an' he's reckless, an' perhaps if I
were young an' hot-bluided masel', I wouldna find so
much fault in what he has done."

"Ye talk as if ye admire the fool f'ae what he's done,
what he wants tae do. *He wants war!*"

"He only wants what is rightfully his, an' his father's."

"God's bluid." Fassefern looked around in dismay.
"There's never been an army invaded English soil in the
past six hundred years! Even if—miracle o' miracles—it
did, who would provision it? The Royal Navy is a thousand ships strong. Unless they all mutiny against the
Hanover government at the once, they'll seal these
bluidy isles off tighter than a whore's arse an' wait till we
all choke on our pride!"

"We've always stipulated the need f'ae King Louis's navy tae keep them from blockading us."

"His navy?" Keppoch guffawed. "We would need his army, too, tae show us how tae fight wi' cannon an' musket, no' just *clai'mor* an' targe. We need trained soldiers tae lairn us the ways o' the English army. We need leaders tae gie us discipline. Christ knows we have the heart an' courage tae carry the fight tae the streets o' London if need be, but wi' an' army o' crofters an' shep herds, who will keep them from worryin' after their homes an' crops after a few months o' war?"

Archibald refilled his glass, topping up Catherine's as he did so. "We should be worried mair about the clans willin' tae turn their backs or their swords against us. The Lord President himsel', Duncan Forbes, is offerin' commissions in the Hanover army tae any laird who will denounce King Jamie an' take the oath tae Fat George. Ye ken The MacDugal? He were given back all the lands an' titles taken awa' in the '15 in exchange f'ae a promise tae wear the black cockade."

"The MacDugal has taken his judas gold an' f'ae that will have tae live wi' his conscience," Keppoch declared. "So will all the ithers who have declared openly that they willna take up a sword f'ae either side. It's the quiet ones, the sneaky ones, the ones we dinna know about an' willna know about until it's too late. They're the ones who would hurt us most, f'ae ye canna build an army on ghosts an' turncoats."

"Like The MacLeod," Jeannie said derisively. "I told ye that bastard could ne'er be trusted. I told ye he would ne'er hold tae his word. He smiles through his arse, that one does. Thank the Christ he has a bairn who's no' afraid o' his own shadow."

"Young Andrew MacLeod? Aye, he'll keep his vow tae fight f'ae the Stuarts, but on his own, wi'out his father tae gie the order, it will be like a single bee leavin' the hive. A single sting instead o' thousands."

"It could well be thousands," Lochiel said dispiritedly,

"if The MacKenzie o' Seaforth follows MacLeod, or The Ross, or The Grant. The MacIntosh controls three thousand in Clan Chattan alone, an' if he accepts the commission Forbes is offerin'—"

"If he takes it," Keppoch predicted, "he'll split the great Clan o' the Cats in two. The Farquharsons will ne'er follow an order tae fight against us, nor will The MacBean or The MacGillivray. They would break awa' from Clan Chattan first."

"Angus Moy is very conscious o' his responsibilities as The MacIntosh. He would never deliberately pit one clan against anither within his own sect."

"Responsibilities!" Jeannie was on her feet again. "A clan's responsibility is tae their chief, an' the chief's responsibility is tae the kirk—tae Scotland! No' the ither way around!"

"What I dinna ken," Keppoch said, ignoring the outburst, "is why these lairds think they'll fare any better if they declare f'ae German George. They canna ha' forgotten how every clan—Whig or Jacobite—was treated after the '15. It didna matter if a clan fought wi' or against The Stuart, they were all orthered tae disarm. They were all stripped o' their weapons an' powers, all treated wi' contempt an' mistrust . . . an' it willna be any different now."

"Most o' the chiefs know that," Lochiel agreed. "An' they dinna want tae see this country torn apart again."

"Men like Duncan Squint-Eyed Forbes should've had a musket fed doon their throats years ago," Jeannie grumbled. "Turnin' men against their own kind! Cowards!"

"His methods may be wrong, but he wants peace in the kirk as badly as we do," Lochiel said. "He disna want tae see brither fightin' brither, Highlander fightin' Highlander. He knows as well as we do that a war now means the end o' any chance we might have o' a free an' independent Parliament in Scotland."

"We may have lost that chance the minute Prince

Charles set foot on Scottish soil," Alex said softly, having held his silence until then. "If he stays, or if he manages to convince even a handful of clans to form up behind him, it will be all the excuse England needs to cross our borders in strength. Parliament has already voted to reinforce the garrisons at Fort George and Fort William. I saw evidence that half of England is mobilizing its militia . . . the other half have never stood down from the alert caused by that fiasco last February when the Prince nearly drowned himself in the Channel."

"The Prince promises us there is an army o' Englishmen waitin' tae join his cause."

"If there is, I didn't see them," Alex said dryly. "What I did see was an army of fanatics warning the common people of the swarms of naked, bloodthirsty cavemen who will be pouring out of the mountains and across the border to rape their women and sacrifice their children to the druids." The ebony eyes bored into the silent figure beside Lochiel. "You will never convince them we only want to be left alone to live in peace. You will never convince them that we shouldn't be conquered and *civilized* as it suits them."

"The Prince already has pledges," Archibald said glumly. "Clanranald, Glenaladale, Kinlochmoidart . . . they've all answered his summons an' fallen f'ae the laddie's charm. Aye, an' a grand charm it is, brithers. He has his father's face, his father's eyes, his father's knack o' lookin' right into yer soul an' twistin' it out yer throat again. Ye were wise tae send me in yer stead, Donald. I dinna think ye could ha' resisted him."

"My mind is firm on where I stand, where the Camerons stand. This I have told him an' it willna change."

"Then dinna go within a mile o' him," Archibald ordered, "f'ae I ken ye better than ye ken yersel', an' if this Stuart prince once sets eyes on ye, he'll have ye weepin' an' gratin' an' doin' whatever it is that pleases him tae have ye do."

Lochiel frowned. "It would please me, brither, tae

share a dram o' that wine ye seem tae be hoardin' tae yersel'."

Archibald chuckled, and the topic slid painlessly into less volatile areas. Catherine hadn't dared look up during the entire exchange; she could scarcely believe they were debating the rebellion so openly, discussing treason so freely, and she could only wonder what kind of men could even dream of challenging the might of King George's armies.

She stole a glance along the table and thought she had at least part of the answer. Alexander Cameron would fight the devil, she was sure, and with little more provocation than a change of mood. He argued calmly, logically, and eloquently against war, yet she had seen firsthand the darker side of him, the violent side. Could such violence and logic coexist for very long inside one man without tearing him apart?

What went on behind those impenetrable, unreadable eyes of his? Had anyone ever been close enough to the man to be able to read his thoughts or understand his moods? Had anyone ever *wanted* to understand him? Each time she thought she had found a flicker of tenderness lurking inside, he proved her wrong. He baited her, he played with her emotions, he teased her unmercifully . . . and yet after the attack on the coach, when he had held her in his arms, she had never felt so safe, so protected in all her life.

Her gaze wavered slightly as Lauren Cameron's laughter broke into her thoughts. The virago was all over Alex, brushing up against him each time she thought of another probing question to ask him about his travels. He didn't seem to be objecting. Another inch or two, in fact, and his nose would become permanently wedged in the cleft between her breasts.

Catherine reached for her wineglass. The *Camshroinaich Dubh*. The Dark Cameron. Dark gods and druids, ghosts in the mist and visions of bloody battlefields . . .

Invade England! How she wished Hamilton Garner

were here in his fine scarlet tunic and white breeches. He would show them all how laughable their plotting and debating was, how useless their speculations. A handful of blustery Jacobites would not even make it as far as the River Tweed without reeling back in awe at the sight of His Majesty's Royal Dragoons!

Hamilton!

Where was he now? Had he recovered from his wounds? Had something terrible happened—infection, fever, or worse? He surely would have come after her if he had been able, for there was no question of him abandoning her to the likes of Alexander Cameron. And *Damien*! Had something happened to Damien? Why had he not been on the road behind them? She had, indeed, left markers and messages, too many for the Highlander to have found them all. Why, then, had there been no sign of pursuit?

She stared glumly at her empty wineglass.

It was too late, that was why. She was irretrievably trapped in this medieval mountain fortress. The inhabitants—some of them anyway—might be friendly enough, but she was nonetheless the intruder here. The stranger. The foreigner. The *Sassenach*. She would be watched wherever she went, whatever she did. Even if rescue *was* just beyond the bend in the road, she had little hope of reaching it.

What were they laughing about now? She concentrated all of her attention on Alexander's mouth, but that was a mistake, for it made her remember how it felt, warm and wet, fastened hungrily around her breast.

She gasped, startled to see a spreading red stain on the linens in front of her.

"Oh! How clumsy of me!" She righted her glass and reached hastily for her napkin to soak up the spill before it ran down onto her skirts.

"Are ye all right, hen?" Rose asked. "Ye look like ye swallowed a cherry pit."

"I . . . I'm fine. Really. I was just . . . clumsy."

"Aye, ye're tired, lass, an' wi' good reason," Lochiel said. "I'm surprised ye insisted on comin' down f'ae dinner at all. We told Alex tae leave ye be."

"She would not hear of it," Alex said, his voice coming from over Catherine's shoulder. She turned around, startled by his sudden appearance by her side, and found herself staring up at two of him.

"I . . . am a little tired," she confessed through a gulp of air.

"Of course you are," Maura said, standing immediately. "How thoughtless of us to keep you here so long. Alex, you must take her up to bed at once."

16

Catherine heard the command and stumbled slightly over the hem of her skirt as he helped her to her feet. He laughingly thanked Maura for the suggestion and bid a good evening to everyone on her behalf, his arm like a steel band around her waist, holding her steady as he steered her through the hall and up the flight of stone steps.

"You do not have to leave with me," she protested, trying unsuccessfully to pluck his arm away. "I would not want to be accused of spoiling your evening."

"How very considerate of you. But I prefer to make sure you get where you are going."

"Are you implying"—she stopped abruptly and swayed dangerously close to the wall—"that I am not in my proper senses?"

Alex smiled despite himself. Her eyes were large and dark, the centers so dilated there was only a thin halo of violet around the rim. She was flushed and warm, and her breasts were fluttering against the confines of her bodice like trapped birds longing to be set free. He had partaken liberally himself at the dinner table, and his blood was not as cool as it should have been—not if he had to resist the lure of those fiery eyes and luscious pink lips for very long.

"I should have warned you the wine was nearly as potent as the whisky. Archibald oversees the making of both."

"You, sir, make far too many presumptions. If anything, I found the burgundy weak and lacking in body, its effects disappointing."

"Disappointing? In that case, perhaps it has just been your father's fine gin you have been missing since we left Derby, not your gallant lieutenant."

"Vile," she seethed, and with a flounce of her wide skirts detached herself from his arm and marched ahead, making only one wrong turn before she located the gallery leading to the west tower. Cameron lagged behind, smoking one of his cigars as he mounted the steps to the bedchambers.

The one Catherine had been occupying was in darkness save for a single beam of blue-white moonlight that streamed through the window. She stood in its path, silhouetted by the shaft, shimmering in a glaze of luminescence.

"Deirdre? *Deirdre?* Sweet Mother Mary, where is that girl?"

"Anything I can help you with?" Cameron asked from the door. His features were in shadow, his broad frame lit from behind by the sconce out on the landing. The blood pounded into Catherine's temples as she saw the tip of ash on his cigar glow brightly for a moment, then fade again.

"You can snuff out that dreadful black weed and light one of the candles," she said sharply. He gave no indication he was about to oblige either request until she sighed and added a grudging "Please."

"Certainly." He went back out to the landing and returned with the taper from the wall sconce. He found the night candle and lit it, then set the taper in an empty stand.

"Thank you."

"You're welcome. And thank *you*."

"For what?"

"For tonight. For behaving as if everything was as it should be. I can appreciate how difficult it must have been for you to sit through the dinner conversation without once speaking your mind."

Catherine regarded him suspiciously, not knowing if she had just been complimented or insulted.

"And despite my earlier reservations," he added, pausing to let his eyes drift across her bodice, "I believe you managed to win me the envy of every warm-blooded male in attendance."

Catherine held her breath. Compliments? Flattery? What was he up to?

"Thank you for escorting me up the stairs. I can manage on my own now."

"Are you sure? I am . . . not unfamiliar with women's clothing and . . . without a maid to help you . . ."

Catherine felt the dark eyes on her breasts again, stroking them like a pair of hands. Was that it? Was he regretting he had not carried through with his threats earlier in the day? Was he wondering, speculating, on just how much effort it would take now to overcome her defenses?

"I assure you, Mr. Cameron," she said with ice in her voice, "I am quite capable of tending to myself."

He shrugged and smiled lopsidedly. "I was only trying to be friendly. If you change your mind, or if you need me for . . . well, anything at all . . . I am right across the hall."

"If I change my mind, sir, I shall fling myself out the window and let the wind undress me."

"An ingenious solution, I'm sure. Perhaps a tad melodramatic, but as always, a credit to your vivid imagination. Good night."

He was still smiling to himself as he walked into the smaller chamber across the hall. The minx had a spark to her, there was no denying. She managed constantly to get under his skin and rouse more than just his anger in these verbal jousts. Too much more and he could not be held accountable for his actions. He had come damned close that afternoon. *Damned* close. And he had been feeling slightly off balance ever since.

The hell of it was, he still could not pinpoint what it was about her that attracted him. They were as opposite in character as a man and woman could be. She was spoiled, proud, haughty, and stubborn. She provoked him deliberately, repeatedly, secure in the belief that she was immune from any manner of retribution, smug in her conviction that she was above anything so base and repulsive as physical desire. Yet there were times— coming more and more frequently—when the icy facade showed cracks. When he sensed she just needed to be taken into someone's arms and held.

Someone's?

His?

No. In spite of Aluinn's rose-tinted view of the world, there was just too much of the past to overcome. The pain, the memories . . . they were too strong. The guilt was still too near the surface even after all these years. Annie would still be alive if not for him. She would not have suffered degradation and pain at the hands of the Campbells if they had not been able to use her love as the ultimate weapon against him. He never wanted to place himself or anyone else in such a position again. Love was a weakness he could not afford.

Suddenly Alex's body ached and his head drummed with a vengeance. So far he had not had an opportunity to enjoy more than a cursory wash or an hour's catnap since his arrival at Achnacarry, and the strain was finally catching up to him. A steaming hot bath. A tall glass of brandy. A soft mattress and twenty-four hours sleep . . . Heaven.

He sighed as he closed the door behind him, but he only progressed a few steps into the room before he drew up short again.

She was lying on the bed, curled there in a pool of tousled lace petticoats. Her hair was spread in gleaming red profusion around her shoulders, accentuating the satiny smoothness of her throat and arms. She had removed her corset, leaving only a slippery wisp of silk clinging to her breasts in a way that was far more enticing than naked flesh would have been. Her shoes and stockings were tossed in a casual heap at the foot of the bed and her petticoats allowed to ride deliberately high above the shapely calves.

Seeing where his gaze was temporarily stalled, Lauren shifted her knee so that the petticoat was displaced further, baring more of the smooth, warm flesh.

With an effort Alex moved forward again, glancing at the night table where a partially full bottle of whisky stood.

Lauren smiled and drained the last few drops from the glass she was holding. "Shall I pour ye a wee dram? Ye look as though ye need it."

Like a cat, she curled her legs beneath her and rose up on her knees. She poured the whisky without waiting for his answer and held it out to him, poised in the candlelight like some heathen nymph. He took the glass from her fingers, conscious of the way the silk molded to her breasts—breasts that were large enough to produce an involuntary dryness in his mouth.

"I suppose . . . I should ask what you are doing here, in my room, in my bed."

She pursed her lips and her eyes feasted openly on the aggressive breadth of hard, muscular chest and shoulder. "Why, I wouldna want tae be accused o' refusin' yer invitation. A fine welcome home tha' would be."

"Invitation?"

"Mair than the one, I warrant." She sidled closer to the edge of the bed. "Though it's hard tae keep count when it's yer eyes doin' the talkin'."

"If I gave you the wrong impression this evening, I'm sorry. You are a beautiful woman, Lauren, and I apologize for looking. But that's all I was doing: looking."

"Mmm." She raised her hands to the silver and topaz brooch that held the length of tartan pinned over his shoulder. She unfastened it and let both the clasp and the wool fall to the floor.

"I am a married man," he reminded her quietly.

"Aye, married. But why are ye here, then? In a separate room, a separate bed? An odd way f'ae a new husban' an' wife tae behave, is it no'?"

Alex glanced down. Her hands had not been idle. The pearly buttons of his waistcoat had been unbound, the jabot loosened and flung to the floor. Her fingertips slid up the fine linen of his shirt and began searching for the fasteners.

"We could just talk, o' course," she suggested with a sigh. "If tha's what ye'd truly rather do."

"What I would truly rather do—" His tongue ran across his lips and his gaze fell to the voluptuous display of firm white flesh. The silk of her chemise seemed to be caught on the jutting, wine-red nipples, and he knew the smallest brush of his fingertips would free them. "What I truly want is to get some sleep. I haven't had much in the past few days."

Lauren purred sympathetically and pressed even closer, using his distraction to peel away the heavy velvet of his coat and waistcoat. She had worked his shirt open to a point below his ribs, and she ran her hands over his bare flesh, her fingers combing through the thick black hairs, her lips parted as if the sensation was too much to bear.

The sultry amber eyes lifted slowly to his, and Alex felt himself being drawn into the smoldering pools of green and gold and hazel. It would, he reasoned, be one way to prove that Catherine Ashbrooke meant nothing to him. A way to prove it was only the tension and excitement of returning home that had stirred his blood, not the thought of sinking himself into all that soft white flesh, of hearing her cry out his name, of seeing her passion shimmer to life in the depths of the dark violet eyes.

Lauren leaned forward and closed her mouth around the dusky island of his nipple, tracing warm, wet circles over the sensitive flesh. Alex grasped her by the shoulders, his fingers tightening reflexively as his body fought the undeniable rush of erotic pleasure.

"I don't think you want to be doing this," he advised, his voice rough and low.

"I ken exactly what I want, Alasdair. What you want too." She groaned deep in her throat and dragged his mouth down to meet hers. Her body pressed urgently against him, breasts, belly, and thighs all joining in the conspiracy to undermine him. There was no hesitation, no modest apprehension as her tongue darted between his lips, taking possession of his mouth with a wanton assertiveness that brought Alex's senses crashing back down around him.

He broke free and thrust her away to arm's length. The glazed tiger eyes looked mildly startled as she stared up at him, her mouth slack and wet.

"What's wrong?" she asked on a gasp. "Why have ye stopped?"

"It isn't difficult to stop something that hasn't started."

Her hands, quick and deft as hummingbird wings, darted beneath the pleated folds of his kilt. "Has it no'?"

"Lauron—" He grasped her wrists and eased her hands gently away. "I am extremely tired. I am also slightly drunk, or I would have turned you over my knee and sent you packing ten minutes ago."

"But ye didna," she said with a sly smile. "An' ye canna tell me ye have a warmer bed tae lie in this night. Ye look tae me like a man in need, Alasdair. *I* need too. I need a real man, one who can take me away from this place. Ye dinna belong here, Alasdair, an' neither dae I. Ye'll never be happy, no' wi' this ruin o' a castle, no' wi' yer simperin', yellow-haired *Sassenach* wife."

"I think I've heard about enough—"

"D'ye know what they dae f'ae a night's pleasure here, Alasdair? They sit around the fire each an' every night an' talk of auld times, o' kings long forgotten an' glories long deid. They live in the past, all o' them. They spoke tonight o' bluid an' courage like as if the glens were full o' both—but they're no'! The kirk is full o' raggedy crofters an' bandy-legged shepherds who've never seen a broadsword, much less raised one in battle. Run wi' me, Alasdair, afore it's too late. Take me away from here!" Her eyes sparkled and her hands wrested free of his grip to stroke brazenly between his thighs. "Ye'll no' regret it, I promise ye."

Alex did not answer. Instead, he walked away from the bed and crossed to the low dressing table. He snatched up a couple of fresh cigars and closed them in his fist as he walked back to the bed.

"You found your way here without any difficulty. I assume you can find your way out again?"

Lauren sat frozen on the rumpled sheets, her eyes narrowing as she watched him pick up the whisky bottle and stalk toward the door. The shock stained her cheeks red and brought her hands up to sit angrily on her waist.

"Where de ye think ye're goin'? Tae yer sweet an' lovin' wife? Ye think ye'll get what ye need there?"

Alex paused at the door and glared back over his shoulder. "What I need is a long, hot bath, and what I want is for you to be gone when I get back. If you're not, I can promise you, I won't be quite so polite ejecting you."

Lauren's hands curled into fists. "Bastard! There's no man alive ever turned me out o' his bed!"

"Then I'm glad I could provide you with a new experience." His sarcasm was rewarded by the smashing of glass as she threw her empty whisky tumbler across the room. It crashed against the wall beside his head and a tiny fragment sliced through his wrist, leaving a thin thread of blood in its wake.

"And a good night to you too," he murmured, pulling the door closed behind him.

The faint sound of breaking glass drew Catherine's attention away from the window, where, seated on the cold stone bench, she had been staring vacantly out at the night vista, not really seeing the loch or the mountains or the swollen, glistening beauty of the Highland moon.

Sighing, she began to pull her hair out of its stiff coils, dropping the steel pins beside her, uncaring as to whether they landed on the seat or the floor. When her hair was loose and flowing around her shoulders, she stood and reached around for the laces that held her bodice bound rigidly in place, but her movements were so sorely restricted that after a few feeble tugs she had to rest her arms and wait for the blood to flow into her fingers again.

On the third attempt—one away from tearfully executing her threat to launch herself through the window—she succeeded in slipping the last knot and unwrapping the layer of shiny green silk. Another minor struggle with more laces and the relief was palpable as the pressure of the whalebone corset and stomacher was released from around her ribs. She groaned aloud as she flung the wretched garment aside, and she spent several blissful moments massaging her flesh and relishing the ability to breathe deeply again.

Leaving a trail of cast-off petticoats, wire panniers, chemise, stockings, and slippers, she groped through the rack of borrowed garments in the armoire until she found a clean nightdress. The giddy effects of the wine had abated and her temples throbbed. She sought out the china basin to splash some cool water on her face and found both the bowl and pitcher empty.

"Oh, Deirdre . . ." Her shoulders slumped wearily and her lips formed around a silent oath.

She took the pitcher and padded barefoot to the door. The circular landing outside her room was dark and the door directly opposite was closed, emitting only a thin blade of light along the lower edge. Seeing a shadow cut back and forth across the light, she tiptoed noiselessly to the fireroom, not wanting to give Alexander Cameron any excuse to come to her rescue again. She was mildly surprised he had not returned to the party downstairs, surprised he had not returned to the fawning attentions of Lauren Cameron. There had been no mistaking the seductive invitation in the large amber eyes, no mistaking his interest, either, each time he drew a breath and pondered the enticing depths of the virago's cleavage.

"What do I care?" she asked herself irritably. "They deserve each other."

She pushed the door to the fireroom carefully open and shut it behind her again, pausing to assure herself she had not been detected. She turned and was several steps into the steaming hot room before she realized her precautions had been in vain. Alexander Cameron was there, relaxing in the brass bathtub, his eyes closed and his head tilted back on the rim as he savored the clouds of steam rising around him. In one hand he nursed an almost empty glass of whisky, in the other, a fresh cigar. The huge cast-iron pots that were kept filled and suspended over the fire were sitting empty on the hearth.

Catherine dared not move, dared not breathe. The door had made no sound on its rope hinges, and her bare feet had not disturbed so much as a dust mote. But even as she hesitated, poised to fly back to safety, the ebony crescents of his lashes rose slowly, warily, the dark eyes rooting her to where she stood.

Fully expecting to see Lauren Cameron standing there armed with her bruised vanity and a more substantial reserve of weaponry, Alex was taken aback to see Catherine, scantily clad and clutching a porcelain pitcher to her bosom as if it were her heart sprung from her chest. He lowered his cigar and checked the flow of resentment that surged through his bloodstream. Two beautiful women in a highly provocative state of dishevelment presenting themselves before him in less than a ten-minute span—if he did not know better, he would swear it was a conspiracy.

"If you have come in here with the intentions of interrupting my bath, I give you fair warning of violence. I have waited the whole blessed day long for these few minutes of privacy and will relinquish them for nothing less calamitous than an earthquake or flood." He shifted slightly, sending more billows of steam into the air as he stuck his cigar back into his mouth and closed his eyes again. "On the other hand, if you would care to join me . . ."

"I *beg* your pardon?"

The whiteness of his teeth flashed in a grin as he lifted his glass. "In a drink, of course. There should be another glass around"—he waved the tumbler absently—"somewhere."

"No," she said on an exasperated sigh. "I do not wish to join you in a drink."

"Mmm. You're absolutely right. You have had quite enough already."

Catherine gripped the pitcher closer, the temptation to throw it almost too much to resist. "I supposed you had gone back to the party."

"The idea of a hot bath and cool sheets appealed to me more."

"Cool sheets? I should have thought you would have taken up the offer of warmer ones, what with all the attention being lavished on you tonight."

The dark eyes opened a sliver.

Catherine moved closer to the fire, blithely unaware that the brightness behind her rendered the cambric of her nightdress all but invisible.

Cameron groaned inwardly and closed his eyes again. "Do I detect another confrontation in the air, madam? If so, be so kind as to fetch the bottle down from the mantel."

"I would sooner say what I have to say to you while you are still relatively sober, if you don't mind."

"I don't mind at all, but if you want me to *hear* anything you have to say, I suggest you move away from the fire. The view from here is extremely distracting."

Catherine glanced down. Then stepped quickly into the shadows by the hearth.

"Thank you. Now . . . what is it you wish to discuss so earnestly? Not my sleeping habits, I warrant."

Catherine set the pitcher aside and clasped her hands

together. "I do not wish to *discuss* anything. I *insist* on knowing exactly when you plan to honor your word and send me home again."

A smile played at the corners of his mouth. "You insist, do you?"

"Yes," she said quietly. "I insist. You gave your word not only to me, but to my brother as well. You promised to send me home as soon as we reached your Archberry safely. Well, we are here and we are reasonably safe . . . although for how long is a matter of conjecture, what with all this talk of rebellion and crusading princelings."

Cameron delayed his response long enough to exhale a long streamer of smoke. "It might please you to know Donald thinks I have exhibited extremely poor sense of judgment by bringing a new wife to the Highlands at this time—a new English wife, at that. He did not put it into so many words, of course, for he is far too thrilled to see the yolk of wedlock fastened around my throat, but he does have an uncanny way of saying a great deal by saying nothing at all. In other words"—the dark eyes smoldered thoughtfully up at her—"even if you *were* my loving wife, and we *were* passionately—or should I say *desperately*—infatuated with one another, there would be little argument or opposition to my sending you back to Derby, at least until the troubles are resolved one way or another."

Catherine chewed her lower lip, trying not to notice how the water made every single muscle across his chest and shoulders gleam like polished bronze. "Is that what you intend to do? Pretend you are sending me away for my own safety?"

"It is a logical solution."

"But one that would leave them with the impression we are still married, even after I am long gone."

"I said it was logical, not perfect."

She watched him reach out and tap the ash from his cigar. His hair was wet, clinging to his neck in glistening black streaks. The steam was blurring his features, softening them, and she had forgotten—or perhaps just refused to remember—the first time she had seen him in the forest glade, how the sight of all that sculpted muscle had taken her breath away. He was a frightening and dangerous man, full of contrasts, full of surprises. A man who could maneuver the graceful steps of a dance as easily as he could execute the deadly steps of a sword fight. The thread separating the savagery from the beauty was fine indeed, and she glanced at the door, suddenly so very far away.

She moistened her lips. "When would it be . . . logical, then . . . to send me away?"

He ignored her, ignored the question, and she laced her fingers tighter together.

"If you haven't the time to deliver me to the border yourself, you could let me send for Damien. He will be worried sick by now, and I'm sure he would sooner come fetch me himself than trust my safety to strangers."

"Are you forgetting the patrol we met on the road?"

"Of course I'm not forgetting. How could I forget? I shall carry the horror of that single day with me the rest of my life!"

"What makes you think your brother would fare any better?"

"I . . . don't understand."

"Come now, Catherine. You may not understand Gaelic, but surely you grasped the drift of what the sergeant and his men had in mind for us? A stupid Englishman and his wife . . . a little fun and entertainment to while away the afternoon. After they finished robbing, raping, and killing us, they intended to blame the ambush on the rebels—popular scapegoats these days, I'm told."

"Damien and . . . and Hamilton will *both* come to fetch me. And Hamilton will bring a regiment of dragoons with him if necessary."

"I have no doubt that man would start the war himself, if necessary, and take the greatest pleasure in doing so.

But your fiancé's misguided ardor is not my biggest concern." He rolled the cigar between his long, square-tipped fingers and studied the curling ash. "Just out of curiosity, has it occurred to you yet that your name and description—everything about you, in fact—is probably known by now by every Campbell, every Watchman, every militiaman and English soldier garrisoned between here and the Tweed? Even if your brother managed to make it through the patrols—and that is a very big if— what makes you think either one of you would make it out of the first glen alive? Do you understand, *Mrs. Alexander Cameron,* what I am trying, in my clumsy way, to tell you? I would imagine the Duke of Argyle and his kinsmen break out in rashes just thinking of what they would do to you if luck were to throw you into their hands."

Catherine stared at him aghast while the last few drops of blood drained from her face.

"Then why?" she cried softly. "Why did you bring me here if you knew . . . if you even *suspected* there would be a chance I could become trapped here?"

His dark eyes avoided her possibly the first time they had done so. "To be quite honest, I have been asking myself that same question since we crossed the border."

Catherine recoiled from the unexpected contrition in his voice. It was another trap, another ploy to make him seem human, to unsettle her, to throw her off guard.

"And?" she demanded, her own voice shrill. "Did you manage to come up with an answer?"

He took a deep breath. "No. No answer."

"No answer," she repeated in a whisper. "You just took it upon yourself to play God. You ruin my life, ruin any chance I might have had for happiness in this miserable world, and then . . . and then you have the arrogance to sit there and . . ."

She backed slowly toward the door, her eyes blinded behind a rush of tears. "Oh, you are cruel and heartless. You bully people and use them thoughtlessly. You prey upon their weaknesses, then throw it in their faces time and again for the pleasure of your own amusement. You ridicule my feelings for Hamilton Garner because you know you are incapable of experiencing or even understanding the purity of such devotion. You are cold and empty, and I pity you, sir. You would not understand any emotion, least of all love, regardless if it stood up and slapped you in the face! Loving you would be a curse, and I would wish it on no other living soul, friend or enemy, for it would indeed be a desperate and fruitless undertaking with only heartbreak, pain, and betrayal as a reward for their effort."

Cameron moved. Through a film of startled tears, she saw him rise up out of the water, saw him step out of the bath and stride toward her, his body shedding moisture in sparkling sheets. She whirled and ran for the door, but he was right behind her. His hand shot out and slammed it shut, his big body crowding hers against the wall so that she had nowhere to turn, nowhere to run. She cringed against the cold stone blocks, her face buried in her hands, her entire body cowering in anticipation of his brutality.

He stood behind her, his feet braced wide apart, his arms held rigid by his sides. She could feel the heat of his body against her back, smell the steam rising off his skin. The impact of hard male flesh was boldly impressed on her body and her mind, shocking her to the very core. And when she felt his hands close firmly around her upper arms, it was like a fork of lightning jolting along her spine. Her limbs were useless, too numb to offer any resistance as he slowly, inexorably turned her around to face him. Her belly flooded with liquid fear as she glimpsed the rage in the narrowed eyes, the unfeeling coldness in the mirthless smile.

"So. You find me cruel and heartless, do you? Lacking any and all emotions?" His voice chilled the nape of her neck and sprayed her arms with gooseflesh. "Well, madam, it might interest you to know how absolutely correct you are in your analysis. And more, that it has taken a considerable effort over the years to achieve such a high level of impunity—impunity that does not come without its faults, I freely admit. You, on the other hand—"

"Let me go," she gasped, twisting her head in a wild, frantic motion that was immediately impaired by the rough pressure of his steely fingers beneath her chin.

"You, on the other hand, admit to nothing," he continued. "You have the body and passions of a woman, yet you flaunt them like a child. You have spirit and courage and a streak of independence as wide as the ocean, yet you persist in playing the role of a spoiled, petulant debutante without the wit to realize your every action has a consequence. I told you this afternoon, madam. I *warned* you in the plainest terms possible that I was tired of playing these games. I also warned you of the consequences should you choose to test me any further."

"Let . . . go of me. At *once*." The shallow whisper was barely audible. Not so the deep and animal-like groan that broke from her lips when she felt him shift forward and press the threat of his body against her thighs. "No," she gasped. "Don't—"

His hands cradled either side of her neck and angled her mouth up to his.

"Y-you gave your word not to h-hurt me!"

"I have no intention of hurting you," he murmured. "And my promise was not to *force* you to do anything you did not want to do."

"I . . . I don't want you to do this. . . ."

"I don't believe you," he said evenly, and his lips brushed her temple. They moved slowly, willfully along the verge of her hairline, sliding down to capture the delicate pink curve of her earlobe, remaining there long enough to feel her pulse quicken beneath his hands.

"Oh . . . no . . . please . . ."

She tried to use her fists to push him away, but her hands were pinned against his chest, trapped against the powerful wall of muscle. The overwhelming presence of all that hot, sleek flesh prompted another cry, so that when his mouth began to rove again, her lips were parted and vulnerable to his assault. His hands kept her face upturned to his while his mouth held her hostage. His tongue lashed and probed with a single-minded possessiveness that produced yet another ragged cry—more of a whimper this time as she realized her fists had ceased pushing and her fingers had spread into the damp black hairs on his chest. Aware of the subtle change, Alex drew her even closer, molding his body, his mouth, to hers so that each bold thrust of his tongue evoked stunningly sharp reverberations deep in her womb. The kiss became the center of her consciousness, all she knew or felt, even as she fought the rising heat of passion—fought it, cursed it, craved it.

"You're a woman, Catherine. Act like one. Tell me what you want."

"Not this. Not *like* this."

"*Exactly* this," he insisted, skimming his hands downward. "Exactly *like* this."

His fingers brushed over her breasts, his palms engulfed the tender fullness and found the nipples already peaked and straining, quivering with a need that etched itself plainly on his skin. With his mouth firmly over hers again, he began to unfasten the chaste row of ribbons over the bodice, and Catherine tried one last time to push him away. But the effort was halfhearted; there was not enough strength in her arms to deter him, not enough conviction in her hands to keep them from exploring the vast, naked planes of brawn and muscle. She had fought his power in the garden at Rosewood Hall and lost. She had fought it in Wakefield and resisted it through ten interminable days and nights of travel. It was wrong and sinful, wicked and shameless, but she could fight it no more. She wanted to feel his mouth on her flesh again. She wanted his heat. She wanted his strength.

He pushed the cambric off her shoulders and Catherine

tore her mouth free on a gasp of unholy pleasure. The blood in her veins turned to quicksilver, hot and molten; her legs were useless beneath her, and if not for the arm that knowingly curved around her waist to support her, she would surely have melted to the floor.

Alex heard a second, shivered cry, and his black eyes flickered up to hers, but what he saw there was not enough to stop him from lowering his head and capturing the taunting sweetness of her breast. The taste had haunted him all afternoon long, the memory had prickled his tongue every time he looked at her along the dinner table, and he took her into his mouth, as much as he could hold, groaning when he felt her rake her hands into his hair and pull him even closer. Her back arched as she thrust her breasts forward for his pleasure; her fingers twisted around handfuls of his hair, bracing herself against the heat and suckling wetness.

Reeling with the effects of this new intoxication, Catherine was barely aware of him stripping away the rest of her nightdress, chasing it down past the rounded softness of her hips. He followed it down, sinking onto his knees before her, his hands on her thighs, his thumbs stroking the golden thatch of downy curls, parting them, probing the tender pink flesh between. Catherine's body stiffened and her lips formed a moist, rigid *O*, but she dared not look down, dared not conceive of the dark head bending to her again, of his mouth pressing into the juncture of her thighs, his tongue lashing and probing with the same determined boldness he had used to conquer her senses elsewhere. She wanted to cry out for him to stop, for it was an unheard-of violation, lewd and sinful . . . but when the pleasure gripped her, then gripped her again, she shamelessly cast all thoughts of modesty aside and pushed eagerly into each new volley of pleasure. This time, when the weakness in her knees became too much to bear alone, she slipped down beside him, her mouth searching feverishly for his, her tongue as bold and greedy to know the taste and feel of him.

Their bodies came together, their movements hauntingly reproduced in the shadows that danced and flickered across the walls. Catherine reveled in the heat of his limbs twining with hers, she marveled at the iron strength of his flesh, the devouring hunger of his lips as they roved everywhere, explored every sweet hollow and curve. A thousand bright shivers of expectation welcomed his hands as they spread her thighs and she felt him settle purposefully between.

Her hands clutched the bulging muscles of his upper arms and her eyes opened wide . . . wider as the incredibly hard slide of flesh began to furrow inside her, stretching, pushing, impaling her as if he meant to split her in two. Her limbs tensed involuntarily, and for a long moment her passion was overshadowed with the anguish of doubt.

Sensing her fear and suspecting the cause, Alex raked his fingers into the golden spill of her hair. He forced her to look up into his face, into eyes that no longer burned with rage or arrogance, but with an entirely new emotion, naked and raw, more utterly devastating than the awesome, desperate hunger in his body. Catherine saw it and her heart soared. She tasted it on his lips, through a kiss that was tender and honest and admitted more than any false whispers or promises. Her hands moved, smoothing down the corded muscles of his back until they settled over the poised hardness of his flanks. Her fingertips were cool and trembling, their invitation as tentative as the sob of assent on her lips as she thrust her hips upward, her eyes squeezed shut through the stab of white-hot pain.

An instant, no more, and the pain subsided.

An instant more and she felt him slide forward, her smothered gasp acknowledging the warm, throbbing presence that marked the end of one identity and the beginning of another.

It was with a sense of wonder that she felt him start to move within her, for she had truly not expected more. Her hands were still molded to the iron sinews of his hips and she left them there, lightly riding the slow and deliberate thrusts that were her introduction to the moist, sensual friction of flesh on flesh. He coaxed her limbs wider and lifted them higher, and she gasped to feel him stroke even deeper. She tried to choke back the unbidden cries of pleasure each measured thrust produced, but it was impossible, and when he lowered his mouth to her breast again, the combined sensations made her arch up beneath him, again and again, meeting each plunge of his hips with an eagerness that took her breath away. A groan lifted him up on outstretched arms, and she knew she had never seen anything so beautiful as the gleaming, sculpted perfection of his body; her gaze moved lower and she saw how her hands grasped him, how her own body arched and strained to pull him closer with each bold thrust.

Now not even the commanding power of his obsidian eyes could hold her. Her head thrashed side to side, fanning her hair in a fine-spun web beneath them. Her nails ribboned his flesh with tiny white scratches and she began to shiver, to quake uncontrollably as a mindless urgency overtook her, an urgency born of blood and fire and consuming desire. His hands were there to lift her and support her as his thrusts came harder, deeper, faster. She sobbed disbelievingly as she neared the edge of some incredible precipice, and her long slender legs twined frantically around his, fusing their bodies together as she rushed headlong over the brink of erupting passion.

She was not aware of crying out his name, but Alex heard it. He heard it through a flood of pleasure that surged through every cord and sinew in his body, that clouded his senses to everything but the lithe, supple body shuddering violently beneath him. Each muscle, each nerve, each pulsing vein screamed for release, yet he forced himself to wait, to resist the lure of the clenching velvet sheath until the spasms grew so intense they robbed him of both reason and sanity. He plunged his hands beneath her hips and thrust himself as deep as life and breath would take him, and as one they soared beyond rapture into the stunning brilliance of ecstasy.

Lauren Cameron pressed herself against the rough stone wall, her eyes closed, her cheeks flushed, her fists curling and uncurling as hatred seethed green and evil within her. Her feet had become rooted to the floor, her nerves singed raw as she listened to the choked cries of unimaginable joy coming from the other side of the fire-room door.

How dare he humiliate her this way! How dare he scorn and dismiss her, then run straight into the arms of his *Sassenach* wife!

Lauren had *not* mistaken the glances and half-smiles he had cast sidelong at her throughout dinner. She had *not* imagined the pressure of his thigh leaning against hers or the riveting suggestiveness in the long, tapered fingers as they stroked and caressed the curved sides of his wine goblet. These actions had been as deliberate and seductive as the knowing glimmer in his eyes each time they sought her reaction. Her reaction? She had felt naked and weak with anticipation through the better part of the meal.

Not invite her? He had practically ravaged her right there at the dinner table. What game was he playing? What game were they both playing—he, the stalwart and untarnished husband, she, the prim and virginal bride so quick with her blushes of modesty. Yet at a moment's notice they were sprawled on the floor, naked and grappling together like dogs in heat.

Lauren had heard them arguing as she had been leaving Alasdair's room. Perhaps he had been boasting about her visit, using it to rouse the yellow-haired bitch into a jealous rage. Perhaps the whole thing—the glances, the touches, the subtle innuendos throughout the evening—had been staged for that very reason.

Lauren backed slowly away from the door, the fury

darkening her eyes. No man used her like that. She was no man's vehicle for winning the attentions of another woman . . . not unless she willed it to be so!

She whirled around and descended the stone spiral with no thought or care for the sound her leather heels made on the steps. Flushed and wild-eyed, she paused at the bottom and glanced along the deserted corridor, hearing the distant strains of laughter and music. She had thrown her clothes on in haste and anger, not troubling herself with laces or bows, and she was in no mood to have to explain her dishevelment to anyone she might meet in the main wing of the house.

Rape, she thought blackly. She could say he tried to rape her before he crossed the hall to ease his frustrations on his simpering wife.

No. That story was only good one time. A second, similar incident would only cast further doubt on the mishap with the MacGregor boy, and if the first charge was questioned, Lochiel might begin to wonder if he had hanged an innocent man. The blame for the theft of his gold and jewels might then shift onto Lauren's shoulders—where it rightfully belonged—and she would be lucky if she could escape with the clothes on her back!

She felt like screaming. Her body was still throbbing, aching, burning with jealousy, and she hurried along the gloomy corridor until she came to a narrow stairwell used mainly by the servants. She fled silently down into the bowels of the castle, pausing now and then to listen for footsteps. She ran the length of the vaulted stone undercroft, and at the northernmost end of the vast storage rooms turned up a well-worn flight of steps that fed tributaries to the pantry, the kitchens, and of immediate interest to Lauren, the guardhouse.

She went unerringly to the third door from the stairwell and tested the latch with a trembling hand. It was not locked, and taking a deep breath, she eased the door open and slipped inside. The room was small and dark, the only light coming from a high slitted window that overlooked the courtyard. It took a few moments for her eyes to adjust, and when they did she saw the shape of a cot emerge from the shadows, and on it, the outline of a male body. He was lying there, one arm folded beneath his head as a pillow, the other draped across his chest.

"Ye should know better than tae creep up on a mon when he's asleep. It's that dark ye could have a dirk atween yer eyes afore they finished blinkin'."

Lauren's pulse quickened, his voice evoking a rush of sweet-hot sensitivity between her thighs. "Ye werena at the party tonight, Struan MacSorley. Ye were missed."

"I'm pleased tae hear it. Did ye bring me ma supper, then?"

Her gaze was drawn to where a bold awakening was visibly and majestically reshaping the folds of the blanket. The blood flushed sluggishly into her belly, swirling there until the heat became almost unbearable.

She lifted her hands slowly and pushed the already loosened halves of her bodice off her shoulders. "I've brung ye somethin' tae suckle on, aye. If ye're hungry."

The glint of his eyes followed the movement of her hands as she peeled away the layers of her outer clothing and left only the sheer wisp of silk clinging to her breasts. The dusky peaks were proudly defined, straining against the fabric with an impatience that caused the blanket to stir again. She moved to the side of the bed and reached down, casually lifting a corner of the wool, skinning it back inch by solemn inch. Her breath dried in her throat as she bared the hard, barrel-size chest, the coarse mat of red-gold hair that narrowed over the belly and exploded in a dark nest at his groin. Her eyes widened appreciatively, and she did not even notice the grin that welcomed her awed stare.

"I'm that hungry, lass," he growled softly, "ye'll not know when one course ends an' the next begins."

Lauren set her teeth against a fierce shiver as one of his huge, callused hands skimmed up beneath her petticoat and without preamble delved greedily into the moist nest of silky curls. She gasped and trembled against the pressure, which only invited the blunt-tipped fingers to seek a bolder intimacy. Sobbing with the instant, mind-shaking release, she crumpled slowly to her knees beside the cot, her mouth agape, her hands clutching his broad shoulders for support.

With a deep chuckle of satisfaction, he tore the silken shield off her breasts and feasted on the voluptuous bounty, his hard body beginning to quiver with an intensity Lauren might have found amusing if not for the shattering distraction of his hands and lips. Her cries were real, her passion genuine. She gave herself willingly, eagerly to the pleasure, knowing that by morning she would be stronger for it, thinking more clearly, whereas Struan MacSorley would not be thinking at all. Not with his head, at any rate. And a man incapable of thinking clearly made mistakes, believed the unbelievable, questioned the most ingrained loyalties, abandoned the most steadfast convictions.

MacSorley had been Alexander Cameron's friend once, almost a brother by marriage. He could not be feeling too comfortable with the idea of a *Sassenach* taking his dead sister's place in Alasdair's affections. His glaring absence at the party tonight suggested he was downright disgusted. And if that was the case, Lauren would play on those feelings, all night and all day if need be, doing her skillful best to acquire not only an obsessive new lover, but a potentially useful and deadly ally.

17

Catherine drifted back to reality, her arms locked tightly around a bunched feather bolster. She stretched slowly, languidly, inwardly noting each pleasurably bruised muscle. Her body tingled with a new awareness. She felt healthy and vigorous and alive, wanting to take back every sour, accusing word she had ever said to anyone in her lifetime and replace them all with laughter and smiles.

She opened her eyes and stared dreamily at the canopy overhead. She was in her bedchamber, ensconced in a nest of fat, cozy blankets. She could not remember precisely how she had come to be here. Her last vague recollection was of curling sleepily and contentedly against Alexander Cameron's warm body, of feeling his arms enfold her and hold her close as if she had rendered him as utterly and blissfully depleted as he had rendered her.

The immodest thought produced such a flooding of guilt to her cheeks that she sank below the line of the covers until only her eyes and the pink tip of her nose were left exposed.

What on earth had come over her last night? What had come over the pair of them—cavorting like debauched lovers, first on the hearth in the fireroom, then in the huge featherbed, carrying on until sheer exhaustion had caused them to collapse into a deep sleep. Sweet merciful heavens . . . the things he had done! The things she had allowed him to do! Eighteen years of propriety, of striving to learn discipline and moral turpitude . . . gone. Gone in the passionate heat of one reckless night.

It never should have happened, the prickling voice of her conscience hissed. *You should have stopped it. Stopped him.*

"I did not exactly encourage him," she whispered aloud.

Didn't you? What do you call parading around in a flimsy nightdress in front of a naked man?

"I did not know he was naked—"

How else does one bathe?

"I certainly did not know he was bathing!" Catherine insisted.

Well, when you found him and saw what he was doing, why did you not run back to your chamber and bolt the door?

She chewed her lip in agitation. It was a logical question and deserved a logical answer. Indeed, had fleeing not been her first impulse?

But you didn't do it. You stood there and defied him again, knowing—knowing, I say—what his reaction would be.

Catherine had no rebuttal, no defense. There *was* no defense; her actions had been utterly irresponsible, unconscionable . . . and just plain *foolish.* She was *weak,* in body and in spirit. So much for the lofty Miss Catherine Augustine Ashbrooke who thought herself to be so far above such base instincts. So much for her righteous contempt for her mother's behavior—for that matter, hadn't Lady Caroline said it was in her blood to make the best of the situation? *What* was in her blood, though? The ability to crave and feel passion, obviously, but was there nothing more? Last night she had become a woman in every sense of the word, yet she felt more childlike, more confused, more helpless than ever before, floundering in a sea of new doubts.

Might I also remind you that last night put to rest a quick and easy annulment along with your virginity?

Catherine groaned and buried her head in the pillow, but the little voice persisted, turning tart with sarcasm.

Lieutenant Garner will not be pleased. He had reserved the honor for himself—would have had it, too, had you simply refused your father and left Rosewood Hall on your own. You could have gone to London with Damien and been Mrs. Hamilton Garner by now.

Somehow, the thought of waking up naked and disheveled in Hamilton Garner's bed did not cause the intensity of blush it should have. Nor did the thought of lying in his arms rouse quite the same stirring inside as did the memory of Alex's arms and body cradling her. The two men were totally opposite, in character and in nature. Hamilton was . . . well, smooth. In every sense of the word. Polished. As if he were a statue or a figure to be admired daily, with every last detail just so—every hair placed just right, every fingernail a clean white crescent. She could not imagine him with a stubble of beard showing or a stray piece of lint on his tunic sleeve, whereas Cameron . . . She quite believed he was capable of tumbling her in a muddy field if the mood came upon him—and making them both wildly happy in the process.

Catherine covered her face with her hands and sank even deeper into the bedding. How could she even think such things? How could she even dare to compare Hamilton Garner's careful precision to the strong, brooding, animal-like recklessness of Alexander Cameron?

Where was he anyway?

She sat up and glared at the empty side of the bed. Surely he must know she would be waking up feeling confused and guilt-ridden. Surely he would have something to say to her, even if it was only—

"Good morning."

The quietly spoken salutation was so unexpected, Catherine gasped and clutched the blankets to her bosom. Alex was standing in the doorway, a small tray balanced in his hand. She had been so absorbed in her own thoughts she had not heard him enter. He was fully dressed, wearing breeches and a plain white shirt, giving the impression he had been awake for some time. His hair was carelessly swept back in a queue. His jaw was clean-shaven, his eyes clear and piercing, showing no signs of either fatigue or guilt. In fact, he looked so refreshed and so obviously satisfied with himself, Catherine allowed her conscience to answer for her.

"We must be waking on different mornings. I see nothing good about this one so far."

A smile tugged at the corner of his mouth. "I was beginning to think we might waken on different mornings at that. It is past two o'clock in the afternoon."

"Two—" Catherine forgot herself and pushed upright. "In the afternoon? But why wasn't I wakened sooner? What must everyone be thinking of me?"

Alex shrugged easily. "They are undoubtedly thinking you endured a long and harrowing journey over the last two weeks. You wouldn't raise any eyebrows if you failed to make an appearance for another two weeks."

"You made the same journey. I doubt if anyone expects you to lounge about all day."

His smile turned wry. "Men are expected to eat, sleep, and think on their feet, didn't you know?"

"Women are able to eat and sleep and think on their feet as well as men. Probably better, since we are also expected to feed, clothe, and provide for their comforts on top of everything else."

On the word *provide* the blanket slipped completely to reveal the two perfect moons of her breasts. Alex's gaze fell involuntarily and his breath departed his lips on a small gust. He was already treading his way very carefully through these first few minutes. He had steeled himself out in the hallway for the verbal confrontation, but had no means of preparing himself for the sight of all that slippery blonde hair spilling over bare white flesh. His senses were already under assault from the lingering, musky scent of their lovemaking; seeing the rose-tipped thrust of her breast, it was all he could do to maintain the balance of the tray.

As she hastened to cover herself, he cleared his throat

and set the tray on the nightstand. "I thought you might be a little hungry. I managed to scare up some chocolate for you and fresh hot biscuits. I didn't bring too much in case you were still asleep, but if you like I can send Deirdre to the pantry for something more substantial."

The violet eyes flicked to the door. "Deirdre! Good heavens, yes. I should have thought she would have wakened me hours ago."

"Actually——" Alex felt her eyes turn to him as he walked over to the window. "She was here earlier. She came into the room this morning and . . . well, that was what woke me. I guess she thought it best not to return until she was sent for."

Catherine's fingers twisted around the blanket. "She saw us? You and I . . . *together*?"

"My fault," he admitted with some chagrin. "I had every good intention of tucking you into bed and retiring across the hall to my own room, but . . ."

Catherine swallowed hard as she remembered. He had carried her from the fireroom and set her on the bed, but somewhere between drawing the covers over her and brushing back the flown wisps of her hair, he had succumbed to the urge to kiss her again, and before either of them knew it . . .

At least he was being civil, she thought as the color ebbed and flowed in her cheeks. He could as easily have been clumsy and belligerent, or worse, casual and crude. If anything he appeared to be almost as uncomfortable as she was.

"It never should have happened," she remarked, her voice whisper-soft.

"My fault again. Entirely. You had a little too much to drink and it gave you a little too much false courage, which I, in turn, took rather shameless advantage of. To be quite honest I probably had more than my share of the dinner wine as well, and I guess the temptation . . . twice in one day . . . was more than I could handle. I am very sorry."

He sounded so genuinely contrite, she felt she ought to at least own up to some of the blame. "You were not *entirely* at fault. You did not force me to drink the wine, nor did you force me to . . . to do anything else against my will."

Alex turned his head from the embrasure, and she was struck by the completely incongruous thought that he should always stand in partly sunlit windows. The light bleached his shirt almost transparent, made his hair gleam like molten metal and his eyes burn a deep, dark midnight blue.

"Whether you had been willing or not last night," he said evenly, "I doubt very much if I could have stopped. It was an act of pure selfishness on my part, and you are absolutely right: It should never have happened."

Catherine laced her fingers tightly together on her lap. She kept her eyes deliberately downcast, although she was aware of every movement, every small gesture or expression he made. For some reason the warmth she had been experiencing since waking had given way to a hollow chill, and she knew, suddenly, what he was leading up to with his penitence and contrition.

"Last night . . . you told me it would be impossible for me to leave Achnacarry just yet. Shall I assume that was also the wine speaking?"

"It will be difficult, not impossible." (Was that relief she detected?) "There has always been a thriving business along the coast smuggling contraband in and out of the country."

She smiled ruefully. "Am I to be considered contraband now?"

"At the moment, very much so. And I am afraid it is the only way to absolutely guarantee your safe passage home."

Catherine's smile stayed in place, though it was tilted oddly to one side. She was so accustomed to being the one to do the rejecting, to dispatch unwanted suitors out the gates, it left her a little bemused to be the one being rejected.

"Home," she murmured, covering her discomfort. "Yes indeed. Father will no doubt be beside himself with joy to see me back in the nest. And Mother will . . ." She hesitated and lifted her thick, honey-colored lashes only to find he was watching her, studying her with eyes that looked as brittle and hard as glass.

"Yes? You were saying?"

"Nothing." She quickly lowered her lashes again. "It doesn't matter. I am sure I can manage them."

The spark of brightness in Alex's eyes faded and died away. "Well, then, I shall see what can be arranged. I have to go to the coast for a few days anyway and—"

"You are going away?"

He had already turned to stare out the window again and missed the look of disappointment on her face. "Donald received another summons from the Prince this morning. It stated in no uncertain terms that he will consider it a direct affront to himself and to his father if The Cameron of Lochiel does not meet with him in person."

"Your brother is going to meet with Prince Charles?"

A nerve shivered high in Alex's cheek. "You can see why this is not the best of times for me to be introducing any new complications into the family."

So. Now you are a complication too.

Catherine frowned. "How long will you be gone?"

"Only for a few days, I hope. A week at the most. I imagine there is a good deal of diplomacy involved in refusing a prince his royal due. At any rate you will be quite safe here so long as you remember to stay inside the castle walls. No riding through the woods alone. Campbell's men may still be in the vicinity, and I would lay healthy odds young Gordon Ross would dearly love to meet with you in an isolated clearing somewhere."

He allowed the warning to sink in a moment, then added, "If you wish to write a letter to Damien, I'll see it leaves on the first available ship. You can advise him of the arrangements I am making, and I will add my own note to let him know the exact date of departure and point of arrival when I learn them."

"I imagine it will be an expensive way to remove me from underfoot."

Alex studied the soft oval face, noting the unrelenting blooms of color high on her cheeks, like the flush of a fever. Her fingers were crushed around the folds of the quilt, holding it like a shield to guard her nakedness. Her eyes were fixed on the bedpost, and she refused to even glance over in his direction. She looked so very slender and fragile in the old warrior's bed that he had to battle a strong urge to cross the few steps that were separating them. He ached to gather her into his arms and kiss away the hurt and shame, but to do so would only compound the host of errors he had committed last night. His emotions were too raw, he was not thinking clearly. His heart was pounding like a drum inside his chest, and his hands were shaking so badly he had to keep them balled into fists by his sides.

"I have been giving the matter some more thought," he said tautly, "and it occurred to me that since Raefer Montgomery ceased to exist in Wakefield, why not take it one step further and kill him off completely? His death would give you the perfect excuse for returning home . . . the bereaved widow, et cetera, et cetera."

"A widow?"

"You would hardly be expected to mourn overlong, having only known the poor fellow a short time. Naturally there would be a considerable estate to . . . shall we say . . . blunt the residual scandal somewhat."

She stiffened. "I don't want your money. I don't want anything from you."

"A noble sentiment now, but when your feet are dancing on English soil again, you might have second thoughts. I will leave the details to you . . . a tragic accident on the streets of London, a headfirst tumble into the

River Thames. In my letter to Damien I will give him power of attorney and a new will."

"You do not have to do that," she insisted, her cheeks flushing darker.

"Yes," he said quietly. "I do. It is little enough, considering . . ." He saw her starting to fight the shimmer of tears and he brusquely changed the topic. "Well, I'll see what I can do about finding Deirdre for you. If you like I will also make your excuses to Donald and Maura so you will not have to be disturbed for the rest of the day. The entire castle is in an uproar anyway, what with Donald's decision to leave first thing in the morning."

"Will I see you before you go?"

His gaze slid helplessly to the pale slope of her shoulders—shoulders he had kissed and caressed and used as a pillow when the ecstasy he had found in her arms had robbed him of the ability to think or move.

"You can just give the letter to Deirdre," he said hoarsely. "She will deliver it to me before we leave."

Catherine nodded, accepting this final rebuff with as much grace as she could muster. She watched him walk to the door and pause, looking back as if he might say something more, but then he was gone and the door was closing firmly behind him. She stared at the scarred oak, willing it to open again, but it did not, and after a few moments she could see nothing at all through the veil of hot, bitter tears.

18

Alexander Cameron stamped his feet to ease the tension, cupped his hands around his mouth, and blew a hoary breath to warm his fingers. The dawn was beginning to lift the gloom, to give shape and substance to the stone and mortar walls that surrounded the courtyards. Clouds of mist, tinted the yellowish hue of goat's milk, rolled over the battlements of Achnacarry Castle and dripped onto the cobblestones in a steady drizzle. It had rained all night and there were puddles everywhere. The cold seemed to soak through his heavy layers of clothing to scratch wet, icy fingers up and down his spine.

Alex wore the *breacan an fheile*—the belted plaid kilt common to Highlanders winter and summer. He was well-armed, with two steel-butted dags belted to his waist, and a saber as well as a basket-hilted broadsword strapped onto his saddle alongside a flintlock musket. He was not alone in the courtyard. A cacophony of horses' hooves rang out on the stones, competing with the efforts of the clan piper to inspire the assembly of men into some sort of order. The lights had blazed from the castle windows all night long as hasty preparations were made for Lochiel's departure. Hardly anyone had slept, and now hardly a single window was empty of the dark silhouettes of excited onlookers.

The mist, thick and nebulous, blotted out most of the upper stories—not that any one particular face could have been distinguished from another, even if that one particular face was the only one surrounded by a halo of long blonde hair. And besides, Alex thought, the windows in the west tower faced the opposite direction . . . and she was probably still soundly asleep, dreaming of home. . . .

Catherine had barely closed her eyes all night long. She had tossed and turned in the huge empty bed, alternately climbing down to pace back and forth to the door and staring unseeing out into the rainy night from an uncomfortable perch on the stone window seat. She had not seen Alexander since his visit to the room earlier that afternoon. She had written her letter to Damien, and Deirdre had collected it as instructed, and the slim hope she had fostered that he would still stop by to see her, even for a moment, faded with the last of the midnight blackness. She knew Lochiel's party was leaving at dawn, and she spent most of the last few anxious hours debating whether or not she should find her way downstairs to be on hand when they departed. As Alex's wife, surely her presence would be expected. As his *complication*, however, she feared his resentment at such a presumption. She did not know what to do, how to feel, how to act anymore. One night—one single, reckless night—and her world had been overturned.

She thought of home, of Derby and Rosewood Hall, of Damien and Harriet—even of Hamilton Garner. But they all seemed so distant somehow, as if they had been part of a life she had lived years, not mere weeks, ago.

What would Damien do when he received her letter? He would be relieved to know she was safe and coming home at last, but would he also be able to read between the lines and know something had happened between her and the man she had sworn to hate to her dying days? Damien had admitted to befriending Raefer Montgomery. What had he said—? That the name might change, but not the character of the man. He had obviously found qualities to like and trust in Alex, and as his lawyer he would surely have been privy to information concerning not only his business assets, but his personal life as well. Was there something *she* should be reading between the lines? Something she had missed in their relationship? Something that did not quite ring true about their confrontation in Wakefield?

Catherine was not permitted to explore the thought further. A soft tapping on the bedchamber door announced the arrival of Deirdre, who seemed surprised to find her mistress awake and sitting by the window.

"Shall I bring you a cup of hot chocolate? It is a dreadful, dreary morning, is it not?"

Catherine stared out the window again. The mist formed an opaque wall she could not see through, but she imagined the still, inky waters of the loch below and the jagged beauty of the mountains beyond. If she tried very hard she could even see a horseman riding along the crest of the clouds, his black cape flowing behind him, a giant black stallion prancing beneath him.

Go to him. The harm is done; what more could happen from a simple farewell?

"Pardon me? Did you say something?"

Deirdre looked over and frowned. "I asked if you wanted your meal up here or if you intended to join Lady Cameron and the others in the breakfast room."

"Oh." She delayed giving a direct answer and sighed. "How is Mr. MacKail this morning?"

"Angry as a mule with a burr under his tail. He actually tried to get up out of bed to join the others, daft man. Dr. Archibald had to pour a whole vial of laudanum down his throat to stop him. I don't suppose it helps, his room being directly over the courtyard with all the noise and fuss."

Catherine pricked to attention. "Can you see anything from there? I mean, the fog is so thick. . . ."

"Oh, yes, mistress. His is a small room only a storey above the ground. You cannot see across the court, but you can see quite clearly into it. And they are making ever so much noise." Deirdre saw the look on her face and ventured to add, "Mr. MacKail is sound asleep. He would never know you were there if you wanted to take a peek from his window."

"I . . . I don't know. I . . ."

"After all, it is rather an important errand they are setting out on. A bit of history in the making, I should think, riding out to tell the Stuart prince to go home to Italy." Seeing Catherine's further hesitation, she took up a velvet robe and draped it over her shoulders. "We would have to hurry if we're not to miss them leaving."

MacKail's room was not very far and the window was, as Deirdre had said, directly above the courtyard. The dripping fog had cloaked everything in a light haze, but there were enough torches lit to burn away the moisture, at least around the men and horses. Impervious to the rain, Donald Cameron stood near the center of the yard, dressed in all the pomp and splendor befitting an influential Highland chief. His hair was tied back with a black silk ribbon, his head covered by a bonnet trimmed with the eagle feather that marked his rank. His jacket, waistcoat, and trews were tartan, as was the voluminous length of wool draped regally over his shoulder, but each was a different pattern and blend of colors so that he glowed crimson, black, yellow, and green from head to toe.

Surrounding him, waiting the order to form and march, were a dozen personal servants, several pipers, the clan bard—who would record every word of the momentous occasion for posterity—and no less than sixty heavily armed clansmen led by the lion-maned giant, Struan MacSorley. Catherine did not envy Lochiel and his entourage their trip over hazardous mountain passes and rocky gorges in this weather. The thickening mist showed signs of returning to a full-fledged rain before too long, and the lingering effects could well hang over their heads for the entire journey.

Inwardly, Catherine could admit to some curiosity over the man they were riding to meet. She had heard all the stories about the Stuart prince—how handsome he was, how witty, how charming and eloquent. She could also not help but feel some sympathy for him, having come all this way only to be told by men like Lochiel that there was no chance for a rebellion to succeed, not without committed help from France and from dissidents in England.

Was there ever a royal family so plagued by misfortune? James I of Scotland had been murdered, James II killed by an exploding cannon, James III slain in a rebellion of his own nobles led by his son. James IV had fallen in battle at Floddenfield, James V had died of shame after his army deserted him at Solway. Mary, Queen of Scots, had been forced to flee her country and her throne, only to be considered a threat by her cousin Elizabeth and imprisoned for nineteen years before eventual execution. Her son James had in turn been named King of England and Scotland after the Union of the Crowns, but both he and his son Charles I ruled so arrogantly and despotically, the Puritans had ousted them in a civil war. After eleven years of suffering Cromwell's purges the crown was restored to the Stuart heirs, but upon Charles's death the throne was taken by his brother James II, a staunch Roman Catholic. In desperation Parliament asked William of Orange, then married to James's Protestant daughter, Mary, to come to England and seize the throne in his wife's name. The invasion of the Orangemen sent James II fleeing to France and brought about a law in England decreeing that all future monarchs had to be of the Protestant faith.

During his daughter's reign, James died in exile. Louis XIV of France was quick to support James's son, the thirteen-year-old James Francis Stuart, as rightful King of England, as much to stir up old hostilities as to win an ally in the exiled youth and his mock court. In

1702 the English throne was again bereft of an heir, but the government ignored James III's claim in favor of Mary's sister, Anne. James was passed over again eleven years later when Anne died without issue, and so desperate was the English Parliament to avoid another Catholic king, they traced back nearly a century to find a descendant of James I's Protestant daughter ruling the state of Hanover in Germany. In 1714 the elector of Hanover was crowned George I, and a year later James Francis Stuart made his first serious bid to reclaim the throne.

It was probably true, Catherine reflected, that the people of England would have preferred the son of James II to the doughty, fifty-four-year-old foreigner who spoke no English and surrounded himself with a pompous German court. But James Francis Stuart was Catholic and refused to appease Parliament by converting to the Protestant faith. Moreover, his roots were firmly in Scotland and raised fears of a definite shifting of power to the north.

The Scots, naturally, took this as a further slap in the face. In the rebellion of 1715, ten thousand loyal clansmen took to the battlefield at Sheriffmuir in support of King James. Catherine's father and uncles had joined most of England in lining up behind King George to defend the Hanover claim, dealing the Jacobites a bloody and costly defeat that had sent the Pretender back to France to lick his wounds.

But how, in reality, had he expected any other outcome? England was master of the sea, boasting an empire of colonies in America, the West Indies, and India. Could it have afforded to allow the comparatively small nation of bristling Scotsmen to displace its king and put one of their own on the throne, regardless if their claim was legitimate or not? Could it afford to do so now?

Catherine knew the answer, just as she was beginning to understand why Alexander Cameron had come back home after so many years away. It had nothing to do with politics, certainly nothing to do with religion. It had everything to do with family, with pride, with his identity and self-respect as a Scot and a man.

Having grown up well-schooled in her father's prejudices and staunch political beliefs, Catherine had been content up to now to recite them blindly, barely giving any thought to whether there was as much wrong on both sides as there was right. She gave it serious consideration now, however, realizing how difficult it must be for proud men like the Camerons and the crusty Keppoch she had met the other night to go to their brave but foolhardy prince and tell him there would be no grand restoration forthcoming.

You are beginning to sound as if you hold some sympathy for these rebels, her conscience chided silkily. *That could be dangerous. Very dangerous indeed.*

Catherine ignored the little voice and leaned forward to press her forehead to the window. She had caught sight of a familiar figure striding through the wisps of fog, and her eyes followed him now, her mind gone completely blank of any other thoughts. He was dressed like everyone else, in a woolen kilt and short frock coat. His head was uncovered and his hair unbound, the long, thick, ebony shock curling against his temples in the dampness. Stopping by Shadow's side, he began to check the tension of the cinches, and the stallion's elongated, graceful head turned, nudging him with affection. Alexander murmured something in the huge beast's ear and produced an apple from somewhere under the folds of tartan slung over his shoulder.

As Shadow munched, Cameron's gaze strayed upward toward the windows. Catherine flinched back, not wanting to be seen, and her attention was caught by a poignant exchange taking place on the torchlit steps. Lady Maura and her husband were standing there, his hand resting lovingly on her cheek as they smiled softly at each other, unmindful of the milling, bustling confusion that surrounded them.

After Maura tenderly kissed his palm Lochiel mounted his dapple gray, giving the signal for the rest of the horsemen to follow suit. The pipers filled their chanters and struck the first few chords of a lively marching tune, the notes swelling and echoing off the wet stone walls.

Alex drew his horse in line behind Donald and next to Struan MacSorley. At the last possible moment there was a flash of titian red, and Lauren Cameron ran out of the crowd of wives and well-wishers. She stopped between the two men and made a demand that won a laugh from both of them. Alex bent over first and gave her a brotherly kiss on the cheek. She looked disappointed and pouted at MacSorley, who roared and scooped her into his saddle with a swirl of skirts and bare, thrashing legs. His mouth plunged down over hers, kissing her with enough enthusiasm to rouse a prolonged and ribald cheer from his men. The hand around her waist slid boldly up to cup a breast, while the other disappeared beneath her petticoats long enough to start her legs wriggling and squirming again in a squealed, falsely modest effort to break free.

Catherine backed completely away from the window and let the curtain fall back into place. Her throat was tight and her eyes ached with a dull throbbing. The previous night she had willed Alexander into Lauren Cameron's arms with haughty contempt, but somehow she did not feel so haughty now, knowing that when she was gone and out of the way, Lauren—or someone else like her—would be more than eager and willing to fill Catherine's place in his bed. He had demonstrated with breathtaking intensity that he was a healthy, virile man with appetites that could not go unappeased too long. The thought of his arms around someone else, of his body straining and thrusting into someone else . . .

She had to put those thoughts behind her. She would need all of her strength, all of her concentration to face the ordeal that surely awaited her at Rosewood Hall. She would also have to deal with the reality that she was no longer Catherine Augustine Ashbrooke, the most sought-after heiress in three counties. She was Catherine Ashbrooke Montgomery, and widow or not, the damage to her reputation had been a *fait accompli* the moment she had ridden away from Rosewood Hall. Had she herself not always been among the first to laugh and gossip with relish over the merest hint of scandal involving any of her peers? Had she not regarded it as a solemn duty to defame a rival's character, however flimsy the evidence of misconduct might have been against her? In this case there would be no shortage of former victims positively drooling for a chance at revenge. Two weeks ... two *hours* in the company of a man like Alexander Cameron would have sealed her fate in stone.

There was nothing she could do about it. Her only defense was stupidity. She had started by flaunting herself at him at the birthday party and compounded each error thereafter by challenging him at every turn, deliberately poking and prodding his temper until she'd left him no choice. She had acted childishly, tormenting him with a naïveté that, in hindsight, she could only regard with wonder. Add to the list ignorance, stubbornness, conceit, duplicity ... all of the fine qualities he had accused her of possessing from the outset. And yet, if he was so clever, why could he not now see the doubts that were tearing her apart?

"It isn't fair," she whispered. "It just isn't fair."

"Eh? Ye want some air?"

Catherine looked up, startled by the sound of Auntie Rose's voice so close to her ear. Even more startling was the fact that she was seated before the fire in the family retiring room, that she had been so totally immersed in her own misery for the umpteenth time since Lochiel's departure from Achnacarry three days earlier that she was unaware of her surroundings or her company.

"Ye look warm, hen," Rose said solicitously. "Aye,

ye've been sittin' here long enough tae roast yer cheeks a rare shade o' pink."

Maura glanced up from her needlepoint. "Would you care for another cup of chocolate, or perhaps some wine?"

"Chocolate?" Rose's button nose wrinkled in disdain. "Bah! Devil's brew, tha'. Pour us oot a wee dram o' *uisque*, there's a good lassie. Do more good f'ae the soul than all the sweet brown coo's milk in the world."

Grateful for the opportunity to stretch her legs, Catherine set her own square of neglected stitchery on the arm of the chair and crossed to the sideboard. She glanced askance in Jeannie's direction, but the doctor's wife was sound asleep in a chair by the window, her mouth quivering open on each rattled breath.

"Some o' us dinna have the stamina," Rose declared cheerfully and bent her snowy head to the length of lace she was tatting.

Catherine smiled and unstoppered the decanter, but before she could finish pouring, her gaze was attracted to the bright square of light glowing through the high, narrow window. It had rained the first two days and nights of Lochiel's absence. As strong and well-fortified as Achnacarry was, the damp had found its way through the doors and windows, rendering most of the rooms—especially those in the more ancient sections—cold and musty and unfriendly. Today, even though the clouds seemed to have lifted temporarily and the fire was blazing hot and crackling, Catherine's mood failed to rise accordingly.

"Pour some f'ae yersel', hen," Rose ordered. "It'll dae ye nae harm on a foul day such as this."

"Lady Cameron?"

"No, thank you, dear. I still have some wine." Her glass from the noon meal sat by her elbow, the contents not diminished by more than a mouthful over the last hour.

"Aye, love, aye," Jeannie said, snorting herself back

awake. "I'll have a wee one. Ma throat's dry as an auld sock."

"Nae wonder f'ae that," Rose commented. "Ye've snorked enough air this part hour tae pipe us all the way tae Glas'gy."

Catherine delivered their glasses, but did not return to her seat. "I think I shall take advantage of the break in the weather to walk outside."

"In this damp? Quickest way tae rot yer lungs, hen," Rose cautioned.

"Nonsense." Maura laid her embroidery aside. "I feel like a little fresh air myself—assuming you would not mind the company."

"Not at all."

Catherine had found herself growing sincerely fond of Donald's wife. It had been at Lady Cameron's insistence that she leave the dreary loneliness of her room and join the others for meals, for the afternoons of sewing, and for evenings of lively conversation. Her discomfort had quickly been eased when she realized the gossip revolved mainly around harvests and sheep shearing, the children's tribulations and education—everyday problems concerning everything from pending marriages to the market price of wool. Normal and civilized. There was the expected amount of discussion surrounding Charles Stuart's presence in Scotland, but, oddly enough, not nearly as much as what dominated the parlor conversations in Derby. For Catherine, who had assumed all of Scotland was frothing at the mouth in anticipation of swarming south and invading England, it came as an unsettling revelation to know that so many advocated peace. They were not warmongers and savage barbarians thirsting for blood. In many ways, in fact, their family lives were more serene, more sociable, less pretentious than those she witnessed in Derby and London.

She thought of the dandies in their tight fawn breeches, stiff neckcloths, wigs, and smelly pomades, and compared them to the Cameron clansmen and neighbors who had gathered to celebrate Alexander's homecoming. Their clothing was drastically different to be sure—there was hardly a frock coat, neckcloth, or scented handkerchief among the lot. But their smiles were honest, their laughter genuine and robust. The Cameron family had shown no reluctance or lasting hostility in welcoming Catherine among them. Would Sir Alfred or any of his influential, socially prominent, *civilized* peers have acted the same had she introduced a black-haired, kilted Scottish renegade to the table at Rosewood Hall?

Catherine sighed and drew a borrowed wool shawl closer about her shoulders. She and Maura exited the castle by a small judas gate and began to stroll along the graveled path of the formal gardens. The air was drenched with the scent of briar roses, their clustered heads drooping with the weight of the recent rains. Rooks and curlews wisely kept to their shelters beneath the arbors, but the sound of their quarreling was as incessant as the patter of dew dripping off the branches at each quiver of a breeze.

Catherine stopped to pick a rose, one that was pure white with just a blush of creamy pink in the center. She tilted her head to the side as she did so and noticed the two clansmen following at a discreet distance. Their eyes were not on the two women, but on the surrounding border of forest, the sloping shoreline, the hills in the distance, and their hands were never far from the dags and broadswords they wore belted prominently around their waists.

"You get used to them," Maura said casually. "You even appreciate them sometimes when you have an armload of flowers or fruit."

Catherine doubted if she could ever get used to the idea of bodyguards and was about to resume walking when one of the men smiled and offered up a small wave. With some surprise, she recognized Aluinn MacKail.

His wound, according to Deirdre, was healing remarkably well, with equal credit going to Archibald's doctoring skills and the stubborn Scotsman's own determination. Twice in the past two days Catherine had seen him wandering the halls of the castle, and while he never remained overlong in their company, he joined the ladies and Dr. Cameron each night for their evening meal. He appeared to be a particular favorite of Rose and Jeannie, being cavalier enough to laugh at their bad jokes and roguish enough to embellish their good ones. His manners were as impeccable as his social skills, for he could pluck a word of flattery out of the air and bestow it on the least-suspecting person with hardly more effort than a quick, easy smile. The children all adored him; the servants fussed around him like royalty. Catherine could scarcely fault Deirdre for falling under his spell. He was handsome, charming, boyishly sincere . . .

Yet he had also demonstrated that he was capable of extreme, cold violence. Even if they had not witnessed his abilities in the attack at the River Spean, the very fact that he had spent fifteen years in Alexander Cameron's company revealed far more about his character than two brief weeks of casual acquaintance would impart.

His loyalty to Alexander was unquestionable, and Catherine was surprised enough by his appearance in the garden to wonder if some of that silent diligence had shifted to her during Alex's absence. Why else would he be out in the cold and the damp, assuming the menial task of a guardian?

"This was always one of my favorite retreats," Maura said, drawing her attention to the ornate iron bench and arbor positioned in the center of the garden. "When it seems the whole world is conspiring against me, I come here and just enjoy the roses and the birds and the vines growing overhead. It is very peaceful, and so very pretty in the sunlight." She laughed and glanced wryly up at the dirty banks of clouds swarming overhead. "Unfortunately that is not the case today."

"I can't imagine you troubled or needing solace from the world," Catherine said shyly.

"When you have four children pulling at your skirts at one time and a husband raging about like a fifth child in a tantrum, I shall remind you that you said that."

Catherine's smile faded and she lowered her lashes, not quickly enough, however, to avoid Maura's soft frown.

"What is it, dear? Is something troubling you?"

Catherine studied the rose in her hand. She wanted very much to confide in someone, to pour out all of her doubts and fears . . . but she simply did not know how or where to begin.

"Men can be such strange creatures," Maura said, guessing at the cause of Catherine's crestfallen mood. "Strong, domineering, and so unbending at times it makes you want to take them by the throat and scream. At others they are so childlike, so lost and groping for a few words of reassurance, it can make you weep. It can make you angry too, especially if you happen to be feeling lost and lonely yourself."

Catherine swallowed hard, but said nothing.

"The Cameron men," Maura continued, "are particularly stubborn and strong-willed. A curse of their bloodlines, I believe. There isn't a one of them who you could say had a true grasp of the word *compromise*, certainly not if it applies to their own behavior."

"Donald seems very loving and gentle."

"Donald? Yes, he is. Loving *and* gentle. But there are times when the sheer strength of that love frightens me half to death."

"How can love be frightening?"

"When it consumes you. When it blinds you to all other considerations. When you can no longer distinguish right from wrong, love becomes a terrible burden and it can destroy you as readily as it can save you."

Catherine pondered the words carefully, then sighed. "I don't think I would ever want to be that much in love."

"My dear, you do not have a choice. Sometimes it just happens, whether you want it to or not, whether it makes sense or not, whether it makes you happy or not. And believe me, the harder you fight it, the harder you fall. Donald Cameron was the last human being on this earth I wanted to find myself falling in love with. I was raised *knowing* all Cameron men were heartless and despicable, all the women wore black and conjured spells over iron cauldrons. Heaven only knows what Donald thought of us Campbells. You cannot begin to imagine the shock waves that tore through both clans when we announced our intentions to marry, but I fought it as long as I could, I truly did. I refused to see him, refused to think about him, I even threw myself wholeheartedly into a courtship with another man. But Donald was always there, standing between us." She paused, and her eyes took on a faraway look. "I agreed to meet with him one last time, thinking I could get him out of my system. I listened to what he had to say and he listened to what I had to say. We argued. We discussed all the logical, sensible reasons why the union simply could not work . . . and then . . . he touched me. That's all he did, he just . . . touched me. Here, on the cheek—" She pressed her fingertips over the faint blush, and her smile blossomed with the memory. "I knew then I would die if he ever took his hand away."

Catherine remembered the scene she had witnessed in the courtyard prior to Lochiel's departure. He had laid his hand on Maura's cheek, and she had kissed his palm in a way that suggested she felt the same way now as she had all those years ago. Not a showy, flamboyant gesture by any means. Not as brassy or brazen as Lauren Cameron's display.

Thinking of Lauren brought another memory to the surface.

"Who was Annie MacSorley?"

"What?" Lady Cameron looked badly shaken.

"I know she was Struan MacSorley's sister, and I gather she and Alexander were betrothed at one time—"

"Handfasted," Maura whispered, her face draining of color as if a vein had been severed. "But I should not be the one to tell you about her—"

"Please." Catherine impulsively took Maura's hands into her own. "I am trying so hard to understand. To understand *him*."

Lady Cameron nodded slowly. "Perhaps we both need to talk about it. I've tried to block it from my mind for so long . . . we all have. But if Alexander is to have any peace, we must all find a way to put the ghosts to rest. Dear Lord, but I wish the men were here. I have a feeling we are both going to need the support of a strong pair of arms before we are through."

Thirty miles to the west at that precise moment, Donald Cameron was having much the same thought. He wished Maura were by his side. She was his strength, his logic, his compassion.

It had taken the slow-moving train the three full days to reach the coast, winding through the luscious green glens of Lochaber and Rannock, climbing and snaking its way around fairy-tale gorges, ravines, and waterfalls only to approach a desolate and wind-ridden coastline that was a smuggler's paradise. In one of the small, rarely frequented inlets, the Prince's ship, the *Du Teillay*, lay at anchor, a modest three-masted brigantine much abused by the seas and offering the barest of comforts to her royal passenger.

Lochiel's entourage had been stopped twice in the descent to the harbor: once by an armed band of Mac-Donald clansmen whose chief had assumed the responsibility of protecting the Prince; once by a dour-faced Highland laird who had himself been summoned for an interview with Charles Edward Stuart.

"Aye, he's a likable enough laddie, Donal'," the old man had said. "A Stuart through an' through. He'll have the royal crest carved on yer arse afore ye even ken there's a knife up yer kilt."

Donald's frown—it had rarely left his face since their departure from Achnacarry—grew bleaker as he studied Hugh MacDonald's belligerent scowl. Known as Glengarry, the laird was an old warrior, a friend and strong ally of the Camerons. His loyalty to the Jacobite cause, like Lochiel's, had never been in question, but also like Donald's, it was tempered by reason.

"Glencoe has already been an' gone," Glengarry continued wearily. "Aye, an' his kinsman, MacDonald of Scotus. We've all told the lad the same thing: Go home. The time's nae right. Aye, we can fight in the mountains an' we can raid oor neighbors tae the south, but it willna be shepherds an' yellow-bellied merchants waitin' f'ae us ayont the Tweed. It will be German George's artillery an' stiff-backed scarlet troops, heavy armed an' eager tae spill oor bluid."

"Does he bring any encouragin' words from France?"

Glengarry screwed up his face. "He brings wha' he wants tae bring. Nae troops, nae weepons, nae gold. Just a blind eye an' a swelled heart, an' faith he'll have an army o' Heelanders followin' him tae the gates o' London."

"Has there been any word from The MacLeod or The MacDugal?"

The old man leaned sideways in his saddle and spit noisily onto the ground. "They didna trouble themsel's tae reply tae the fairst two letters Wee Tearlach sent them. The third time it were young Clanranald hisself took the summons tae Skye, an' he come back wi' a message f'ae the bonnie laddie tellin' him since he came wi nae troops, nae guns, nae money, he shouldna be surprised tae find nae army waitin' f'ae him."

Lochiel felt a crushing pain in his chest. MacLeod and MacDugal had been two of the most outspoken Jacobite supporters, boasting about how many men they could bring into the field to lead a Stuart uprising. With them both reneging so openly it meant others of lesser conscience and means would not hesitate to follow their lead, placing the greater burden of responsibility on Lochiel and his fellow moderates.

Confirming Donald's worst fears, Glengarry touched the side of his nose. "There are more than a few good men waitin' tae see how ye call it, Donal', afore they commit their own minds one way or t'ither. Dinna lead them wrong. Dinna choose in haste or we all suffer f'ae it. If ye believe we can fight an' win, so be it; we're wi' ye. If ye dinna think we have a whore's prayer f'ae saintdom, then we willna think any the less o' ye f'ae yer courage in tellin the lad it's so. I'm an auld mon, a foolish mon who dreams o' seein' a Scottish king on a Scottish throne again. I'd pledge ma soul tae the devil just tae see the *Sassenach* bastards driven back across the border where they belong. But I wouldna want tae be doin' it just so's the wee prince can sip his wine in comfort in Winchester."

Donald's heart had been leaden as he watched Glengarry ride away. If every laird in Scotland felt the same way, if that was all they were being asked to fight for—a free and independent Scotland—how different the circumstances would be! There were thirty thousand fighting men in the Highlands alone. United behind that single purpose, they could form an impenetrable wall across the border that no English—or German—king in his proper senses would dare challenge.

But that was not the Stuart dream. They wanted all of it: Scotland and England united under one monarch. It was an unrealistic goal and the one that was doing the most harm to the Prince's cause. And in the eyes of the English it was also the single most damning factor, one that would unite all of England against them.

Glengarry had said a dozen lesser chiefs had eagerly pledged their support already, but only because—he suspected, unkindly—they knew their numbers would not influence the greater scheme of things one way or the other. It was an unfair judgment, for their homes and lands and responsibilities were taken every bit as seriously as his own, but the harsh reality was that these same lairds could only pledge perhaps a hundred, two hundred, men at most. And two hundred fighting men out of thirty thousand simply did not tip the scales. As chief of the Camerons, Lochiel controlled the lives and destinies of five thousand men, women, and children. He could not enter into any commitment lightly, even though it galled him to think that someone, somewhere, might regard his act of caution as cowardice, his efforts at diplomacy merely a ruse to ingratiate himself with the Hanover government.

"Ah, Maura, ye were right," he whispered. "All those years ago ye were right."

Alexander leaned forward, and Lochiel waved his hand in a dismissing gesture. " 'Tis naught but somethin' Maura said tae me on our weddin' night. She said we Highlanders possess the pride o' lions. Like lions, we have nae fear tae temper our actions, only pride tae govern them."

Stubborn Scottish pride, Catherine thought and dragged the stiff horsehair brush through her hair so furiously the strands crackled and flew about in a spray of sparks. Why had he not told her the truth behind the murder charges? Why had he not explained the reasons for his exile and the persecution by the Campbells that made it necessary for him to travel in disguise? The story of Annie MacSorley's death had stunned Catherine. Where she had once feared to discover Alexander Cameron's human qualities, she now knew he was not only human, but deeply scarred and terribly vulnerable.

Snatches of conversations and arguments came back to haunt her. The wretchedly caustic voice of her conscience, so recently awakened, gleefully took advantage of her new flood of guilty feelings and reminded her of each insult she had hurled, each accusation she had spat, each occasion when she had called him cruel or heartless or incapable of expressing an emotion. Cruel? Heartless? Without emotion? He had killed two men for the love of a woman, accepted banishment from his home, his family, for the sake of averting a bloody clan war, and then tried his utmost to exorcise the demons that had haunted him by throwing himself into every reckless, dangerous enterprise he could find.

Catherine sighed and stared at her reflection. It was too late. What good did any of this remorse do her now? Nothing had changed. The same pride that had kept him silent before would continue to keep him silent now, even though he might be suffering from the same confused feelings she was having.

Why don't you just admit you are in love with him?

Catherine's eyes widened in shock. "No! I'm not!"

Oh, I think you are. And I think you have been fighting it for some time now . . . since the moment you saw him in the forest.

"Don't be ridiculous. There is no such foolery as love at first sight. For all I know there is no such thing as love. Not for me. Certainly not for him."

Two of a kind, are you?

"Two complete opposites, as he has told me often enough."

People say all manner of things in anger . . . or self-defense. And as virginal as you may have been in body, you must know his actions were not those of a man who simply craved a night of pleasure. You saw it in his eyes, remember? You saw it, and you reached out to him as desperately as he reached out to you.

"No!" She pushed away from the dressing table and paced to the window. The storm that had been threatening earlier was lashing across the land in full force. The heavens cracked time and again with lightning; the thunder rolled over the castle battlements like muted cannonades. Trees were bent, whipped in half by the wind's fury, and the loch was churned white with spume, the surface bubbled with the driving rain.

"Love has to be more than just pleasure," she insisted quietly. "And besides, if he . . . if he felt anything at all for me, why would he send me away? Why would he not ask me to stay, or suggest we try this marriage for real?"

Pride, Catherine. Or perhaps he doesn't know how you feel.

"How *I* feel?"

A jagged fork of lightning streaked across the night sky, strafing the crust of mountains, illuminating the landscape, and causing the castle foundations to tremble with the impact. Catherine reached out to catch the window shutters and lifted her face to the icy pinpricks of rain and wind.

Could you do it? Could you give up the parties, the seasons at court, the social prestige? Could you forfeit the simple things, like new ribbons for your hair whenever the fancy took you? Could you forsake all of it for a chance to share the life of a man like Alexander Cameron?

"I . . . I don't know if I'm strong enough—"

You can be strong enough if you want him badly enough. It isn't only his pride standing in the way, you know.

Catherine opened her eyes and stared out at the raging storm. The front of her dress was soaked, her hair was wet and plastered to her skin.

"If I thought . . . if I dared believe . . ."

Believe it, Catherine. And tell him before it is too late.

"Too late?" she whispered. "What do you mean, too late?"

There was no answer. There was only a sudden, blinding flare of lightning, so bright she had to throw her hand up to shield her eyes. It left an image seared on her mind of the same battlefield she had glimpsed once before. Standing alone, surrounded by a sea of clashing swords, was the same tall warrior she had seen the first time, only now, as he turned toward her, she could see his face. There was no mistaking the square, rugged jaw or the blazing midnight eyes. And no way to warn him of the glittering ring of steel closing in around him as he raised his fists and clawed the sky with the bloodied talons of his fingers. . . .

19

It seemed to take an eternity to dispense with the formalities. Lochiel had been welcomed into the crowded great cabin of the *Du Teillay* with the enthusiasm accorded a long-lost relative. The Prince and his staff of seven advisers who had embarked with him from France had lavished food and drink on the Cameron chief, who, along with Alexander and a half dozen envoys from neighboring clans, were charmed and disarmed by his humble graciousness.

Charles Edward Stuart was the perfect host. He had deliberately dressed to downplay his heritage, wearing plain black breeches and a coat of cheap broadcloth. His shirt and stock were made of cambric, not very clean; his wig was sparsely curled and fit poorly over the pale copper hair beneath. He was a handsome man, a fact that added to the romantic aura that surrounded him, at least where the Jacobite ladies were concerned. His blue eyes were large and expressive, his nose thin and prominent, his mouth as prettily shaped as that of a woman. There was a calmness about him, an assuredness unhampered by his youth or inexperience. It was the confidence of royalty, of knowing his cause was right and just and that there could be, should be, no possible argument against it.

He was also a very clever prince, playing with the emotions and sentiments of his guests as if they were instruments to be finely tuned prior to a performance. The opening chords were struck without warning, without preamble, shortly before midnight.

"Now that you have toasted your loyalty to my father's

cause, my faithful Lochiel, perhaps you will tell us what manner of support he may count upon from the beautiful glens of Lochaber."

One by one the voices around the dining table fell silent and the earnest faces turned toward Donald. Even Alex, who had been aware of the subtle manipulation of the conversations all through the evening, looked to his brother to see if the experienced statesman had been expecting the trap to be sprung.

Alex had to admire the young man's audacity. The dinner had been sumptuous; the wine had flowed like water. And now the regent planned to serve himself along with a hefty side dish of sentiment for dessert. He was, after all, a prince born to the royal house to which Lochiel had pledged eternal allegiance. This same royal prince had embarked against all odds, armed only with the might of his personal convictions and the hope of persuading—or shaming—his father's subjects to join him in a holy war.

Lochiel set his empty glass on the table and waved away a servant who rushed over to fill it. "Perhaps, Yer Highness, ye could tell us first what support we might expect from yer cousin King Louis, an' when it might arrive."

The Prince's smile did not waver. "As you know, my father's cause has the full support of the French government. Even as we speak, Louis is conferring with his ministers to finalize the plans for a full-scale invasion of England, to be coordinated, naturally, with our own army's march south."

A rousing cheer was prompted by one of his advisers, the Reverend George Kelly, in a tactful attempt to forestall identifying exactly which army the Prince was referring to. This time Alex was not alone in glancing along the table, firm in his opinion of their host's poor choice of companions. Kelly was thin-lipped and bald as an eagle, with the same predatory instincts. The Irishman, O'Sullivan, boasted some military experience, but discreetly avoided giving references to specific battles fought. Sir Thomas Sheridan was seventy years old and had been Charles's classroom tutor. William Murray, the exiled Marquis of Tullibardine, was so crippled by the gout he could not walk without a stick. Aeneas Mac-Donald was a Paris banker whose only function as far as anyone could determine was to enlist the aid of his elder brother, the chief of Kinlochmoidart. Francis Strickland was the sole Englishman in the group, a Roman Catholic from Westmoreland whose family had always been loyal to the Stuarts. At the moment both he and the seventh member of the elite assembly, Sir John MacDonald, appeared to be more interested in the quality of the claret than the conversation—as if they had heard it all before.

These were the men closest to the Prince, the men who had vowed to see him claim the throne of England in his father's name. Of the seven, O'Sullivan seemed to be the slipperiest, exchanging frequent glances with Charles and prompting him with either a nod or a shake of the head.

Alex lowered his gaze and wiped at the beads of sweat that had formed on the outside of his tankard. He could not say anything. Protocol demanded his silence, but inwardly he was screaming for Donald to be on his guard.

"I am glad the French are sendin' troops," Lochiel continued. "We can well use their trainin' an' experience tae organize our own efforts."

"As I said, the King of France will need assurances that we have an army willing to support my father's holy cause."

"Which ye canna raise, Highness, wi'out some show o' good faith from France. An army needs swords an' muskets, lead f'ae shot, an' gunpowder—"

"The cargo bay of this ship is full of muskets and broadswords," the Prince interrupted hastily. "Bought on my own initiative."

"Aye, but a broadsword canna stop a cannonball,"

Lochiel pointed out gently. "An' the English army has cannon by the score. We have but a few rusted weapons an' none who ken how tae fire them."

"Men can be taught to fire cannon," O'Sullivan said wanly.

"Aye." Lochiel looked at him. "They can be taught how tae light a fuse, but learnin' how tae aim an' hit a target takes practice, an' we have neither the powder nor the shot tae squander."

The Prince surged to his feet. "Were you or were you not the chief instigator of the committee formed to entreat my father to return to Scotland?"

"I were on the committee," Lochiel agreed freely. "I still am, so far as I know, an' will be until we find a *realistic* way tae bring King James home."

"You doubt my sincerity in this venture, sir?" the Prince asked stiffly.

"On the contrary, I find ye a remarkable young man. Furthermore, I believe if anyone could lead an army tae victory in Scotland, it could be you."

The Prince flushed under the compliment and sank slowly back into his chair. "Then why do you hesitate—you who have the power to sway half the clans in the Highlands in our favor. Why?"

"The men's hearts are wi' ye, Highness, but their heids—" Lochiel threw his hands up in a gesture of helplessness. "After the calamity last year—"

"Surely you cannot hold me to blame for that? We had twenty-two ships bulging to the seams with men, guns, and supplies . . . all of it collected through *my* persistence."

"Aye, an' most o' it lost through French incompetence."

"The fleet encountered a storm in the Channel—"

"Any fool knows the worst storms o' the year are in February. I ken yer hands were tied; ye had no choice but tae sail when the French decided they were ready tae sail—but by the Christ, the Royal Navy knew tae the day, the hour, the minute when the first ship left port an' where it was bound."

"There are spies in every conflict," O'Sullivan declared.

"Aye. An' ours tell us the French have as yet made nae move tae send help. In fact, they tell us the King's ministers are so dead set against any further involvement wi' us, they have drawn the treasury purse strings shut."

Two red splotches colored the Prince's cheeks as he stood again. With a visible effort he forced himself to remain calm, to turn from the table and pace the length of the cabin until he stood near the multipaned gallery windows. Light from a brass lantern poured over his head and shoulders, gilding him in an aura that could not have been more unnerving had he been standing in a church nave.

"We must not bicker amongst ourselves," he said tautly. "Indeed, we must not quarrel, especially over an incident that occurred better than a year ago. The main thing to remember is that we set sail then with seven thousand French troops. There are at least that many again waiting to embark at the first word of our army marching south."

Lochiel steadied himself, astounded by Charles's refusal to admit he had entered into this present endeavor without the slightest proof of solid support from either side of the Channel.

"Highness—" He laid his hands carefully on the table. "There will be nae army marchin' south. At the most ye could raise two, three thousand men—*maybe*—but it still couldna be called an army, for ye'd have nae weapons, nae food, nae money tae pay them—"

"Would we have their loyalty?"

Lochiel's face flushed at the quiet inquiry. "I can speak only f'ae masel', an' in that ye have ma most passionate loyalty. But loyalty canna buy guns. Loyalty canna grow men out o' the ground tae fill the ranks o' an army."

"We were led to believe we could rely upon twenty, thirty thousand faithful Highlanders."

"Then ye were poorly advised, sir. A damned sight

more poorly advised than even the English garrisons posted here, f'ae they can tell ye within ten men how many each clan could put intae the field, how well they would be armed, an' behind whose standard they would march."

"I have heard the rumors, sir, that our cause has suffered grave losses to the lure of Hanover gold. Still others remain silent, too ashamed, I must surmise, to acknowledge their king's plea for help. Others have had to be cajoled to come down out of their mountain strongholds to appease me with their patronizing bromides." He paused, watching the insult darken Donald's complexion. "I tell you now, I will not be patronized. I will not be swayed by cowards and naysayers. The time is right to strike, and to strike hard! The main bulk of the English army—including its artillery—is across the Channel fighting in Flanders. The few regular troops that remain are not sufficient to withstand a Highland army, regardless of whether it is but one-tenth the promised strength.

"All we need," Charles continued, addressing his rhetoric to the rapt and silent group, "is a single victory to prove to the whole country that we are committed to our cause. All of our friends who have doubted us would come forward; all the foreign aid we might need would pour into our borders. Gentlemen"—he squared his shoulders and faced them fully so that the dazzling light from the lantern spilled over his regal countenance, making it appear to glow from within—"this is my home. This is my country. These are my Highlands as much as they are yours. The blood of my ancestors stains the soil beneath my feet, and their voices cry to me through the glens and mountains. I will not go back to France in defeat again. I will stay and fight to restore honor to my father's name though not another single man has the courage to stand by my side!"

A sickening wave of humiliation drained the blood from Donald's face, yet he still groped for threads of reason. "Aye, Highness, aye. Perhaps ye should remain in the kirk. Perhaps, wi' time an' care, ye can win over yer detractors, prove tae them ye are indeed committed tae victory. In the meantime, I would personally guarantee yer safety, f'ae as long as it takes—"

"My safety? You think I care one whit for my safety? And would you have me skulking from cave to cottage to avoid the hounds the English would undoubtedly set after me while we waited for an army formed out of pity to grow around me? No, my good Lochiel. I will, indeed, stay in Scotland, and I will, indeed, walk these glorious hills, but not as a criminal, not as a thief in the night, not as a beggar seeking alms. In a few days, with the few friends I have, I will erect the royal standard of the House of Stuart and proclaim to the people of Britain that Charles Stuart has come home to claim the crown of his ancestors—to win it back or to perish, if need be, in the attempt."

A round of furtive glances was exchanged around the table. Only one pair of dark, midnight eyes did not waver from the ashen face they had been watching throughout the Prince's impassioned speech. Alex saw the tears in his brother's eyes and the small half-circles of blood cut into the flesh of his palms where his fingernails had forced him to maintain his silence.

Slowly, the Prince looked directly at Donald also. "You say I have your loyalty, Lochiel, and so I believed or else why would I have been drawn so relentlessly to these shores? You and my other faithful Highlanders filled me with such hope . . . with the heart to keep on going even though man and nature pitted their fury against me. *My* Highlanders, for we share the same blood, the same courage, the same quest for honor . . . *or so I thought*."

The golden head tilted up again, angling the angelic face into the full sphere of light. "I would force no man to stand by my side if he lacks the faith or trust to do so. Lochiel may stay at home if he finds he has so little hope for me and my cause. There he may learn the fate of his prince from the newspapers . . . and perhaps offer a toast or two in our favor. Surely that would not be too much to ask?"

Donald Cameron stared unblinkingly at the gilded prince. He rose slowly to his feet, his body rigid and trembling, the tears falling in two shiny streaks down his face. Through a sluggish wave of helplessness, Alex heard his brother's voice break the crystalline silence.

"No, by God. I will not keep tae my home while ma prince fights alone f'ae ma king . . . nor will any man over whom nature or fortune has given me power."

There was more, but Alex did not hear it. He found himself thinking, irrationally, of an avalanche he had witnessed once. One small step had sent half a mountain exploding down upon an unsuspecting village. He had the same feeling now, that he was poised to take that one small step, and if he did, the only way to go was down.

20

The storms that had plagued the skies over Achnacarry finally dissipated, and on the fifth morning of Lochiel's absence the sun made an appearance over the horizon. The mists were reluctant to leave the coves and inlets of the loch, and the forests rained dew for another full day before they, too, relinquished the dampness and began to steam dry. Catherine took long walks in the garden and along the shoreline. She ventured bravely into the woods with Deirdre and their shadow of silent guards to pick wild berries, and while there discovered a narrow stream that looped its way through the saplings, its waters flashing silver with salmon.

She startled Aluinn MacKail one morning by joining him unexpectedly in the courtyard and requesting to be allowed to accompany him on one of his rides. After a brief debate and a longer delay to arm a mounted escort, they rode up into the hills, where she was afforded a breathtaking overview of the castle, the loch, the seemingly endless rolling sweep of Highlands. Seeing the appreciation in her eyes, Aluinn told her some of the Cameron history. He pointed out the ruins of an ancient keep nearby and filled her imagination with stories of medieval battles and feuds. He spoke of Alexander and hinted at a misspent youth, but never broached the subject of his exile, and Catherine did not give any inclination that she knew. By the end of the first morning they were both relaxed and laughing, and she hoped somehow that she had gained an important ally should the need for one arise.

As the days stretched into a week, so, too, did Catherine's patience stretch to the breaking point. She was still wracked with doubts, confused by what she was feeling, but as bad as it was suffering alone, she suspected the real trial would begin when and if Alexander came home. To that end she rehearsed whole speeches and thought of countless arguments to present both for and against the idea of her remaining at Achnacarry. She walked the gardens tirelessly, one turn convincing her she was a fool to even entertain the notion of staying in Scotland, the next convincing her she would be a greater fool to leave. Always at the back of her mind was the very real possibility that she was debating with herself needlessly. Alexander Cameron was as stubborn as he was proud. If he had already made up his mind to send her away—and had she not badgered and insisted repeatedly that he do just that?—no amount of rationalizing would budge him.

Also at the back of her mind was the recollection of his telling her he had a distinct and everlasting aversion to marriage. What made her think a single night of passion had changed his opinion? He must have spent many similar nights with many other women over the years. Perhaps she was reading far too much into a few murmured phrases, a too-soft caress, a dark promise in the depth of his eyes. Perhaps it was nothing more than what he had so bluntly told her the next morning—a matter of too much temptation combined with too much wine.

She simply did not know anymore. There were no storms to affect her senses now, no providential bolts of lightning to frighten her into seeing something that was not there. What had seemed so clear then was, in the stark reality of daylight, a confusing and hopeless situation. He did not want her. He could not possibly love her. Perhaps she should go home, if only to get away from the mystic beauty of the mountains and the treacherously hypnotic effects of heather and peat smoke. Would she be so willing to cast her lot to the wind if she found herself back at the River Spean confronting a dozen filthy militiamen?

The answer was a resounding no. She would die of sheer terror if she had to endure what lay beyond these thick stone fortifications. She *was* soft and she *was* pampered, and she honestly did not know if she wanted to change, or if she could change.

Always sure of herself in the past, she now felt mired in doubt and uncertainty. She wanted to stay. She wanted to go. For the first time in her life she wanted someone to tell her what to do, but even the obscure and tinny voice of her conscience remained stubbornly silent.

"Cow piss," Rose announced, her voice almost causing Catherine to spill her wine. "Take ma advice, hen: A wee tot o' cow piss an' vinegar each mornin' an' yer bairns will all be laddies. I ken. I've had six o' ma own."

"Cow piss me arse," Jeannie countered derisively. "All that'll gie ye is a sour belly an' no' much more. Beetroot jelly. Tha's what ma mither told me, an' all *twelve* o' ma bairns are laddies. Ye take a wee dram, ye see, an' muckle it on his nether parts just afore—"

An abrupt roar of laughter interrupted the dissertation, and Catherine glanced gratefully to the door of the retiring room. Archibald Cameron stuck his head into the room and thundered for their attention, as if the trembling of the walls had not already alerted them to his presence. He swung an arm wide in a sweepingly flamboyant gesture and stood aside as two tartan-clad, bedraggled figures who had obviously ridden long and hard through the night and morning walked past him into the room. Catherine's heart needed but a second to flutter with recognition.

"Alex," she whispered.

The dark eyes found her immediately, but any greeting he might have offered was drowned in a swell of anxious voices.

"Alex! Struan!" Maura grasped each man's arm in

welcome. "Thank God you have come back to us safely. We've been hearing all manner of rumors—"

"What has been happenin' at Arisaig?"

"Did ye see the Prince? Did ye speak wi' him?"

"Where is Donald?"

Alex held up his hands to staunch the flow of questions. "Donald is a day or so behind us, nothing to worry about. Struan and I came ahead with a few of the men. . . ." His voice trailed away and his gaze strayed back to Catherine.

Drinks were thrust into their hands and both men were ushered closer to the fire. They were relieved of their heavy sword belts, bonnets, and plaids, then questioned as to the last time they had eaten. Both men looked exhausted. Struan's glorious mane of hair was stringy and limp, his beard thick with the dust and grime of traveling. Alex fared little better. His hair was stuck to his neck and brow, his jaw was blue-black with several days' growth of stubble. His eyes, normally so clear and piercing, were heavily smudged with dark rings of weariness.

"Ye look like hell, brither," Archibald announced with his usual aplomb. "Has the war started wi'out us?"

He had asked the question half as a joke, but at the look on Alex's face, Archibald's normally jovial smile faded and the light in the pale-blue eyes became bright with alarm.

"Out wi' it, lads," he ordered. "What news f'ae Arisaig?"

"The clans meet ten days from now at Glenfinnan. The Prince plans to raise the Stuart standard and proclaim himself regent of Scotland in his father's absence."

Jeannie let off a whoop of excitement and executed a quick dancing jig before her husband could glare her into silence.

"A gathering of the clans?" Aluinn asked quietly. "Who is he expecting to join him there?"

Alex drew a deep breath and tossed back the contents of his glass before answering. "Clanranald and Kinlochmoidart are already arming; Glenaladale and most of his MacDonalds; Keppoch, and Glencoe, of course—"

"Keppoch? But he would never commit unless . . ."

"Unless the Camerons were committed," Alex finished grimly. "The same holds for the Stewarts of Appin, the MacLeans, Glengarry, the Grants, the Frasers . . ."

"My God—" Maura whispered in horror.

"They have all pledged?" Aluinn asked.

"They will all have to search their own consciences and make their own decision now that the gauntlet is thrown." Alex looked almost apologetically at Lady Cameron. "Donald did everything but get down on his knees to beg the Prince to return to France or at least to wait for a better time, but—"

"How is he?"

"Donald? Oddly enough, I think he's relieved that the waiting, the arguing, the endless debating is over. It was his decision to make and he made it, committing himself one hundred percent."

"Everything?"

Alex knew what Maura was asking. There were lairds who would agree to send half the clan under a son or a brother to fight for the Stuarts and thereby honor their oath of allegiance to the exiled king. They would also send a token force to pledge for Hanover, thus ensuring that regardless of the outcome their titles and estates would be protected. But Donald would no more consider dividing his loyalties than he would give half an oath.

"Refill yer man's glass, hen," Rose whispered in Catherine's ear, loud enough to win the attention of the dark eyes again.

All of her carefully rehearsed greetings deserted her, and Catherine was suddenly aware of how she must look. She had spent the morning taking a leisurely walk along the shore, and her hair was scattered every which way around her shoulders, loosened from the glossy blonde braid that hung down her back. She raised a hand to smooth the tendrils back from her face, but there were

too many and his eyes were too sharp. Her flush deepened and spread down her throat. Her ability to move, to
think, to speak had all but deserted her.

Rose prodded her with an elbow and she walked halt-
ingly forward. She was aware of his eyes on her all the
way, the heat from them coiling through her belly and
between her thighs like silken ribbons.

Somehow she managed to carry the bottle to where he
stood without dropping it, but it was all she could do to
lift the decanter and rattle it against the edge of his glass.
He eventually raised a hand to steady it.

"Have you been well?"

"Yes," she answered in a whisper. "Very well,
thank you."

"Alasdair! Struan!" Lauren Cameron came running
into the room, skidding to a halt in a breathless swirl of
flying red hair, yellow skirts, and excited laughter. "I've
just heard the news! Is it true? Is cousin Donald raisin'
the clan f'ae Prince Charlie?"

"Aye, lass," Struan said, swelling his massive chest
proudly. "Lochiel has pledged the Camerons tae fight
f'ae King Jamie."

The tiger eyes lingered on Alex's face a moment
longer than they should have before she smiled to
acknowledge Struan's remark. "When? When are we
marchin' tae meet the Prince?"

"As soon as Donal' returns, he'll be tellin' us all about
it," Archibald said. "Nae sense workin' yersel' up till
then. By the Christ, but this calls f'ae a toast. Aye, there's
a bonnie wife. Fill ma glass, Jeannie, then fill all the
rest."

Catherine refrained, as did Maura. Alex joined the toast
in silence, then returned his emptied glass to the tray.

"If no one objects, I've lived in these clothes for a
week now—half that time in the pouring rain. Struan, I
thank you for your company. Aluinn—can I speak to you
out in the hallway for a few minutes?"

Catherine watched Alex lead MacKail out of the room,

then was distracted by Maura clapping her hands for order in the mild pandemonium of voices. Luncheon, she suggested, should be delayed long enough to give the men a chance to freshen up. Lauren was dispatched to tell the cook, and Struan, after a hastily murmured excuse, prowled after her a few minutes later.

Aluinn came back alone. The smoky gray eyes held Catherine's for a moment before he joined Archibald and Maura by the hearth.

Catherine forced her legs to move, to carry her out of the room and along the sunlit hallway. She told herself she was only going to change her own clothes and brush her hair into some semblance of order, but as she started up the stairs to the west tower, her footsteps lagged and she had to firmly grip the carved stone banister for support the rest of the way to the top.

The doors to all three rooms were closed, and she thought of a game she had seen played at a country fairground with walnut shells and a dried pea. The gamester had hidden the pea under one of the shells and taken ha'penny bets from the onlookers, who tried to guess where it had ended up. She had no excuse to enter Alex's room, nor did she want to confront him in the fireroom if he was in the tub again. She would go into her own room and leave the door ajar. That way, if he wanted to see her or speak to her in private, he would know where she was.

Resigned to the wisdom of her strategy, she entered her bedchamber and adjusted the width of the door opening twice before she was satisfied. The single narrow window at the end of its recessed bay did little to alleviate the gloom, which seemed darker than normal, and she had walked to the dressing table and begun to unwind the long plait of her hair before she realized Alex was standing in the embrasure, his broad frame slashing the beam of sunlight into hazy, dust-laden streamers. She stared at his reflection in the mirror, her hands frozen on the separated strands of hair.

He moved, shifting the play of shadows and sunlight

again as he leaned casually on the stone casement. "Don't let me interrupt you."

Catherine bade her hands move and they obeyed, resuming the process of combing out the braid.

"Aluinn tells me you have been venturing outside the castle."

"He took me riding, if that is what you mean. I was beginning to feel like a prisoner."

He frowned instantly, "Has anyone said or done anything to—"

"Oh, no," she said quickly. "No. I only meant . . . I mean, the walls were beginning to close in on me a little, I guess. No . . . everyone has been extremely hospitable."

He pursed his lips and looked down at his hands. "Archie seems to think there is Scottish blood in you somewhere. He is quite taken with you."

"I . . . rather like him too. He is—" She groped for an appropriate word to fit the recalcitrant, outspoken doctor, but failed to find one.

"A bit unorthodox?"

"He is a very fine doctor," she allowed. "He has worked a minor miracle on Mr. MacKail's shoulder."

"He should be good. He was trained in Edinburgh and graduated at the head of his class."

"Archibald?" She could not keep the incredulity out of her voice, and he smiled.

"Every family has an eccentric or two hiding away in a closet. In our case, we have Archie."

"And Jeannie," she murmured, matching his shadow of a smile.

"Ah, yes, Jeannie. She is another matter altogether. Good solid farm stock, not the least impressed by the Cameron name or position. She would be as happy stomping around in a sod *clachan* as she would living in Holyrood House."

Catherine glanced surreptitiously at him in the mirror's reflection. Oddly enough, the week-long absence had sharpened her intuition, and she could hear the faint depression in his voice, see it in the slight stoop to his shoulders. He was more upset, more shaken by Donald's capitulation than he let on. All this trite, casual small talk was hiding the fact that he was worried, frightened, almost . . . lost.

To cover her own nervousness Catherine took up the hairbrush and began dragging it through the length of her hair, smoothing the tangles, taming the heavy cascade into the sleek ripple over her shoulder.

"Your letter to Damien got away safely," he said after a moment. "We managed to find a ship that was just leaving—"

Their eyes met in the mirror and there was a breathless little silence between them. He was thinking how lovely she looked standing there, her face dusted pink, her hair bright and flowing softly over her shoulders. Even the plain cotton dress she wore took on a certain elegance for simply being graced with her form. He had tried not to think of her too often over the past week, and for the most part he had been successful. Only when he closed his eyes did his willpower fail him. If he had hoped to exorcise her from his blood that night, or sought to use the week away from her to regain his perspective, there, too, he had failed miserably. He was drowning, floundering in the perfume of her hair and skin, and if she did not stop looking at him that way . . .

Catherine no longer saw the man who had kidnapped her, frightened her half to death, and introduced her to horrors she had never dreamed existed. Instead, she saw a very vulnerable man who had survived his own private hell and emerged strong and vital and on his guard against any further possible damage to the heart that beat so formidably within his chest. And she was thinking, if she could steal but a portion of that strength, a small part of that heart . . .

Alex clenched his fists tighter, his whole body fighting the desire to stride across the room and take her in his arms. He turned and looked out the window.

"One of the reasons we left Arisaig ahead of Donald," he explained, "was to make a detour down along the coast to meet with a smuggler Struan knows quite well. After a good deal of haggling and a few threats on both sides, we managed to arrange passage for you and Deirdre as far as Blackpool."

The hand holding the brush faltered over the span of a few quick heartbeats. "When?"

"The end of the week, Saturday." His voice was strained, the words so low she almost could not hear them.

"I see."

"Under the circumstances it is the smartest, safest route . . . and it is imperative that we get you away as quickly as possible." The sound of the brush falling on the dressing table drew his eyes back in time to see her walking toward him. "Naturally, there are still risks traveling by sea, but . . . the captain assures me he pays the coastal revenuers an exorbitant sum to keep them looking the other way."

"Will you be taking me?"

"To the coast, yes. After that you will be well-protected, don't worry."

Catherine wasn't worried at all. She was remarkably calm, in fact, as she joined him by the window.

"And you?" Her hand toyed absently with the laces that crisscrossed her bodice. "What will you do now that your brother has decided to go to war?"

He was silent, his body immobile, his arms taut with the knowledge they could reach out and touch her, stroke the soft white curve of her cheek.

"I am a Cameron. I cannot turn my back on that fact regardless of my personal feelings. Sometimes . . ." His voice trailed away, and his eyes fell involuntarily to where her hand lingered over the dusky cleft of her breasts. "Sometimes there are larger issues than a man's private convictions."

She looked directly up into the clear midnight eyes. His expression might have been carved from stone, but her senses were absorbing very different undercurrents. She let them flow over her, warming her, stirring her with subtle, unspoken messages that were far more arousing than any physical act of touching. The blood flushed through her limbs, and she swayed slightly with the tension, knowing beyond a doubt that he was fighting the same strong urges. As she watched, a thin white line formed around his mouth and a pulse began to beat in his temple—the same temple scarred in his duel with Hamilton Garner. The duel where he had won her as his wife.

"I am a Cameron too," she reminded him. "You made me one."

She stepped deliberately closer, bringing the ripe, sweet musk of her woman's body tantalizingly near. Every one of Alex's nerves tingled, every small hair in every small pore stood on end.

"Catherine, I don't think—"

She pressed even closer—close enough that the heat of her body paralyzed him. His fingers clamped a rigid warning around her arm, but she ignored it. She raised both hands and curled them around his neck, the contact sending a visible shiver through his big body.

"You don't know what you're doing," he began, but he felt her breasts cushion enticingly against his chest and he saw the bright violet shine of desire defying him to push her away. He started to. By God, he started to. And his lips parted, intending to offer a final warning, but with a soft rushing breath her mouth was there, moist and supple, sweeter than anything he had imagined or remembered tasting in his lifetime. The pink tip of her tongue flicked between his lips, teasing him, taunting him in a way he himself had taught her, and her hands tightened around his neck, forcing him to bend, forcing him to respond in kind.

With a deep-throated groan he sank his fingers into the glossy waves of her hair and crushed her to him, casting aside all of his good intentions, his honorable resolutions, his firm and noble determination not to further enmesh either one of them in a dilemma that could have no happy solution. He kissed her with lips that were bruisingly hard; he held her in arms that trembled like those of a schoolboy. The rasp of new beard on his chin chafed her tender skin, but Catherine did not seem to notice. She responded with an eagerness that flamed his need beyond all caution and reason.

Alex lifted her and carried her to the bed, his hands tearing at her clothing almost before he had set her down. He bared her breasts and his mouth plundered each straining peak, devouring the last of her doubts even as he unleashed an urgency within her as great and ungovernable as his own. His hands abandoned her, but only for as long as it took to release the yards of pleated tartan from around his waist, and when they returned it was to press her down onto the bedding, to feverishly brush aside the remaining barriers of her clothing and thrust himself as deeply inside her as sense and passion would allow.

A cry was shocked from his throat as the pleasure gripped him instantly. The hunger that had haunted his every unguarded thought engulfed him now, driving him to a possession that was forceful and unyielding. He tried to hold himself back, to check himself, knowing it was too soon . . . too soon . . . but Catherine sensed his weakness, shared it as she drew him deeper, held him tighter while the hot torrent of his ecstasy surged and erupted within her. She writhed with the joy of it, clawing her hands into his flesh, into the bunched muscles of his back and shoulders as he shuddered again and again. Blindly, convulsively, she arched herself higher, opened herself wider so that his life force throbbed and pulsed at the very heart of her soul.

Her name was on his lips as he shook the last of the mighty spasms free and collapsed, gasping, on top of her. She lay absolutely still, stunned and splintered with wonder. She raised a hand and combed her trembling fingers through the waves of raven hair, her skin tingling everywhere under a wash of utter contentment as she pressed her lips to his temple and soothed him, calmed him. Reluctantly, he slipped into an exhausted sleep, his arm fast about her waist and his head pillowed between the soft mounds of her breasts.

Catherine drifted back from a dreamless slumber sometime later. She and Alex were still curled together, although their positions had changed somewhat. Her head was now nestled in the curve of his shoulder. One of her legs was lying carelessly across his, whether to pin him down or to offer protection was unclear. She raised her head slowly, tentatively, but he did not stir except to release a deep and untroubled breath. It occurred to her that she had never seen him sleep before—in fact, she had often wondered if he ever slept at all. How different he looked! Gone were the brooding lines of worry, the stern set to his jaw. The thick black crescents of his lashes lay like fallen wings on his cheeks, and his hair, swept back from his forehead, looked like strokes of black paint against the whiteness of the sheets.

In their haste to reach the bed, neither had completely disrobed. Catherine still wore her chemise and bodice, although both were loose and gaped open over her breasts. Her skirt had been discarded, but his impatience had allowed him only to push her petticoats above her hips and free one slender leg from the pantaloons. Alex still wore his shirt, the linen spread open across the breadth of his chest with the excess shoved up beneath his arms.

Her eyes wandered lower and she stared. Despite their previous night of passion, when she had been left with the distinct impression there could be no possible secret or mystery yet to discover, she realized she had never seen a man's naked body in the full, uncompromising light of day. By candlelight, or by firelight, her modesty had been greatly spared. There was no such vestige of charity now, and her cheeks flushed a hot, bright crimson as she studied the sleeping male form, measuring it and charting it as might an artist who was planning to transfer the bold contours to canvas.

Aside from the sheer physical beauty of Alexander Cameron, there were harsher realities revealed by the daylight. Dozens of scars, both fine and wide, threaded their way across the hard surface of his flesh. The thigh cut by Hamilton Garner's saber bore an older welt, the skin shiny and pulled flat over the surrounding tissue. His ribs, his arms, even his belly wore the telltale signs of the life he had led in his fifteen-year absence from Achnacarry.

The love in her heart swelled to epic proportions, and she could not resist stealing a tender kiss from the wide, full lips. She carefully disentangled herself from the circle of his arms and left him to sleep, deciding she would make his excuses to the family and bring him a tray of food later.

Moving quietly so as not to disturb him, she slipped her skirt back on over her petticoats and repaired the froth of confusion he had made of her chemise and bodice. A quick glance at the mirror told her she would never be able to offer simple conversation as an explanation for their prolonged absence, but she worked a few minutes with a brush and comb to restore at least a modicum of propriety to her appearance. In truth, she did not care if the whole world knew what she and Alexander had been doing in the tousled arena of the bedchamber. Nor did she feel the least bit embarrassed that she had shamelessly seduced him into her bed. If there had been any lingering question as to how she felt about herself or her husband, it had been answered most thoroughly in his arms, and that was all she knew or cared about.

She had professed to love Hamilton Garner, but that love had been as phony and pretentious as the rest of her sorry existence. Her heart had never beaten wildly out of control at his approach, her skin had never prickled at the sound of his voice, her bones had never seemed to melt from within at his touch. All these things happened, and happened with shocking intensity, whenever Alexander was near her—even from that first moment she had laid eyes upon him in the clearing. She could no longer deny it or argue the logic of it: She was in love. Honestly, completely, painfully in love. And such a sweet pain it was! Sweet and all-consuming, from the tenderness between her thighs to the ache within her heart. She would gladly forsake anything to hold on to this feeling. She would willingly live in a little sod cottage if he asked it of her and if he was there to share it with her.

She finished her repairs and was crossing on tiptoes to the door when she saw Alex raise a hand and rake the hair back from his temple.

"Catherine?" His voice was slurred, heavy with fatigue.

"Go back to sleep," she whispered and went over to the bed. She pulled the quilt over his body and, on a sudden impulse, bent down and kissed him squarely on the mouth.

The dark eyes showed surprise . . . and pleasure.

"What was that for?"

"You," she said simply. "Because you thrive on challenges."

"I do?" he asked warily.

"Indeed. And here is a new one for you: I love you, Alexander Cameron. More than common sense or decency should allow. Your strength frightens me and your stubbornness angers me, and I believe you to be a truly dangerous threat to a woman's inbred gentility, but there you have it. And unless you are prepared to give me several honest and convincing reasons why I should do otherwise, I intend to remain here at Achnacarry as your wife, as your lover if you will have me, as the mother of your sons, of which—please God—there will be many."

His eyes widened and he started to push himself upright, but Catherine was already at the door. She heard him call out, but she dared not stop or go back. She had said it and she meant it, and it was up to him now whether they used the smuggler's ship to send out a second explanatory letter to Damien or a bound, gagged, and screaming Catherine Ashbrooke Cameron.

Her heart was pounding and her hands were shaking as she ran through the long gallery and down the narrow secondary corridor that opened into the courtyard. She ran across it and through the judas gate into the rose gardens, slowing down only when she entered the path she normally followed to the tranquil solitude of the shoreline.

When she was into the small band of trees that fringed the banks of the loch, she heard footsteps coming swiftly up behind her. She took a deep breath to brace herself for the inevitable arguments and turned steadfastly to confront her husband—but it was not Alex who came to a grinning halt behind her. It was not Alex who reached out his arms to her, and it was not Alex who clamped a brutal hand over her mouth to stifle her scream of horror.

Alex cursed as he threw back the quilt and swung his long legs over the side of the bed. A wife! A lover! A mother, goddammit! Where had all that come from?

"Catherine!"

The roar of his voice died away without producing any results, and he cursed again as he spread the six yards of tartan on the floor and rolled himself in the pleats, securing it about his waist with a leather belt.

She loved him, did she? She was going to stay at Achnacarry, was she? Didn't she know there was a war about to break out? Didn't she know her position here in the Highlands could only get worse, not better, regardless of whatever support and protection his own immediate family might be able to offer?

What the hell had happened during his absence?

He sprang to his feet, flinging the surplus length of tartan over his shoulder as he bolted out the door.

She loved him. Of all the stupid, untimely . . .

His mind replayed her impassioned speech word for word as he ran through the gallery and checked several of the main rooms. A startled servant gaped at his bare chest and his bare feet and pointed out a window, telling him she had seen Catherine run out into the garden, and in a swirl of crimson and black plaid he followed.

He was not entirely blameless, he reasoned as he pushed through the judas gate. He never should have touched her. He should have cut off his hands first before surrendering to the temptation of all that silky white flesh. He never should have kissed her. He never should have looked into those treacherously beautiful eyes of hers and imagined seeing a plea there . . . a plea to be taken and held and loved.

His footsteps slowed on the gravel path.

So he had bedded her, what of it? He had bedded dozens of women over the years, some equally as lovely and seductive as Catherine Ashbrooke. What made her different? What set her apart from the rest? Why the devil had he gone through with the marriage when he could easily have slipped away into the night and never seen her again? And why, in God's name, had he gone up to her room today? He had wanted her too badly, needed her, truth be known, in ways he did not even want to think about . . . and hadn't thought about until just this minute.

A wife? A lover? A mother for his children? Not since Annie's death had he even allowed such thoughts to enter his mind.

Annie. There was the real hell of it. He could hardly remember her face anymore, aside from the impression of sweetness and sunshine. When he tried, all he could see was Catherine dancing under the glitter of candlelight at Rosewood Hall, or Catherine in the forest, standing in a pool of sunlight, or Catherine looking up at him, her eyes round with wonder as she discovered ecstasy in his arms.

Aluinn had said it was time to let the ghosts rest. Perhaps he was right.

And she would be safe here. Achnacarry could be changed into a fortress at the turn of a key, isolated and inviolate. . . .

"Catherine?"

He listened for a reply, but there was only the furious squawking of birds in the trees somewhere off to his left. He ignored the irritating little prickle at the nape of his neck and listened to his heart instead. It was beating against his breastbone, demanding to be heard. He had kept it prisoner too long, denied it the softness and tenderness and trust. . . .

"Catherine?"

The breeze snatched his voice and carried it into the stand of trees. He saw the glitter of sunlight reflecting off the water of the loch, and he pictured Catherine sitting by the shore, prim and stiff with rebelliousness, waiting for him to present her with all his righteous arguments as to why he should send her away and why she should go.

He paused at the edge of the garden and plucked a snow-white rose.

A wife, a lover, a mother for his sons . . .

Alex stopped. This time the uneasy feeling was too insistent to ignore. He stared hard into the trees on either side of the path and tried to determine what it was that was out of order, but he could see nothing. He could hear nothing but the faint lapping of water against the shore and the incessant screaming of the birds.

His hand fell to his waist and he gaped down in shock as he realized he had been so distracted in his haste to dress and chase after Catherine, he had neglected to bring along a weapon of any kind—a precautionary habit that had become as instinctive to him as eating or breathing during the past fifteen years. And looking down, he saw something else. A bright patch of color where there should have been only the drab brown and green of the hedgerow.

Alex bent down and clutched the dainty satin slipper in his fist, and again his eyes bored into the maze of trees and glittering slivers of sunlight. There was no movement, no sound. He pushed aside the bushes that bordered the path and almost missed it: a long, shiny thread of silver-blonde hair caught on a branch.

"Catherine—"

There was more. Freshly scuffed earth and the clear imprint of boots had left evidence of the struggle that had taken place before they had managed to quiet her. Alex whirled and ran back to the garden, shouting the alarm to the guards on the castle walls before he had even cleared the trees.

21

Struan MacSorley was just pacing himself toward the final rush of orgasm when he heard the alarm sound in the courtyard. His eyes bulged wide and he sucked in an enormous breath as he caught Lauren midstroke and tossed her summarily off his thighs. She gasped and scrambled blindly to reseat herself, but he was already off the cot, unmindful of his nudity or glaring tumescence as he took up his sword and flung himself out the door.

He was back less than a minute later.

"What is it?" she cried. "What's wrong?"

"Get yersel' dressed an' out o' here, lass," he ordered sharply. "There be Campbells on the land."

"Campbells? Here at Achnacarry? But how—"

"Are ye deif, woman? Dinna stan' there askin' daft questions." He flung himself on his tartan and rose seconds later fully covered. "I said get dressed. They'll be countin' heids in the great hall an' yers had best be among them—wi' all yer claythes *on*."

Lauren glanced down along her flushed and gleaming body. "Surely they havena come tae attack the castle? An' how did they get so far onto Cameron land?"

"The point is tae no' let them get off again—an' no' wi' Alasdair's wife."

"The *Sassenach*? They've taken the *Sassenach*?"

"Aye, that they have, sneakin' thievin' swines."

Lauren sank back against the wall, her eyes shimmering with the excitement that raced through her body.

She could scarcely believe it. She could scarcely believe it had happened so swiftly.

"Gie us a wee kiss f'ae luck, lass," MacSorley demanded, scooping her lustily into the circle of his arm. He was about to promise a finish to what they had begun, but halted when he saw the malicious little smile playing on her lips. "Here now, why d'ye look so pleased wi' yersel'?"

"Pleased?" She blinked and tried to concentrate on his craggy face. "I'm no' *pleased*, Struan MacSorley. But I'll no' lie by sayin' I'm sorry it were her they took instead o' . . . instead o' Lady Maura, f'ae instance. Or one o' the ithers. Or even *me*."

"Aye, well . . . the *Sassenach* is still a Cameron," he grumbled, "an' it shouldna be so easy tae lift her out o' the gardens."

"Nae wonder they took her there; it's where she spends most o' the day. She has naught tae do wi' anyone ither than tae peer at us down her long English nose an' laugh ahind our backs. Why, she thought I were a laundress the fairst day she were here. Told me so tae ma face, she did, an' me there tae lend her claythes an' welcome her tae the family. Welcome her, hah! She never wanted tae come tae Achnacarry; she were brung here against her will. Kidnapped, she was, an' used as hostage tae see Alasdair an' Aluinn through the patrols."

Struan's eyes narrowed. "What are ye talkin' about? What do ye mean she were brung against her will?"

"She didna come tae Achnacarry by choice," she repeated tersely. "She has neither a love f'ae Scotland nor a love f'ae Alasdair. She keeps a separate bed an' bars the door at night. I heard them fightin' the fairst night. I heard her talk about her *fiancé* back in England. A sojer! A lieutenant in the dragoons! She threatened tae send f'ae him, tae send f'ae her fancy sojer an' his whole regiment o' lobsterbacks if Alasdair didna let her go home!"

The wiry froth of Struan's beard split over an ugly

scowl and he gripped her tightly by the shoulders. "Ye're speakin' through yer teeth, woman. Why would he bring her here an' call her his wife if it werena true?"

"I dinna ken the answers, Struan, only more questions. Were I you, I'd be askin' them too. I'd be askin' how the sojers knew tae find them by the Spean. An' why did the *Sassenach* stop Alasdair from killin' Gordon Ross Campbell when he had the chance? I might even go so far as tae ask how the Campbells knew she'd be alone in the garden today, an' how they were able tae take her wi'out a sound in the full daylight."

"I dinna like what ye're sayin', lass," Struan hissed, his breath hot on her face.

"I dinna like the idea o' the pair o' ye ridin' out after her, wi' most o' the men still away wi' Lochiel an' scarcely a han'ful left tae chase after God only knows how many Campbells. I dinna like tae think it might be the *Sassenach*'s way o' winnin' her revenge, tae set a trap f'ac Alasdair an' turn him over tae Argyle."

He relaxed his grip and stepped back from the cot, his every instinct fighting against the ring of truth in her words. But the facts were there. Had he and Alex not spent the better part of two days negotiating passage back to England for the lass and her maid? Struan had not questioned his reasons and no explanations had been offered, but Alex had seemed almost relieved when the arrangements had been finalized—as if he could not wait to get his bride out of Scotland.

Something was not right, Struan admitted, but just what that was he couldn't say.

Lauren studied the changes in his expression intently. "Are ye thinkin' on Annie, yer own sweet sister deid these many years? Are ye thinkin' on what she would make o' such a shameless bed o' lies?"

"I'm thinkin'," he said evenly, "that ye'll wish it were you an' no' the *Sassenach* stolen by the Campbells if I hear ye've breathed one word o' this tae anyone else. *Anyone,* d'ye hear me?"

"Aye, Struan, I hear ye." Rising onto her knees, she pressed her moist, imploring lips over his. "Struan . . . dinna be angry wi' *me*. I couldna bear it if ye were angry wi' me f'ae speakin' the fear that were in ma heart."

His eyes lost some of their fierce glaze and his hands closed around her arms again, this time lifting her so that her mouth was crushed brutally against his. She clawed her fingers into his shoulders and matched the violence of his kiss, groaning as she did so.

"Ye will be careful, will ye no'?" she cried softly. "If it *is* a trap—"

"If it's a trap it will be sprung on the one who laid it. Now, get dressed. Lady Maura will be needin' ye."

Lauren watched him snatch up his blue woolen bonnet and set it on a slouching angle over the straw-colored hair. Without a glance he left her, his angry steps fading away on the cobblestones.

She released a long, pent-up breath and massaged the tender flesh of her upper arms, cursing him for the bruises that would be there come the morning. She did not particularly relish a lover with an unpredictable temper. A violent passion was one thing, threats of violence against her person were quite another.

Deep in thought, she dressed and slipped out of the guardhouse unnoticed. Instead of following instructions and making her way to the great hall, she veered toward the dingy, sooty structure that housed the castle smithy. There was no one working over the coal pit, no clang of hammer on anvil, and she moved on quiet feet through to the small chamber in the rear.

He was there, asleep in a curled fetal position, an empty jug of whisky cradled in his arms. Lauren stared at the thin, bony frame of the man and felt a shudder of revulsion ripple through her. She could scarcely believe she had let him crawl over her body or that she had allied herself with such a vile, foul-smelling creature. But it had been a necessary evil. Doobie Logan was the lowest form of life imaginable to a Highlander—a clansman who spied and informed on his own kin to their enemies. Logan was paid well by the Campbells to keep them abreast of the comings and goings at Achnacarry. Lauren had passed him the odd tidbit—like the decision to send young Iain Cameron to London to meet the *Camshroinaich Dubh*—and she had been paid *extremely* well, though the price Logan had demanded in turn for keeping her secret as a fellow conspirator had made her scrub her body raw afterward.

She approached the snoring figure, and her hand crept stealthily beneath her skirt. She experienced a cool shiver of gratification, almost sexual in nature, as she withdrew a wickedly sharp dirk from its hidden sheath and plunged it deeply, repeatedly, between the jutting plates of his shoulder blades.

Catherine did not regain consciousness until her kidnappers had carried her several miles away from Achnacarry. She was on horseback, supported roughly on the saddle by a bare-armed, barrel-chested Highlander who smelled abominably of old sweat and rotten teeth. The garron they shared was one of the short, stout ponies common to the mountainous reaches of Caledonia, but the animal's surefooted attack of the path they were on was no consolation for the view of the steep and jagged cliffs they were climbing.

There were three of them, one riding ahead, one behind. There was very little light left in the sky, only the post-sunset hues of murky purple and blue that distorted the shadows and made the ground they covered seem twice as ominous. The features of the man who rode in the lead were already distorted, but not by the shadows so much as by the beating he had taken beneath Alexander's fists. Catherine had never thought of Gordon Ross Campbell as a particularly handsome man, and now, with his nose flattened across the bridge, his teeth cracked off at the gums, and his eyes sunken in deep hollows, he looked simply ugly. He had not shaved in many days—possibly because of the gouges, cuts, and scabs that still showed through the dirty stubble. Whatever youth he had possessed—or pretended to possess—had vanished, and she would not have recognized him in the garden had it not been for the hatred blazing from the cold blue eyes.

The shock of seeing him at Achnacarry, of realizing too late she had dashed out of the castle without alerting any of the guards, had delayed the reflex to scream long enough for Campbell's filthy hand to clamp viciously over her mouth and smother it completely.

She had kicked and squirmed, her nails had torn at the flesh of his forearms, but he had simply dragged her through the hedge and whistled softly to the other two men lurking behind the trees. One of them carried a large burlap sack, and seeing it, Catherine had bitten the flesh of Campbell's palm so hard her mouth had filled with blood. But he had only grunted and brought his other fist down against the side of her head—once to break the hold of her teeth, a second time to knock her soundly unconscious.

They were moving very fast, with no thought to spare for their captive's comfort. They all rode with one hand on the reins, another on the muskets that rested warily over their hips. Who they were was apparent, where they were taking her was a matter of conjecture, and what they planned to do with her once they got there was something she did not care to contemplate. Obviously they had been watching the castle and knew Lochiel and most of his men were away. They had watched and waited, and she had presented them the perfect target for a quick raid—something she had been warned about time and again, though not that it could happen so close to the castle itself.

The shiver of apprehension that coursed through Catherine's body did not go unnoticed by her captor. He shouted something to Gordon Ross Campbell in Gaelic, and at the first reasonably wide ledge in the hazardous trail they were following, the young Campbell called a brief halt. He drew his horse alongside Catherine, and she tensed inwardly at the leer on his broken, battered face.

"An' so we meet again, Mrs. Cameron."

"Where are you taking me? Why are you doing this?"

His grin was little more than a dark, evil slash. "Where we're takin' ye is o' nae concern ither than f'ae ye tae behave well enough tae live tae see it."

"Alex will never let you get away with this. He will come after you."

"Aye, I'm prayin' he does. I'm countin' on him followin' us all the way tae Inverary, where there's a hangman's noose waitin' on him."

"And ten thousand gold crowns waiting for you?"

"That'll sweeten the pot some, I'll no' deny it. But then so will *you*, an' it'll be a fine choice I'll have tae make in the next wee while on whither I sell ye back tae the Camerons or back tae yer own kin. But here . . . I thought ye werena opposed tae the idea o' collectin' the reward yersel' at one time?" He narrowed his eyes and let them slide down to the firm thrust of her breasts. "Mayhap, if ye're nice tae me, I wouldna mind sparin' a few coins yer way."

"I would rather be nice to a ground slug," she said coldly. "As for your coins and what you can do with them—"

He laughed coarsely and leaned forward. He grabbed a fistful of her hair and jerked her forward, twisting her head painfully to one side. Her cry of pain opened her lips to the revolting feel of his mouth sucking wetly at hers, and she gagged; she brought her fists up and tried to beat him away, but the man in the saddle behind her chuckled lustily and caught them, dragging them painfully around to the small of her back.

Campbell had his fill and released her with another husky laugh. "God's teeth, ye're goin' tae be a worthy hellcat tae tame. Aye, an' if ye're good—or even if ye're na'—I'll pass ye 'round the rest o' the lads tae have a go."

The third rider edged closer, muttering something under his breath, and Catherine did not require a translation of the words to know he was questioning the need to wait any longer before they could have some fun. Campbell's eyes were on Catherine's face as he laughed and nodded, but before the debate could continue, their amusement was cut short by the sound of hoofbeats on the mountain path.

"It looks like they joined up wi' someone here," MacSorley said on a grunt, pointing to the impressions left on the cold ground. "Fifteen, mayhap twenty men in all."

He straightened and cast the light of the torch around the ledge, waiting calmly for Alexander Cameron to decide their next move. It had taken nearly an hour to assemble a dozen well-armed men and retrace the kidnappers' steps from the garden to the hills where the Campbells' horses had been concealed. By then the dusk was well upon them, and more precious time had slipped past as they were forced to move slowly and carefully over the well-worn trails that wound away into the hills. It might have been downright impossible to follow had it not been for the heavy rains that had washed away all but the most recent signs of traffic.

Alex swore under his breath. "Twenty men, you say?"

"Coincidence?" Aluinn stood beside him, his features illuminated by the flickering light of the torch. He had insisted on coming on the hunt, though after several hours of hard riding his shoulder was beginning to feel like a small torch burning all on its own.

"I stopped believing in coincidences a long time ago," Alex said grimly. "Gordon Ross Campbell said he had twenty men waiting for him across the Spean. *Goddammit!*"

"Don't crucify yourself. I had the same opportunity to kill him and I didn't take it."

Alex was not appeased. "For every five minutes we lose verifying their tracks, they gain fifteen on us. We'll never catch them this way, not at night."

"They're smart," Aluinn agreed. "They're keeping to the high ground, winding back and doubling around to confuse the trail. Struan—you know the lie of the land better than anyone else—have you any ideas?"

"Aye, I ken the land," MacSorley said after a lengthy pause. Lengthy enough to earn inquisitive glances from both men.

"And?"

"And . . . I wisna sure until the past hour, but ye ask me, I'd stake ma soul they're gonny cut through the mountains at Hell's Gate. It's the shortest route tae Inverary. Tae go around would cost them two, three days."

"They will never make it through the Gate at night!"

"Fast as they're goin', they'll be at the mouth o' the pass wi' an hour or two tae spare afore dawn. Slow as we're goin', they'll be through the pass an' dug in f'ae as fine an ambush as the devil himsel' could set afore we get there."

"Is there no other way over this bloody mountain?"

Even though it was dark and nothing much was visible in the night sky, all three men turned to stare up at the formidable wall of granite that reared up before them.

Struan weighed his words carefully before he answered. "Nae man could fault ye f'ae doin' as much as ye have already tae try an' fetch the lassie back."

Alex turned slowly to stare at the big Highlander. "Are you suggesting we give up and turn back?"

"I'm suggestin' . . . she's *Sassenach*. The Campbells willna harm her. Seems tae me ye could save yersel' a purseful o' gold by lettin' them send her back tae England f'ae ye."

Alexander's expression was unreadable in the shadows, but he appeared to hesitate, to start to turn away, and he did, but only a few degrees—the better to channel all of his strength and fury into the fist he drove upward into Struan's bearded jaw.

The giant staggered back a step, his head whipped violently to one side by the blow. His response was instinctive and deadly. His left arm lashed out to block a second punch while his right delivered a crushing blow to Alex's midsection, the power behind it lifting him up and hurling him several feet into the darkness. The frustration MacSorley had been harboring, the anger he had been feeling over his doubts and misgivings exploded on a curse, vibrating off the face of the rocks as he stalked after Cameron.

"Jesus! Struan! What the hell!" Aluinn tried to block his path, but a swing from the trunklike arm sent him sprawling facedown in the dirt.

Alex had regained his feet by then and lunged out of the shadows to meet the Highlander, the two of them coming together like enraged bulls. The torches were brought forward, but the shadows swallowed them time and again, leaving the stunned onlookers with only the thud of fists on flesh to mark the action. Grunts and curses punctuated the scuffle of feet; flying pebbles and clouds of dust were left roiling in their wake as the two men grappled together, the smell of sweat and rage steaming the air between them.

Aluinn staggered to his feet, shouting at the rest of the men, and it took three of them to pin Alex to the rocks, seven of them pulling and pushing at Struan to stop his forward momentum.

"Goddammit!" A frankly astounded Aluinn MacKail stepped into the swirl of choking dust and cradled a hand over his bruised jaw. "What the bloody hell is going on here? Struan? Alex?"

Alex strained against the men who were holding him and spat out a bloodied chip of a tooth along with an indecipherable curse.

Struan surged forward, dragging his keepers with him

as if they were mere annoyances hanging off his arms and limbs.

"I said *enough*!" Aluinn drew his pistol. "The next bastard who moves is going to earn an ounce of lead for his trouble!"

Both men tested their restraints a moment longer before grudgingly shaking them off.

"Now, then: Struan, you seem to have something on your mind. Would you care to say it in plainer words that we can all understand?"

"There are some things what need explainin'—"

"Explanations?" Alex erupted savagely. "I don't owe you or anyone else any damned explanations!"

"*Alex!* Leash that goddamned temper of yours for one minute and hear what he has to say. Struan, you say you want explanations. For what?"

"F'ae what we're doin' out here in the middle o' the night."

"We've come to take back Alex's wife, for God's sake. Why does that need explaining?"

Struan spat out a wad of bloody spittle. "*Is* she his wife?"

"*What?*"

"Is she his wife?" Struan demanded. "Is the lass here by her own choice, or was she brung tae Achnacarry against her will?"

Alex surged forward again, but Aluinn straight-armed the gun, aiming at his chest to pull him up short. With one eye on Cameron, he glanced at Struan. "Now *you* had better explain."

"I were told the *Sassenach* didna come tae Achnacarry o' her own free will. I was wi' him when he spent two days an' half a thousan' in gold tryin' tae find a ship tae carry her home. We're out here in the middle o' the night walkin' smack intae a trap that couldna be set nor sprung wi'out help from somewhere. . . ." He paused and his chest heaved with repressed emotions. "It has tae be asked, an' it has tae be answered: Is the lass yer wife or

no'? *Is she a Cameron . . . or has she gone willingly wi'
the Campbells?*"

Alex was so stunned by the question, it drained the
remaining fight from his body. "Struan, for the love of—"

"Answer him, Alex," Aluinn said abruptly, his voice
as cold and level as the gun he still held between them.
He saw the question in Alex's eyes as they turned to him,
but he could also see, where Alex could not, the taut
expressions on the faces of the other wary clansmen.
They knew MacSorley would not dare make such an
accusation unless there was some doubt, some basis for
suspicion. "Answer him," he said again, softer this time.
"Unless you are not sure of the truth yourself."

Alex's dark gaze turned to Struan. He remembered, as
clearly as if it had happened yesterday, the big Highlander coming into the stables one night, catching him
and Annie together in a tangle of naked limbs and panted
caresses. Struan had drawn his knife with every intention
of gelding Alex, despite the fact that he was Lochiel's
brother, and despite the fact that the burly guardsman
completed the handsome threesome of Cameron,
MacKail, and MacSorley when there was brawling to be
done and whores to be tupped. Tupping Struan's sister
was quite a different thing, and Alex had seen his life
flash before him in the gleam of a bone-handled dirk. But
he had stood his ground and faced his giant friend
calmly. He had told Struan that he and Annie were handfasted, that they loved each other as purely and honestly
as any man and wife, and that the only reason they had
not pledged their vows before an altar yet was that Annie
had been too terrified of her brother's reaction to seek his
permission before she came of legal age the following
spring.

He also remembered that it had been Struan, and only
Struan, who had been able to coax Annie's lifeless body
out of his arms. And it had been Struan who had held him
like a baby and wept with him over their loss.

"Catherine and I were married three weeks ago in

Derby," he said, looking directly into the Highlander's eyes. "And you are right, she did not want to come to Scotland. For that matter she did not want to marry me, nor I her, but we were forced by circumstances to oblige. Yes, I brought her with us to help us get through the patrols, and yes, she tried her damnedest to foil us every step of the way ... but somewhere between then and now—and I'm damned if I know when or how it happened—we stopped fighting one another." He paused and wiped at a trickle of blood leaking from his lip. "She told me today that whether I liked it or not, whether I wanted her or not, she was going to stay here at Achnacarry as my wife, my lover, and as the mother of my children. I heard her say that and"—he looked down at his bloodied, scraped hands—"a part of me came back to life. A part I thought I had buried fifteen years ago." He looked up again and shook his head with the helplessness of it all. "I loved Annie, Struan. I always will. I would have gladly given my own life to save hers or bring her back, but I couldn't. And now ... it's happening again, and I can't stand by and let anything happen to Catherine, not even if I have to fight my way to Inverary myself."

MacSorley's gaze had not wavered from Alex's face since he had started speaking; it did not waver now as he clenched his fists and walked slowly forward. He stopped close enough for some of the long bristles on his beard to touch the other man's chest ... then reached forward and grasped him by the upper arms. "Ye've told me more than I deserved tae hear. Aye, we'll catch the bastards long afore they ever get a whiff o' Argyle air. An' ye'll no' have tae fight alone, no' while there's a breath left in ma body."

Alex clasped MacSorley's arms, and the tension in the torchlit circle drained visibly as the two men hugged and clapped each other soundly on the shoulders.

"Does this mean you *do* know of another way across

the mountain?" Aluinn asked lightly, resheathing his pistol.

"Aye." MacSorley grunted. "I ken a way only the goats are daft enough tae use, an' then only if the devil has their balls atween his teeth."

Alex and Aluinn both noted the glances the other clansmen exchanged. The desolate range of mountains they were attempting to cross was shrouded in superstition, believed to have been thrown down to earth on a day when the Creator had been in a rage. Hell's Gate, a narrow pass aptly named for its sheer drops and torturously steep corries, was the only way across that anyone knew of within a ten-mile stretch in either direction.

"Can you take us through by night?"

"Better at night," Struan said without guile. "Then ye canna see where ye're goin'. Mind, f'ae his trouble, the madman who takes it will be waitin' on the ither side o' Hell when the Campbells ride through."

Alex glanced at Aluinn, who only shrugged and passed the decision back to him.

"All right. We'll do it."

Guessing that some of the men might not be especially eager to take the additional risk, he suggested asking for several volunteers to remain on the Campbells' trail, hopefully getting close enough to them by morning to keep them from suspecting they were no longer being followed.

But there were no such volunteers forthcoming. In the end, four men had to be chosen—choices that seemed random at first, but a closer scrutiny revealed them to be the four with the largest families and most number of dependents waiting for them at home.

Catherine was faint from cold and terror. The trail they were following had deteriorated to hardly more than a sheep track and had descended into a narrow gorge devoid of any living thing as far as she could see beyond the flickering torchlight. Even the sturdy little garrons

balked at the sight of the bleached spines of trees leering
out of the darkness and the jagged projections of rock
that suddenly thrust forth from the shadows. Catherine
even thought she detected a genuine sigh of relief from
the man whose horse she shared when Gordon Ross
Campbell gave the signal to halt for the night.

The animals were staked around the stump of a
gnarled old tree but remained saddled. The torches were
doused, the rations limited to a couple of unleavened oat-
meal biscuits and a mouthful of sour water. No one
thought to provide Catherine with a blanket or a length of
tartan. Her body ached from an untold number of bruises,
and her temples throbbed with an appalling rhythm all
their own. She gingerly tested the lump on the side of her
head, just above her ear, where Campbell's fist had
silenced her. The skin had been broken, and her hair and
cheek were crusted with old blood that had left muddy,
sticky streaks down her neck.

The moon was a crescent-shaped sliver rising over the
top of the mountain peak like a scythe. Stars hung suspended by the millions, but the light they shed did little
to alleviate the sinister shapes and shadows that distorted
the landscape. She was glad she could not see more than
a dozen or so paces in any direction, and as she edged her
way around the large boulder they had dumped her
beside, she hoped the Argylemen were as blinded by the
darkness and as disoriented as she was.

The rough stone scraped her hands and wrists as she
felt her way around the boulder. She had lost her other
slipper somewhere along the way, and the ground was
littered with sharp pebbles that cut into the bare sole of
her foot. She kept moving, inch by inch, keeping the
stone at her back, moving away from the circle of
arguing men. They were arguing over her, she imagined,
arguing the order of succession. Catherine's hope for a
speedy rescue had died when the three men had been
joined by the larger force on the hillside, as had any
chance of her being able to reason her way into being

delivered unharmed to the Duke of Argyle. One of the newcomers in particular stared at her as if she were fresh meat set before a pack of wolves. He was big and reeked of unclean body parts.

Even if Alex had come after her, even if he was within reach, what could he do against so many? Lochiel had left a skeleton guard at Achnacarry; the most-experienced fighters had gone with him to Arisaig. But even if Alex had a hundred skilled troops with him, how could he possibly follow or hope to find her in the pitch blackness?

Catherine reached the far side of the boulder and groped at the darkness that lay beyond. She kept her eyes and ears trained on the guttural voices nearby, and her panic mushroomed when she heard Gordon Ross Campbell's laugh rise above the others. He was asking for her, demanding the prisoner be brought to him; it was a matter of mere seconds before they would discover her missing.

Catherine leaned farther out, but her hand found nothing to grasp but air. She heard the scratch of tinder on flint and guessed that a torch was being lit that they all might watch the coming amusement; she had seconds, fractions of seconds, to find a path and hide herself away in one of the hundreds of fissures that riddled the walls of the gorge.

Taking a desperate chance, she pushed away from the boulder and ran into the blackest part of the shadows. She ran with her arms outstretched, and one of them smashed painfully into stone, bringing the sting of tears to her eyes. She forced them back and kept running, kept scraping her way from rock to rock, tumbling and twisting as the cold stone teeth bit into her feet, her legs, her arms. Her skirt snagged on an outcrop and she cried out as she was jerked to an abrupt stop, halted long enough to hear angry shouts of pursuit from behind. She tore at the folds of linen and ran forward again, managing to stumble only a few feet before she felt hands reaching out to grab her. Flung sideways in the darkness, she lost her balance and went down hard, her head cracking against the rough stone, the pain exploding across her temples moments before she was plunged into a black void of unconsciousness.

The pass Struan led them to was not much more than a crevice slashed between two mighty spirals of contorted and overlapped rock that rose hundreds of feet into the sky above them. The entrance to it was covered with brambles and thorn bushes so that in daylight, from more than a score of paces away, it appeared to be a sheer cliff of unbroken stone. As it was, in the darkness, it took MacSorley over an hour to hack his way through the undergrowth and locate the opening.

The chasm was just wide enough to accommodate the breadth of a horse's flanks. Shadow, by far the largest of the animals, balked at the entrance, his nostrils dilating, his muscles quivering with undisguised fear. Alex stroked the gleaming neck and soothed the stallion as best he could, but even he had to fight back a strong and intense revulsion to the idea of entering the black maw. Struan's torch threw ghostly illumination off the slime-covered rock overhead; the air became thick with smoke and made the men's eyes water until the ceiling lifted and a draft sucked the fumes upward. Then there came an even more terrifying assault on the senses: Thousands of bats began to screech and scream and stir the air into a black boil of stinging wings.

Alex kept Shadow moving forward, kept his eyes fastened on the flare of Struan's torch ahead of him. His knees were scraped raw on the walls of stone, and he did not want to think of what might happen should the torches fail or the horses become stuck, or the mountains shift suddenly and crush the jaws of the trap closed. His eyes were burning from the smoke and his ears rang from the high-pitched shrilling of the bats. He did not turn around to see if the next man in line was faring any better, for his own nerves would not bear too much more pressure before they snapped and he screamed as loud as the bats.

Fifty yards into the bowels of the mountain, a chilled, wailing wind forced each rider to lower his head to protect his eyes from flying bits of dirt and grit. The flames of the torches streaked straight back, and Alex followed Struan's example and held his tartan up to protect the light. He found that he was holding his breath; his skin was clammy and cold, and there was an uncontrollable urge to void his bladder, like a child caught in the grip of some unimaginable nightmare.

One hundred yards . . . two hundred yards . . . and the men's brains began to feel as if they might explode from the pressure. Two of the four torches had been snuffed, and the men shouted back and forth, encouraging each other, encouraging the petrified animals.

Three hundred yards into the howling chasm and the walls began to relent. The wind stopped as abruptly as it had started, and although any exposed skin still felt as if it was being whipped and sliced into bloody strips, the men could sit straighter in the saddles and ease the terrible strain on their spines.

Alex wiped the streaming moisture from his eyes and saw that they were entering a chamber of sorts, an oval cavern hollowed out of the rock, twenty paces across by perhaps forty paces in length. In the middle was a still, glasslike pool of water. Huddled around the rim was a silent audience of gruesomely emaciated stone pillars, some so lifelike in size and shape that they appeared to shuffle uncomfortably in the glow of the torchlight. Some boasted faces hewn out of the rock, grizzly distortions of half-rotted noses and sunken eye sockets.

"A hellish sight, is it no'?" Struan whispered. "Legend claims these are the men turned tae stone by the dark gods f'ae their lack o' courage."

Alex glanced at MacSorley and was mildly surprised

to see the same fat beads of moisture shining on the soot-stained brow as he felt dripping off his own.

"Hellish indeed. How do we get out of here?"

There were cracks in the walls of the cavern every few feet, none of them seeming wide enough to afford an exit.

Struan relit the doused torches and grinned easily as he led the way toward one of the fissures on the far side of the pool. As he passed between two of the stalagmites, he reached out and patted one of them on what might have been an incredibly well-endowed bosom.

"Take heed o' Beulah the Bitch if ye ever need come this way again. Mind ye gie her a wee pat on the teat f'ae lettin' ye go through. She'll remember if ye dinna an' she'll change the stones on ye out o' spite."

Alex had no reservations whatsoever about leaning over and caressing the rough stone breasts. Each man in line did likewise until the last one was swallowed into the vastness of the mountain tomb again.

22

When the sun poked its bloodshot eye over the horizon, the Cameron clansmen were in position at the southern exit of Hell's Gate. They had ridden most of the night, but true to MacSorley's promise they were settled into a perfect ambuscade where the Campbells would least expect to find them. Alexander, Aluinn, and MacSorley waited out the dawn at the mouth of the pass, keeping sharp eyes on the distant column of men as they coaxed their reluctant animals through the last half mile of treacherously broken terrain. Campbell had wisely chosen not to attempt the Gate at night and their encampment had been invisible in the darkness, but as the sky began to spill color down the side of the mountain, the tiny figures could be seen moving through the rock and bracken. The gorge, heavily pocketed with mist, was below them; three keen pairs of eyes were above.

Alex stared hard at each horse and rider as they moved closer, and he noticed the bright splash of yellow hair at almost the same instant as Aluinn's finger jabbed out over the boulder.

"There," Aluinn spat. "Right in the middle."

"I see her," Alex murmured. The relief he had expected to feel on seeing Catherine alive and relatively safe did not accompany his nod. Instead, he felt an annoying, itching sensation at the back of his neck, as if there was something more down there he should be seeing but was not. The closer they came, the more persistent the itching grew; his nerves tautened and his instincts were screaming at him to look . . . *look!* . . . but whatever he was supposed to see eluded him.

He glanced at Struan and saw that the big Highlander had stiffened as well, like a wolfhound catching the scent of fresh blood. What was it? What was it they both sensed but could not identify? Something was out there, something deadly and dangerous and evil.

"Good God," Aluinn whispered.

Alex saw him then. Second in line in the column, sitting fat and squat on a pony whose back and belly sagged beneath the bulk of the man. Half of his face looked human enough under the cocked blue bonnet, but the other half had the texture and appearance of lava spewed from some demonic volcano, left to cool around the distorted crater of an eyeless socket. His nose was a misshapen mass of darkly pigmented skin, split with spidery red veins. His hair was greasy and parted around a diagonal welt of a scar that ran from the crown of his head to the hollow of his throat. His arms were so thick they were held away from the trunk of his body; his legs were like tree stumps, the flesh as scarred and ridged as bark where it showed between the hem of his kilt and the top of his hose.

"Where the bloody Christ did he come from?" Aluinn asked through the grate of his teeth.

Alex could not answer past the smothering constriction in his throat. A wave of hatred, black and burning like acid, boiled up from some hidden depth of his soul, flushing through his blood and cramping the muscles in his belly and thighs.

"Malcolm Campbell." The name was squeezed through taut white lips. "I should have known. He never would have trusted such a prize to another man, bastard son or not."

As if Campbell heard the words spoken out loud, he jerked on the reins of his horse and called an abrupt halt to the forward motion of the column. The single reptilian eye narrowed, almost disappearing into the porous folds of skin.

He has picked up the scent too, Alex thought with malicious pleasure. He's feeling it crawl along his skin, but he doesn't know what it is, or where it's coming from.

Gordon Ross Campbell edged his horse alongside his father's.

"Sum'mit smells wrong here," Malcolm snarled, his voice like the sound of two marble slabs grinding together.

Gordon Ross studied the formidably steep peaks of the surrounding mountains, but sensed nothing other than the desolation of barren rock.

"Are ye certain there's nae ither way around?"

"No' unless a man sprouts wings an' flies," Gordon Ross said confidently. "Asides, they canna be in two places at the once."

Malcolm Campbell kept his eye trained on the shadows and corries even as he grunted in grudging agreement. The men they had left in the rear had reported seeing the Cameron trackers closing on their heels—a remarkable feat in itself, all things considered. To think they could have somehow passed them in the night did not even warrant the flattery.

He had to think it was just the sweet taste of revenge that was starting the glands in his mouth watering. It was likely just the anticipation of finally confronting his hated enemy after all these years that had the sweat squeaking between the leather of his saddle and the flesh of his bare thighs.

The great *Camshroinaich Dubh* within his grasp at last! A legend—*faugh!* He, Malcolm Campbell, would be the legend before this day was through. He was already a minor miracle, was he not, for having survived a wound that would have killed any other mere mortal. Cameron's sword had hacked the flesh from the bone, tearing half his face away and severing the muscles from the left side of his chest. A clansman had roughly stitched the gaping flaps of gristle back in place as a courtesy to his family, but they had dug three graves that day, carved three names into the stone cairn laid to mark his fallen brothers, Angus and Dughall. Through it all, through the shock and the fever and the infections, through the weeks of delirium, only one thought had kept Malcolm Campbell alive: *Revenge.* He had nurtured that same hatred, that same desire for retribution in his son, and together, by God, they had done it. Before the day was through they would have their victory. They would have the head of the *Camshroinaich Dubh* and the fear of every Cameron who believed their legendary prodigal to be invincible. It only remained to get through the pass and position themselves on the other side of the granite wall, to settle in and wait for the mighty Alexander Cameron to ride into their swords.

A quarter mile away, Alex thought he detected a smile on the cruel, twisted lips. MacSorley touched him on the shoulder, beckoning him away from the rocks, and the three men raced back through the narrow gulley to where their horses were tethered. They galloped down the rutted slope, stopping several hundred yards beyond a wide avenue carved into the rock and scrub. It was the perfect spot for an ambush. Where the trail cut through the tumbled boulders, it was just wide enough for two men to ride abreast. The banks on either side were chest high and covered with a wild hedgerow tall enough and thick enough to conceal a man. The overall gloom—if the sun obliged by delaying its appearance into the world from behind the slow-moving bank of clouds overhead— would make discovery unlikely until the full troop of Campbell's men was bottled in the avenue.

Knowing this was undoubtedly the same place Malcolm Campbell would have chosen to set up his own ambush, Alex took particularly primitive delight in the loading and priming of his steel-butted dags. Aluinn was hunkered down beside him, gently massaging his stiffened shoulder, his gray eyes calmly watching without comment as the paper cartridges were torn open and measures of black powder poured into each barrel. The actions of the long, lean fingers were steady and precise—almost loving—as if the man tamping down the wadding and balls knew exactly where each solid round of lead shot would be placed.

"There are twenty-five of them," MacKail remarked dryly. "Only eight of us."

"Aye, well," Struan commented from behind, "they're only Campbells. We have tae gie 'em some kind o' advantage, else they'll run off bleatin' like stuck pigs."

Aluinn crooked an eyebrow. "Still, it wouldn't hurt to have a man up higher in the rocks with spare rounds of ball and powder. We will have only a few seconds of surprise wherein every shot will have to count."

Struan chuckled grimly. "Dinna fret yersel'. I've a wee surprise already planned f'ae those deservin' o' a quick an' painless death. Mind, there are ithers who warrant nae such mercy."

Alex stared at the battered face, knowing his own was hardly in better shape. "Malcolm Campbell is mine," he said quietly. "I am still holding you to your bond."

MacSorley's eyes narrowed. It had nearly killed him fifteen years ago to pledge on his honor not to hunt Malcolm Campbell down like the dog he was and finish the job Alex had started. A score of times he had sucked the last drop out of a whisky jug and staggered off in search of vengeance only to turn back, cursing his own words. But making that pledge had been the only way he could coax Alex to relinquish Annie's small, lifeless body after a ten-hour vigil that had bordered on madness.

"Aye, lad. I made ye that promise. An' he's yers . . . but I'll be directly ahind ye, tae be sure he disna cheat Auld Hornie again."

"Fair enough. Aluinn—" Alex turned to MacKail. "As

soon as the first man falls, they'll know it's a trap and they'll be turning their guns on Catherine."

Aluinn nodded. "I'll get to her first, don't worry."

"Aye," Struan grunted. "An' I'll be directly up *yer* arse as well, count on it."

A shrill whistle from the lookout warned the men of Campbell's approach.

Forcing his mind to go completely blank, Alex ducked into position. He placed his musket beside him on the rocks and checked to make sure his sword was belted securely around his waist. He waited, both pistols cocked and ready, and out of the corner of his eye he could see the other clansmen crouched in their places, not a muscle or hair twitching to betray their presence. Every instinct was tuned to the stillness of the air, every breath was held lest a rising puff of mist betray them.

The first of the riders entered the cloistered avenue, the slow, plodding hoofbeats echoing off the hard ground. Alex raised both pistols and curled his fingers around the triggers. He waited until the flanks of the lead horses were directly in line with his barrels before he leaped to his feet and discharged both flintlocks point-blank into the startled faces of the Campbell clansmen.

They were not the faces he wanted to see, but Alex did not stop to question the whereabouts of Malcolm or Gordon Ross Campbell. He flung the empty pistols aside and snatched up his musket, remembering to suck in his breath and brace himself for the tremendous recoil of the Highland firing piece as he pulled the trigger. The cloud of smoke from the exploding powder stung him blind for a few precious seconds, but by then he had also discarded the musket—it would take far too long to reload—and was leaping down from his perch on the rocks, his sword flashing in his hand.

His throat vibrated with the roar of a battle cry as old and savage as his Highland ancestry. All along the curve of the avenue the *cath-ghairm* was echoed as his men flung themselves out of the cover of the bushes and met

their enemies head-on. The first volley of gunshots had
been effective—half of Campbell's men lay either dead
or dying beneath the panicked frenzy of horses' hooves.
From the rear of the avenue, high on the rocks, came
Struan's surprise: a steady stream of wickedly barbed
arrows that proved to be deadly efficient in adding to the
carnage of writhing bodies and thrashing horses.

Alex slashed his sword across the saddle of the next
man in line, cleanly severing an arm at the elbow. The
man's sword, with his hand still gripped around the hilt,
flew off into the rocks, spattering them red with blood.
A second slash went to MacSorley's aid, relieving the
man—who was about to shoot the Highlander—of both
his pistol and his life.

"I'm that glad tae see ye've no' forgotten how tae fight!"
MacSorley roared, baring his teeth with fearsome glee as
his *clai'mor* split open the skull of an Argyleman. "But I'd
no' be worryin' so much on ma back as on yer own!"

Alex whirled and lunged out of the way only moments
before a terrified horse bolted past him. He had barely
regained his balance when a second animal thundered
toward him, this one driven by a screaming, sword-
wielding Campbell. He ducked as the blade hacked down
in an arc across his shoulders, and was never certain if it
was his own sword that brought his attacker crashing to
the ground or the well-placed arrow that skewered
cleanly through the man's throat.

Alex dashed a hand across his brow to keep the sweat
from rolling into his eyes. He vaulted over two writhing
bodies and ran down the avenue. No more than a minute
had passed since the first shots had been fired, but
already the ground was red underfoot, the air was choked
with dust and acrid smoke. Horses were rearing and
blocking the lane in their confusion, their screams adding
to the general chaos that had erupted. He saw a flash of
yellow hair up ahead and pumped his legs faster, but a
sword came at him from nowhere and he spun into the
rocks, his blood splashing the stone as he turned.

* * *

When the shooting began, Catherine was trapped in the middle of the column. She felt the arms of her captor go limp as a carefully placed shot tore away the back of his skull. As he slumped forward she pushed him to the side to free the saddle, but his foot caught in the stirrup and he hung grotesquely over her thigh. Too terrified to stop and think what she was doing, she leaned over and began to tug and pry at the stuck foot. It would not budge, and the dead weight was beginning to pull her off balance when a pair of strong, lean hands came to her rescue. Aluinn freed the foot and shoved the body off the pony, but before he could give Catherine more than a brief smile of reassurance, he was turning away, reacting to her screamed warning.

Aluinn spun like a dancer, his sword flashing as he brought it up to block a thrust from Gordon Ross Campbell's *clai'mor*. Campbell's blow was deflected with a sharp ringing of steel, but since his weapon was much heavier than the elegantly thin saber, he lost valuable seconds recovering his momentum to strike again. Aluinn's cut was faster, his blade slicing across the younger man's throat before he could finish screaming the Campbell *cath-ghairm*.

Catherine's pony shied from the spray of warm blood, and she scrambled to hold on to the reins, to keep her seat as he reared and pawed the air. A hoof flayed wildly in Aluinn's direction, catching his shoulder in the same place the bullet had torn through the flesh. He fell back, his lips frozen around a cry of agony, and staggered heavily to his knees, his hand clutching at the wounded shoulder.

Catherine wheeled the horse around and managed to slip out of the saddle before the animal bolted into the clashing mêlée of swords. She ran to Aluinn's side, but he was beyond movement, beyond feeling or knowing anything apart from the blinding pain in his shoulder. He did not feel the slender arms circle his chest and try to help him to his feet; he did not see her spin away or hear her strangled cry as a pair of trunklike arms reached down and dragged her up onto the back of yet another short, stout garron.

Malcolm Campbell wrapped his arm tightly around her waist and thrust the snout of his pistol sharply up beneath the curve of her chin. His first thought was to kill her then and there, but he knew the moment he did so he would have no leverage against the stinging flights of arrows or the slashing swords. As he watched the last of his men fall to the ground beneath the Cameron onslaught, his anger rose in his throat. Images flashed in disjointed sequences across his mind—a stable turned from one moment to the next into a bloody battleground; his brothers Angus and Dughall split open and spilling their guts on the straw; his own hideous wounds; the first time he had dared look into a mirror . . .

He roared again, and this time there was an answer.

"It's over, Campbell! Let her go!"

Malcolm's head swiveled in the direction of the hated voice. It was him. It was the black-eyed devil responsible for his pain, his disfigurement, his *humiliation*!

"Cameron, ye *bastard*!" He screamed and cocked the hammer of the flintlock. "I'll kill her! So help me Christ, I'll kill her here where ye can watch her brains fly up tae feed the bluidy ravens!"

Catherine squeezed her eyes shut as she felt the nose of the pistol dig deeper into her throat. She had a hand clawed around his forearm, but it was like trying to scratch stone. Her other hand groped instinctively to maintain her balance, and her fingers struck cold metal. It took a moment for her to absorb and identify the shape— it was the hilt of a knife Campbell wore tucked into the top of his hose.

"Let her go," Alex repeated calmly, evenly. "This is between you and me. It always has been."

"If that's so, then yer men will listen when ye tell them tae put their weapons down an' move away back."

One by one the Cameron clansmen looked to Alex for direction, and one by one they dropped their weapons and slowly shifted back against the rocks. Campbell watched them, alert for any sudden movement, and then his single rat eye flicked down to where the body of his son lay sprawled and still twitching on the blood-slicked mud.

"Ye've just added tae the price ye'll be payin', Cameron," he hissed. "Ye've added tae it twofold."

The midnight eyes did not waver from Campbell's face. Ignoring the snarled threat, he directed his words, soft and low, toward the pale and trembling figure of his wife.

"It's all right, Catherine, I'm here. Don't be afraid; it's almost over."

She opened her eyes, but her head was tilted at an impossible angle that allowed only a view straight up into the sky.

"Alex?" she gasped.

"I'm here, love. I'm right here."

Campbell's voice echoed with fifteen years of seething hatred. "I must gi'e ye credit f'ae yer taste in lassies, Cameron. This one was just as sweet an' soft as the ither. Aye, sweet an' wet an' bonnie enough tae please most o' ma men, though I foun' I had tae take her twice afore she stopped squirmin' long enough tae take all the seed I gave her. A pity we had tae teach her manners, but the cuts an' bruises were well-earned. She's a rare hellcat, as ye must know."

Catherine tried to turn her head to see Alex's face, but the muzzle of the gun prevented it. She tried to call out to him, but could not manage more than a dry gasp past the terrible, aching pressure across her throat. Above her the clouds were drifting away from the sun. In a few moments it would burst free. She curled her fingers tighter around the hilt of the dirk and prayed the sunlight would blind her to the final pain.

Campbell grinned and nudged his heels into the garron's flanks, easing the animal away from the avenue and back up toward the mouth of the pass. Alex followed, step by rigid step, his hand clenched around the hilt of his sword so tightly the veins rose along his forearms like blue snakes.

Campbell waited until the last possible second, luring his enemy far enough away from his men so that his escape would be only a matter of a few galloped strides into the pass. When he judged Alex's position and patience to be at their limit, he brought the pistol down from Catherine's neck and aimed it toward the Highlander's massive chest.

At the same instant the sun broke from behind the foaming white clouds and Catherine jerked her hand up, bringing the sharp little stiletto with it. Alex saw her hand move, and the cold shock of seeing the dirk clutched in her fist, coupled with the colder shock of realizing what she was about to do, brought forth a violent roar of fury from his throat. He launched himself forward just as Campbell pulled the trigger.

The horse reared as the gun discharged inches from his ear. Catherine slipped sideways and her aim missed . . . but so did Malcolm Campbell's. Cursing, he flung the empty gun to the ground and kicked the horse in the direction of the pass, but Alex was by his side in three long strides, his fists catching the saddlecloth and hauling it back. Campbell's arm was still around Catherine's waist and she started to slash at it with the knife. She heard another loud curse explode in her ear, and the next thing she knew she was being shoved to one side and thrown to the ground, her fall breaking the grip Alex had on the saddlecloth.

The pony responded at once to Campbell's furious commands and galloped up the hill, but before they had covered more than ten paces an arrow struck the animal's neck, just behind the hard bone of the skull. Horse and rider went down hard in a crush of flailing legs. Campbell was thrown clear and did not attempt to stop his fall, but rolled with it so that he was on his feet and running as the next arrow ricocheted harmlessly off the rocks beside him. He retrieved his broadsword and threw himself into the mouth of Hell's Gate, mindful of the pounding steps that pursued him into the gloomy chasm.

Crouched low and drawing on every fiber of speed and muscle in his powerful legs, Alex hurled himself through the air like a human catapult. He caught Campbell by the shoulders, and together they slammed into the jagged face of the stone wall. Alex's arm was scraped bloody to the elbow as Campbell's bulk trapped him momentarily against the rock, and seeing his enemy down, Campbell raised his sword and turned, roaring obscenities as he carved a glittering arc through the air.

Alex rolled to one side with a hair's breadth to spare as the blade missed his throat and clanged loudly on the cold stone. He avoided a second windmilling slash and was forced to retreat out into the sunlight, only then discovering he had lost hold of his saber in the mad charge. Campbell came after him, his broadsword raised and clenched in both hairy fists.

A bright sliver of steel came stinging through the air and stuck in the hard ground inches from Alex's foot. He heard a bellow from over his shoulder and recognized MacSorley's enormous *clai'mor*, but he had no time to shout his thanks as Campbell screamed in for the kill. Grasping the five-foot length of bloodied steel, Alex pulled it free and raised it, barely in time to block the jarring impact of a direct strike. There was no finesse, no grace involved in dueling with the heavy weapons; power and brute strength were all that mattered, and a man drunk on the scent of blood was far more dangerous than a man defending his skill and reputation. Alex had forgotten more than he cared to admit about the tremendous weight and awkward balance of the Highland weapon, and he paid for his ignorance with two successive slices across his ribs and shoulder.

Sensing the weakness in his adversary, Campbell grinned malevolently and pressed forward, advancing

with a killer's bloodlust to slash at an arm, a thigh, the
exposed belly and neck . . .

Alex staggered back from the force of the attack, his
breath labored and dry, burning along his throat,
scorching into his lungs. He felt the sword slip in the
wetness of his palms, twisted loose on a wrenching blow
that left his fingers and arm numb from the recoil. He
grasped the hilt in both hands and swung with all his
might, but Campbell was fast, despite his bulk. Steel
scraped on steel as their blades crossed, and for a long
moment the two men stood face to face, eye to eye, the
muscles in their arms bulging, their sweat and blood
splashing each other.

In a sudden downward lunge, Alex canted his blade
forward, breaking the tension in Campbell's wrists and
trapping the edge of Malcolm's sword in the ornate
scrollwork of MacSorley's finely wrought basket hilt.
He forced the blade down and turned it inward, feeling it
bite through hard flesh as he dragged it up and along the
straining muscle of Campbell's inner thigh. He heard
Campbell scream and felt the hot spurt of blood as an
artery was severed; at the same time he released his hold
on the *clai'mor* and brought his dirk up hard and fast,
thrusting it deep into the stubbornly beating muscle of
Campbell's heart.

Campbell slumped forward, his single eye gaping in
outraged disbelief as he stared down at the handle of the
knife protruding from his chest. His hands clawed
upward and curled around Alex's throat, but there was no
strength left in the fingers to do more than score a few
bloody scratches into the side of Cameron's neck.

Alex supported the sagging weight of his enemy long
enough to hiss a curse in his ear, then shrugged it aside
and stepped back, his chest heaving, his hands red and
dripping. A soft cry from behind made him tear his eyes
away from the bulbous corpse, and he turned in time to
catch the slender body that came running up the slope
behind him.

Catherine threw herself into his outstretched arms, weeping his name over and over and sobbing a great wet patch onto the front of his shirt.

He stroked the blonde silk of her hair and closed his eyes, gathering her close enough to feel her heart beating against his own. "It's over," he promised her. "It's all over."

"I was so frightened." She buried her head deeper into the curve of his shoulder. "I was so frightened you wouldn't come."

"Wouldn't come?" His hands cradled her face and tried unsuccessfully to tip it up to his.

"I thought . . . I thought you would not want me back," she sobbed, her words muffled against his throat.

He let her hide there a moment longer, then angled her face upward in strong, sure hands, and pressed his lips over hers. "Well, now you know better."

Aluinn came up beside them. He was holding his shoulder and gently massaging the wounded flesh, but when he looked at Alex and Catherine a smile broke through the gray mask of pain. "It's about bloody time you two acted like man and wife."

Alex ended the kiss on a sigh. "She's stubborn, for a *Sassenach*."

"And he's extraordinarily obstinate and proud, even for a Highland barbarian," Catherine responded, her face turning into his throat again.

"You will hear no arguments from me," Aluinn said, "on either count."

Both men sobered and looked down at the sprawled form of Malcolm Campbell.

"All these years," Alex murmured. "He's been like a cloud over my shoulder all these years."

"Yes, well . . . the sun's out now." Aluinn tipped his head up and narrowed his eyes against the dazzle of sunlight. The lofty, windswept vista that stretched out before them seemed too regal a setting for such carnage as lay at their feet, and then he noticed a scarred, gaunt tree as old as time itself standing alone some distance down the slope. Collecting on its gnarled, spiny limbs were hundreds, perhaps thousands, of black-winged ravens, silently watchful, smugly awaiting their bloody repast. Aluinn looked up at the mountain again and a cold chill shuddered over the surface of his flesh as he realized that one of the peaks that formed Hell's Gate was also known as Clach Mhor.

The ravens will drink their fill of Campbell blood three times off the top of Clach Mohr.

The prophecy had come true. First Angus, then Dughall . . . now Malcolm.

"Why don't we get out of here?" Aluinn suggested, bending to retrieve Struan's sword. The big Highlander was standing a short distance away, shaking his hand to rid it of the gore flowing down his arm. The other Cameron men were retrieving their weapons, assessing their own wounds, of which there appeared to be many.

Alex, by far the most seriously injured, lifted Catherine gently in his arms and carried her, despite her protests, down the slope to where the horses were tethered. He placed her on Shadow's back and swung himself up behind her, rearranging the folds of his tartan so that they were both wrapped within the warm cocoon.

He was so gentle with her, she felt her throat swelling with tears again. "Alex?"

"Hush. Don't talk. There is a tiny hamlet a few miles down the glen where we can——"

"He did not touch me. None of them did." The wide violet of her eyes turned to his. "He only said it to make you angry. I earned these bruises and cuts myself trying to run away last night. I didn't get very far because I slipped and fell halfway down the mountain, but—— Why are you laughing?"

"You are a great deal of trouble, you know. One of these days a man will be clever enough to tie you hand and foot to the bed before trusting you on your own."

A flicker of a challenge sparkled in her eyes. "Will that someone be you, my lord?"

He traced the tip of a finger across her lips and smiled. "I believe I have another method in mind for keeping you in bed."

23

The crofter's cottage was small and primitive, huddled in the lee of an imposing overhang of rock. The structure was built of sod and thatch, windowless aside from ventilation slits above the stone chimney. The floor was dirt, the fireplace large and smoky and hung one end to the other with assorted pots, forks, and dried meats. The farmer, recognizing the Cameron tartan at once, set out food and drink, boiling vast quantities of water to wash and care for the men's wounds. A bathtub was an unheard-of luxury in the glen, but Catherine was thrilled with a pan of warm water and a soft cloth. Her torn dress was replaced with one of simple homespun, many times repaired but obviously the best the family had to offer.

Word of the *Camshroinaich Dubh*'s presence in the glen spread, and within the hour men and women arrived at the cottage bearing baskets of food, bread, ale—whatever they could spare. The clansmen who had won such a resounding victory over the Campbells were toasted time and again, and as dusk began to settle over the vibrant green of the fields, fires were lit, stories were told, and songs were composed to mark their triumph.

Catherine slept through the afternoon and most of the evening. She wakened briefly each time she felt Alexander's presence in the room with her, but the fear, anxiety, and shock had taken their toll and she could do little more than acknowledge his gentle questions with reassuring murmurs and fall back asleep.

Alex insisted all of the other men have their wounds tended before he allowed the crofter's wife to strip him of his shirt and cluck over the tears and cuts in his flesh. One particularly nasty slash that wanted cauterizing and a poultice of mustard and cobwebs earned him a long lecture in muttered Gaelic when he refused.

"Thank you, Old Mother, I'll be fine."

"Ye'll be deid, ye dinna get some sleep," she warned.

"I will," he promised, his eyes wandering to the slender form already asleep on the single, straw-filled mattress. "Soon."

"*Alano.*" The old crone was reed-thin and if she stretched she might possibly stand level with Alex's waist, yet she had a tongue as sharp as an executioner's blade. "The puir wee lamb's exhausted. She disna need ye climbin' all over her wi' yer lusty thoughts."

Alex was permitted no defense, no chance to deny the charge as a bony finger was thrust toward the hearth to indicate where he could spread his tartan. "Mayhap when she wakens, an' when the thoughts come frae *her*, ye can gie her a wee cuddle. But no' afore."

Alex retreated gallantly, but before he could give way to the overwhelming weariness that gripped him, he went outdoors and spoke to Struan and Aluinn for nearly an hour. When he returned he stood over Catherine, watching her sleep for some time before he spread his tartan in front of the fire and rolled himself in its warm folds. He did not close his eyes for some time, however. He stared at the small bundle of blankets on the bed and relived every moment of every day they had spent together, every look, every touch, every whisper that had changed the course of his life over the last three weeks. He relived them and hoarded them next to his heart, secure in the knowledge he was making the right choice. The only choice.

Catherine woke with a start and for several panic-filled minutes did not know where she was. She heard the crackle of flames in the grate and smelled the musky sweetness of burning peat, but it was only when she saw the outline of the old woman bending over to stir the contents of one of the large iron pots that she remembered.

She was safe. The horror was over. Alex had rescued her, had ended the nightmare, and had admitted to wanting her back—a declaration that almost made the terror of the past twenty-four hours worthwhile.

She stretched carefully, testing the aches and pains that flared along her body. She did not know how long she had been asleep or whether it was day or night. The door to the cottage was closed, but she thought she could see tiny particles of light floating through the smoke that sought escape through the ventilation slits.

"Excuse me?" With one hand she pushed herself carefully into a sitting position, while with the other she held the thin blanket modestly high to cover her nakedness. "I beg your pardon?"

The old woman looked up from the fire.

"My . . . husband. Is he nearby?"

The crone frowned and said something unintelligible.

"Mr. Cameron." Catherine tried again. "Is Mr. Cameron nearby?"

"Aye, aye. *Camshroinaich.*" The woman beamed and patted her shrunken breasts, confirming herself to be of the clan. She bowed her head over the cauldron again, babbling away to herself in Gaelic.

"Oh, dear." Catherine gathered the blanket around her shoulders and climbed up off the pallet. The woman glanced over and the volume of what she was saying increased, but Catherine only shrugged helplessly and pointed to the door. "I only want to speak to him. Actually, I . . . I just want to see him."

The woman clamped her toothless gums together and jutted her chin in a gesture of disapproval as she watched Catherine take short, stiff steps to the door. It was held closed by a crude wooden latch, and as she drew it aside, the door swung outward. Catherine raised a hand instantly to shield her eyes from the flash of bright sunlight; it blinded her for some few seconds, as did the sight of clean blue sky overhead and brilliant green foothills surrounding them. The air was crisp and clear, filled with the sounds of insects buzzing, cattle lowing, and children playing somewhere off in the distance.

It was such a different and welcome scene than what she had wakened to the previous morning, she felt tears spring to her eyes. She let them flow unchecked and could not have moved from that spot had she wanted to, not even when the three men seated beside the narrow sluice of a stream stopped their conversation to turn and stare at her.

Alex stood up immediately and walked up the gentle slope to the cottage. Seeing the shimmering heather of her eyes, he said nothing; he simply took her into his arms and held her until the last of the tremors had faded from her body.

"Has anyone told you you are an exceptionally lovely woman?" he asked softly. "Even when your eyes are running and your nose is red?"

Catherine sniffled and smiled. "And you, sir, have a most unpleasant habit of not being around when I wake up in strange places."

"Ah. Married life," he murmured. "The nagging begins."

" 'Tis a small price to pay," she countered, and unmindful of the curious eyes watching them, she rose on tiptoe and kissed him purposefully on the lips. She raised her hands to his shoulders, carrying the edges of the blanket with her so that her slim and naked body was pressed urgently to his. She felt his quick intake of breath and melted willingly against him as his arms moved to draw her even closer. His lips were warm and hungry, his eyes dark and, for once, clearly readable in their intentions.

Their gazes locked, he murmured something in Gaelic to the old woman, and Catherine heard a chuckled

response. The crofter's wife brushed past them, cackling
with feigned disapproval as Alexander scooped his wife
into his arms and carried her inside.

The firelight cast a soft pinkish glow on their bodies;
the heat from the flames was strong enough to reach the
corner of the cottage and keep the drafts from chilling
their damp flesh. Catherine moaned appreciatively as her
hands slipped over his gleaming muscles; she shuddered
and bowed her head over the vast plane of his chest, letting her hair sway and drag across his skin. Her mouth
reached greedily for the hard bud of his nipple and she
sampled it with slow, swirling probes of her tongue. His
hands were on her hips and she felt him rise up beneath
her, his flesh seeking her moist sheath even as she teas-
ingly wriggled away. She slid lower on his body, her fingers tunneling through the luxuriant mat of black hairs on
his chest. Her lips roved shamelessly onto the flat surface
of his belly, and her teeth nipped playfully at the
descending bands of steely muscle.

For two days now they had rarely left the cottage.
Alexander seemed almost desperate to make up for lost
time, for the squandered days and nights when they had
fought instead of loved. From the quiet comfort of
walking hand in hand through the dusk, to the stretching,
thrusting power of his body taking her to incredible
heights of ecstasy, Catherine was kept in continual awe
of her husband, discovering facets to him she had not
known existed in any man, let alone the one she had married. But however idyllic her newfound love, she suffered under no illusions. There were still a good many
secrets and mysteries surrounding Alexander Cameron,
and certainly he would not change overnight into someone who could bare his innermost feelings to scrutiny.
Neither could she. But with time she hoped she could
break through that formidable wall he had built around
his emotions. Already, almost hour by hour, she was
coming to know and interpret each glance, each special

half-smile, each moment of exquisite stillness that prefaced the urgent hunger in his body.

She felt his urgency now as her lips moved lower and the mighty body tensed beneath a volley of tender, erotic caresses. It was her pleasure to shock him, to feel him curl every one of his ten fingers into her hair, to hear him shiver her name free on a disbelieving breath, and to prolong the rapturous agony until he could no longer bear it. With a deep and heartfelt oath, he groaned and drew her mouth back up to his, rolling with her, silencing her throaty laugh with one powerful thrust after another until she grew faint from the thrill of it.

His cry was harsh, torn from his chest, as she turned to quicksilver, growing hotter and hotter, tauter and more insistent with each vaunted stroke. He could feel the passion rising within her, feel her flesh, warm and sleek as satin, squeeze around him and share a single bright spark of perfect fusion before they were plunged headlong into a whirlpool of colliding sensations.

They clung together, rocking gently in their mutual wonderment as the last of the shimmering vibrations dissipated. Their limbs remained possessively entwined; only their lips gradually relinquished contact as their bodies collapsed, limp and drained, onto the tousled bedding. Catherine was panting lightly into his shoulder, the flutter of her lashes brushing against his neck. Her body glowed and throbbed within his arms, the musk of her skin soaked his senses like an exotic perfume, and Alex felt the unaccustomed prick of tears behind his eyes.

She was so lovely. So young. So untouched by the harsher realities of life—and yet time and again she seemed determined to prove he was the innocent, the more naïve of the two. He had thought her weak and helpless, yet she had saved their lives at the Spean bridge. He had thought her pampered and temperamental, yet there were untapped reserves of strength and courage in the slender body. She had remained brave and levelheaded during the ordeal in the mountains, and by

God—he tightened his arms, and his body ached with love for her—she had been willing to sacrifice herself so that he could end once and for all time the nightmare that was Malcolm Campbell. All that, and she could forgive him his ignorance and stupidity, she could tolerate his pride and stubbornness and defy him not to love her. He wished he could take her and run with her. Run far away from the troubles of the world and find a niche of fairytale happiness somewhere where she would never be hurt or frightened again.

Catherine traced her fingertips lightly over the armored muscles that sculpted his chest and listened to his heart thundering beneath, content to know that at least a small part of it belonged to her now.

"I never really loved Hamilton, you know," she whispered softly.

"I know." He stroked a hand through her hair and kissed the golden crown. "I would have killed him if I thought you did."

Catherine propped her chin on her fist and studied him intently. "How did you know? I mean . . . how did you know this would happen?"

The midnight eyes narrowed as they drank in her naked beauty. "I could be clever here and say I knew it the moment I took you in my arms and kissed you on the terrace. And thinking back, that was probably the precise moment that did us both in. Where did you learn to kiss like that?"

"I was about to ask you the same question."

"I have led a sullied and tarnished life these past long years—or haven't you been listening to what you have been telling me all these weeks?"

"People—" She paused and bit her lip, trying to recall a mote of wisdom she had heard somewhere. "People say all manner of things in anger . . . or self-defense. Or when they're trying to hide their true feelings."

"Ah, but in this case you were not far off the mark. I *am* stubborn and pigheaded, arrogant and conceited. I have made a career out of searching for the hard life, of putting my anger and my selfishness before all else."

"True," she agreed with amazing alacrity. "And thus you should not strive for sainthood now."

The dark eyes narrowed further. "You should also know that I have had a dozen mistresses over the years—scores, for all that I have lost count—few of whom would have a kind word to say on my behalf. I am a bastard to live with, a man who has spent fifteen years avoiding any kind of commitment, even to myself. During this time, I have never pictured myself in a domestic situation, never wanted to be held accountable for another human life."

"I suppose you dislike children and kick small dogs?"

"I abhor children and kick animals of any size if the mood comes upon me."

"Then it will be enough, I think, if you can reconcile yourself to the fact you have a wife now."

"A wife I did not ask for," he reminded her, "but won in a duel."

She inched higher on his chest and let her thigh slide suggestively over the top of his. "You may have won me in a duel, my lord, but I am no mere trophy to be placed on a shelf and forgotten. Take heed as well that I will not endure any further confessions of past misdeeds—especially those concerning females of loose moral persuasion."

Alex eased his lips free after a long, leisurely kiss and gazed deeply into the sparkling violet of her eyes. Why could he not have stumbled upon Catherine Ashbrooke six months, a year ago? So much wasted time. He would have liked those six months to try to tame her, to be tamed . . .

"Why are you smiling?"

"Can a man in love with his wife not smile?"

A shiver raced through her body and caused her to suck in a small, tremulous breath. Her chin quivered and her lashes quickly fluttered down.

"What is it? What have I said wrong now?"

"Nothing," she whispered.

He tucked a finger beneath her chin and waited for the huge eyes to meet his again.

"It's just . . . you have not said it outright before."

He took a deep breath and drew her forward. "Words and I often trip over each other, you must have guessed that by now."

She nodded and his fingers stroked the curve of her cheek, feeling the warmth generated by his admission.

He kissed the tip of her nose, the soft pout of her mouth. "For some reason, though, at this precise moment, I have never felt less clumsy and so I can admit quite freely that I love you, Catherine. With my body if you will have it, my heart if you will trust it, my soul if you will take it into safekeeping."

Catherine could do little more than stare, wide-eyed, as his mouth reinforced his words. The scent of him, the feel of him, the taste of him combined to send her senses reeling, spinning out of control even as the words echoed in her mind and made her body flush with pride. He loved her! *He loved her!*

Alex caught her by the shoulders and pulled her down beneath him, his hand twining itself in the long strands of her hair and forcing her head to arch gently back. His mouth was there, plundering the creamy smooth flesh of her throat and breasts, then it traveled down, repaying her for her previous mischief by reducing her to a quivering, helpless bundle of raw sensations.

The joining that followed was swift and tumultuous, the ecstasy more intense, more protracted, more consuming than she thought a person could bear without perishing from sheer excess, and Catherine reveled in the knowledge that they gave and received equal pleasure.

"Catherine?" His breath was hot against her throat, his voice broken with emotion. "Do you *believe* that I love you?"

"Yes . . . oh, yes." She curled her body against his, her

heart brimming, her flesh still pulsating gently everywhere he had touched her.

"And if I asked you to do something for me, would you do it without question, without argument?"

"I thought I had been doing just that these past two days," she murmured shyly.

A wry gust of breath stirred the fine hairs across her neck. "Just because you have proven yourself to be a wanton at heart, young lady, do not presume to lay the blame at my feet."

"And I suppose you are completely innocent of my corruption?"

"Completely. The skills you have displayed have left me frankly astounded."

"But pleased?"

"Euphoric," he admitted, pressing another small sigh into the curve of her shoulder. He allowed the mood of gentle bantering to fade before he repeated his question.

"Without argument?" She pondered the possibilities. "You are not going to ask me to endear myself to someone who is beyond endearment—" She thought of Lauren Cameron, whom they had discussed from opposing viewpoints over the past two days. "Or perhaps tell me for the thousandth time I mustn't wander anywhere without a regiment of bodyguards? Believe me, you will hear no arguments on that point. When we get back to Achnacarry I shall probably remain locked tight within the castle walls until I am old and shriveled and of no use to anyone but you . . . and quite happily too, I might add."

"Catherine—" He folded his arms firmly around her. "I am not taking you back to Achnacarry."

"Not taking me back? Where are we going?"

For a brief, blissful moment she thought he was going to say he was taking her away—far away—from Scotland, from England, from anything that might threaten to destroy their newfound happiness. But in the next dreadful heartbeat she knew that was not possible. He had already told her he would stand by his brother's decision to join the fomenting rebellion. He had pledged his word, his honor, and she knew him well enough now to realize he would never break such a bond with his family, not when he had traveled all this way, endured such risks and dangers just to stand by their side. And if that was the case, if he was not proposing to run away with her, and he was not taking her back to Achnacarry . . .

"Oh, no. No! No, Alex . . . *you cannot mean to send me away!*"

"Catherine—" His arms prevented her from jerking up and pulling away from him. "Catherine . . . *listen to me!*"

"No! I *won't* listen! And I won't go! You cannot make me go!"

"I can and I will," he said evenly. "We are a two-hour ride from the coast. The ship I made arrangements for you to sail on should be docking sometime before midnight and leaving again within a few hours. You are going to be on it."

"No. No. No! *Nooo!*"

"Catherine—goddammit, will you stop squirming and listen to me! There is going to be a war!"

"I don't care. I'm your *wife*! I belong *here* with you!"

She twisted frantically to break out of his grip, but he only wrestled her flat on the pallet and pinned her down with the weight of his body. "Yes, you are my wife. And I would be a pretty damned poor husband if I did not do everything in my power to see that you were safe."

"I will be safe at Achnacarry—"

"As safe as you were the other day in the garden?" He waited until the hot flash of anger in her eyes passed. "Catherine . . . a castle is only as strong as the men who guard the gates, and there will be precious few men left behind to do so. Donald has pledged to raise every clansman who can bear arms to join the Prince in a show of strength. *His* clan, *his* strength. But there are others who do not share his sense of honor. Clans will be fighting against one another; boundaries, territories, laws, and loyalties will cease to exist—"

"I don't care. I ... I'm not afraid. And I doubt if Donald will be sending Maura away, or Archibald will dispatch Jeannie to some safe haven."

"Maura and Jeannie have lived with blood and violence all their lives. They know what to expect and they can accept it."

"Tell *me* what to expect and I will accept it too. Haven't I just proved I can survive the worst life has to offer?"

"Catherine ..." His voice became softer, more desperate. "I never want you to have to prove anything to me again. Only that you trust me and love me enough to know this is what is best for you. For the both of us. I want you to be safe. I want to know you are safe and warm and protected—"

"Please," she sobbed, her hands trembling where they cradled his cheeks. "Please don't do this. Please don't send me away, Alex. Please ... *please* ..."

He lowered his mouth to hers, kissing her with all the tenderness and passion it was within his power to impart. Her pleas were tearing at his heart and his weakness was so acute he knew he dared not look into her eyes again or the resolve he had been building so carefully over the past few hours and days would desert him completely. She had no idea, could not conceive how Highlanders went to war. Scotland was known as the birthplace of valor, but it was also renowned as a country of wars. The Campbells would see this rebellion as an opportunity to swarm across Lochaber's borders and put the torch to everything that could burn. The English would send their fine, well-trained infantry and cavalry; they would bring heavy guns that could blast holes through stone and mortar as if it were paper. They would not stop to ask the nationality or political leanings of any man or woman who stood in their path, but they would surely leave a trail of bloody, broken bodies in their wake.

When the kiss ended, he laid his head between her breasts and prayed to feel her arms close around him. One last time. Just one last time. He did not *want* to send her away. Dear God, he did not want to let her out of his sight for even an instant . . . but he knew it was what he had to do. He had to send her out of harm's way at all costs, even if it meant destroying her love for him.

Catherine stared unseeing at the thatched roof over their heads. All of the joy, the peace, the sense of belonging she had been feeling, learning to feel, had vanished, leaving her numb and empty inside. He was going to send her away. He was going to send her away, then go off to fight a war, possibly to die.

"You knew all along it would come to this, didn't you?" she asked woodenly. "You knew, and yet you didn't tell me. Instead, you let me believe . . . let me *hope* you loved me enough that it wouldn't matter who or what I was."

He raised his head and frowned.

"That's it, isn't it? It's because I'm English. A *Sassenach*. An embarrassment to the great Clan Cameron."

"Your being English has nothing to do with my decision," he said evenly, "and you damned well know it."

"At this exact moment I do not know anything anymore. I only know you are sending me out of your life without giving me a real chance to try to belong *in* it."

"Catherine, this is the wrong time—"

"Yes, yes. I understand all about your valued sense of timing. Yesterday and today you needed time to prove you were capable of feeling and acting like a human being—a caring, compassionate, loving human being. Tomorrow and the days and weeks after that, you'll be going off to play at war, and the only needs you will have then are the need to kill, maim, and brutalize—all in the name of family honor. Well, thank you, perhaps you are right. Perhaps I shouldn't be here to see that happen. Perhaps I shouldn't be here to see you degenerate into something less than a man."

She pushed away from him and stood up, and he did not try to stop her, not even when he saw how badly she was shaking as she gathered up her clothing. He watched her slip her arms into the cheap cotton chemise, and he longed to reach out and stop her. She stepped into the single petticoat and drew it snug about her waist, then shrugged the shapeless homespun frock over her shoulders and laced it tight over the bodice . . . and he could not resist standing behind her, placing his hands on her shoulders, smoothing the wild curls of her hair.

"I love you, Catherine. I know you are angry with me now, and you may not believe it absolutely, but I do love you. What is more, I swear on that love—and on my life—that I will come for you as soon as I possibly can."

The slender back remained like a solid, impenetrable wall before him; her hands continued to tug on the laces of her bodice as if she had not heard—or did not choose to hear.

The impending sense of loss drove him to lean forward and place his lips tenderly over a fading bruise that marred the soft white flesh of her neck. He turned away to dress, so ridden by his own inner turmoil that he did not see the terrible shudder that swept through her body and sent her nails gouging into the flesh above her heart.

24

Catherine stood on the beach watching the last of the longboats being loaded with contraband. Highland wool was at a premium in Europe, along with the heady amber spirits distilled and taken for granted in nearly every castle and bothy in the kirk. Incoming goods reflected the suspicions of intrepid businessmen and merchants: gunpowder, flints, lead, and weaponry of all kinds, which would command exorbitant prices in the months ahead.

The captain of the *Curlew* was a short, wiry bristle of a man who appeared to have gone through most of his life without ever having laid a hand to soap and water. Blackpool, she had been informed in no uncertain terms, was not one of his regular stops, but as a personal favor to The Cameron of Lochiel he would set her ashore in a small inlet he knew of about four miles down the coast. From there, two of Alexander's most trusted men would accompany her into the city and stay long enough to arrange a coach and escort to Derby. Catherine recognized one of the men from the group who had rescued her from the clutches of Malcolm Campbell. The other was Aluinn MacKail.

Part of the reason for their delay in the shepherd's glen became apparent when Struan MacSorley reappeared after a two-day absence. He rode at the head of a sizable column of armed clansmen he had collected from Achnacarry. And riding in the middle of the burly Highlanders was Deirdre O'Shea.

Lochiel, they were told, had returned to the castle and was already making preparations for raising the clan.

Struan carried with him a packet of letters, hastily written, from Maura, Donald, even Archibald, wishing Catherine a safe journey and praying for her swift return. Not one of them argued with Alex's decision, not one ally among them suggested what she might say or do to change his mind.

Catherine blinked to keep the tears back as she looked up at the hazy rift of moonlight breaking through the clouds overhead. A crisp, salty breeze cooled her cheeks and stirred the sand underfoot into tiny whirling dervishes. She was wrapped in a broad swathe of tartan that kept out all but the most persistent drafts, and yet she shivered. Her mind brimmed with pictures and images, yet she thought of nothing. The numbness she had felt in the cottage was deeper, colder now that she had the waves lapping at her feet.

"It's time," Alex said softly, startling her, for she had not heard his footsteps in the sand.

She looked up and saw his face in surprisingly sharp detail: his eyes, his nose, his wide and sensual mouth, the truant locks of black hair that insisted on curling forward on his brow . . .

"You will give Maura and Jeannie my fondest regards?" she began. "And your brothers and Auntie Rose? You will tell them this wasn't my idea?"

"If you want me to, I will."

She bit down on the fleshy pulp of her lip and gazed out over the water. The waves were clear, luminous where they rose and curved over a wash of foam, glittering under the moonlight as they ran up on the shore and slipped back again.

"I was thinking how ironic it was. How I pleaded so hard for you to send me home, and now that you are . . ." Her voice faltered. He reached out a hand to touch her, but she saw the movement and flinched out of range. "Please, don't. I never was very strong when you touched me . . . but then, you knew that, didn't you? You relished that particular little hold over me, used it rather shame-lessly at times too, I daresay."

He looked down at his hands . . . and curled them into fists. "The captain tells me the winds are fair. You should have clear sailing between here and Blackpool."

"Assuming the revenuers do not interfere. Then again," she sighed, "what new adventures could a battle at sea possibly provide over what I have already experi-enced thus far? I should think it would prove tame by comparison."

"The captain is an excellent sailor. I doubt you will even see another ship on the horizon."

Their eyes locked for the span of a brief, strained silence before Catherine turned to the sea again. "Yes, indeed, the little man looks anxious to be away. I should not delay him any longer than necessary."

"Catherine—"

His voice was thick and low, and the sound shivered across the nape of her neck. She did not face him again, but stared steadfastly out across the water so as not to let him see the tears collecting along her lashes. She would not let him see her cry. If it was the last thing she did on this accursed shore, she was determined to keep the shreds of her pride intact.

He pressed a rolled, sealed, and beribboned set of documents into her reluctant hand.

"The letters I promised you," he said softly. "The choice as to whether you return to Derby a wife or a widow is still yours. In any event, these papers will give you legal access to the accounts . . . and the estate . . . of Raefer Montgomery. Aluinn has copies of everything; he will send them on to London."

"I told you once before I did not want your money."

"Then safeguard it for me. This also—" He took her hand and she felt something cold and hard glide onto her finger. It was a ring, a huge amethyst stone surrounded by a fiery circle of diamonds.

"It belonged to Sir Ewen's wife, and before that, his

mother, and so on back a couple of generations. I had almost forgotten about it until Maura reminded me it had been a bequest for my wife."

"It . . . should stay at Achnacarry," she whispered.

"It should stay exactly where it is."

Catherine averted her face from a particularly cutting gust of wind and found herself looking up into her husband's dark eyes. The ache in her chest grew until the pressure threatened to smother her, and without another word she turned and stumbled toward the two pots of burning tar that marked the landing area for the longboats. Deirdre was already seated in the bow, her hands clasped around the portmanteau she had guarded ever since leaving Derby.

With the water crawling up the sand and licking at the hem of her skirts, Catherine braced herself for the final farewells. The expressions on the faces of Aluinn Mac-Kail and Struan MacSorley were grim and uncomfortable, the latter looking as if he wanted to grasp two heads and knock them together.

"I am sorry to have been the cause of so much trouble," she said quietly, "and I do appreciate everything you have done for me. I . . . I cannot honestly say I wish your venture well, but I do wish you personal success . . . and safety."

She moistened her lips and cast a final glance along the craggy shoreline. She had been less than a month away from Derby, yet she felt as if she had aged by a score of years. Sights she would never forget had been forged onto her memory: Did the moon ever balance so brightly in the sky over Rosewood Hall as it had over the ancient battlements of Achnacarry? Was the mist as eerie and secretive, the grass as green, the moorlands as pungent with heather and peat? True, she had spent the most frightening days of her life in Scotland, but she had also found happiness and meaning . . . and love.

The captain cleared his throat impatiently, prompting Catherine to turn her back on the shore and step into the longboat. Alex stood rock-still, his face expressionless, his fists held down by his sides. Aluinn regarded him with an impotent sense of frustration, knowing there was nothing he could do or say to ease his friend's pain.

"I'll take good care of her," he promised and clasped a hand around Alex's arm.

Cameron nodded, but before he released Aluinn's grip he reached beneath his coat and withdrew a slim, sealed letter.

"When you arrive in Blackpool, give this to Deirdre. Ask her, in your most cavalier manner, if she would pass it on to Damien for me. You may assure her the contents are purely personal—a simple request from me to my brother-in-law."

"I'll see she delivers it." He stepped into the longboat as the oarsmen prepared to shove it into the surf. He tossed a wave of his hand in Struan's direction and, as an afterthought, shouted, "Don't start the war without me."

MacSorley laughed and returned the wave as the little boat cut into a shallow trough of water. "Bah! We'll have it fought an' won by the time ye find yer way back!"

Alexander remained on the glittering shore, his broad frame bathed in the bluish moonlight, his hair whipping in the salt air. His gaze stayed fixed on the bobbing craft until it was absorbed into the blacker shadow of the waiting *Curlew*. Within minutes the sheets of wide canvas were unfurled on her two tall masts, swelling and straining eagerly forward as they filled with the stiff southerly wind. The ship glided soundlessly out of the narrow inlet, bending her bow gracefully into the larger waves beyond the jagged point of land. By morning they would be clear of the most dangerous stretch of water and out into the open sea-lanes. Two days, three at the most, and they should be close off Blackpool.

"I will come for you, Catherine," Alexander whispered. "I swear I will come for you, though hell might stand between us."

The wind snatched the vow and flung it to the heavens

as he turned away from the water's edge, his convictions pounding solidly in his chest. But it would be many months before he would find himself on the road to Derby again. And then not as a husband seeking to reclaim his wife, but as a soldier in the Highland army seeking to reclaim a throne for his king.

Special Advance Preview
from the stunning sequel to The Pride of Lions

The Blood of Roses

Coming soon from Dell Books

Excerpt from *The Blood of Roses*

It had been because of an almost desperate need to feel the sunlight on her face, to smell the crisp, clean air, and to escape to the haunting beauty of the still, silent forest that Catherine had ridden away from Rosewood Hall that morning.

Somewhat calmer now, she led her horse along the dappled pathway, the only sound being that of the hoarfrost crunching underfoot. Why she found solace and comfort in retracing the steps that had led to her initial meeting with Alexander Cameron she did not know. Was it because, secretly, she hoped to find him in the clearing again? Or that she thought by some miracle he had come back to her and was waiting to carry her away just as he had promised?

No. If that was what she thought and hoped, then she was dreaming again.

Her heart and thoughts heavy, she rounded the final copse of evergreens and stood at the outer rim of the clearing, almost in the exact spot she had halted the first time she had seen Alexander. The pond where he had been bathing was crusted with a thin rime of ice, the mossy banks were frozen and coated brown with fallen leaves. Even though it was winter now and the trees were stripped to their bare branches, the sunlight was still mottled where it touched the ground, the beams broken and stippled with shadows.

Catherine could still feel his presence. She could still recall with startling clarity every detail of their first encounter—her shock at seeing a half-naked man bathing by the pond; the first riveting moment when their eyes had met; the seemingly endless eternity before her heart had commenced beating again. In her confusion and foolishness she had accused him of trespassing, poaching ... anything that came to mind in the heady rush of excitement. It had been a defensive measure, taken against an intoxication the likes of which she had never felt before and doubted she would ever feel again.

Catherine closed her eyes, reliving the sensation of his hands stroking down her body, of his mouth winning her capitulation. He had possessed her completely, body and soul, flesh and spirit, and had branded her forever a woman. *His* woman. Even if he never came back into her life, he had spoiled her for all others. His passion, his strength, his tenderness could have no equal. Never.

"Catherine?"

She opened her eyes slowly, not daring to move or breathe. It was a trick of the wind, it had to be—a torturous murmur of frosted air that carried the echo of a voice, nothing more.

"Catherine?"

She gasped and whirled around. Louder this time, the voice had not been a trick of the wind nor a taunt of her imagination. It was real!

"Alex?"

"Catherine, are you here?"

With a sob she ran back along the path. She saw a cloaked figure standing partially concealed behind two tightly interwoven evergreens and hesitated the merest fraction of a second before flinging herself into his outstretched arms.

"Damien! Oh, Damien, it's you! You've come home! You've come home!"

"Good heavens." Her brother was taken aback as he cradled the sobbing bundle against his chest. "For a greeting like this I would make a point of coming back to Derby every other day. Here now, what's all this? I know it's been almost two months since I removed myself to London, but—"

Catherine lifted her tearstained face from his shoulder. For a long moment his confusion was genuine, but then he looked around and cursed his own stupidity.

"Damn, Kitty. I'm sorry. I should have waited and called at the house, but I wasn't thinking. I saw you ride out of the stables and wanted to see you alone, without Mother or Father badgering me with endless questions . . . and, well . . . I guess I just didn't think."

Catherine sniffed loudly and wetly. Having brought no handkerchief with her, she patted Damien's breast pocket and relieved him of his. She held the linen to her nose and blew, looking up into her brother's face as she did so and nearly gasping aloud. He looked dreadful! His complexion was sallow and unhealthy, his eyes were clouded with fatigue that could not be the mere result of a hurried trip from London.

"Dear God," she cried. "Has something happened to Harriet?" Reaching out, she clutched his arm, nearly tearing the seam of his cloak in her anxiety. "Is she ill? Has something happened to the baby?"

"No! No, Harriet is fine. Honestly. She's fine. A little plumper around the middle, but otherwise shamelessly content."

Catherine swallowed a deep gulp of air to regain her composure. "Then what is it? Why are you sneaking about the woods like a thief?"

Damien arched an eyebrow wryly. "I think I prefer your first greeting, thank you. And since when is it a crime to seek out the bosom of one's own family on one's own land?"

"Damien Ashbrooke, the only bosom you have cared to seek out for the past few months has belonged to Harriet." She finished wiping away the streaks of tears from her cheeks and glared up at him accusingly. "And what leads you to believe Father would badger you with anything less than a trowel after the argument the two of you had following the happy occasion of my wedding? You have been carved up and served for dinner *in absentia* more often than a joint of mutton."

"I gather he is still angry over my decision to take permanent residence in London? It never seemed to bother him before I was married."

"Before you were married and while you were sowing your wild oats all over hell and gone, he was perfectly content to keep you and your scandals in London. But, may I remind you, you are his son and heir. You are respectably—if somewhat hastily—married, with a possible son and heir of your own on its way. He assumes there is just as much law to be practiced in Derby as in London, and as much determination in your soul to preserve the fortunes of Rosewood Hall as there was in the souls of twelve preceding generations of Ashbrookes."

"Kitty—" He sighed. "I am abandoning neither my heritage nor my duty. I am twenty-four years old, hardly the age to consider retiring into dotage. I have a thriving practice in London, which I am not prepared to forfeit just yet. I am fully aware of my responsibilities as an Ashbrooke—good Lord, they have been drummed into me since birth—but I am also concerned with my responsibilities to my wife and child."

"Bravo." Catherine smiled. "Well said, my brave and beautiful brother. And said well in the seclusion of the forest."

"I have said the exact same thing to Father's face."

"Indeed, you have. Unfortunately, he isn't nearly as astute or sympathetic as the trees, nor as perceptive as your little sister. There is something more going on behind all this skulduggery, and if you don't out with it soon, I shall go after you with a trowel of my own."

Damien laughed softly. "Obviously, my concerns for your welfare have been unfounded; you haven't lost the edge to your wit yet. Has all been forgiven, or have you just managed to stay out of Father's way?"

It was Catherine's turn to sigh. "He has been so damned civil since you confided the extent of the absent

Mr. Montgomery's wealth that one would think he had orchestrated the whole affair himself. Hearing him wax profound on his new son-in-law even has me listening in awe sometimes and wishing I could meet the fellow myself."

"Better that than the alternative. Father can be a self-righteous swine when he wants to be."

"Swine is hardly the word I would have used to describe a man who forces his only daughter into marriage with a complete stranger. He should just dare to lecture me on my behavior."

"Meaning . . . what?"

She glared up at him again. "I haven't been following in dear Mother's footsteps, if that's what you are asking, though not for any lack of opportunity."

"It never occurred to me that you might. You do, after all, have Alex."

"Do I? Where?" She looked around angrily. "Are you seeing someone here that I am not?"

"Kitty—"

"Don't *Kitty* me. And don't patronize me either. I haven't seen Alex, haven't heard one single word from him in over three months."

"He hasn't exactly been languishing on his laurels all this time. And if you love him—"

"If I love him? *If* I love him?" She clasped her hands tightly together in frustration. "You have no idea how many times I have asked myself the same question. Do I love him? Do I even know him? I spent less than four weeks with the man—half of the time plotting how to turn him over to the authorities and collect the reward! The rest of the time . . ." Her shoulders slumped and she shook her head slowly. "The rest of the time I was so frightened I think I could have convinced myself I loved Attila the Hun if he had rescued me."

"Kitty . . . you don't mean that."

"Don't I? Maybe you're right. Maybe I don't know anything anymore. Who is to say I would not have been just as happy—or as miserable—married to Hamilton Garner? At least I would know where he was and know what he was doing all these miles from home. Every time I turn around someone is talking about Hamilton Garner. Lo—the brave hero! Did you know he was promoted to major? I could have been the wife of a respected army officer, boasting night after endless night of my husband's accomplishments. Instead, I find myself spending so much time in my rooms I have begun to tat the cobwebs into lace. Have I spent one moment at Rosewood that hasn't been plagued with doubts and fears? Is my husband alive? Is he dead? Did everything happen the way I remember it, or am I seeing things, believing things that just are not true, not even real? Does he think about me? Does he wonder how I spend my days and nights? If I have enough food to eat? If I'm warm or cold? Am I one-*tenth* as important to him as . . . as . . ."

"As he is to you?" Damien provided softly.

She looked up at him and scowled. "Do not put words in my mouth, Damien Ashbrooke. Especially when you cannot possibly be sure of what they are."

He sighed expansively. "Very well. I guess I was wrong. I guess I should not have told him you wanted to see him."

Catherine grew very still. It came together, like two tin pans crashing in the silence, why Damien had followed her into the woods instead of meeting her at the house, why he looked so tired, so haggard, so . . . worried!

"You've seen him. Has something happened to him? Has he been hurt?"

"No! I mean, yes, I've seen him, but no, he hasn't been hurt. Well, not that you'd notice at any rate. He was wounded at Prestonpans, but—"

A roaring filled Catherine's ears. The roaring was Damien's voice and she could see his lips moving, but the words were running together in a series of distorted sounds and echoes.

She swayed forward slightly and he had to reach out

and catch her about the waist to prevent her from falling. He led her to a nearby tree stump and made her sit down. Watching the color come and go in her cheeks, he searched beneath the frilly jabot at her throat until he found and unfastened the top three buttons on her jacket.

"Wounded?" she gasped. "You said he was wounded?"

"He has a few new scars to show you. Nothing serious. Nothing missing, nothing broken, nothing twisted out of shape or disfigured. My word of honor, Kitty. He's fine."

"Wh-where did you see him?"

"He showed up in London a few days ago. Completely unannounced, of course, and walking bold as brass through Piccadilly Square as if he owned the place. He stayed a few hours, gave me a list of errands as long as your arm to run, then vanished again, him and that great bloody stallion of his."

"Alex was in London?" She repeated it slowly, her heart hammering against the confines of her tightly laced stomacher. To reach London he would have had to pass by Derby . . . wouldn't he?

"His business was urgent," Damien said, reading the question in Catherine's eyes. "He could not afford to stop or delay on the way there. However—"

"He is coming here on the way back?" she cried.

"That, uh, was his intention. Until I, in a more rational state of mind, managed to dissuade him."

"You did *what*?"

"Well, for one thing, there is the trifling matter of the two companies of militia Father has so generously invited to encamp on our grounds." The point, well-made, was also thickly coated in sarcasm. At the first news of the Pretender's intent to march south, Lord Alfred Ashbrooke had run, wig askew, to Colonel Half-yard's headquarters and demanded armed protection for his property. "A tinker cannot get close to the house without running a gauntlet of questions and accusations. I was stopped four times in the final mile."

"I could meet him," she gasped. "Anywhere!"

"Anywhere and everywhere is swarming with soldiers. And I wasn't the only one who followed you away from the stables. A rather priggish-looking lieutenant stopped me at the edge of the forest and would have run me through with his saber if I hadn't been able to convince him I was your brother. If you don't believe me, look behind you . . . *carefully*. You can just catch a glimpse of a red tunic through the trees. Lord help both of us if we don't walk away from here arm in arm singing praises to the King."

Catherine felt a surge of anger. "Father! How dare he have me watched!"

"Undoubtedly for your own protection," Damien said placatingly. "But a distinct nuisance, nonetheless."

"A *damned* nuisance," she retorted, jumping to her feet. "And one that shall end here and now."

"Frankly, I wouldn't say anything about it if I were you. The old Catherine Ashbrooke we all knew and loved would probably have demanded an entire regiment to escort her on a walk through the gardens. You wouldn't want to lapse too much out of character now, would you?"

Catherine opened her mouth to toss back a retort, but thought better of it and sank back down onto her seat on the log.

"Was I really so troublesome?" she asked, chewing on the tip of a gloved finger.

"You were just young and foolish and more in love with who you were supposed to be than who you actually were."

"A sage observation, brother dear. Considerate of you not to mention it before now."

Damien shrugged. "I had hopes it would pass. And I can see by the look in your eyes every time you say your husband's name that it has."

"Alex," she whispered. "Oh, Damien, I have to see him. I just have to!"

"He'll be relieved to hear it. I got the distinct impression he was not altogether certain what to expect by way of a reception. He seemed to dwell particularly upon the chilliness of a certain young lady's departure from Scotland and her reluctance to acknowledge even the tiniest bit of good judgment on his part for taking such swift action to see to her safety."

"He thinks I am still angry?"

"In truth, I think the two of you have more in common than you realize. He paced a rut in my floorboards telling me how it would have been better for all concerned if he'd never accepted the challenge from Hamilton, never taken you out of England, never so much as spoken to you let alone touched you. I told him he was absolutely right, of course."

Catherine's heart missed a beat. Her chest, her shoulders were suddenly so heavy under the weight of her emotions, she felt doubled over. "Is that why he did not come here?" she asked softly. "Is that why he went to London first?"

"Actually . . . he went to London because he wasn't sure you were here."

"Not here? Where would I be?"

"Considering half the shires are evacuating before the descending hordes, it was not an altogether unreasonable concern." He paused and tilted Catherine's chin higher so that she was forced to meet the rarefied blue of his eyes. "He wasn't even sure if you were living here as a widow or as the wife of an absentee merchant."

"He didn't know? All this time and . . . *he didn't know*!"

"How could he, Kitty? He has been fighting a war, remember?"

"Well, yes, but . . . he should have *known*. He promised. He gave me his word of honor. He should have known I would wait for him. Damien, please . . . you must take me to him. You must!"

"I can't do that—" He held up his hand and pressed a fingertip over the protest forming on her lips. "Not because I don't want to, but because I don't know where he is."

"Then how—"

"He, on the other hand, knows where I will be staying tomorrow night—"

"Tomorrow!"

"—after I leave here. And that is where he will go in search of your answer."

"Answer? Answer to what?"

"To this—" Catherine stared, her eyes rounded with disbelief as her brother reached to an inside pocket of his frock coat and withdrew a folded, sealed sheet of paper. She gaped at the letter, then up into his handsome face, and his expectant smile faded under the hot flare of violet sparks that burned in her eyes.

"Do you mean to tell me you have been standing here for ten minutes with this in your pocket?"

Without waiting for a reply she snatched the letter out of his hand and pressed it to her bosom for a long, breathless moment before daring to break the wax seal. Her hands were shaking as she unfolded the single sheet, and she had to read the opening salutation twice before her eyes would focus properly to continue.

My dearest Catherine . . .

She stopped, clutched the letter to her breast again, and felt Damien's arm circle her shoulder.

"I'm all right," she gasped. "I'm all right."

He kissed her tenderly on the forehead, then walked a few paces away to give her some privacy.

My dearest Catherine,

I pray Damien has found you well and in good spirits. We had heard most of the gentry were relocating, and so I did not hold much hope of seeing you. I was happy enough and relieved just to hear that Mrs. Montgomery was visiting at Rosewood Hall while her husband is out of the country.

Somehow, a piece of paper seems hopelessly inade-

quate for expressing what I want to say. I should have had Aluinn's talent for poetry to know how to properly tell you what is in my heart. Instead, I shall simply have to be content with the truth, blunt as it may be. Not one single hour of one single day has gone by wherein I have not thought of you. I sometimes find myself wondering if it was all a dream, if I only conjured you out of a desperate need to have something warm and loving in my life again. If I am dreaming, I pray I never wake up. If I am awake, then I pray you dream me into your arms and, one night soon, God willing, we shall waken together.

Your devoted servant, A. C.

Catherine's lips trembled as she read it a second and third time. "Damien . . . Damien, I must go to him. Take me with you when you leave tomorrow. We can take precautions, we can—"

"I can't do that, Kitty. It isn't safe."

"I don't care! I'm tired of being safe! I am going back with you, and there is nothing you can say or do to prevent it! I listened to logic and reason and concerns for my safety once before, and see where it has gotten me?"

"If you won't think of your safety, then think about his. Kitty—" He took her hands into his. "I have had more inquiries in the past two months as to the whereabouts of the mysterious Raefer Montgomery than I could tally on five pairs of hands."

"Good gracious, what has that to do with—"

"Some were just the usual curiosity seekers, those who had heard about the duel and wanted the gory details. But there were others not the least bit interested in the duel, but damned persistent when it came to questions about his current and past affiliations—including his lovely new wife. At the same time I'm hearing another name discussed in the coffeehouses and men's clubs— Alexander Cameron—complete with questions and curiosities."

Catherine felt the warmth drain out of her face. "What do you mean?"

"The Camerons are a large and important clan. Without Lochiel backing his cause, the Prince might not have found himself ten men willing to support a rebellion, let alone thousands. As for Alex's importance, well, it might interest you to know that your husband has won himself a great deal of attention. He and his men were responsible for sending our valiant dragoons cantering away from Colt's Bridge; they were instrumental in taking Perth, Stirling, and Edinburgh. At Prestonpans, it is said he single-handedly led a charge against heavy artillery, and instead of being blown to hell and gone like any other mortal man, captured more Hanover cannon than they have men knowledgable enough to shoot them. Shall I go on?"

"You seem to be quite well-informed about what goes on in the Jacobite army," she said tersely.

"It is my luck to be privy to information London prefers to keep close to its breast, including the stories and rumors of a certain legendary figure who is quickly assuming the title 'invincible.' The result, my dear sister, is that any lobsterback worth his salt ration would trade his firstborn son for the honor of capturing or killing Alexander Cameron."

"I still don't see what that has to do with me."

"Frankly, I'm worried that it may have a good deal to do with you. And Alex was worried as far back as August, when he sent you out of the country in hopes of throwing the hounds off the scent."

"Damien, for heaven's sake, will you stop talking in riddles."

"You are a clever girl, Catherine, figure it out. You married a tall, strappingly handsome, black-haired rogue whose skill with a sword was sufficient to win honors from the Master of His Majesty's Royal Dragoons. Moreover, after the much-celebrated duel and much-gossiped-about nuptials, the pair of you disappeared without a trace for over a month. Coincidentally, during the same four-week period Alexander Cameron—another tall, strappingly handsome, black-haired rogue—reappears in the Scottish Highlands after a prolonged absence on the Continent. Once there, does he keep his presence low-key and unremarkable? Heavens, no. He acts out a fifteen-year-old vendetta against the nephew of one of the most powerful Hanover chiefs in Scotland, doing so while in the act of rescuing his beautiful, golden-haired English bride."

"Damien . . . *you* know all the details and *I* know all the details, but who on earth is going to take the trouble to run back and forth between Scotland and England to link the two stories?"

"You met some of the Duke of Argyle's kinfolk," Damien said bluntly. "And you still require an answer to that?"

"But it was a personal matter between Alex and Malcolm Campbell. Campbell is dead now; that should be the end of it."

"Should be," Damien agreed. "Would be if we were talking about proper English gentlemen here, but we're not. We're talking about a race of people who were born fighting. Highlanders take their honor very seriously; an insult to a fourth cousin twice removed is still an insult to the clan chief. The reward on Alex, in fact, has doubled to twenty thousand gold sovereigns. I'm hearing nasty rumors laced with words like 'assassin' and 'paid killer,' and if that is the case you can bet they'll be probing for any obvious weakness in our valiant friend's armor."

"Meaning me," she said softly.

"Meaning *any* weakness. You just happen to be foremost in my mind, for obvious reasons."

"I know how truly worried you must be, but . . . you also know I must see him. I *must*, Damien. Even if it is only from a distance and only for a few brief moments."

Damien smiled wryly. "Oddly enough he said almost

the exact same thing ... and I did not believe him either."

She flushed and caressed the letter where she still held it against her breast. "Well then, big brother, what do you suggest we do?"

"*We* do nothing. *You* return to the house and go on about your business as if nothing untoward has happened."

"But—"

"I, in due course, shall meet with your husband as per his instructions, and together we shall decide the best and safest way to arrange a meeting. I want your promise on this, Kitty. I want your word that you will not try anything foolish like following me or venturing out on your own." He tilted her face upward again, his hand as firm and uncompromising as the stern set to his jaw. "Alex knows what he is doing. And we both know, if there is any chance in hell of him getting you alone for five minutes, he will."

The fire was little more than a sporadic ripple of flames at the ends of the half-charred log when some faint scratching sound disturbed the silence of the sleeping house. Catherine stirred and sought a warmer hollow in the mattress, not wanting her dream to be interrupted. It had been the same for the past two nights since she had seen Damien in the forest, the dream so vivid, so real, she could feel the searching fingertips skimming over the taut peaks of her breasts, the naked, heated flesh pressing against hers, the long, wickedly skillful fingers stroking deftly into the aching juncture of her thighs.

She also knew the dream would not last, and she whimpered softly in her sleep. All the craven sensations, so long denied, were flooding her loins, coursing through her body like waves of thick, rich cream. There was pressure where she longed most to feel it, and she parted her thighs willingly, undulating against the insistent, probing tension until the sheer silk of her nightdress was wet with her need.

The pressure was so real—the pleasure so intense—she cried out and pushed herself closer to the source of warmth. And for as long as it took her to realize that it was *not* a dream, that she was *not* alone in the bed, her body continued to respond, to plead for a deeper intimacy. But then her eyes snapped open. The very real presence of muscle and bone and hard male sinew brought a jarring halt to all sensations in her body, and a scream of pure terror bubbled to her lips. She struck out with her fists, pushing and writhing against the great wall of naked muscle that threatened to crush her. She managed to land a solid blow to his temple and was gathering strength for another when she heard a softly murmured Gaelic oath.

Her fist froze in midair and her eyes widened. Certain her mind was playing some dreadful hoax, her body tensed and her heart skipped several beats.

"A hell of a greeting for a wife to give her husband," Alex murmured, his hand firmly in place over her mouth. Indeed, as she continued to stare up at him in shock, the hand slid around to cradle the side of her neck, and the pressure of his fingers was replaced by the possessive warmth of his lips.

"Alex?" she gasped. "Oh, God . . . *Alex?*"

"You were expecting someone else perhaps?"